PERFECTLY IMPERFECT SERIES
SPECIAL (DISCRETE COVER) EDITION

PRECIOUS

hazard

NEVA ALTAJ

Perfectly Imperfect Reading Order & Tropes

1. Painted Scars (Nina & Roman)
Tropes: disabled hero, fake marriage, age gap,
opposites attract, possessive/jealous hero

2. Broken Whispers (Bianca & Mikhail)
Tropes: scarred/disabled hero, mute heroine, arranged marriage,
age gap, Beauty and the Beast,
OTT possessive/jealous hero

3. Hidden Truths (Angelina & Sergei)
Tropes: age gap, broken hero, only she can calm him down, who
did this to you

4. Ruined Secrets (Isabella & Luca)
Tropes: arranged marriage, age gap,
OTT possessive/jealous hero, amnesia

5. Stolen Touches (Milene & Salvatore)
Tropes: arranged marriage, disabled hero, age gap, emotionless
hero, OTT possessive/jealous hero

6. Fractured Souls (Asya & Pavel)
Tropes: he helps her heal, age gap, who did this to you,
possessive/jealous hero,
he thinks he's not good enough for her

7. *Burned Dreams* (Ravenna & Alessandro)
Tropes: bodyguard, forbidden love, revenge, enemies to lovers,
age gap, who did this to you, possessive/jealous hero

8. *Silent Lies* (Sienna & Drago)
Tropes: deaf hero, arranged marriage, age gap, grumpy-sunshine,
opposites attract, super
OTT possessive/jealous hero

9. *Darkest Sins* (Nera & Kai)
Tropes: grumpy-sunshine, opposites attract, age gap, stalker hero,
only she can calm him down,
he hates everyone but her, touch her and die

10. *Sweet Prison* (Zahara & Massimo)
Tropes: age gap, forbidden romance, only she can calm him
down, opposites attract, he hates everyone but her, touch her and
die, OTT possessive/jealous hero

11. *Precious Hazard* (Tara & Arturo)
Tropes: arranged marriage, age gap, enemies to lovers, grumpy/
sunshine, opposites attract, touch her and die,
OTT possessive/jealous hero

12. *Frozen Heart (Iris & Adriano)*
Tropes: opposites attract, age gap, stalker hero, forced/arranged
marriage, only she can calm him down, opposites attract, touch
her and die, OTT possessive/jealous hero

DEDICATION

For Andie,

Thank you for being there for me from the very first word to the final letter. For your help and guidance on every messy page, through crunched and misaligned timelines, and the overall chaos I throw at you each time, that you somehow manage to sort out. Thanks for your insights, encouragement, and unwavering support that have shaped not just this book, but my entire journey as a writer. I wouldn't be the author I am without you.

Thank you for walking beside me from the beginning, my friend. <3

Glossary

Puttana – *Whore* (Italian)

Gattina – Little cat or kitten (Italian)

Madonna Santa – Holy Madonna, but as an exclamation, the expression is akin to "Dear God" (Italian)

Ma sei impazzita! – You are crazy! (Italian)

Svadba – a wedding celebration; does not apply to just the act of getting married, as people could be married in a church or a city hall one day, but have their *svadba* on the same day or much later (Serbian)

Pasulj – A simple Serbian dish made with beans; an old-time, home-cooked, favorite meal

Sljamu nalickani – An insult with no literal translation, loosely means "a scumbag who puts too much effort into his looks, overdoing it" (Serbian)

Sunce ti jebem – No literal translation, but loosely means "fucking hell" (Serbian)

Isuse! – Jesus! (Serbian)

Slava – Serbian family celebration to honor their patron saint

Sarma – Serbian stuffed cabbage rolls

Gattina nera – Black kitten (Italian)

Ma lasciami dormire – Let me sleep (Italian)

l'Onore – Honor (Italian)

Famiglia – Family (Italian)

Rispetto – Respect (Italian)

Gattina mia – My little cat (Italian)

Stronzo – Asshole (Italian)

A note about the flowers: It is a Serbian custom that when flowers are presented as gifts (for example, for birthdays or romantic occasions), the bouquet must contain an odd number of flowers (e.g., 3, 5, 21, etc.). Arrangements consisting of an even number of blooms are only appropriate as a gift for the deceased (i.e., brought to a funeral).

Author's Note

Dear Reader,

If you've followed the recommended reading order for the Perfectly Imperfect series, you have probably noticed that the last two books were slightly darker than the stories that came before. There was a lot of focus on internal Mafia politics and plenty of intrigue that showcased the world. That's what those stories demanded, but to be honest, I missed the lighter side.

When I started writing Precious Hazard, I wanted to have a little fun. I chose to explore the characters' dynamics and enjoyed the way they evolved before my eyes. Therefore, you'll find this book is a bit more airy, with significantly less dark business involved.

My hope is that you will find Tara and Arturo's story as entertaining as I did while writing it.

Love,
Neva

Author's Note

Dear Reader,

If you've followed the recommended reading order for the Perfectly Imperfect series, you have probably noticed that the last two books were slightly darker than the stories that came before. There was a lot of focus on internal Mafia politics and plenty of intrigue that showcased the world. That's what those stories demanded, but to be honest, I missed the lighter side.

When I started writing Precious Hazard, I wanted to have a little fun. I chose to explore the characters' dynamics and enjoyed the way they evolved before my eyes. Therefore, you'll find this book is a bit more airy, with significantly less dark business involved.

My hope is that you will find Tara and Arturo's story as entertaining as I did while writing it.

Love,
Neva

CONTENT WARNING

This book contains content that some readers may find triggering or disturbing, such as mentions of an immediate family member's death, kidnapping, as well as graphic descriptions of violence, torture, and gore.

Please keep in mind that this is a work of fiction, where the author has taken creative license in depicting certain scenes that would be considered risky and are not advisable in the real world. Do not attempt to replicate these under any circumstances.

PRECIOUS

hazard

PROLOGUE

Arturo

Fifteen years ago
(Arturo, age 20)

I T STARTS AS A SMOLDER, DEEP INSIDE MY CHEST. THEN, A spark flits to life, bursting into a tiny flare that slowly fills the hollow cavity. Like a dry open wilderness, soon enough, I'm consumed by a raging firestorm. It's hard to imagine such wrath can be born from a mere strike of a match. A delicate flame that oftentimes can't even withstand a gentle breeze. Yet here I am. With an abundance of fuel to feed my fury, the blaze in my veins is ready to destroy everything in its path.

Because the bastard sitting smugly before me wants my sisters. Wants to rip them away from me.

The don takes a puff of his cigar, dropping the extinguished match into a nearby ashtray. He's perched in an enormous wing-back chair at the center of the room, momentarily transfixed by the Cuban in his gnarled, age-spotted hand. With his dry, loose skin and thinning hair, he has always reminded me of a decaying corpse. And tonight, if he insists on taking my sisters from me, I'll turn him into one.

"The girls will need a woman's guidance, Arturo. Surely you understand that." Another puff gets dragged into his tar-infused lungs, and I can't help but wish he'd choke on it. "And who could do a better job of caring for them than your mother's sister?"

That goddamned fucking bitch! I knew that *puttana* would be behind this. And it has nothing to do with her being a worried aunt. After Cosa Nostra all but renounced her when she married a man from outside of the Family, she's been trying everything she could think of to get into the don's good graces. Especially since her husband died two years ago. And now, she's found the perfect way.

Over my dead body!

"I will be taking care of my sisters," I growl while scorching ire races through my blood, whipping the raging fire within me into an inferno. "No one else."

"Oh, come on, my boy... You're barely twenty. How can you expect to raise two five-year-olds and also fulfill your obligations to the Family? To me?" The don gives me a patronizing sneer.

My hands fist at my sides, nails digging into the calloused skin of my palms. The urge to wrap my fingers around the self-absorbed motherfucker's neck and kill him on the spot is excruciating.

"I'll manage," I say through my teeth.

"Vittoria loves the girls. She's already started to decorate their rooms in her home. Your aunt is very excited to have them live with her."

Sure she is. The only thing that conniving hag is concerned about is revamping her own life. If she becomes Sienna and Asya's legal guardian, she'll stand to greatly benefit from their eventual marriages. She'll sell my sisters off to the highest bidders.

"I'll fight for custody." Somehow, I manage to spit out the words despite the giant lump lodged in my throat. Despair is pressing on my chest like a boulder.

"No, Arturo. You'll do no such thing."

Every cell in me is boiling. My blood has turned into molten lava, ready to incinerate the fucker leaning back in his chair in front of me like he's on a goddamned throne. Less than ten feet separate me from the don. If we were alone, I would've already snuffed the life out of him.

But we are not alone.

All of the Family higher-ups are present. The hoard of their muscle in perfectly-fitted suits lined up like fucked-up toy soldiers along the wall. To guarantee I don't step out of line in front of the don, I guess. Salvatore Ajello, someone I consider a friend despite the fact that he's never shown any similar esteem toward me, is among them. His piercing glare is trained directly on me.

We might be friendly at work, but I have no doubt he'd off me without hesitation if I made a move to kill the piece of shit currently ruling the New York Family. That poor excuse for a don, one who does little to nothing to protect his people. Who has now stooped to wrenching grieving five-year-old girls out of their home just days after our parents' deaths. Which means I don't fucking care... So-called friend or not, if Ajello stands in my way, I'll find some way to get past him and kill the bastard trying to steal my sisters. Sienna and Asya are everything that matters to me. Without them, I'll have nothing left to lose.

"You may go now." The don stubs his cigar out in the ashtray. "I've made my decision. Make sure the girls are packed and ready to leave tomorrow morning."

Red.

All I can see is fucking red. Rage blankets my vision in a thick haze as I flex my hands and take a step forward, prepared to commit the highest treason, regardless of the consequences to me.

The don is a dead man.

I move a step toward him when, out of nowhere, pain explodes through the right side of my jaw and my head snaps to the side. It takes me several heartbeats to blink away the blur that clouds my vision and then to recognize Ajello's broad form blocking my path.

"Turn around and walk out." He grabs the front of my shirt, shoving me backward. "Right the fuck now."

Not happening. I push him off and land a jab to his chin, just as he did to me.

"Move," I rasp.

Ajello simply wipes the blood off his split lip with the back of his hand. His face remains completely expressionless while he grabs my shirt again and leans into my face.

"I'll fix this." His words are only just audible, too low for anyone other than me to hear. "I give you my word."

Too stunned by the earnest look on his face that implores me to trust him, I'm still processing what he said when Ajello buries his knee in my diaphragm. The force of his strike sends me stumbling back.

"Get lost, DeVille," he barks. "And do as you've been told."

Struggling to draw air into my lungs, I stare at Ajello in confusion. I'm fairly certain the dick just broke one or two of my fucking ribs. With him being a member of the don's personal security, I'm not the least bit surprised by his protection of the old man. But if he's carrying out his duty, why is there a strange look in his usually stolid depths? Why are they blazing at me, but not in anger? There's an almost reverent plea in the normally cold depths. One utterly at odds with his ready-to-fight stance.

A barely-there movement of his mouth attracts my attention, but no sound leaves Ajello as we continue our blatant standoff. He repeats the motion. Much slower this time, allowing me to read his lips.

Trust me.

I've never seen Ajello show any measure of care for another person, but as he regards me with his back turned to the room full of snakes, I realize what that look in his eyes is.

Concern.

For me.

Can I trust him? This weird, unemotional guy? Despite being only a year older than me, he makes men twice our age wary because of this freakishness. Why the fuck would he give a shit about me, or my sisters? It doesn't make any fucking sense.

My gaze sweeps over the men gathered around the room. Most of them have their hands on their weapons, ready to kill me on the spot if I make one wrong move. Even if I get past Ajello, it would mean nothing. Someone will drop me for my insubordination before I ever get close to the don. Taking a deep breath, I lock gazes with Ajello again.

I have no choice but to trust him.

I nod.

"Go." He gives me a nod in return.

While my ribs scream in agony, I straighten and leave the room. Desperately clinging to a slim hope that he'll keep his promise.

CHAPTER
one

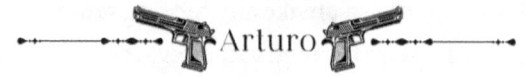 Arturo

Present day
Salvatore Ajello's office, New York
(Arturo, age 36; Tara, age 24)

"SO?" AJELLO ASKS, LOUNGING IN HIS ARMCHAIR ACROSS from me. "Do you have anything to say?"

I glance at the stemware in my hand, rotating it, watching crimson liquid swirl and splash on the inside. The faint traces of wine left clinging to the bowl remind me of blood.

I've bled for our cause more times than I can count. During drug deals gone wrong. Gang skirmishes. Confrontations with rival organizations. I don't regret a single drop. I've always known what I signed up for. The blood I spilled for Cosa Nostra hasn't been wasted. Today, though, I might end up bleeding because of my pure stubbornness.

"I do." I bring the glass to my lips and take a sip. "I am not marrying Tara Popov, boss."

Ajello's right eyebrow rises ever so slightly. That must be the most significant show of emotion I've seen him display in years. Excluding his behavior around his wife and daughter, of course.

After knowing him for more than two decades, I'm still not entirely sure he's actually human.

People believe that Salvatore Ajello is psychotic, but he's not. What he is is a man who doesn't concede the middle ground. It's all or nothing with him. He might think of me as a friend. Maybe? Who can tell with Ajello? But I do know that he'd take a bullet for me. Without a second thought.

None of that holds any sway in his decision regarding my current situation, though. He's *the* Don of New York, and I have just refused to follow his direct order. Killing me for insubordination would be perfectly justifiable.

"Why not?" Ajello's brows pinch together, creasing his forehead. "Drago's sister may be a little high-spirited, but I'm confident you two would make a perfect match."

"A *little* high-spirited? The woman tried to take my head off with a tray of appetizers. If her brother hadn't thrown her over his shoulder and hauled her away, I'd have strangled that psycho right where she stood."

"My point exactly. You need that kind of challenge, Arturo."

"I'm touched by your concern, boss, but I'm fairly certain I have enough challenges in my life. Especially now, with this endeavor we're partnering with Boston on. I don't need to add a batshit crazy woman to everything else I need to deal with."

Rising and grabbing his own drink off the side table, Ajello walks up to the floor-to-ceiling window overlooking the city skyline. That's his usual tell when he's pondering a particularly delicate matter. Or planning someone's demise.

Minutes stretch in silence as he simply stares at the view.

"I don't get close to people, Arturo," he finally says. "It's just not something that works with my personality. Out of everyone I've ever met, you are the closest thing I have to a friend. The only man I'd even consider slapping that label on."

"Alright." I nod, slightly perplexed by the new direction our discussion has taken. And the fact that I'm still breathing.

"You've been my underboss for more than a decade," Ajello continues, turning around. "As my right hand, I trust you more than any of the others, and I've given you nearly free rein on a multitude of business decisions. I have full confidence in you to do what's right for the Family, no matter how complex or delicate the issue might be. You've never failed me."

"So what's the problem?"

"The problem is, you've walked too far into the weeds, Arturo. You insist on being present for every deal. Whether it's seeing to the details of a pivotal contract involving a major drug shipment or supervising a routine job that one of your lieutenants can easily handle. What's more, none of our building projects can get rolling before you personally sign off on the plans and examine the blueprints, even though you know shit about construction. And, a week ago, Nino told me you demanded to be consulted about shift schedules for the security guys at the warehouses."

"I like being thorough. I don't see anything wrong with that."

"I know you don't." He takes a sip of his wine. "When was the last time you got laid?"

I nearly choke on the sip I just took. "With all due respect, boss, that's none of your business."

"It is if it impacts your performance. You've been drowning yourself in work. Sometimes, you don't even go home to sleep, just crash on the couch in your office. Working nonstop because you simply don't know what to do with yourself these days. With Asya and now Sienna married and gone, there's no one left for you to watch over. To protect. No one needs you to save them anymore. You're a nurturer by nature, Arturo. And you have no idea how to deal with your new reality."

I grind my molars, jaw flexing. Somehow, the cunning bastard never fails to dredge up the inner worries most people would prefer to keep buried. He makes you face them, whether you're ready and willing or not. The man may be emotionally detached himself, most of the time, but he's got a real knack for stirring up a shit ton of emotions in others. Ajello never misses his mark. Watching him unleash his "voodoo," especially when it makes our rivals squirm, is a beautiful thing. Having him dig around in *my* psyche? Not so much.

"So you decided to burden me with a wife?"

"Cosa Nostra holds family values in high regard. As my second-in-command, it's expected that you'll be an example to others. As a man of tradition, you get that, right?"

"Why her?" I ask through my clenched teeth. "If it's so important that I get married, I'd happily accept a girl from the Family. Someone nice and meek. With all the available Italian women, why would you pick a Popov banshee instead?"

"Your animosity toward Drago has reached its peak, and it's jeopardizing our collaboration. I need you two to settle your differences and get along."

"He's a presumptuous, bad-mannered asshole who somehow brainwashed my sister into marrying him!" I snap. "Regardless of how things are between them now, I will never forget that. And I will never get along with that dick!"

"Indeed. At least, not until the two of you are on even footing. I'm giving you that chance." Ajello's gaze lies heavy on me. "He got your sister. You get his. Problem eliminated."

I stare at my boss, lost for words. Leave it to Ajello to come up with the most outrageous solution that somehow actually makes sense.

"And as far as nice Italian girls are concerned," he goes on, "I don't think that option is in your best interest. Most of them already worship the ground you walk on, so where is the challenge in that? Tara Popov, on the other hand, is the perfect woman for you. She won't be so easy to charm."

I burst out laughing. "And I thought you didn't have a sense of humor, boss."

"Yeah. My wife shares your opinion on that." He turns back toward the bright lights of the city beyond the window. "I've already booked a suitable wedding venue. All expenses are on me, of course. My gift to the happy couple."

"I'm *not* marrying Popov's sister," I growl again.

"Of course you are. The alternative is me executing you for disobeying my order. Your sisters won't take your death well. Not after they've already suffered so much tragedy in their lives." He sips his wine before he continues, his tone completely relaxed and emotionless. "Asya will undoubtedly cry, but with time, she'll find a way to deal with it. She's always been the strong one, even though it may not seem so from the outside. But Sienna... Poor Sienna," he sighs. "I'm not sure she'll ever get over losing you. Losing people she loves has always been her deepest fear. Much like yours, I might add." He turns around again, leveling me with a look. It's piercing, yet the man himself remains calm, casual, and confident. "Do you know why she agreed to marry Drago?"

Rage ignites inside me, so blazingly hot that I'm barely able to form the word. "No."

"I told her I'd kill you if you opposed the marriage arrangement. It all worked out well in the end, of course, but it doesn't change the fact that she was willing to sacrifice herself for you. What kind of brother wouldn't do the same?"

I'm gripping the arms of the chair so hard I expect the blasted things to crumble to smithereens at any second. Motherfucker! I *knew* his underhanded tactics had to have played a role in Sienna's decision to hitch herself to the Serb. The only reason I'm still rooted in my seat instead of storming across the room to punch the son of a bitch in the face is because of what he did for me all those years ago.

If it wasn't for Ajello, God only knows what would have happened to Sienna and Asya. Neither came through completely unscathed under my watch, but I shudder to think what could have happened if my sisters had been taken away from me when they were five.

Strange that Ajello isn't using his actions back then as leverage against me now.

"You won't insist that I'm indebted to you?" I bite out. "That I owe you my loyalty and obedience because of what you did for my family?"

"Both obedience and loyalty should be inspired by respect, Arturo. A man who would ask someone he considers a friend to do his bidding as repayment for help freely given is not worthy of that respect. What I did, I did because it was the right thing to do. You are in no way indebted to me for that."

My gaze slides back to the glass of wine I set on the side table earlier. Ajello's calmly spoken words have shaken me to the core.

Leaders like Salvatore Ajello are rare in our world, and I would wager nearly unheard of if one considers that world to be the dark underbelly of legitimate society. He's the type of man who never retreats from the battlefield if it means leaving his men behind. One who has always put the welfare of his people, the Family, above all else. He nearly died for it. The crazy fucker.

That is the reason I respect him, the reason he's always had my fidelity. There's never been a time I did not follow Ajello's command.

Is refusing to marry Drago Popov's sister worth turning my back on this man? My leader? My friend?

"Are you really going to put a bullet in my head if I don't do it?"

He looks at me over the rim of his glass. "No. But I'd greatly appreciate it if you'd just agree."

I close my eyes and take a deep breath.

Honor.

Loyalty.

Commitment.

Along with traditions, those are the principles I've followed throughout my life, even before I swore my allegiance to Cosa Nostra at eighteen. A decade ago, when I accepted the privilege of being Ajello's underboss, I pledged my fealty and duty to him as the Head of the Family. I've taken great pride in doing so.

But my loyalty toward Ajello goes beyond my dedication to him as my boss. I'll be eternally grateful to the man, even though he's made it clear I don't owe him a thing for his help. Not that it matters how he feels about it, he's earned my unwavering support.

"Wanna hear something?" I ask. "The day of Popov's atrocious wedding carnival—"

"*Svadba*, you mean?"

"Yeah, that. Once I parked my car and was headed toward his mammoth house, a black cat crossed the road right in front of me."

"Don't tell me you believe in foolish superstitions."

"I didn't. Not until that day, that is. Ten minutes later, though, I met Drago's sister." I shake my head. "A pack of rabid dogs is less of a menace than she is. So you tell me there's nothing to that bad omen."

"Some cultures believe that black cats bring you good luck."

"I guess I'll find out soon enough."

"Should I take that to mean you'll marry the woman, then?"

"Yes." A sigh escapes me. "But Tara Popov will never agree. She hates me. Probably even more than I hate her."

"Hmm. Maybe you shouldn't have tried to kill her brother. You'll need to find a way to fix it. Flowers might help. Compliments, definitely. Try asking her out for coffee first."

I squeeze my temples, groaning on the inside. Salvatore Ajello giving me advice on how to court a woman? "Because that worked so damn well for you, boss?"

"Well, you could always threaten to annihilate everyone she holds dear. When flowers failed, that's what got me Milene. Eventually. As far as women are concerned, the key is not to go soft around them."

Ajello's phone starts ringing, and he shrugs as he takes it out. "*Cara mia*, you're still up? ... No, I didn't have time to get the cat food, yet. I'll do it as soon as I'm finished with Arturo. ... Yes, I'm aware that Kurt has been throwing up since yesterday. The damn pest probably ate another gross bug and—... What do you mean he scratched you?" Spinning around, Ajello races toward the office door. "Stay put. I'm coming up right now. I'll call Ilaria on the way. ... I don't care if it's just a nick! ... No, I'm not overreacting! What if it gets infected?"

A draft rushes through the room from the force of Ajello yanking the door open. He pauses at the threshold, phone still plastered to his ear, and glances back at me. "You have two months to convince your future bride to marry you."

The door slams shut in his wake, but I can still hear the sound of his fading voice while he continues making a fuss about his wife's damn scratch. Jesus. If anyone had told me a few years ago that Salvatore Ajello would be such a goner for a woman, I'd have laughed in their face. It's a tragedy, really. At least no one would ever catch me losing my mind like this. Especially over an *unwanted* wife.

Am I seriously going along with this circus?

Yeah, I am. I gave my word, and no one can make me go against it. Most of all, not Tara fucking Popov.

Grabbing the phone out of my pocket, I dial Nino Gambini. As our head of security, he keeps a close eye on anyone who might impact the Family. Considering the significance of our collaboration with the Serbian organization, he must know Popov's sister's whereabouts. Since Ajello has already kicked things off, setting this ridiculously short deadline before the nuptials, I need to get into gear immediately. Finding out what my wife-to-be is up to these days is the first step in getting my shit rolling.

"I need to know where I can find Tara Popov," I spit out the moment the call connects.

"Hold on. Let me check the logs in her file." The rapid taps of a keyboard drift across the line.

"You have a *file* on her?"

"We have files on everyone we've been in contact with over the past decade, and on anyone who's been deemed a *special interest*." The tapping and clicking continue until Nino blurts, "Here it is. For the past week, Ms. Popov has been filling in as a server at her brother's club. What's today?"

"Wednesday."

"Her shift ends at midnight."

Pulling up my sleeve, I glance at my watch. I've got just under two hours to get my ass to Naos. "Thanks, Nino."

My long stride carries me across Ajello's office. I pause briefly to grab my jacket off the back of the couch, and then I'm out the door.

Heading to meet my prospective wife.

While she's waiting tables at a damn nightclub.

Fucking great.

New York traffic sucks.

"Will you fucking move, you idiot?" I hit the steering wheel with the heel of my palm.

The car in front of me doesn't move. Of course it doesn't. There is a line of at least ten others clogging the lane. The one beside me isn't any better. If I don't get to Naos in the next five minutes, I'll miss my *fiancée*.

"Fuck it." I crank the steering wheel to the right and floor the gas pedal, sliding into a back alley between a couple of walk-ups.

I don't actually have to see Tara Popov tonight, but I want to get this marriage deal ironed out as soon as possible. If I don't, this shit is going to hang over my head, haunting me in my sleep. I can't have that, not with all the other crap that's been keeping me from getting any decent shut-eye lately.

Our buyers are breathing down my neck because our most recent drug shipment was delayed. But instead of dealing with that, I'm fielding stupid-ass noise complaints at one of our buildings in Chinatown. Our workers have been gutting the basement, and Wang, that Triad motherfucker, is demanding we limit demolition to three hours per day. Three fucking hours! It'd take months to finish the custom storage space at that rate, and I needed it done yesterday.

Those are the *real* problems that have me dragging my ass come the break of dawn. I'll be damned if I let myself lose even a minute of sleep because of that woman.

With my foot heavy on the gas, I fly through the narrow alleys in my Land Rover SUV. Typically, I'm a safe driver, preferring not to draw unwanted attention to myself. But with everything that's been going on lately, my patience has worn thin. Traffic jams aren't helping my mood, either. I've already picked up a couple of speeding tickets in the past month; one more and I'll get my license suspended. Somehow, I can't bring myself to care about that today.

I'm nearing Drago's club when a scrawny black cat leaps off the dumpster up ahead, landing in the middle of the road.

"Fuck!" I slam on the brakes and lay on the horn.

The blasted thing doesn't even move. It stands frozen in place with its back arched and tail all bushy, while my headlights reflect in its wide eyes. My tires screech as I throw the car in reverse and then gun it, yanking the wheel to the right and shooting out of the alley onto the main street. If I end up missing Tara because of a cat, a goddamned *black cat*, I'll—*Fuck!* There's only a couple of minutes left until the end of Tara's shift, so I step on the gas, eyeing Naos's main entrance less than a block away.

The yelp of a siren sounds behind me, followed by the cherries and berries lighting up my rearview. A quick glance in the side mirror confirms a police cruiser on my tail.

I groan. "You've got to be fucking kidding me."

CHAPTER Two

 Tara

Next day
Club Naos, New York

THURSDAYS ARE USUALLY SLOW. NOT THAT NAOS TURNS into a ghost town, that never happens, but the high rollers who tend to frequent my brother's upscale club prefer Friday and Saturday nights to cut loose. Unfortunately for me, tonight the entire club has been reserved for a private function. However, instead of the typical bespoke suits and designer dresses, the space is filled with a throng of bodies in leather and ripped jeans.

Local bikers, whose leader happens to be Drago's buddy, have decided to throw a birthday party for one of their members at our club.

Yay me.

"If you continue to stare at my tits, I'm going to kick you in the balls, Johnson." I smack the bearded dude on the chest with my notepad and head toward the bar. That's easier said than done since I first need to somehow squeeze through a wall of sweaty men. Empty beer bottles and glasses rattle when I lift my tray above my head to slide between two tall tables crowded with more bearded guys, all singing along to a song blaring from the ceiling-mounted speakers.

"Tara!" the bartender yells over the clamor. "These highballs are going flat over here!"

"Fuck you," I mumble under my breath and slam the tray onto the counter.

These guys can drink a river dry, apparently. My feet are killing me, and I'm beyond done with the cheesy one-liners I've been suffering through. What I wouldn't give right now to deal with the usual pretentious bimbos and overbearing alphaholes that hang around here. Most of the time, the clientele numbers around eighty, each with deep pockets filled with the spoils of their shady underground businesses. Tonight's horde of nearly two hundred is a far cry from that. Aside from the illegal shit, that is.

I'd love to kill my brother when I get home for making me do this crap, but he and Sienna are in Chicago right now, visiting Sienna's sister. My revenge will have to wait.

I know, I know… Being forced to take "disciplinary leave" from my position as the general manager of Drago's diamond smuggling *is* a fair punishment for causing a scene at his and Sienna's delayed wedding reception. The whole thing makes me feel like I'm back in high school and have been suspended again. But I get it. I embarrassed him. Spoiled the perfect day for my sister-in-law. Yeah, I fucked up. *Again.* But making me work at Naos? That blows!

To make matters worse, I couldn't get a regular job somewhere else while serving my "sentence." Not because I didn't want to or didn't try, but because of a "security risk." Seems Big Brother has decided to make another bold business move and might have pissed off someone else in New York, so me being on my own is a huge no-no at the moment. I've been wondering if it has anything to do with the Greek Syndicate, because Drago totally flipped out when he heard I've been dating Stavros.

Stubborn, overprotective boar!

After a twenty-minute lecture on how I should have my shit to-gether by now, Drago laid down the law. I am to fill in for whoever calls in sick at his club. Waitress, bartender, janitor… it doesn't mat-ter. I've been relegated to stand-in at this point. A Jill Of All Trades! Master of none, it seems.

So far, I've inventoried everything in the storage room. I had to go on a middle-of-the-night "hunting trip" to buy limes when we unexpectedly ran out. And, I even got the chance to have the Tom Cruise *Cocktail* experience by working behind the bar for a few nights. That was fun, until I screwed up a mix and one of the patrons ended up in the ER.

Fuck. My. Life.

I'm a waitress now, and I despise that even more than doing in-ventory. But I promised myself that I would prevail. I will not fuck this up! God knows I've fucked up pretty much everything else so far.

"This is for the gentleman in the reserved booth." The bartender sets a bottle of Dom Perignon and two flutes on a silver tray and pushes it toward me.

"There's a *gentleman* among these Neanderthals?"

"VIP. He's in number twelve."

I push the tray back. "Jelena and Maja are serving everyone who's hanging around in the booths."

"This guy requested you specifically." He leans over the wooden counter, smirking. "I didn't know you were into Italians, Tara."

"Ha! Hell would freeze over first." I grab the tray and make my way across the dance floor toward the far end of the section of semi-private booths.

The middle of the club is packed. Bodies swaying and grinding to the driving beat. The thumping bass reverberates through the floor, sending pulse after relentless pulse to the center of my chest. It's almost impossible to push my way to the VIP booths. At least I recognize most of the faces. I've gone with Drago to a few meet-ups held by this MC. They are a rowdy bunch, but having so many of these bikers around doesn't bother me. Much. In general, though, I don't do well in a big crowd of people I don't know. I always feel as if everyone is staring at me, waiting for me to fuck something up. I can't stand it.

Keeping the tray as steady as I can, I push between two guys ogling one of the other waitresses. The last thing I need is to drop this damn bottle of vintage champagne. I bet it costs more than my car.

Granted, I'm still driving the old POS that I used in my college days. I'm good with other people's money but suck at handling my own. I never did manage to save enough to buy something better. So I'm stuck with Old Betsy because Drago refused to buy me a new car while I was in school, telling me I had to earn it. That's his Balkan personality, through and through. We may have moved to the States two decades ago, but he never lost even a smidge of the lessons from the old country.

Ugh, if I didn't love my brother so much, I would've said *fuck it* and moved back into my apartment once he fully recovered from being shot. I might have, too, if I hadn't gotten evicted because I forgot to pay the rent. In my defense, I was more worried about my brother's life than bills at the time. Regardless of yet another blunder by me, I respect Drago enough to humor him and his security concerns. Although I'm still not convinced that anyone would actually try to hurt *me* just to get to him. Who would care about me, honestly? But, fine, I've agreed to stay put.

The luxurious booths that go for fifteen grand on a regular night fringe the dance floor in a wide arc. The frosted glass walls separate each seating area and provide a semblance of privacy to the lofty occupants lounging in the inner sanctum. Designated servers are typically stationed at the entry point, ready to wait on these VIPs hand and foot. Booth Twelve is Drago's personal space. No one but him is normally allowed to use it. But tonight is not a *normal* night. And it seems that the bastard currently sitting there has decided to screw with my evening even further.

The two lamps at either end of the white leather sofa are dimmed, making the space murkier than the rest of the club. Spinning around a couple gyrating at the edge of the dance floor, I don't even look at the booth occupant as I walk up and set the tray in the middle of the low, glass table. "Your champagne, sir."

"Well, well… looks like she has some manners after all." The rich baritone rumbles along my skin, setting off an unexpected shiver.

My head snaps up, eyes zeroing in on the man relaxing with his arms outstretched across the back of the sofa. The white leather sharply contrasts with his entirely black attire. The top three buttons of his fitted dress shirt are undone, revealing a sliver of chiseled bronzed chest. Light reflects off the thick golden chain and the cross that hangs around his neck. I let my gaze wander higher, to the painfully gorgeous face I hoped to never see again. The lower third is covered by short stubble that makes it look like he's perpetually sporting a perfect five o'clock shadow. The neat trim doesn't hide his strong chin or wonderfully angular jawline. His nose is straight, and his deep brown eyes are framed by thick, dark lashes. And then there's that slightly wavy hair, impeccably styled and so black that it practically absorbs the light around him.

Goddamned Arturo DeVille.

Sienna's brother.

Fury fills me as I take in his flawless features. I wish I could get away with marring them just a little. Or a lot. I'd call it payback for leaving my brother with a scar across his cheek when the two of them tried to kill each other. I know DeVille didn't get away unscathed, but it wasn't enough. I'm completely positive that Drago would have been able to kill the bastard if Ajello hadn't appeared and broken up their little clash. Fate could be a real bitch sometimes. I'd like to kick her ass, along with DeVille's. My brother is the only family I have left, and the thought of anyone hurting him makes me go ballistic.

Oh, right... If I needed a reminder of how I got to where I am now, there he is.

The devil incarnate.

"What the fuck are you doing here?" I ask through my teeth.

"That's more like the real you." Arturo's lips pull into a condescending grin. "Take a seat, Tara."

I smile back as wide as I can. "I think you're forgetting where you are, DeVille. You don't get to give orders around here. And it's Ms. Popov to you."

That grin disappears, transforming into a scowl. "Will you just fucking sit down, woman? I need to talk to you about a serious matter."

"We have nothing to discuss. Nothing you'd say is of any interest to me."

DeVille pinches the bridge of his nose and lets out an exasperated sigh. "Ajello might have been right. I should have brought flowers. But you likely hate flowers, don't you?"

"Ajello?" I raise an eyebrow. "Why would your boss have any opinion on my preferences? He doesn't even know me."

And why wouldn't I like flowers? I love flowers. There's a giant pot of peace lilies next to my bed. Drago got it for me after one of his tirades about how I don't take my responsibilities seriously. That one was when I dropped out of college. My third college. But the plant is still alive and well! *Okaaaay...* the "well" part may be a bit debatable since, the last time I checked, it only had a couple of green leaves among a multitude of dried ones.

"Will you please just sit?"

"Nope. I'm quite fine as I am, thank you."

"I should have ordered whiskey." DeVille shakes his head as he reaches for the champagne bottle. "Fine. This is how things stand. The Cosa Nostra don has expressed his wishes to have the two of us join in holy matrimony. I came here tonight so we could agree on terms and move forward with finalizing the finer details. Your *preferences*, for example."

I gape at him, processing the nonsense that just left his mouth. A marriage. To him? An uncontrollable giggle explodes from my chest. I try to wrangle it in so as not to draw too much attention to us, but it's just so damn hilarious.

"You really had me there for a moment," I snort. "Did Sienna put you up to this? Is this her way of getting back at me because I pranked her with that story about her favorite shoe boutique shutting down? You can tell her we're even. Bye!"

Still laughing my ass off, I turn around to get back to work but DeVille's annoyingly sexy voice washes over me again.

"Tara." That throaty timbre should be illegal, or at least come with a warning label. It's dangerous to the unprepared.

I throw a glance over my shoulder. By all outward appearances, Sienna's brother is still lounging comfortably against the back of the sofa as he sips champagne from his flute. However, there isn't a trace of ease or softness in his features. His jaw is set in a hard line, and his forehead is furrowed as he watches me over the rim of his glass. I'm not sure how I know this, but I'm convinced that the man is a primed powder keg. A clogged magma chamber that's ready to erupt. That look in his eyes? That's the look of tightly contained rage. It could incinerate me right where I stand.

"I'm dead serious. Ajello even booked the venue."

What?

Grabbing the edge of a nearby armchair, I drop onto the leather seat.

Salvatore Ajello is the most feared man on the Eastern Seaboard. I've seen grown men—gangsters and thugs—nearly shit their pants when Ajello's name is brought up. How the hell did I end up in his crosshairs?

"Excuse me?" I choke out.

"It's a done deal. The don wants to strengthen the ties between our organizations, so it's not up for debate. Our job is to settle on how we're going to handle this situation."

"Oh? It's a done deal, is it?" My voice is steady, and I manage to keep my tone calm. But as I lean over the table to bring my face right up to DeVille's, I'm brimming with anger. The pressure spiking my blood might just rival that of the man proclaiming himself my intended husband.

Holy shit, this can't be happening.

"Well, let me tell you how we're going to handle this situation, DeVille," I say through gritted teeth. "I'm gonna go get myself a double shot of tequila, and then I'll carry on with my shitty night. And you…" I point my finger at his chest. "You're going to return to your deranged boss and tell him that he's welcome to order his little minions, like yourself, around. Arranging marriages and other nonsense to his heart's content. But I'm not one of them. So, I would like both of you to kindly fuck off."

I keep my eyes locked on DeVille's and get up from the armchair with as much grace as I can muster, straightening out my apron as I rise. A smart person would do anything to stay off Ajello's radar, fearful of ending up in a body bag for pissing off the don. Too fucking bad I've never been accused of being wise.

"Tara…" DeVille's voice seems to have morphed. It has dropped several decibels and gotten somehow deeper, gaining an almost purr-like quality. The gravelly undertone gives an impression that he's a hair's breadth from losing his shit. It's not so much a warning as a promise of my demise.

"Your drink is on me, DeVille." I nod toward the bottle on the table, then turn on my heel and walk away.

I feel the weight of his stare as I traverse the full length of the crowded dance floor. It can't possibly be real because there are so many people between us, but as I reach the bar and slip under the counter flap to get to the back, the feeling of being watched, watched by him, stays with me. It's like his glare is burning a hole through me while I reach for a bottle of tequila and pour myself a double shot. That scorching sensation persists as I down my drink in one go.

I shift, trying to catch sight of him. There are glimpses as the mob of happy and drunk bikers moves. He's still in the booth. Still reclining on the sofa as if he owns the place and everyone in it. Why isn't he leaving, damn it? Goose bumps race across my exposed skin as if chasing the path of his heated gaze. I'm imagining things, I know it, but I swear his gaze sizzles over my flesh like a physical caress.

It leaves me rattled.

Holy fuck, I have never met a more infuriating man in my life. He carries himself as if he's the most important person in the room. His tone is always authoritative, like every sentence he speaks is an order he expects to be obeyed. And unless you're a part of his beloved Cosa Nostra, he seems to view you as if you're somehow beneath him. Everything, every fucking thing that man does irritates me to no end.

Whatever possessed his boss to think of me for this harebrained marriage idea, expecting me to even consider spending more than a minute in DeVille's company, is not my problem. It's Drago's. He got himself into the scheme with the Italians, so he should be the one to handle this mess. I wish I could call Drago right now to speak with him about it, but my brother doesn't do phone calls. This, too, will have to wait until he gets back from Chicago. But I have no doubts. Drago will fix this. He always does.

I almost lost him when the Romanians attacked our home, and Drago got shot… My heart nearly stopped beating. My big brother, well, he's my rock, the glue that holds me together, the most important person in this world to me. He's taken care of me almost my entire life. No matter how many times I've screwed up, he's been there.

But this… Fuck. This isn't on me. So I know he'll make it right. And I just want to go home and put it all behind me. Too bad this night is far from over, though. I need to get back to work, but I'm cemented in place, weighed down by Arturo DeVille's scalding stare.

It's a real physical effort on my part to get moving, to make myself focus for the rest of my shift.

For the next three and a half hours, I rush around the club. I double down on getting everyone their orders, keeping busy as I try everything in my power to avoid glancing in the direction of the VIP booth. There's no actual need for me to look over there to see if Sienna's brother has left. That searing sensation that dogs my every step is proof enough that he hasn't.

"Tara!" Jelena howls across a table crammed with four bikers chugging beer as part of some immature game. "Stavros is in the back, asking for you."

Bloody perfect. Hopefully, no one will mention it to Drago. The last thing I need is for him to find out my ex showed up here tonight.

"Tell the bouncers to throw the jackass out and not let him in again," I grumble while trying to fit another empty glass on my tray.

"Ah, okay. I was afraid you two were back together."

"Nope. I don't make the same mistake twice." A tiny lie. It usually takes three fuckups before I learn my lesson. But it sounded cool.

She laughs. "Yeah, alright. Hate to say *I told you so*, but I knew nothing good would come out of that relationship. You've got dreadful taste in men."

Like I don't know.

Yet, I still try to underscore that fact with every guy I date.

I knew Stavros was a tool from the moment I met him, but I still agreed to go out with him. The expensive sports car and fancy suits couldn't hide the truth. The guy is a moron. I'm not sure he has two functioning cells in that brain of his. He constantly flashes the ugly-ass seal ring on his pointer finger and brags about the pricey trinkets he buys with his money. The money he earns by working for his dad. Stavros's main interest, though, is his workout regimen, which he insists on telling me the details of. Every. Single. Time. So, money and gym, that's all he ever talks about. He's the only man I know who's that full of himself without having an actual reason to be. We dated for the last two months, and I wanted to break up for at least the last month and a half of that. But I didn't. Maybe I'm a masochist. Or just plain stupid.

Yesterday, though, Stavros took me out to dinner at an exclusive restaurant. Before our appetizers even arrived, he was prattling on about his big dream in life: to find a perfect woman, one who is a match for him in every way, so she could bear him a bunch of perfect little babies who would inherit his spectacular genes. Excuse me, but the world has enough idiots. I made my apologies, saying I needed to use the facilities, and then took my ass as far away from the imbecile as I could.

Okay, so I didn't *technically* "break up" with him, but I think my message was loud and clear.

Besides, that's my usual MO. I run away a lot.

Mostly from myself.

Too bad I can't seem to escape Arturo DeVille's stare.

Because his eyes are STILL BURNING HOLES THROUGH MY BACK!

Half an hour later, with closing time swiftly approaching and the crowd starting to dissipate, I tell Jelena that I'm taking off and slip away into the staff room. After grabbing my purse and jacket out of my locker, I leave Naos through the kitchen door, desperately trying to avoid a certain someone and his scorching gaze.

Leaning on the side of the building, with the dumpster shielding me from the view of anyone who might come out into the alley after me, I relax my shoulders for what feels like the first time in hours. "Finally."

It's still the dead of night, but as they say, New York never sleeps. The chilly air rejuvenates my tired senses, and breathing becomes much easier without the constant pressure of so many eyes on me.

Especially a particular pair of dark-brown irises searing through my last nerve tonight.

I straighten out, ready to head to my car, just as a wave of profound loss sweeps over me, and for the teeniest instance, I miss that smoldering heat.

"Definitely stupid," I mumble, then make my way to the parking lot. Leave it to me to forget my key fob at home today and not be able to get into the underground garage at Naos.

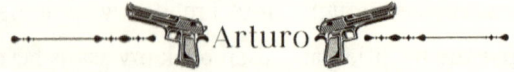Arturo

I slide into the back seat and slam the door shut. Damn that woman!

"Mr. DeVille?" Riggo glances at me from the driver's seat of the fully decked-out BMW stretch sedan I've decided to use since I can't drive my Land Rover. "Did you have fun? Any good-looking chicks in there?"

"Hardly."

"What? But I noticed at least a dozen, maybe two, going in while I waited. Including a blonde who was wearing the shortest dress ever, and she had the sweetest laugh. Did you see her?"

Not a chance. All night, my focus was solely on the tiny brunette in her cute little apron, smacking people around with her notepad. And the worst part? I was inconceivably enthralled.

"Just start the car."

"Absolutely, Mr. DeVille. On it. Oh, Nino called. He's been trying to reach you, but your phone is turned off?"

I pull my cell out of my pocket. The battery is dead. Fucking perfect. "What did he want?"

"He mentioned that there's an issue at the Brooklyn site. He's waiting for you at the location."

"It's two in the fucking morning," I sigh, squeezing the bridge of my nose. "Alright. Step on it."

Our newest construction property is half an hour away, and I spend the entire drive wondering how Tara Popov managed to slip from my sight at Naos.

Considering the ongoing tension between me and Drago, cornering his sister in front of his people after she stormed away from me was out of the question, so I kept my distance, waiting until the time was right. My gaze, however, followed her for the remainder of the night as she ran around serving a rowdy bunch of bikers I never imagined I would see at Drago's upscale club. What the fuck was that all about? Drago has been as erratic as his sister with some of his business choices lately.

One of those choices resulted in a bullet lodged in his chest. If it wasn't for Cosa Nostra, the man would be six feet under instead of a constant irritation in my life. But, maybe I could use his continued breathing as leverage, get him to agree to let this marriage between me and his sister proceed just as Ajello has planned. Maybe. I truly never know what to expect when dealing with this Serbian lot.

Case in point... His sister. Any sensible woman would understand that matrimony will strengthen the ties between our organizations. And a sane woman would never even have considered outright rejecting the directive of the Cosa Nostra don. The ramifications of such an action could only spell doom for her and her family. Despite Popov's gang being sizable enough, it's no match for the New York Family. In a direct confrontation, we'd wipe them out. Tara Popov surely must know that. Ignoring such a threat only confirms what I already knew. She's clearly certifiable.

The file on her that Nino provided me didn't have a lot. Seems she's only been classified as "mid-level important" over the past four years, since Ajello decided she's worth keeping an eye on. Nino was able to gather some basic info about the schools she attended, her employment history, and a bit about her personal life.

It appears that during her freshman year, she was expelled from her initial high school, but she managed to graduate from another with only a suspension on record. "Illustrious" post-secondary years followed after that. Tara's journey to higher education took her through three different colleges before she dropped out, without ever completing her liberal arts degree. Then came a stint of short-lived odd jobs that got her nowhere, at which point her brother must have stepped in. Since that time, she's been working for him, and although she spent a few years as some kind of admin for his precious gems operation, it seems that also didn't go well for her, since now she's serving tables in his club. That only proves it... Tara Popov is irresponsible, uncommitted, and obviously a foolish person. One I'm expected to spend a lifetime with. Jesus fucking Christ.

While her professional path is less than impressive, the woman certainly made sure her love life has been eventful enough. Although lacking full details, Nino's file included a list of the names, and at times occupations, of men that Tara has been linked to romantically. That list reached double digits, but her relationships never lasted longer than two months. If that alone wasn't enough to illustrate her poor life choices, the fact that her most recent boyfriend is noted to be Stavros Katrakis, the stupid as fuck son of the man currently leading the Greek Syndicate, takes the cake.

"We're here, Mr. DeVille," Riggo says as he stops next to Nino's SUV, twenty feet from a dilapidated building that we'll be demolishing starting tomorrow. Fuck. Later *today*.

Illuminated by an industrial LED spotlight mounted along the roofline at the corner of that same structure, three men appear to be engaged in a heated discussion, their raised voices carrying all the way to me. A car I don't recognize is parked close by.

Not knowing what I'm getting into here, I pull my gun out of the holster beneath my jacket and slip it into my waistband at my back. Easy access.

"Have your weapon ready, just in case," I tell Riggo, then exit the car and head toward the group.

Nino is on the right, and the other two men are facing him. The shorter one is in the middle of a tirade, gesturing with his hand as he continues to press whatever it is he's pissed about. His back is turned to me, so I have no clue about the trespasser's identity as I draw nearer.

"… and I demand that you halt all work until this issue is resolved!" the man yells in a slightly accented voice.

Nino notices me approaching and relief briefly flashes across his resigned face. In matters of security, Nino's skills are top-notch. But his patience for dealing with people's bullshit is practically nonexistent. Which is why I know that despite outward appearances, Nino has had just about enough. He hardly ever gets involved in our business matters because his trigger finger is all too tempted to resolve every confrontation.

"You need to discuss this with Arturo." Nino nods in my direction. His even-keeled delivery tells me the situation is hardly expected to escalate. Unless he's made to continue this conversation.

The frustrated guy turns around. My forehead furrows the moment I recognize him. What are the odds? Tobias Katrakis. What the fuck is the Greeks' top man doing on our property? Aside from a small drug deal between us six months ago, Cosa Nostra hasn't done any business with the Syndicate. Their group is mostly involved in loan-sharking and running dodgy self-storage complexes around the tristate area. A lucrative business for them, but peanuts compared to what we're into. Typically, our interests do not intersect.

"Katrakis." I come to stand beside Nino. "What seems to be the problem?"

"This." He motions with his hand, indicating everything around us. "This land is mine, and you must stop what you're doing immediately. There's been a big mistake and it needs to be resolved."

"There's nothing to resolve. We bought this lot months ago. I signed the contract of sale myself. The paperwork was clear; there were no other claims on the property. I also didn't see the Katrakis name anywhere on the real estate purchase agreement."

"Yes, well… The ownership was *temporarily* transferred from us to another firm for reasons I'm not willing to disclose to you. And therefore, this property should never have been put up for sale in the first place. I want to buy it back."

"Yeah, that's not going to happen." I motion with my head toward the exit gate. "Now leave."

"I have many connections in this city, DeVille. Many important people come to me when they need funding, and sometimes, in return, I accept the fulfillment of a favor instead of money. Several of my debtors have dealings with Cosa Nostra."

I narrow my eyes at the slimy little asshole and take an aggressive step toward him. There's virtually no way he can't see just how much his words have pissed me off. "Are you fucking threatening me? Please, say you are so I can make my shitty day just a tiny bit better by snapping your miserable neck."

Katrakis's bodyguard draws his gun, but Nino gets ahold of the dickwipe's wrist and twists the man's arm. A gunshot pierces the air, and the bullet ends up somewhere in the dark. It's immediately followed by a pained grunt when Nino throws the bodyguard to the ground and shoves his knee between the useless piece of shit's shoulder blades. Before the guy even realizes what just happened to him, the barrel of Nino's Desert Eagle kisses the back of his head.

Katrakis's attention bounces between his incapacitated man and me. I haven't even bothered to pull my own weapon. A single punch to his ugly mug would send him straight to la-la land.

"Get the fuck off my site, Katrakis!" I bark.

The bastard gives me a curt nod and heads toward his car. Nino releases the worthless guard, and the man trudges after his employer while Nino keeps him in his sight. Then, we both wait until their taillights disappear through the gate.

"Aren't you supposed to be the cool head?" Nino grumbles while we make our way to our respective vehicles. "You know the Greeks have their claws in the city's administration."

"It's almost three a.m., Nino. I'm fucking tired, hungry, and more than a little pissed off."

"Mm-hmm. I take it the meeting with Drago's sister didn't go as planned?"

"No, it didn't."

"So you figured you'd vent some steam by dragging us into a dick-measuring contest with the Greek?"

"I didn't drag us into anything. Katrakis and his goon showed up uninvited on *our* land. But yeah, I guess you're right. I could have handled that better," I admit. "See if you can dig up who's behind the offshore company that sold us this lot."

"I'll try."

"While you're at it, locate Katrakis's boneheaded son for me. His father might not be open to sharing how the land he had no intention of selling ended up on the auction block, but I bet that idiot put it up as collateral in one of his dumb schemes. Which means, whoever sold the deed has put us in this fucked-up position and they'll need to be dealt with."

"Sure. You know Stavros been seeing your future wife?"

I scoff. "Yeah, I read the file. She'll have to end that immediately. Or I'll end it for her."

"Be careful. Katrakis might be a small fish, but he's got teeth. The Syndicate is resourceful. We don't want any entanglements with them. At least, no more than we've already gained, apparently." He gives me a slight shove with his elbow. "So, how is she anyway? Popov's sister?"

"Stubborn, reckless, and absolutely unreasonable."

"But beautiful, yes? I've only seen her from afar, but"—he whistles—"she's a babe. I wouldn't mind doing her if you two don't end—"

My fist flies as if of its own accord, slamming right into Nino's face.

"What the fuck, man?" he groans, pressing his hand over his busted lip.

"Watch your damn mouth," I growl, then take off at a clipped pace toward my car.

Yeah... *What the fuck* was that?

CHAPTER
Three

Tara

I 'M GOING TO BE LATE FOR MY SHIFT. AGAIN. AND SATURDAYS are the busiest nights at Naos. I snatch my coat off the hanger in the foyer and rush outside.

"Drago was very clear in his instructions, Tara," Iliya, one of my brother's men, comments as I sprint past him on the driveway. "You should be taking one of the guys with you whenever you work the night shift. Especially while the boss man is away."

"Then it's a good thing you won't be telling on me." I wink, throw my purse and coat on the back seat of my beat-up car, and slide behind the wheel.

The straight shot from home to Naos generally takes a little over an hour, but not when I drive. To avoid heavy traffic, I tend to take a lot of side streets rather than main roads. Not tonight, though. I'm already fifteen minutes behind, so I hit the interstate.

I make it through that gauntlet and even manage not to miss my exit, but now's when the real fun starts. The closer I get to the club, the more congested the streets get, and I need to concentrate so I don't run over any idiotic pedestrians who cross the road wherever they fucking feel like it or hit the bike couriers who whiz dangerously close between the cars. With the traffic light changing to green, I'm about to make a left turn when a pickup, coming the other way, blows through his red. I slam my foot on the brake in the middle of the intersection. Mad honking explodes behind me.

"Fine. Fine." I wave at the jerk riding my bumper and step on the gas. Old Betsy gives a little sputter, and the engine dies.

Fuck!

I turn the key again and again, getting nothing but rapid clicking in response. The blasts of horns continue from all sides, echoed by the furious screaming from the asshole behind me sticking his head out of his window. A common enough scene in New York, and it shouldn't bother me, but my shoulders tense with every honk, every curse word lofted at me. Each blast underscores just how incompetent I am.

My anxiety ratchets up. I picture other drivers leaving their cars, or marching up to mine and shouting every obscenity on earth at me. By the time my car finally starts, sweat beads along my hairline, and my hands tremble.

Taking deep breaths usually helps to calm me down, but as I cruise down the street, the nerves don't leave me. Adrenaline is running rampant in my veins. I'm still about ten minutes from Naos, but I can't keep my focus on the road.

My fingers flex around the vinyl of the steering wheel, and I turn onto the nearest side street, belatedly realizing the road is closed up ahead due to construction. Whatever. Works for me since it appears to be completely deserted at this hour. As soon as I see it, I pull into what seems to be a dead-end, narrow alley. On my right there's a building that's clearly undergoing some renos. Big tarps cover half of its facade. On my left is a three-level public garage, but it too is closed and utterly empty. In the distance, I can still hear the hum of traffic, the ever-present noise of the city. But all around me is a peaceful, calm night.

Just what I need to get myself under control.

I park and step outside, leaning against the car door for stability. My limbs feel weak and unsteady while my chest remains tight, with rapid puffs escaping my lungs. The chilly air helps, though. I take a deep, slow breath, trying to visualize a serene environment. A green field. Wildflowers. The cheerful chirping of birds.

I exhale a shaky breath. Nope. It's not working. I need something else.

Instead of soothing images, my mind conjures up Arturo DeVille's angry eyes from two nights ago, glaring at me over the rim of his flute of champagne. As pissed off as I was at him that night, I loved seeing the usually uptight prick lose a bit of his composure. I saw his superiority slip off him like an ill-fitted mask. It gave me perverse satisfaction to ruffle the devil's scales.

Jelena told me he's been at Naos the last two evenings. He likely returned, intending to press the moronic marriage deal again. The man must not understand the meaning of "fuck off." I'm almost sorry I agreed to switch shifts with Jelena, working the afternoons instead. I would have loved to wipe that smug grin off DeVille's annoyingly handsome face by once more telling him how he can stick Ajello's brilliant idea up his own ass. It might've been the last time I could've seen those pretty features unmarred because, when my brother gets back, he will surely beat the shit out of him for even suggesting this dumb plan.

A tiny smile pulls at my lips. Imagining the demise of Arturo DeVille is proving more therapeutic than the calm influence of singing birds. All of a sudden, it's way easier for me to breathe.

Feeling better, I turn to get back into my car, but a bruising hand wraps around my arm and pulls me away.

"You bitch!" an angry male voice booms into the night.

"Stavros?" I cry out. "What the fuck? Let go of me!"

"You thought you could get away from me, yeah?" My ex shakes me, his fingers and the band of his ugly seal ring digging into my skin. "Make a fool out of me? Tell your bouncer buddies to throw me out like I'm some sorta trash? And then you send me your stupid little breakup text today?"

"Stavros! You're hurting me!" I try to shrug off his hold, but he plants his other palm on the side of my car, caging me with his body.

"I waited for you to get back from the restroom for almost an hour," he barks, squeezing my upper arm hard enough to make me wince. His face is red now, and the look in his eyes is homicidal. "Every damn server at that place was snickering behind my back! I've never been more humiliated in my life!"

I shove on his chest while trying not to panic. The bastard must have followed me here. Dread pools in the pit of my stomach. A minute ago, I thought this quiet location was my salvation; now it's become the site of my latest, and maybe biggest, mistake. There isn't a soul in sight. No chance of anyone venturing this way or helping me.

Damn it, I should've listened to Drago! He ordered me to break up with Stavros when he found out I was dating this moron, but I told my brother to fuck off and to stop butting into my personal life.

Another mistake.

Big mistake!

"I'm sorry!" I shout, trying to placate the quickly unraveling man before me.

"You should be very sorry, you fucking bitch! My father is friends with the owner of that restaurant, and now everyone knows how some stupid cunt dumped me without a word."

Pain explodes in my head as his palm connects with my cheek.

The entire side of my face feels as if it's on fire. My fists fly up, pounding on Stavros's front, while hot tears well in my tightly closed eyes.

"You think you're something special?" he snarls. "Better than me? You think you can make—"

A muted bang bursts into the air just as something splashes my face.

My body goes completely still. A moment later, I realize I'm no longer being pinned against the car. My arm feels like it weighs a ton as I lift my hand to wipe my eyes. Slowly cracking my lids, I focus on my trembling fingers.

They are covered in blood.

"Stavros?" I choke out. He was right here in front of me and—I look down, gaping at the man slumped on the ground at my feet.

Oh my God.

I rear back, gaze transfixed on Stavros's body. The side of his head is bloody, and he doesn't seem to be breathing. Filling my own lungs with oxygen becomes a problem. I can't seem to swallow around the big lump stuck in my throat.

What the fuck happened?

With my back plastered to the car door, I freeze like a deer in headlights.

Footsteps.

Coming toward me out of the dark corner of the dead-end alley. Out of the shadows where the flickering street lights don't reach.

Getting closer.

I need to get back into my car, lock the doors, and drive away as fast as Old Betsy can manage to go. *Turn around, Tara!* My instincts are screaming at me, pushing me toward safety. But is being trapped in a car that might not start the safest bet? Maybe it will, though. Then again, with the luck I've been having lately, it's likely a definite *not*.

Shoving down every impulse that tells me to flee, I fix my focus on the dead body and try to calm my skyrocketing heart rate. If anything, having a man who leads a powerful criminal organization in New York City for a brother has taught me to never act before thinking.

Stavros worked for his father and had plenty of enemies, I'm sure. It's possible that one of them decided to take him out. I have no desire to know who made that hit or to become an unfortunate witness.

One who will then need to be disposed of.

But if I don't see the shooter, I stand a better chance of making it out of here. Alive.

Tap. Tap.

Tap. Tap.

Steps drawing ever closer. A crunch of broken glass under a heavy sole. Coming from my right.

I bite my lower lip and squeeze my eyes shut.

"I haven't seen anything," I say, loud enough for the shooter to hear me. "Please. Don't come any closer. I can't divulge anything I don't know."

Tap. Tap.

Tap. Tap.

Slow, measured footfalls. Relaxed, as if out for a nightly stroll. Closer. Closer.

"I don't know who you are. And I don't care." My voice turns shrill. My throat starts to close up, and I'm left fighting for air. "I haven't seen or heard anything!"

The steps halt right in front of me. Instantly, a rich woody scent with a bit of spice fills my nostrils. Then, a light touch seizes my chin. Fingers tilt my head up and turn it to the side.

With no hope left, I squeeze my eyes even harder. "Please, I just want to go home. I promise I'll keep my mouth shut."

"I find that promise very hard to believe, Tara." A rich, velvety baritone reaches my ears.

My eyes snap open.

"You!"

Arturo

I ignore Tara's furious glare and focus on the welt spreading across her left cheek. The motherfucker hit her hard. "Does it hurt?"

"Yes!" She pushes my hand away. "What the fuck, DeVille? I thought you were someone my ex had threatened or tangled with. Maybe a schmuck who couldn't pay back his loan and decided to kill the messenger instead. And I figured I was next!"

I look down at the dead guy. Stavros Katrakis. The stupid son of a bitch I followed after Nino's guys managed to sneak a tracker on the little shit's car for me. This pencil-dick owed me answers. Answers I now won't be able to get. Fucking great. As if our existing problems with the Greek Syndicate weren't enough. I just made them infinitely worse.

Truth is, I didn't give a damn about who I was shooting when I pulled the trigger. I saw that asshole slap Tara, and rage unlike any I've ever known boiled in my veins.

"What if you missed? Had you considered that?" she continues to jabber. "Your crazy ass could have killed me, DeVille! And what the hell are you doing here anyway?"

It sure didn't take her long to get back to spitting nails. Just moments ago, she was shaking like a leaf. I push the thought aside. Now is not the time to examine why seeing her scared and hurt made me lose my head. Killing the Katrakis pup wasn't exactly smart, not that I regret it. But if I were thinking more clearly, I would have chosen a different way to make him pay.

"I don't miss, Tara." Reaching into my coat, I take out my phone and dial my driver. "Pull the car to the end of the street."

"It's dark! And Stavros's head was like… inches from mine. And now look at it! There's a rather large hole in his skull. Why in the hell did you shoot him?"

There's no way I'm admitting I offed the bastard for raising his hand at her. "Are you always this hysterical?"

"I'm not—"

The rumble of an engine and the squeal of tires interrupt Tara's diatribe. My car turns the corner and comes to a stop right next to the body, narrowly missing Stavros's right hand. What douche needs to wear a seal ring simply to let others know about the authority he's been given by his daddy?

"Mr. DeVille!" Riggo erupts from behind the wheel and rushes around the front of the stretched luxury sedan, almost stumbling over Katrakis's lifeless form. "I've just—What—Oh shit! This guy is dead!"

"Your deductive reasoning never ceases to amaze me, Riggo," I sigh, reminding myself that he's just an excited, nineteen-year-old kid. "Put the stiff in the trunk. We'll drop Ms. Popov at home, and then you'll get rid of the body."

"You're not dropping me off anywhere," Tara snaps. "My car is right here. Besides, I'm late for work."

I feel the twitch in my left eye. The fucking thing starts whenever my temper is hanging on by the thinnest thread. I take a deep breath and try to keep my tone calm and even. "You're not getting behind the wheel tonight."

She might pretend to be unperturbed, but people can rarely

hide shit from me. The foolish woman is barely keeping it together. She'll likely get into a wreck heading to Naos, home, or wherever else she might decide to venture. Maybe I should just let her drive herself to her own doom. It would solve this whole "marriage problem" quite effectively.

"Who the fuck do you think you are to order me around?"

"You're in shock," I snap. "Your hands haven't stopped shaking. Consider me a Good Samaritan and get in the fucking car. Now, Tara!"

"I'm fine. I'll call an Uber." She turns around and, stepping over the body, grabs her purse from the back seat. There's hardly so much as a wobble to her brisk stride as she then rushes toward the mouth of the alley.

"You're covered in blood!" I yell.

"Screw you, DeVille!"

I watch her for a few seconds, admiring the agility with which she traverses the uneven pavement in her platform heels, then turn to Riggo. "You have ten seconds to stuff that body in the trunk," I bark and take off in pursuit of my unwanted future wife.

She's rather quick, but her legs are much shorter than mine. I reach her just before she gets to the corner. Taking a page out of her brother's book, I grab her by the waist, then throw her over my shoulder. With her pert ass saluting the night sky, I turn to head back to the car while my arm wraps around her thrashing thighs.

"What the—Let me go!"

"Keep your voice down."

"I will not keep my voice down! I'll scream if you don't let go of me this instant!"

"Should I remind you that we have a dead guy and you're covered in his blood?"

"I had nothing to do with that! You killed him."

"Exactly. And I'm going to kill you unless you shut up."

"Ha! You wouldn't dare."

I stop and meet her gaze over my shoulder. "Want to test that theory?"

She scrunches her nose and huffs.

"Yeah, I didn't think so."

By the time I walk up to my vehicle, Riggo has managed to stuff Katrakis's body in the trunk and is now holding the back passenger door open. I lower the grumbling woman to the ground and nod toward the seat. "Get in."

Something hard pokes into my stomach. I look down to see my own gun pointed at my gut.

"I am not getting into that car with you, DeVille."

I must really be losing my edge if I didn't notice her pulling my Sig from the back of my pants while she was dangling upside down. Or maybe I was too distracted by her ass mere inches from my face.

"Do you even know how to use a gun?" I ask.

"Care to find out?"

I sigh. The safety is still on. I'm done with this standoff. Grabbing the barrel, I slowly pull it up and press it to my chest. "Either shoot or get in the damn car."

Glaring at me as if she could eviscerate me with her eyes alone, Tara begrudgingly lets go of the weapon. Then, will miracles never cease, she actually does as she's told and gets into the car.

I give Riggo the address and directions to Popov's mansion before popping open the trunk. Stavros's body is cramped inside, his arms slumped at strange angles. This bastard is lucky he isn't alive, otherwise he'd be hurting something awful come morning. I throw the gun in, and it hits Stavros's head and bounces off to fall somewhere behind the body.

"A town car and a chauffeur," Tara mumbles as I slide onto the seat next to her. "I should have guessed. Is driving yourself beneath you, DeVille?"

"No. I'll get my license back in a couple of months."

"Say what now? How did a rule follower like you manage to lose your license?"

"Speeding."

I hit the button to raise the privacy divider. Once the barrier is fully up, I turn to face the pint-size hellion.

She's moved as far away from me as possible, curling up with her head leaning on the side window. As we cruise along the illuminated roads, the intermittent glow of street lights falls on Tara's face. She's a rather cute little thing. But only by outward appearances.

Her long, dark-brown locks are gathered into a high ponytail that somehow emphasizes her delicate facial features. The most striking of which are her big, round eyes lined with long black lashes. Their color is the most vibrant shade of green. Like a springtime forest. Or emeralds. They remind me of the irises of the cat that leaped in front of my SUV the other day. That feline's peepers glowed in the dark. Witch's eyes. But Tara's are bright with her stubborn resolve. And then, there's her lower lip… Slightly fuller than the upper one, giving her a permanent pouty look. Her nose is small and slightly upturned, sprinkled with a multitude of tiny freckles. Knowing her personality, however, I would've expected her to sport horns, not freckles. I'm not yet fully convinced that she doesn't, despite her innocent looks.

"We need to finish our discussion from the other night, Tara."

"The marriage nonsense? I thought I made myself perfectly clear."

"Yes. But it appears that I have not. We are getting married. The decision has been made, and there's nothing either of us can do about it. You are, however, encouraged to share your preferences regarding decorations and catering."

She twists in her seat, practically launching herself within inches of my face. "There's no way in hell—"

I press my finger over her mouth, silencing her. "You shouldn't have killed the Katrakis heir, Tara."

"What? You shot Stavros, not me!"

"Really? Then why are *your* fingerprints all over the gun used to kill him?"

Those alluringly green eyes widen, watching me with an expression that hints at confusion and alarm. And for just an instant, I lose myself in their mysterious depths.

So pretty.

Like dawn-kissed dew shimmering on a blanket of young grass. It's hard to pull myself back to the here and now.

"I'm a very careful person, *gattina*. I clean and wipe down my weapons every evening. You won't find my prints on any of the guns I use. Not if I can help it. After all, you never know when one of them may turn up as a murder weapon."

Tara's face morphs into a mask of horror as she watches me remove my leather gloves and throw them on the side console.

"You have a choice to make, Tara. Make the wrong one, and you'll find yourself facing one of three potential outcomes. Option number one: Stavros's body is discovered by New York's finest, along with the murder weapon with your prints on it." I seize her chin, letting the pad of my thumb brush over her lower lip.

So soft. Much softer than I imagined it would be.

"Two… I'll simply kill *you*. Make your body disappear without a trace. That would certainly solve more than one of *my* problems." The death threat is a bluff, but I let her see the truth of my next words. "I *will* not have my loyalty or commitment questioned. I *will* obey my don and marry the woman of his choosing. But that won't be necessary, of course, if my intended bride isn't among the living anymore."

That plump lip beneath my thumb starts quivering. Tara blinks, and two tears slide down her cheeks. My eyes trace their paths over her flawless, rosy skin. Not so tough, after all. I knew she wouldn't be. Although, in the minute after I shot that son of a bitch for hitting her, she surprised me. She stood perfectly still. Didn't scream. Didn't flee like most other women would have.

But the two glistening droplets making tracks across her flesh don't lie, even though Tara remains mute.

"So my advice to you is to take option three," I continue. "In less than two months, you'll walk down the aisle. You'll smile, and when prompted, you'll say 'I do.' Do you understand?"

Another tear breaks its confinement, falling like scalding acid on my skin. Any second now, her tough girl act will dissolve, and she'll go into a complete meltdown. She'll agree to the marriage, and she'll beg me to get rid of that gun.

Her lips part ever so slightly, like she's ready to utter the words. For a fleeting moment, the tip of her tongue connects with the pad of my thumb. That faintest touch sends a jolt of electricity straight to my cock.

It takes me several heartbeats to register the pain. It's not in my dick, but rather my thumb, trapped between Tara's sharp, white teeth. The crazy woman bit me! I yank my hand back and lunge toward her, wrapping my other hand around her throat. Leaning into her face, I growl, "You're a damn savage. Just like the rest of your lot."

"Fuck you!" she snaps while her hands fly to my face and she tries to jam my eyes back into my skull with her thumbs. "You tricked me, you bastard!"

"*Ma sei impazzita!*" I grab her wrists, pulling her hands off me.

My actions force her off-balance, and she falls forward, bumping her forehead into mine.

"Ouch!" she cries out and tries to free her hands.

I tighten my grip on her slender wrists, not enough to hurt her, but sufficiently so she can't escape. Her forearms get trapped between our bodies as I pull her against my chest.

A big error on my part.

Our foreheads are still pressed together, and the tip of her tiny nose is brushing mine. I have no choice but to stare directly into the mystical green orbs that are a mere hairsbreadth away. They stare back.

The sweet scent of her strawberry shampoo engulfs me, further fucking with my mind. I would have expected the stench of brimstone and burned sage from a witch like her, definitely not mouth-watering summer berries.

Her warm, rapid breaths fan my face, setting off tingles across my lips. Trying to kill the sensation before it spreads, I scrape my tongue and teeth over my bottom lip. The only thing it does is make me yearn to find out how she tastes. Sweet or bitter? Probably a fusion of both.

And then, a different craving surfaces. I want to know what it would be like to have this hellcat in my bed. Would she purr? Mewl sweetly? Or would she hiss and scratch my back?

Knowing Tara as little as I do, I'm betting on *both* in this, also.

"Let go of me, Satan," she sneers through her teeth.

I raise an eyebrow. "Satan?"

"DeVille. Devil. Satan. Suits you to a tee."

A corner of my mouth twitches. I shouldn't find her so damn amusing. She's feral, rude, and childish. The exact opposite of the women I'm attracted to. So why the fuck am I fantasizing about having her under me? About ravaging that sassy mouth just to shut her up?

Reluctantly, I release her. The moment she's free, she pushes away, scooching as far from me on the seat as possible. Her short-sleeved white top is spattered with blood, and there are smears on her face, too. I grab a box of tissues and a bottle of water from the door pocket and set the items on the seat between us.

"Use this to clean yourself up."

She doesn't look at me as she pulls out a tissue and begins to gingerly wipe her left cheek. The one that's reddened by Katrakis's hand but unmarred by his blood.

I clench my teeth and grab another tissue, splashing a bit of water on the napkin. "Look at me."

"Nope."

"Tara."

"What?" She turns toward me.

I seize her chin once more, holding her head in place as I clean the blood off her smooth skin.

The woman glares at me the entire time I carefully swipe the wet tissue over the right side of her face and around those luminous, green eyes. I work slowly, lingering as I gently wipe her chin, nose, the shell of her ear… everywhere, even after all traces of blood have been removed.

Tara says nothing, just continues to stare at me. She stays motionless, but the air around her is constantly shifting. It's almost as if a skittish, feral cat is frozen in place in front of me. Tiny goose bumps have broken out across her arms, making the fine hairs there stand on end. Just like a cat's fur tends to do moments before the creature pounces.

"You cold?"

"Yes."

I discard the soiled tissue and shrug out of my suit jacket. "Here. Put this on. I'll turn up the heat."

A look that's part disgust, part longing crosses her face as she glances at the jacket in my hand. She flattens her lips, then snatches the garment and puts it on.

"Better?"

"A little," she says, turning away. "Why do you care if I'm cold?"

"I don't. But you ending up sick and bedridden doesn't work with my plans."

Tara hums and wraps the jacket tighter around herself.

The rest of our drive passes in silence. Popov's place is outside the city, in the middle of bumfuck nowhere. The air around us remains charged.

"I've got a few business things I need to handle in the next couple of days," I say as we're nearing the Serb's compound. "But I'm free on Tuesday. I'll pick you up at seven."

"What for?"

The BMW stops at the massive gate blocking the entrance to the grounds. I lower the privacy partition and let Riggo know that I'll handle getting us in.

A security guy approaches, but before he can knock on the driver's window, I slide mine down and catch the man's attention.

"Ms. Popov had a slight car problem tonight, so I'm dropping her off."

The guy glances at Tara, then gives me a nod and yells something over his shoulder in Serbian.

"Why would you be picking me up, Satan?" Tara asks again once the car advances past the guardhouse.

"Dinner."

"I'm not going to dinner with you."

"Of course you are. Otherwise, Drago might get suspicious when, in about a month, we tell him we're getting married. As it stands, our secondary meet-cute sparked undeniable attraction between us, and we're eager to see where it leads."

"Do you really think that my brother will believe that crap?"

"He will. Because, let's be honest, you're not exactly known for your thought-out decisions, Tara. Trust me. The background we have on you is very thorough."

The car slows down and stops in a circular driveway in front of a four-story mansion. I get out and come around to open Tara's door. Ignoring my outstretched hand, and with her lips tightly pressed together, she all but sprints out of the vehicle toward the house. At some point during our tussle, her hair must have come undone. Or maybe she yanked the tie out herself. However it happened, her dark strands are now whipped up in a blustering gust of wind.

Just before she reaches the front door, she stops and turns on her heel. The coldness of the glare she directs at me easily rivals tonight's breeze. Standing there, essentially drowning in the too-big jacket, bathed in the warm glow of the windows on either side of the main door, her scowling expression gets kinda spoiled. But my balls still ache at the resultant view.

She's beautiful.

A vengeful she-cat, bearing her canines and sharp claws.

"Mark my words, Arturo DeVille." Her vitriol carries on the wind while she points her finger at me. At least, that's what I imagine she's doing. It's hard to tell with the sleeves of my jacket swallowing her entire hand. "I'm going to make your life a living hell."

"Of that, *gattina*, I don't have the slightest doubt."

The streetlights are out, and not a single window is lit. Only a sliver of the moon, mostly hidden by clouds, provides enough light to guide my steps. The air is crisp, hinting at imminent snow. It's freezing.

"Asya!" I yell as I run down the deserted, pitch-dark alley.

The ground is hard and cold. My limbs are numb, even though I've been running for hours. Searching.

"Asya!"

My toe catches on something on the concrete, making me stumble and lose my stride, but I recover and continue running. Shouting my sister's name.

Weeks. It's been weeks since she vanished without a trace. The days and nights have bled together, becoming an endless, horrifying oblivion I can't escape. I've questioned, bribed, or beaten every rat in this damn city who could possibly shed light on her whereabouts. All without success. No one has seen her. No one has a clue. She simply disappeared into thin air.

"Asya!" I shout at the top of my lungs.

There is no answer. Just the wind blowing empty soda cans and scraps of paper along the desolate road I blindly run down.

It's my fault. I should have protected my sisters better. Should have had tighter, twenty-four-seven security around them. Then, the girls never would've been able to sneak out. They're my responsibility. Mine to watch over. Mine to keep safe.

I failed.

So I run. Searching in the dark. Searching until I find something. Until I get her back.

I can't stop. I have to find—

I spring up in bed, covered in sweat. Heart jackhammering against my ribcage. It's still dark outside, without even a faint ray of moonlight to break the murk. Reaching for the nightstand, I grab my phone to check the time. Four a.m.

"Great."

Tossing the phone on the covers beside me, I drop back onto the pillow. Five more hours until I need to be at the office. Might as well use the time to check my emails or go over the new contract that dropped into my inbox yesterday. There's no way I'll be able to go back to sleep now. Not after that dream.

Nightmares have plagued me since the day Asya went missing. Intensified tenfold when Sienna swallowed half a bottle of sleeping pills because of her grief and nearly died. They continued for months, long after Asya was found safe and sound. Before tonight, I haven't had one in over a year. Something must have triggered it.

I just don't know what.

CHAPTER
four

 Tara

MY BEDROOM DOOR FLIES OPEN.

"You got another one!" Sienna screeches from the threshold, happily bouncing on the spot. Several red petals dislodge from the bouquet in her hands, falling onto the hardwood floor.

I take in the enormous arrangement of red roses in her arms and roll my eyes. The thing is so huge that the only part of Sienna I can see is the big neon-green bow at the top of her head.

"Yay." I try to smile but it probably comes out as a grimace, so I quickly lower my head and focus on my book.

"You know, I had no idea my brother is such a romantic," my sister-in-law chirps as she hauls the flowers across the room. "Wow. A hundred red roses! Arturo must really be taken with you. I don't recall him ever buying flowers for anyone else. And—" She comes to a sudden stop. "Where are the orchids?"

"Orchids?" I mumble distractedly. The hero is just about to save his girl from the kidnappers. It's the best part of the book.

"The ones from yesterday. The white and pink ones, in the pretty gold vase you promised to give me later."

Oh shit. Quickly shutting the book, I scrounge my mind for a plausible explanation. "Um… I took them to work."

"To Naos?" Sienna scrunches her nose at me, then sets today's bouquet on top of the vanity. The same spot where the orchids used to sit. "But why? They looked so good here, in your room."

"Well I… I just wanted to look at them while I was working?"

Crap. That shouldn't have come out sounding like a question, but I'm a horrible liar.

I actually buried the flowers in the backyard, just behind the doghouses. There was no way I could simply throw them into the trash. Too risky. Someone might find them and start asking questions. But the minor inconvenience and a bit of elbow grease turned out to be a good thing. I kinda like the idea of Drago's hounds pissing and shitting all over Satan's present.

"Oh, that's adorable!" Sienna singsongs. She takes another look at the roses, and after a soft sigh, jumps onto the bed beside me. "I'm so happy that you guys are dating. I wanted Drago to invite Arturo over for dinner, so the four of us could have some family bonding time, but he refused. He's convinced that you and my brother aren't actually going out, and that Arturo has been sending you flowers simply to piss him off. Maybe you could talk to Drago? If this is serious, that is. I mean… is it? Serious?"

"I'd say it's pretty serious." Unfortunately.

"Gotta admit, I never saw it coming. Especially after the whole fiasco that happened at my wedding. Oh, and… um… you're not exactly his type."

"What?"

"Yeah. Arturo is very conservative. I used to laugh and tease him that he missed out. If he'd only been born a few decades earlier, he could have gotten himself a Stepford wife. That's the type of women he's dated."

"Oh?" I arch my brows. "And were there… many?"

Why did I ask that? I don't give a fuck about DeVille or his sexual escapades.

I mean dating history.

Nope. Not thinking about sex and Arturo DeVille.

"Not really. At least, as far as I know." Sienna shrugs. "No one he was serious about, or that he actually brought to the house to meet Asya and me. But, whenever he did have a date accompany him to a Family gathering or event, she was always someone prim and proper, with her spine ramrod straight as if she had a pole stuck up her ass. Picture this—hands folded demurely on her lap when seated. Never uttering a word unless she was asked a specific question," she gripes and mimics throwing up by sticking her finger in her mouth. "I have no idea where he found those chicks. I didn't know women like that still existed! But, I guess, Arturo is just used to being in control, barking orders all day and expecting them to be followed. He demands that of his men, so maybe it's not so strange that he'd do the same with the women he was seeing? Does that sound crazy?"

"Hmm. I didn't peg him as a chauvinist. He's not, right?"

"No. But he is a bit of a traditionalist, and the silliest things get on his nerves."

I bite the inside of my cheek to hide my grin. "What kinds of things?"

"God, where should I start?" She giggles, getting more comfortable on the bed next to me. "Overseasoned food. People who sleep half their day away. Um… Cursing, in public, mainly. Actually, Arturo says that *women* shouldn't curse. The whole no-swearing thing doesn't seem to apply to his own potty mouth, apparently… Oh! The weather, when it gets too hot." Her eyes bug out comically like she's inwardly laughing at her brother's ridiculous pet peeves. "He can't stand fast food. Wet towels…"

Check. Check. Check. I keep a mental list, gleefully adding ideas to my *How to make Satan despise me* plan. Maybe I could get him to change his mind?

"…or when an outfit is just plain old frumpy," Sienna prattles on. "He would never go out unless his clothes were perfectly pressed. Don't get me started on his obsession with his *special* dry cleaner. Evidently, no one else can get the job done right. Even a single wrinkle on his suit would be a crime against humanity!" She looks at me then. "That's how he feels about his dates, too. God forbid a girl wears a short skirt or anything that's too revealing. Nothing but impeccably elegant attire that's appropriate for the venue and event for the lady on my brother's arm."

"Of course." I nod eagerly. "Go on."

"Social media. He really hates that. If it was up to Arturo, he'd get rid of everything except LinkedIn."

Create an IG account. ASAP. Check.

"He's such a grumpy bastard," I snort, then quickly add, "It's so cute."

"It is!" Sienna exclaims. Leaning closer toward my ear, even though we're alone in the room, she whispers, "No one knows this, but beneath his grumpiness, his growling and constant scowls, Arturo is actually a big, sweet teddy bear."

My eyebrows shoot skyward. Objectivity is not my sister-in-law's strong suit. "He tried to kill Drago, Sienna. Or did you forget that little detail?"

"Meh. Arturo would never have followed through. It was just a misunderstanding between them. And Drago did rile him up by mocking his loyalty to the don. That's the one subject my brother is super sensitive about."

"So... is the 'big, sweet teddy bear' really that devoted? Would he follow any and all orders from Ajello, regardless of what they are?" I ask.

Sienna sighs, her gaze wandering to the window. She no longer seems like her cheerful self. The silence between us drags on for so long, I don't think she's going to answer.

"You are not a member of Cosa Nostra, Tara, so you can't possibly understand," she finally says. "Honor is everything. That's the ideal that's held above all others in our society. When members swear fealty to the Family, they make a vow to respect the leadership of and always be loyal to the don. Refusing to follow the don's commands is akin to spitting on your own honor."

Great.

"And... and in Arturo's case," she continues, her voice becoming quieter, "his allegiance to Ajello transcends the Cosa Nostra code." Tears well in her eyes, hovering just at the brim, ready to spill over. "You know how our parents were killed during a raid on the casino where they worked?"

I nod. Drago told me what happened to Sienna's parents. She and her sister were five at the time. After the tragedy, they were raised by their brother. Single-handedly, supposedly. But, I'm finding that difficult to believe about the jerk who's currently ruining my life.

"Arturo petitioned to be our legal guardian. However, the old don decided that our estranged aunt should get custody of Asya and me. Don's word is the law. He's the highest authority. We... Our... What was left of our little family was being torn apart. We were going to be forced away from our brother and sent to live with a woman we'd never even met, Tara. And there was nothing Arturo could do to stop it."

Taking her hand, I squeeze it lightly. I'm well aware of what it's like to lose loved ones at such a young age. Sadly, my and Sienna's histories are very similar. That's probably why the two of us bonded so quickly. We both lost our parents when we were kids. We both survived that unimaginable heartbreak. My pain was amplified by the death of my twin sister, who died at the same time as our mom and dad. Drago was the only family member I had left. Until Keva, that is. The two of them got me through those dark times. I'm not sure if I would have made it had I been separated from them. Just the thought of that possibility makes me physically sick.

"But you weren't?" I choke out. "Taken away from your brother?"

"If it wasn't for Ajello, we certainly would have been."

"Salvatore Ajello?"

"Yes. We were moments from departing when Ajello arrived. He told Arturo to unpack our stuff, saying simply that the old don had changed his mind. That was it. A minute later, he turned around and left. To this day, I have no idea what exactly happened. As I heard, the old don was not prone to going back on his decisions, so it had to be Ajello's doing. But he's never brought it up. Like, ever."

"Well… I'm not sure anyone really knows how Ajello does the things he does."

"Yeah. That man scares the shit out of me," she chuckles. "So, you see, that's the true reason why Arturo is so loyal to Ajello. It's not only the principle that mandates his obedience to Cosa Nostra. For Arturo, it's because he feels beholden. He owes a personal debt to Ajello, and no matter what, my brother will never go against the don."

A heavy weight settles in the pit of my stomach. This is bad.

"Oh! I almost forgot!" Sienna jumps onto her knees and claps her hands with glee. It's so like her. Sad one moment, excited the next. "The first draft of my hockey romance is done. Will you have time to read it and give me some feedback?"

"Um… sure. Need me to count limbs again?"

Sienna is amazing when it comes to the overall plot of the story and creating well-developed characters and settings, but she's terrible with pesky little details. Fact checks. Consistency. That sort of thing. Which means, in every sex scene she writes, she seems to end up with at least two extra hands somehow.

"Please! I'll email it to you in a sec."

I watch her dance out of my room on the tips of her sparkly turquoise house slippers, then slump in bed and stare at the ceiling. In no time at all, my laptop pings with an incoming email. I pull it off the nightstand and onto my stomach, opening the attachment Sienna sent. After repeated attempts, I give up trying to read it. My head's not in it; I can't make myself focus on the text.

What am I going to do? I spent the past three days hoping that the arrogant devil would come to his senses and back out of this idiotic plan to get hitched. In truth, I haven't fully wrapped my mind around the fact that I'm being forced into marriage, so for now, I'm simply going with the flow. The temptation to tell my brother what happened and rely on him to get me out of this mess is overwhelming. He'd probably kill DeVille for me. Maybe. I can't imagine he'd hurt Sienna like that. And, even if he'd be willing to do it, I don't think I could bring myself to ask that of him. Plus, I'd have to explain how my damn prints ended up all over a murder weapon, and then ask Drago to clean up yet another one of my messes. Again.

Like the time he had to pick me up from a police precinct after my friends and I got busted for disorderly conduct. A bunch of us left piles of turds outside a high-end boutique. In my defense, they were selling fur coats. *Real* fur coats made from endangered animals' pelts! Since I was deemed the ringleader, and because I used school grounds to organize this little "protest," I got expelled from that particular school in my freshman year.

My stint at my second high school wasn't much better. Drago had to pay to decontaminate and renovate an entire chem lab after

I accidentally spilled a dangerous substance while trying to rescue a resident guinea pig that escaped from the neighboring biology classroom. I only got suspended for that, and only because of Drago's deep pockets. I'm sure he bribed school officials to get me off the hook, too.

Being older, one would think I'd wise up. But nope. Last year, my brother had to "rescue" me once more. Drunk as a skunk, I got on the wrong train, fell asleep, and ended up in the middle of nowhere good. Not surprisingly, my wallet and phone did not arrive with me. Luckily, that's the worst of what happened. I had to beg a stranger to let me use their phone to get a message to Drago. He was spitting mad when he came to pick me up, practically ready to strangle me for disobeying him. He specifically told me to get ahold of him when I was ready to leave the bar and go home. But I knew he'd been exhausted, and it was very late, and I simply didn't want to wake him.

God! I'm so tired of being stuck on this merry-go-round. As sick as I am of always fucking up, Drago must be reaching the limit of how much he's willing to put up with. He's got a wife now. His attention should be on taking care of her, not cleaning up after me.

And that leads me to the other major worry on my mind. I'm terrified of Drago's reaction if he finds out the truth. What if he challenges Ajello? The last thing I want is to put my brother in danger because I managed to get myself into another clusterfuck.

I'm staring blankly at the ceiling, contemplating my options, when a sudden commotion breaks out on the driveway. It must be something substantial because several raised voices followed by the rapid slamming of car doors reaches me. I rush to look outside just in time to see Drago getting on his bike and peeling out like his tail's on fire.

"Adam!" I call out after I crack my window open. "What's going on?"

My brother's childhood buddy, and now his head enforcer, shifts his mighty frame to look up at me. "Special agents from the IRS just showed up at Naos," he says while yanking his motorcycle helmet onto his head.

"Shit."

"Yeah." He flips down his visor and, in the next breath, takes off on his bike, too.

Getting back on the bed, I grab my laptop again so I can check the admin files for Naos, just in case there's something that I'm unfamiliar with. Drago might need my help to deal with whatever it is they're investigating. My phone starts ringing, and I answer it without glancing at the caller ID, too distracted by opening one folder after another.

"I hope you didn't forget about our plans tonight, Tara." The deep, polished voice rumbles across the line, setting off a slight shiver down my spine, even from a distance.

"Now's not a good time, DeVille." I hit that red circle on the screen and throw the phone on the nightstand. It starts ringing again as soon as it lands on the wooden surface.

"Jesus." Grabbing the damn thing, I press it to my ear. "I told you that—"

"Don't ever hang up on me again."

"Noted." After disconnecting the call, I turn off the phone completely. I can't deal with this asshole right now, not when we might be facing a debacle at the club.

Over the years, I've asked Drago several times to allow me to oversee Naos's accounting, but apparently, I'm not responsible enough. Can't say I blame him for being reluctant, considering my track record. Pretty much at every job I've had, I somehow fucked up. Dealing with people is really not my thing. Words, on the other hand, and numbers, those are putty in my hands. And, I'm excellent at spotting inconsistencies.

The first folder I dive into contains copies of invoices from our suppliers. Alcohol distributors. Produce wholesalers. The list goes on and on. These are mostly our partners who inflate their prices, allowing us to show greater expenses on the P&L statements. At a quick glance, everything appears to be in order. Still, I pull up each invoice for the current year and track it against our main database. Once I'm done with kitchen and bar records, I move to guest services, diligently reviewing booth reservations and nightly cover charge intakes.

With IRS CI Agents on our doorsteps, it's likely they are looking at tax evasion or money laundering. Keva handles the money laundering through the club and has been doing it for years. She's great, but in recent months, she's been stretched too thin. What if she missed something? Drago could be in serious trouble.

Halfway through the stack of February receipts, there's a knock on my door.

"Tara." Jelena pokes her head in, holding up her phone.

"Not now."

"Um… I have Arturo DeVille on the line for you."

My head snaps up. "How the fuck did he get your number?"

"No idea, babe. But he doesn't sound happy." She throws the phone at me, and I nearly fall off the bed trying to catch the thing.

"Um. Some privacy, please?"

"Absolutely." She gives me a wink. "Lover's quarrels are the cutest."

I groan. More than half of my brother's crew lives in this house. That's over fifty people under the same roof. Which means, about twenty seconds after the arrival of the first bouquet from Satan, every single person knew I was "dating" him.

"What?" I snap into the phone.

A thick, throaty sound comes from the other end of the line.

"Did you just growl at me, DeVille?"

"You have three minutes." A pause. "To get your ass downstairs." Another pause. "Or my friend from the IRS Criminal Investigation Division will start asking the kinds of questions no one at Naos wants to hear."

"You bastard! You sent them?"

"I figured you'd need an incentive," he snaps. "Three minutes, Tara."

Nothing but dead air greets me after that not-so-veiled threat. I glance at the phone, confirming what I already knew. *Call ended* is flashing on the screen. All I can do is grit my teeth so I won't scream in frustration.

I hate you, Arturo DeVille!

Arturo

"Everything okay, Mr. DeVille?" Riggo asks from the driver's seat.

"Yup. Fucking perfect."

I throw the phone onto the plush, leather seat cushion and squeeze the bridge of my nose. No other person in my thirty-six years has ever made me lose my shit as fast as that insufferable woman.

"You sure? You have a very strange look on your face. Maybe you're experiencing side effects after that blood donation? My sister told me it could happen, especially if they take too much…"

I groan inwardly. The only reason I made Riggo my driver while my license is suspended is that I didn't want to waste anyone else on this stupid job. The kid is eager to help out, but he's a royal pain in the ass who talks all the damn time. His sister works at the clinic with Milene Ajello, and that somehow led to the boss asking me to find a job for the guy.

"…such a noble act. Saving the world one drop at a time, yeah? I heard Dr. Ilaria say you do it regularly. She says your O negative blood saves a lot of our guys. Especially with some of them getting shot so often and all that. Hey, do you know who's going to get your blood next?"

"You. Unless you stop talking."

"Oh. Okay," he chokes out. "Um… So, where are we headed from here?"

"Del Vecchio's Grill." It's a gem of an Italian chophouse, hidden away in Brooklyn. The only place my medium-rare steak hasn't been screwed up at some point.

With all the shit I've had to deal with in the past couple of days, I don't even remember the last time I ate a decent meal. Having to wrangle Drago's infuriating sister after wading knee-deep through the crap Wang keeps flinging, is the last thing I want to do. But, to sell this charade for the benefit of trigger-happy people, sacrifices must be made.

I push up the sleeve of my jacket and peek at my watch. Twenty seconds. If she doesn't—

The car door opens, and the bane of my existence gets in. I look her over, from the tattered gray sweatpants to a cropped T-shirt that leaves her stomach bare and shows off a sparkly belly button piercing. Finally, my gaze halts at the top of her head.

"Are you fucking kidding me?"

"You said I had three minutes," she says nonchalantly while adjusting one of the orange velcro rollers in her hair. "I had just enough time to pee, grab my purse, and put on my shoes. So—"

"We're headed to dinner."

"Oh, I know. Don't worry, I'll have the curlers out by the time we get there."

Closing my eyes, I start counting to ten, hoping that will quell the urge to kill her. "Riggo. Change of plans. Back to the house."

"What? I'm not going with you to whatever hell pit you call home."

Madonna Santa, give me the strength and patience not to end this day in bloodshed. Taking a calming breath, I pin her with my stare.

"You're going wherever the fuck I tell you to go. I'm fed up with your childish behavior, so you better get a grip and start playing along. Or, I'll make this situation way, way worse for you. Do. You. Understand?"

"I don't think it can get any worse than it already is. Fucking Satan."

"Stop calling me that!"

Tara crosses her arms over her chest and looks away. With her attention directed at the scenery beyond the window, she starts mumbling some nonsense to herself. I don't catch all of what she's on about, hearing only words like "fluffy" and "bear," followed by a choice expletive or two.

Whatever. Taking out my laptop, I open my emails and dive into work. Completely ignoring the furious woman beside me.

"You hungry?" I ask as I throw my jacket over the back of the couch.

"I won't be breaking bread with an enemy, especially under his roof."

Pausing on my way to the kitchen, I throw a glance over my shoulder. Tara remains standing in the middle of the living room. With her hands on her hips, she's slashing me with an irritated look.

Shrugging, I head to the fridge. "Then starve."

The last couple of days, it's been one meal out after another, so my choices for a decent home-cooked supper are limited. I grab a package of chicken breasts and some cremini mushrooms, setting them by the cutting board while I busy myself with getting everything else to make a classic Italian-American dish ready.

While I work—cutting the poultry into strips, then season, dredge in flour, and get them into a hot skillet filled with melted butter and oil—I throw a quick glance at Tara. She strides around the living room, checking out Sienna's various knickknacks scattered on the bookshelves. Each time she picks one up to examine it, she sets it back, but never in the original place.

"I wouldn't have guessed that you like mermaids."

I look up from flipping the chicken in the pan to find Tara hovering near the TV stand with a snow globe in her hand.

"It's Sienna's. She loves leaving her glittery shit all over the house," I say. As soon as the words leave my mouth, I feel the need to make a correction. "Used to, I mean." At times, I forget that neither of my sisters live here anymore.

"And you've kept it in place?"

"Yeah."

Tara returns the decoration to the stand, but on the opposite side of where it was before, and continues her perusal. She's sporting a slightly bewildered expression while unabashedly snooping through all my things. My guess is that she assumed I'd be a quintessential bachelor, with a preference for minimalistic decor. If truth be told, that ultra-modern style showcased in the magazines Sienna used to leave lying around doesn't appeal to me in the least. Those featured rooms always looked sterile, staged to be seen and nothing else. A home should look and feel lived in, not like some damn interior design ad.

Crossing the room to the breakfast bar that separates the kitchen from the living area, Tara pauses by the pictures hanging on the nearby wall.

"This one is broken." She points to a framed photo of a twelve-year-old Asya.

"I know. Your brother slammed my head into it. I haven't had a chance to replace it, yet."

"Mm-hmm. I hope it hurt."

Now that the chicken marsala is done simmering in the pan and the creamy sauce thickened, I start chopping a bit of parsley to finish off the dish. "Probably less than the cut I gave him. How many stitches did he need?"

"Several. Luckily, he was on the mend within days rather than weeks. How's your wrist, by the way? Did it heal alright?" The concern on her face is as fake as the compassionate tone she's speaking with. She walks up to the fridge and takes out a bottle of water, then returns to the breakfast bar and sits down facing me. "I hear recovery from a wrist fracture can be very difficult and takes a long while. And, even after, the healed bone is simply not as strong as it once was. Pity."

My hand, attached to the recently mended wrist, stills mid-chop on the cutting board. I know she's riling me up on purpose, but I don't understand why it's getting on my nerves so much. *Ignore her,* I tell myself. I won't stoop to her level or give her the satisfaction of getting the reaction out of me she obviously wants.

"For someone in your line of business, it's crucial to have a full range of mobility and top-notch reflexes," she continues to chirp in a honeyed voice between sips of her drink. "I'd hate to hear that the damage my brother caused to your wrist has left you with a handicap."

I grit my teeth and focus on the parsley, which at this point is a bruised mess after my aggressive chopping.

"Your fine motor skills do seem to be suffering a bit in terms of your finesse, to be honest. That poor parsley looks all but ground down."

Son of a—

My self-control snaps. I fling the knife up, catch the tip of it as it flips in the air, and send it flying. The blade sails mere inches from Tara's ear, all the way across the living room until it strikes the solid wood of the front door.

"Huh." I cant my head. "You might be right. I'm half an inch to the left of my target."

When my gaze shifts back to Tara, she is staring at me open-mouthed, shock etched on her remarkable features.

A pang of guilt hits me. *I didn't want to scare her, damn it!* I just... the hell if I know what. Never have I been so bothered by anyone before. Is it because I haven't come to grips with Ajello's sly meddling in my private life? Has she simply become a convenient mark for me to take out my frustrations? Or am I just that fucked up?

Momentarily shutting my eyes and squeezing my temples with the pads of my fingers, I sigh. "Listen, Tara, I'm sorry. I—"

Cold liquid hits my face.

"Don't you dare come within a mile of me, you sick fuck," she sneers. Then, she throws the empty bottle at my chest and dashes toward the front door.

Shit.

"Tara!"

I take off after her, catching up just as she's reaching for the handle.

"Stay away from me!" she screams, pushing my hand off her forearm when I attempt to stop her. Grabbing the handle again, she tries to yank open the door.

I thrust my arm out over her shoulder, and my palm connects with the wooden surface, slamming the door shut. My chest collides with her back, effectively trapping the hissing spitfire. She has nowhere to go.

"Tara. I'm trying to apologize."

"I don't need your apologies." She's pulling on the handle so hard that a grating creak joins the sounds of her heavy breathing. "I need to leave!"

With the way she's wriggling, she is grinding her perky ass right over my crotch, which makes my dick hard as fucking steel.

"Tara. I need you to listen to me."

"No! I might be a screwup who can't do anything right, but I won't be terrorized by an overgrown nutjob with anger issues!"

Right.

Change of tactics.

Wrapping my arms around her knees and back, I scoop her up and head toward the living room.

 Tara

My heart thunders against my rib cage as I futilely struggle to escape Satan's hold. Even with all my kicking and screaming, he just casually strides to the couch. His viselike grip doesn't waver, even as he sits down and leans back. The way he's positioned me, quickly securing my limbs with his body, doesn't allow me any wiggle room to even attempt to punch him in the face.

"Alexa," he says. "Put on the ambience playlist."

A moment later, the room is filled with a combination of a classical piano melody and the soothing sound of rain.

"Are you for real?" I gape at him. Our faces are so close that I can see droplets of water clinging to his eyebrows and beard.

"I've said it. But I'll say it again." He leans in even closer. "I'm sorry.

For earlier. I didn't mean to scare you like that. I just… snapped… a little."

"Because I wounded your male pride?"

"Maybe?"

"That's fucking pathetic."

Something akin to a smirk plays on his lips. They look kind of nice. His lips. Not overly full, but with a well-defined cupid's bow, adding to his striking appearance.

"I know. Can we please have a civil conversation now?"

"Let me go, and I'll think about it."

His hold on me loosens. I immediately scramble off his lap and take several steps back.

"There's no point in fighting a battle you can't win, Tara. We're getting married, regardless of how you feel about it. Why won't you just accept the situation for what it is?"

Because I can't! My life has been a revolving door of self-made disasters. Constant screwups and gross mistakes. Even when I tried to do the right thing, I couldn't stick with it.

My relationships haven't gone any better because I just keep choosing to date one loser after another. I'm like a magnet for every fuckwit and cheater around. If they're lucky, they just stomp on my heart and split. If they aren't, they end up dead. Dating me seems to be hazardous to a guy's health. Exhibit A: Stavros. Exhibit B: Petar, who died in a confrontation with Cosa Nostra nearly three years ago.

That kind of track record doesn't bode well for finding the love of my life. The one man who'd love me despite my faults. Whose love for me would rival the greatest romance stories ever told. And we would spend our days and nights being happy.

That's what I want. What I dream of. But now, that dream is being crushed by some asinine idea the New York Cosa Nostra don cooked up. And then further ground down by this bullheaded Satan hiding in gorgeous flesh. For whatever reason, the two figured they had the right to dictate my life. To stomp out every possibility of me finding my own happiness, all for their heartless whims.

I can't let that happen! Can't give up the fight. I want my "happily ever after!" And Arturo DeVille is definitely not it!

"Go ahead and turn in that gun with my prints," I whisper. "I'd rather rot in prison than marry you."

"You sure? Because time behind bars wouldn't be the worst of your problems. Word on the street is that old Katrakis is going apeshit, looking for his son all over the tristate area. Maybe I should send him a tip about your ex's whereabouts?"

"Be my guest."

DeVille leans forward, bracing his elbows on his knees and propping his chin up with his clasped hands. His dark depths sear me from beneath his pinched brows.

"One year," he says after a while.

"One year... what?"

"We'll stay married for one year. Then, I'll give you a divorce."

My eyebrows shoot up. "And what would your beloved don say to that?"

"Ajello believes that the marriage between us will fix my relationship with your brother. And... some other things. When his gambit doesn't pan out, and when he realizes that you and I will likely kill each other, he won't oppose it."

"Really? I had no idea your don is such a reasonable man."

"He's not, but he is pragmatic. With nothing to gain, he will yield."

I bite the inside of my cheek. "Two months," I counter.

"A year. Not a day less."

"Why?"

"Ajello isn't the type to be easily convinced he's wrong. It'll take a year, at minimum."

I tap my finger on my lips while a myriad of thoughts race through my mind. "What if, on our wedding night, I try to slit your throat? Would that convince him that us being married is a bad idea faster?"

"Nope. He'll just say we weren't trying hard enough." He drops his head and seems to stare at nothing on the floor.

It's evident that he doesn't want this marriage to happen any more than I do, but he's hell-bent on following through with it. He is entirely willing to sacrifice everything *he* wants in life to honor his commitment to the don. I would admire the man and his loyalty and determination if his steely resolve weren't ruining *my life*.

For the thousandth time, I wish I could kick myself. What the hell possessed me to grab his fucking gun? If I hadn't, he'd have nothing to blackmail me with. No prints. No threat to hold over my head. It's not like I was going to shoot him. He is Sienna's brother, after all. And, my love for her surpasses even the hatred I feel toward him. Fuck!

"Alright. One year. And only if it's a civil ceremony. I'm not getting married to you in a church." I jut my chin. "And, I want half of *all* your assets, not just marital property, in a divorce. You can put that in a prenup."

He bursts out laughing. "Not happening."

"If I'm being forced to be your wife, I expect compensation. Substantial compensation. Half of everything you own sounds fair."

"I'm not handing over five hundred million to you, Tara."

Whoa. I blink. I had no idea Sienna's brother is *that* loaded. "Fine. I'll take twelve. A million for each month we're married."

There's no way he'll agree to this. The only thing Cosa Nostra men value, apart from their beloved *Family,* is money. He'll weigh the pros and cons and see that it's simply not worth it. Too steep a price for his pride.

No. Come on, let me hear it. N-O.

DeVille grits his teeth. His gaze scorches me as he leans back against the couch cushions, spreading his arms along the top edge. He posed exactly the same way at Naos. Arrogant prick. That posture screams *I'm the king, and you should bow down to me.* Except it doesn't quite work with his current scowl and the dark look of frustration on his face.

What's he waiting for? Is he actually considering it?

Nah, DeVille is too stubborn to compromise.

But as much as his overbearing traits have been clear from the get-go, he has managed to surprise me with one thing. I never would have guessed Arturo DeVille is a man who'd be partial to tattoos. He rolled up the sleeves of his dress shirt when he started cooking, and now I'm nearly mesmerized by the dark ink on his ropey, thickly muscled right forearm.

"Alright." His deep voice explodes into the silence of the room. "I accept those terms."

"What?" I reel back, confused.

"One year. Twelve million dollars. You got yourself a deal, *gattina.*"

Bile rises in my throat. No. No. No. I don't want his damn money! I don't want anything from him except for him to disappear from my life. "I... I wasn't serious. I just—"

He leaps off the couch and closes the distance between us so fast that I don't even get the chance to finish the sentence.

"You what? You're just fucking with me again?" His eyes darken. "No one fucks with me, Tara. You laid out your offer. I accepted. So don't even think about going back on your word. Because if you do, I'll destroy you. Piece by piece. Along with everyone you hold dear. You got that?"

I swallow as a sour taste fills my mouth. My stomach roils and then drops to the floor. There's so much hostility and conviction in his eyes that I don't doubt a single word. He's serious. The pressure behind my eyes means I'm seconds from losing my composure. But I'll be damned if I ever again let even one tear slide in front of this bastard.

Lifting my chin, I meet his unrelenting stare. "I want to see the prenup as soon as you have it drafted. The twelve million is to be deposited in my account the day our divorce is finalized."

"Fine. The venue is already taken care of, but do you have any interest in choosing decorations or other wedding shit?"

"*Zer-oh.*"

His eyes fall to my lips when I enunciate the *oh* sound.

"Perfect," he barks. "This will be a high-profile event, attended by the elite of Cosa Nostra. I won't have you embarrass me like you tried to do tonight. Make sure your wedding dress is nice and elegant. No slits up to your ass or plunging necklines where your tits fall out. No flashing your garters so every Tom, Dick, and Harry can picture you in your lingerie. Understood?"

I arch an eyebrow. He noticed my outfit at Drago and Sienna's *svadba*? I thought he might have been too busy dodging the hors d'oeuvres I threw at him. However, considering he just described what I wore that day in exact detail, I can't help but think that he did. "I'll make sure it covers me from head to foot. Wouldn't want to offend your delicate sensibilities."

"Glad we're on the same page. Thursday. I'll pick you up at noon, for lunch. Dress appropriately to be seen in public, and"—he looks pointedly at the top of my head—"preferably, keep your hair... *accessory... free.*"

"Of course. If that's all, I'll see myself out. Don't worry, I'll call a cab."

"That. Is. All," he growls. "But I'm driving you back."

CHAPTER
five

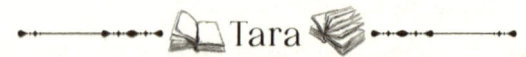
Tara

One week later

"SOMETIME THIS CENTURY, TARA, IF YOU'D BE SO KIND."

I glance up, meeting Keva's scowl. She's leaning on the edge of the stove with her arms crossed over her chest. The steam rising from the pot of stew behind her makes it seem like she's fuming.

"What?"

"Potatoes." She points a long wooden spoon toward the bowl before me. The one I used to prop up my book so I could read. I guess I got a little sucked in by the story.

"Oh. Sorry." Putting the paperback away, I resume peeling the spuds.

If it was anyone but Keva interrupting my reading I would have told them to eff off. But I can't do that to Keva. She's practically a mother to me.

After our parents and sister died, Keva brought Drago and me to the US, fleeing Serbia to protect our lives. We too might have ended up dead if she hadn't smuggled us out. Working multiple jobs, she put a roof over our heads and made sure we had food on our table. Until Drago's business kicked off and his successes allowed him to purchase this house, only then did Keva finally quit her outside jobs. But instead of putting her feet up and enjoying a well-earned rest, she took over managing the household filled with almost half of Drago's people. Every day, she feeds over fifty mouths, tends to everyone's wounds, and on top of that, launders the money for Drago's operations. She's been doing that for years, all while nurturing a pseudo-adopted daughter who's given her more than a few gray hairs along the way.

I smile. It's the times when Keva calls me out on my shit that I truly appreciate how incredible she is. There's no way I could love her more than I already do.

"Are you ever going to take that vacation Drago has been bugging you about?" I ask, grabbing another potato. My brother has been trying to send Keva on an all-expenses-paid trip. Every few months, he buys a first-class plane ticket and books the most luxurious accommodations for her, only for Keva to cancel the whole kit and caboodle.

"Ha! Do you know where he tried to send me last month? The Maldives!" She laughs while stirring the stew. "What the hell would I do in the Maldives? Those fancy overwater resorts are not for me. And anyway, you lot would starve to death or kill each other without me around."

"I'm sure the girls could manage. And I would help."

Keva glances at me over her shoulder. "Tara, you don't even know how to make *pasulj*."

"Of course I do!"

"Sure. But it tastes like dishwater, dear."

"That's not my fault! Every time I asked you to teach me, you just shooed me out of the way."

"Because your nose was always in one of your romance books!

You didn't listen to a word of my instructions, too busy ogling those half-naked men on the covers. Besides, it's hard to cook with one of those things glued to your hands. You almost never actually put down your book."

"That's not true."

Her eyebrows jump toward her hairline, and her gaze moves pointedly to the paperback on the counter. I didn't even realize I had reopened it. It's just… Sienna got me this one yesterday. She said it's the best enemies-to-lovers novel she's ever read. And I'm at the climax of the story!

"You need to get your head out of those and into the real world, girl. That kind of obsession is not healthy."

"I know." I shrug. "But it's so easy to lose myself in the fantasy where characters always, somehow, manage to make the right choices. Especially the cute but shy heroine. She doesn't let anything drag her down, just calmly deals with her shit while holding her head high. And everyone can't help but love her because she's so damn perfect. And then, there's her superhot, brooding love interest. He's so rough around the edges and totally unyielding. But that's just a front. Secretly, he's crazy about the sweet, perfect heroine, and can't wait to steal the stars from the sky so he can lay them at her feet. I mean, what's not to love?"

"There are plenty of good, *real* men around here, Tara."

"Yeah, sure. And all of them are just waiting for me."

"You could find out if you'd break up with the Italian grump."

I snort. Keva is not a part of Satan's fan base.

"It's amazing that you're not charmed by him like all the other women in the house seem to be. They constantly gush about what a gentleman he is for sending me flowers every day."

"Ha! He sent you white lilies last night. Those are funeral flowers. And the day before yesterday… yellow hyacinths. Those symbolize jealousy. A *gentleman* should know these things. And just don't get me started on the hundred roses! Couldn't have added one more, could he? Shame on him!"

"Well, he'll be here shortly to pick me up, so I'll encourage him to do some thorough research on the meaning of flowers in Balkan cultures so he's more informed in the future," I laugh.

This morning, I woke up to a text from an unknown number. All it said was: *1 p.m. Be ready.* It wasn't signed. The jerk probably thinks everyone on the planet should be able to recognize his royal decree; no need for him to actually identify himself. He didn't even bother asking if, perhaps, I had other plans today. Oh no, *His Assholeness* just assumed I'm sitting around waiting for his summons so I can jump and do his bidding.

"What the hell are you doing with that man, anyway?" Keva continues, stirring the stew with enough force to whip it into a pudding. "Are you actually dating him or is this a new way you're trying to piss off Drago? Because it's working."

I bite my lower lip. I'm so damn tempted to confess. To tell Keva that Arturo DeVille is threatening to pin a murder on me—a murder he committed!—unless I go along with this sham of a relationship and become his wife. I know if I told her the truth, Keva would hug me, pet my head, and let me cry on her shoulder. But then, she'd march straight to Drago and tell him everything!

Ugh! That would be a disaster. I can easily picture how it would unfold from there. My brother would be livid and would try to kill DeVille. But if he somehow managed to keep his wits about him, remembering that Satan happens to be Sienna's brother, Drago would then set his sights on Ajello.

And then he would end up dead!

No. I can't risk it. I won't allow Drago to get hurt again because of me. He carries enough scars on his body as a daily reminder that he nearly died in the fire he saved me from.

Never again.

"Drago doesn't get to tell me who I should date." I lift my chin, hoping to convince her. "And I don't need him to sign off on my boyfriend. It's my life."

"He's just worried about you."

Yup. Everyone is always worried about me. It's as if I'm incapable of living independently, or something. Someone constantly needs to hold my hand so I don't screw up while putting on my "big girl pants."

Jesus fuck. Drago's "the world is a dangerous place and I have many enemies" rant is still ringing in my head from when he forced me to move back into the mansion. Never mind that I can shoot a fucking gun better than some of his men. In truth, it's one of the very few things I'm actually good at. But my brother still thinks I can't take care of myself.

"Well, he shouldn't be worried. I'm fine. In fact, I'm feeling pretty damn amazing." I drop the last of the peeled potatoes into the bowl and storm out of the kitchen.

Somebody calls after me as I run across the entry hall, but I ignore them. I need some fresh air before I lose my goddamned mind. Flinging the front door open, I barrel outside, only to immediately smash face-first into a cluster of soft, red petals. The honeyed, floral scent of roses invades my senses.

"What the—" I push off with my hands, trying to repel the flowery onslaught on my nose, sneezing in the process.

"I should have expected this," an irritatingly sexy voice comments from directly above my head. "You can't even accept flowers normally."

Shoving the blasted bouquet away, I glare at the uninvited guest.

The midday sun brings out a bluish tinge in his slightly wavy black hair. He wears it softly swept away from his face, giving it a somewhat mussed look. The gray three-piece suit fits him like a glove, same as every other outfit I've seen him in. It really is a shame that a drop-dead gorgeous guy like him is such an asshole. So much wasted potential.

"It's not even noon," I grumble. "What are you doing here?"

"Courting you. Isn't that obvious?"

"*Courting*? Are you a Regency-era escapee or something?"

Arturo's eyes darken. "Trust me, I'm not enjoying this any more than you. I'm putting in an effort for the sake of appearances. And so should you. Take the roses."

He tries to hand me the flowers, but I shove them back. "Can't. I'm out of burial spots. You keep them."

"Tara?" My brother's voice booms behind me. "What's going on?"

Damn it.

Swapping the scowl on my face for a beaming smile, I swipe the bouquet out of DeVille's hands and crush it to my chest like it means the world to me.

"Look at these lovely roses!" My voice might as well be coated in sugar crystals. Knowing that Drago won't likely hear me clearly, I spin around so he can read my lips. "Isn't my man simply wonderful for bringing me such beautiful flowers?"

"Mm-hmm." Based on the look of disgust on my brother's face as he glances at the roses, one would think they were entrails instead. But then, his attention shifts to his brother-in-law, and Drago's glare turns chilled and stony. "And why is the pretty boy buying you flowers again?"

"It may come as a surprise to you," Satan replies in a

condescending tone, "but a man with manners does that when he picks up his girlfriend for their date."

"*Girlfriend?*" Drago narrows his eyes.

"For now. Soon, hopefully, much more than that."

In a flash, my brother closes the distance between us. A menacing growl leaves his throat as he reaches past me and fists the front of DeVille's shirt.

"*Sljamu nalickani!*" Drago snarls.

"Christ!" I throw the flowers to the side and wrap both my arms around one of Drago's, trying to yank my brother off DeVille.

But Satan uses that to his advantage, shooting out his own arm to wrap his hand around Drago's throat. "Get your fucking paws off me," he hisses.

The two end up in a deadlock, holding each other at arm's length. My head ping-pongs from my brother to my "boyfriend" and back. These guys have been silently waging a cold war ever since Arturo tried to meddle his way into Sienna's marriage to Drago. Going by the murderous expressions on both their faces, that frigid conflict is seconds away from getting really, really hot.

"You're doing this just to piss me off even more, aren't you, you fuck?" Drago roars.

"Contrary to what you may believe, the world doesn't revolve around you, Popov!" DeVille barks back.

"Oh, for the love of God!" I release Drago's arm and slip between their massive bodies, turning to face my brother while I hook my arms on their anchored limbs. The result is me hanging off their strained forearms like a ragdoll, with my feet dangling several inches off the ground. "Stop this! Let go, both of you!" I yell, hoping my weight will make each of them drop their grip.

"No!" The two voices erupt simultaneously, rattling the rafters in the entry hall.

Shit. I have no choice but to spit out the words I'd rather choke on.

"Drago!" I shout. Then, when he looks at me, I continue, "Please, stop. I'm… um… in love with him."

Acid practically floods my mouth.

My brother blinks. His gaze darts back to Arturo, then returns to me. "I don't believe you."

"What? Why?"

"You're the worst liar I've ever met, Tara. Drop this fuckery, right now!"

"But I'm telling the truth!"

"Oh yeah? Until a few weeks ago, you were referring to this mofo as 'that pretentious Italian asshat.' And now, you're suddenly all lovey-dovey with him?"

Well, crap.

I open my mouth. Close it. My brain kicks into overdrive, searching for a way to convince Drago. Meanwhile, he keeps on glaring at me.

He needs to believe this farce. Everything depends on my brother never suspecting that I've been forced into a relationship with Satan. There's too much at stake. I won't let my latest screwup endanger my family. *Clean up your own messes, Tara.* I repeat the mantra in my head.

"Yes, I am." Abandoning my useless hold on the men's forearms, I let go. When my feet hit the ground, I stay wedged between them, giving each a push apart. Not really expecting that my shove would do anything, I'm surprised when both drop their arms and take a step back.

Swallowing the lump lodged in my throat, I turn to face my nemesis. There is a wicked smirk dancing on his sexy lips as he meets my gaze. My legs are heavy as I draw closer and lift to my tippy-toes. I slide my hands upward over his chest and hook them behind his neck.

"I detest you," I whisper. Then pull his head down and smash my mouth to his.

It was supposed to be a rough press of the lips. Just long enough to convince Drago that I was telling the truth, but not so long that I'd want to puke later. That's the only outcome I could foresee after sharing such intimacy with Satan.

As always, though, my instincts and intentions prove shitty.

The moment our lips connect, my brain basically short-circuits, as if a hundred and ten volts zip straight through our touch. I'm reduced to nothing but nerve endings. Made to feel… everything.

Blitzed.

The spicy scent of his cologne is pulling me under. Its faint, earthy notes are driving me insane. Ravenous. Lustful. Maybe it's because I didn't expect a domineering man like him to have such soft lips. Or possibly because he thrusts his tongue into my mouth at that very same instant. Surely not because of his strong hands wrapping around my ass and lifting me to be crushed against his hard male body.

My fingers rake through his perfectly swept-back hair, tangling in the silky strands. He devours my mouth without allowing me a chance to catch my next breath. My bottom lip gets pulled between his teeth; the sting of the bite is both painful and euphoric. If I were capable of a conscious thought, I'd be mortified by the needy moan that escapes me. The kiss is brutal, and bruising, and… dear fucking God… the best I've ever—

"*Sunce ti jebem.*"

My brother's loud curse hits me like a bucket of cold water.

I freeze, and then slowly lift my face, separating myself from the most luscious lips in existence. Reluctantly, and with dread at what

I might see, I open my eyes. Two espresso-colored orbs stare back at me, a wicked glint shining in their depths.

"Tara," Drago's agitated voice roars behind me. "Climb off him. Right. The fuck. Now."

I grit my teeth. "Let me down."

"You're the one clinging to me, *gattina*." Smirking, DeVille dips his head to whisper in my ear. "If I didn't know better, I might believe you enjoyed that."

Blinking to clear the cobwebs from my mind, I quickly untangle my legs from around his waist and unlock the boa-like grip my arms have on his neck and head. The devil's hands remain on my ass cheeks as he keeps me plastered to his torso while I slide slowly down his body.

"Considering the stakes, I'm quite invested in the deal we made," I whisper as my feet land on the polished floor tiles.

Forcing myself to lean on DeVille's chest, I turn around to face my brother. "Drago, you really need to stop butting into my personal life. I don't owe you an explanation for my feelings for my boyfriend. But since you insist, I'll have you know all that hate between us ended up being quite a turn-on. Would you like a demonstration? If you want proof, he and I can just fuck right here in front of—"

"Enough!" Drago growls.

"I'm glad we agree. Now, we have a date to get to, so if you don't mind…"

"Go wait for your… *boyfriend*… in the car. I need to have a word with him. Now, Tara."

"Hey! Don't—" I start protesting, but a flash of worry in Drago's eyes makes me falter.

I know that look. It has nothing to do with him trying to boss me around. Rather, it's a sliver of strain that all too often invades my brother's life. Last year, he wore it for days after I slid off the road and crashed into a tree in the middle of a thunderstorm. At first, I figured he was pissed about the wreckage, but soon enough it was clear he didn't give a shit about that. He was worried about what could have happened to me.

And before he *allowed* me to pick up my car from the mechanic, I had to endure more than five minutes of nonstop ranting on the dangers of driving. It was like he lost his mind and was too afraid to let me get back behind the wheel. I watched the battle he fought with himself before eventually relenting. And I understood that no matter what, my brother's fears would forever include losing me. He might be overprotective and insufferable at times, but I know exactly what it stems from. And when I see that flash of dread in his eyes, the best thing I can do for him is let him say his piece.

"Fine." I shrug and scoop the now rather disheveled bouquet of red roses off the floor. Taking a long, deep inhale of their scent, I head out.

Arturo

My gaze is stuck on Tara as she crosses the hall. I take in her dark, luscious locks as they cascade like a shimmering waterfall down her back, gently swishing from side to side with the sway of her hips while she heads toward the door. Swallowing hard, I can't help but stare at her ass, admiring the way it fills out her skinny jeans. Christ. I drop my gaze, letting it slide along Tara's toned legs and all the way to the pair of white Converse All Star high tops she's wearing. Each step she takes carries her further away, leaving a trail of crushed rose petals feebly falling onto the marble. The vision she presents is simply uncanny. A warrior departing a battlefield, with the blood of her enemies dripping off her blade.

It's sexy as hell.

Not even two minutes ago, I was confident that I had every-thing under control. Masterfully directing this situation. Tara can't act for shit. I could read her intentions well before she grabbed my neck and pulled me down to her mouth. She was utterly incapable of hiding the look of disgust on her face before our lips connected. Not that it did me any favors.

But at the press of her soft lips, I felt like a lightning bolt went through me. Every cell in my body came alive, charged by a weird form of energy. The current raced along my veins, tightening each of my muscles. Everything... everything tingled, as if after years of numbness, life was suddenly coursing through me. And heading straight for my fucking cock. The only thing I wanted was to have the aggravating woman in my arms. So I pulled her closer, crushed her against my chest. And kissed her. Momentarily forgetting it was fake.

What the fuck is wrong with me? I've never had such an intense reaction to a woman before. Especially after a single kiss. And after she insinuated the two of us are having sex, I couldn't get the image out of my head and almost fucking combusted. I can't have that. I need this unwanted desire gone. Being attracted to Tara Popov is simply out of the question.

With significant effort, I finally rip my gaze away from the door she disappeared through.

"I want you to stay away from my sister, DeVille," Drago barks, getting in my face.

"It's a good thing I don't give a fuck what you want, then," I grumble. "Should I remind you that just a handful of months ago, we were in a similar situation? Only then, *my* sister was set to marry a demented asshole. You!"

"My point exactly. And you"—Drago shoves his finger into my

chest, snarling—"her dear brother, whose duty it was to protect her, did nothing."

He's got some gall, insinuating that I don't care about my sister as much as he does for his. As if I wouldn't give my life for Sienna, or for Asya. I would, without blinking an eye.

My fingers curl into a fist, but I force myself to stay focused. I need this dick to believe our goddamned lie. Romance. Love. Wedding. That's the ball game. The rules are murky, but I can't get called on an offside.

"Sienna is a grown woman, capable of making her own decisions. Just as Tara is. Based on what I've seen from her so far, she can hold her own," I say.

"Really? Well, let me tell you a few things about her that you may not have noticed. My sister is the most bullheaded creature on this earth. She's stubborn, loudmouthed, and convinced she can accomplish anything she sets her mind to."

"Yeah, I noticed."

"Of course you did. But here's the rub. Most of the things she tackles on her own end up a fucking disaster." A tick works in his jaw, and he draws a deep breath before continuing. "Tara is a beautiful mess. But there's nothing she won't do for someone she loves. If they needed a lung transplant, she wouldn't hesitate to ravage half the world to locate a suitable donor. She'd maim, mangle, or kill if she had to, and she'd do it without remorse. Using her bare hands, she'd rip that organ out and present it to a surgeon atop her still blood-soaked palms. Except, she'd be holding a goddamned liver. Not a lung."

I burst out laughing. Yup, I can fucking believe it. Can totally picture her doing that.

"Mm-hmm. That. That condescending guffaw is exactly what I mean," Drago sneers. "The only thing you got out of that story is that Tara would royally screw something up. The rest didn't even register. The fact that she'd be willing to murder in broad daylight for the sake of someone she loves. You get that?" His lip curls as he glares at me. "My sister deserves a man who will love and cherish her. Just as she is. A man who will not diminish the things she excels at simply because she makes a mistake or two along the way. And you… You are not that man, DeVille."

The grin dies on my face as the meaning of his words hits me.

"So go on your little date or whatever," he continues. "God knows, Tara doesn't react well to being ordered around, so I won't bother trying to strong-arm her into dumping your ass. Soon enough, she'll realize it herself. She'll see that you're not worthy of her."

As Popov strides away, heading across the entry hall toward the interior of the house, my fist itches to connect with his self-assured face. While I'm trying to quell the urge to chase him down and ram his accusations into his ugly mug, a joyful giggle rings out on the upper level. I glance upward, spotting Sienna skipping down the wooden stairway. She's in her blinding red-and-yellow onesie thingy that sparkles in the blazing sunlight. The glow on the sequins rivals the twinkle in her eyes as she leaps off the second stair straight into Popov's open arms. As if she doesn't need oxygen to breathe, she bursts into nonstop chatter about matching raincoats for the dogs. That's my Sienna.

A tightness grips my chest as I look at my sister with her husband. They are so… happy. Carefree. In love. I can't deny it. This asshole really does love my sister. They have… something that isn't in the cards for me. That all-consuming desire and devotion. A marriage filled with passion, with love.

I loathe to admit it, even to myself, but Ajello was right. I have been keeping busy just to escape the sudden emptiness in the house.

But that's not the main reason for my lack of a social life. I fuck. Here and there. Like every other red-blooded guy, I need an occasional release. Hell, sex is sex, but what it isn't, what I won't ever allow it to become, is an excuse to form an emotional attachment. I've gone to great lengths not to catch feelings for any of my partners. I simply don't have the capacity to let myself care for anyone else anymore.

After fifteen years of being the sole parent to my sisters, worrying and obsessing over all the possible ways they could get hurt because of me, my line of work... After living in constant fear that I'll somehow fuck up... I can't. I can't allow myself to feel that much. Especially not since Asya was kidnapped and missing for months. And then Sienna tried to kill herself. I lost my fucking mind then.

Never again.

Thank God both Asya and Sienna are now happy with men who would willingly lay down their lives for them. They are safe. I'll always love them, will always be there if they ever need anything from me, but I'm not looking to replace taking care of my sisters with caring for anyone else. In particular, a wife. I don't need a relationship that would bring on that crippling fear again.

But knowing how hell-bent the Family is on upholding traditions, I always knew an arranged marriage was a possibility. If it came to that, I assumed it would involve a woman who was raised aware of what would be expected of her. Someone meek and obedient, someone suited to be the spouse of a Cosa Nostra underboss. Someone I'd be able to keep at arm's length.

Despite outward appearances, most arranged marriages in Cosa Nostra are loveless matches. Oh, the couples put on a good show to convince everyone otherwise, but the unions are nothing more than business transactions. And that kind of setup is right up my alley because love isn't for me. Never will be. But knowing that... it doesn't diminish the bitter burn scorching my throat.

Swallowing down the acid, I turn on my heel and step out of Popov's home.

My car is parked on the other side of the driveway, with an awed-looking Riggo behind the wheel, staring straight ahead. As I figured, Tara isn't inside. With her arms crossed over her chest, still gripping the tattered bouquet of roses, Drago's sister is perched on the hood of the car, scowling in my direction. This woman seems to be suffering from a compulsion of not doing as she's told. It's one of the many things we'll need to address before she can be presented to the Family as my chosen bride. Pressed into the marriage or not, Mrs. DeVille will need to behave as is expected of her standing.

"You appear to be unharmed," she mumbles as I approach.

"And you seem unhappy about it."

"I guess. I hoped Drago would rough you up, even if just a bit."

"That's a rather cocksure attitude you have there. Did it never occur to you that it might be your brother who ended up worse for wear?" I open the car door for her and nod. "Get in."

Graceful as a gazelle, she leaps to the ground. Then, she makes a show of sweeping her eyes from the top of my head to my feet, and back up again until our gazes collide.

"Oh please. What would you have done? Threatened to smack him with your award for the *Most Uptight Man of the Year*? Or maybe smear your hair gel in his face?"

"I don't use fucking hair gel," I snap.

The corners of her lips lift into a smirk. "Hmm, could have fooled me."

I grip the door handle so hard that I nearly rip it off. Closing my eyes, I take a deep breath. *Madonna Santa, please have mercy and give me the strength not to choke this woman to death before our wedding day.*

CHAPTER
six

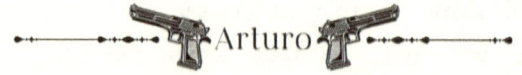 Arturo

One week later

"OH WOW! A COZY FAMILY-RUN RESTAURANT IN THE suburbs," Tara comments, looking around as I lead her to my usual table in the far corner. It's a secluded spot that's mostly hidden from prying eyes, so I can dine in peace. At least, most of the time.

"Hmm, and here I was expecting you to take me to another ridiculous fine-dining establishment where my choices are 'Beluga caviar this' or 'something, something in white truffle sauce that'. God, I think I've had enough *gourmet cuisine* in the past week to last me a lifetime."

"Exquisite flavor and aroma aren't reserved exclusively for fine dining. Besides, everyone knows that there's only one way to leave a place like that." I glance at her while pulling out her chair. "Hungry." Giving her a nod, I clear my throat. "And, they emphasize a certain dress code."

"Oh, yeah. I forgot about that."

I watch her lower herself onto the chair, crossing her leg over her opposite knee. The washed-out skinny jeans hug her delicate curves like a second skin. Her simple navy-green collared shirt is tied into a knot at her navel. The top two buttons are undone, showing a sliver of her lacy bra underneath, the color of which matches her outer layer. Other than two giant golden hoops in her ears that remind me of a fortune teller at the fair, I don't see any sort of jewelry on her.

No hair accessories this time, either. Her long, dark mane is left loose in a silky veil hanging more than halfway down her back. There's so much of that gorgeous, wavy mass that it simply defies logic. More hair on this one woman's head than I would have imagined, enough for at least five people. The sight of all those tresses is making the tips of my fingers itch. The urge to reach out and touch her hair again is overwhelming. To wrap the thick cord of it around my wrist, squeeze the ends in the palm of my hand as I tilt her head back and plunge—

"Why are you staring at me, DeVille?"

"You should tie your hair back," I grumble, quickly taking a seat across from her. "It looks wild."

She raises one perfectly arched eyebrow. "Do I look like I give a fuck about how you see me?"

Nope. Then again, even with her massive hoop earrings, no makeup, and entirely casual outfit, she looks beautiful. Fuck!

"I need to be back in the office in a couple of hours. Let's order." I grab the menu from the center of the table, where it was left for us. "I assume you don't read Italian, so I'll translate for you."

"No need. I'll have a cheeseburger, fries, and a side of ketchup." She grins.

I glare at her over the menu. "This is an authentic Italian restaurant. The owners run things here the same way they did back in Tuscany. They don't serve cheeseburgers. Or fries. And most certainly, no ketchup."

Her smile widens. "I know. I did my research on what Italians consider the biggest food-related faux pas." Her eyes light up with a mischievous glow. "I want a large cappuccino, too."

I sigh. "It's past noon. Cappuccino isn't offered after eleven. Choose something else."

"Nope. I want a *real* cappuccino."

"Well, you're not getting one. It's considered bad for your digestion to have milk-based drinks after lunch. Ordering one could be viewed as uncivilized."

Tara sets her elbows on the table and leans forward, placing her chin on her clasped hands. "Don't tell me the omnipotent Arturo DeVille can't order whatever and whenever the hell he wants, social and cultural rules be damned."

I tighten my hand around the menu and take a deep breath.

While I'm struggling to remain calm, the owner of the restaurant approaches. An older man wearing a black apron over his crisp white shirt and dark slacks. He fidgets with his hands as he stands expectantly next to our table.

"Signor DeVille." He bows his head, speaking in rapid Italian. "We are so honored to have you as our guest again. May I offer you today's specials? Or perhaps you'd like—"

"*Bistecca alla Fiorentina* for me," I cut him off. "And a cheeseburger for the lady."

"Certainly. I'll have the chef—Apologies. Um. I think I may have misheard. The lady would like…?"

"Cheeseburger," I say through my teeth. "And fries with ketchup on the side."

The proprietor blinks at me, his facial features pulled into a slight grimace. "I… Well, um… I'm so terribly sorry, but we don't have ketchup, Signor DeVille."

"Then have someone go buy it." The thick paper of the

menu crumples in my hand. "And the lady also wants... a damn cappuccino."

"Of course." The man nods. "Absolutely."

Once the stunned owner retreats, I glance back at my future wife. Her lips are pursed as she pouts into the phone in her outstretched hand, just as she's done during every other "date" we've gone on in the past few weeks. I pretended not to give a fuck about what she was doing then. Just as I refrained from commenting every time she added heaps of salt and pepper to her food. Once, she ground so much pepper onto her dish, she ended up coughing from the abundance of spice. But I didn't care. Not then, not now. Her shenanigans don't concern me in the least.

She sweeps her hair over her shoulder, tilts her chin up, and pouts into the camera again. Snapping pictures. For what? To send them to someone? Sienna maybe? Or... to another man? Surely she wouldn't be sending pictures to some guy while having lunch with me? Whatever. I don't care. I DO NOT—

Pout. Smile. Air kiss.

"What are you doing?" I snap.

"Taking a selfie." She uses her free hand to open the collar of her shirt further. "I'm still building my following. Need my content to be more engaging." A flip of her hair sends a waft of air carrying the scent of strawberries in my direction.

"Following?"

"On Instagram. Did you know that photos where I'm pouting get ten times more likes and comments than if I smile? See?" She turns her phone toward me.

I stare at the image of Tara in a skin-tight black minidress. With a champagne flute in her hand, she's leaning back against the banister. Her chin is tilted to the camera, and her sinful blood-red lips are pursed as if she's blowing a kiss.

"Delete that thing," I growl as a zap of electricity shoots straight to my cock. "Now."

"Don't tell me you're exactly like my *savage* brother, as you refer to 'our lot.' Do you have a problem with me being on social media just like Drago did with Sienna? Did you know that he actually got her account shut down? You would never lower yourself to that same barbaric level, would you?"

My left eye starts twitching.

"I guess not. So, hey, when they bring our meals out, don't start eating right away. I wanna take a few shots. Pictures of food are almost as popular as the ones of me pouting."

"Showing off what you eat online so a bunch of people you don't even know can comment seems beyond idiotic to me," I grumble. Still, that's infinitely better than having sexy photos of her online for countless horny men to ogle and drool over what belongs to me.

I hate the idea of agreeing with my brother-in-law's actions, but I need to find out how he managed to kill Sienna's social media account. Because I have to do the same for my soon-to-be bride. Without her realizing my involvement, of course. The last thing I want is for her to think I'm jealous or something. It's simply common decency. I can't allow the Cosa Nostra's second lady, for all intents and purposes, to saturate the internet with provocative photos of herself, now can I? Thankfully, she was appropriately dressed. Well, at least in the picture she showed me.

Wait.

What if she's posted nudes, too?

My blood pressure skyrockets.

"Your newspaper, Signor DeVille." The waiter sets a folded *New York Times* on the table for me. As I've been a regular patron here for years, the owner is well aware that I like to browse the news while I dine.

Picking up the paper, I open it to the financial section, hoping that the latest on the markets will distract me from my current train of thought.

"Good God, DeVille. Are you for real?" The woman living rent-free in my gray matter laughs. It's an annoyingly sexy sound.

I clench my jaw. "What?"

"An actual fucking newspaper? What are you, ninety? Hasn't anyone told you that everything is online these days?"

"I'm not interested in clickbait journalism. Our world has become addicted to digital content. Some call it 'news,' but most of it is garbage. The widespread dissemination of misinformation will likely lead to the downfall of our society. And I'd appreciate it if you'd refrain from cursing in public."

She snickers again. It comes out sounding like a purr. Seductive. Smooth. Like a stroke of her tongue against my own.

"Okay. I just have to know one more thing."

I turn the page to the overview of stock prices. "I'm listening."

"Do you wear drawers under your breeches? You know, those thermal long johns to keep your kidneys warm. In the era you think you live in, it was considered scandalous to leave your home without them."

The newspaper tears along the center fold, leaving two tattered halves dangling from my fisted hands. I pin Tara with a glare while fuming at her audacity. Meanwhile, she's giggling like a total nutjob, pressing her hands over her mouth and struggling to properly breathe.

Damn her.

She's being ridiculous. And cute.

The corner of my mouth quivers. Then, completely against my will, it quirks upward.

"Since we're on the subject of my clothes, you haven't returned my jacket," I deflect, hoping this reminder will cause her to stop laughing because it's proving to be annoyingly contagious. "I want it back."

"Yeah, sorry. I kept forgetting at first, but then I decided to wash it. I was taught to always return whatever I borrow, cleaned. And, well, I left it in the dryer."

I stare at her. "You *washed* it?"

"Don't worry. I threw it in the delicate cycle."

She put my Ermenegildo Zegna jacket in a *washing machine*. Perfect.

"Now I wish I remembered to grab it." She shudders and wraps her arms around herself. "It might have come in handy. You Italians do seem to like keeping things on the chilly side."

"It's not that cold in here."

"I like to be warm."

She likes to be warm. Great. Inwardly groaning, I get up and shrug off my jacket. Tara watches me with awe as I take a couple of steps and drape the garment over her shoulders. Her eyes flare as I bend and bring my face to hers. "No washing this one. Got it?"

"Yup."

"Good." I resume my seat and get back to my newspaper. The left half of it, that is.

CHAPTER
seven

 Tara

"**A**LRIGHT. HOW ABOUT THIS ONE?" I GRAB THE HANGER with my brown dress on it. "The hemline falls just above my knees."

Sienna wrinkles her nose. "Definitely not. You're going to a fundraiser with snobs. Nothing other than a floor-length gown will do."

My shoulders sag. "This is the most conservative dress I have, Sienna."

"Let me see what we have to work with." She nudges me out of the way and plants herself in front of my closet, pushing the hangers to the side one by one.

"Too short."

Swoosh.

"Boring."

Swoosh.

"Way too short. Dreadful color. Too much cleavage."

Swoosh. Swoosh. Swoosh.

My butt hits the edge of the bed, and I fall back on the mattress, closing my eyes.

That cute pink dress that barely brushes my thighs and the

four-inch fuck-me stilettos that I planned to put on would have
sent Satan's conservative ass straight into a meltdown. But as soon
as Sienna burst into my room, insisting that she absolutely needed
to help me pick my outfit for today's event, my devious plan went
out the window.

"Tara? Why do you have five men's suit jackets in your closet?"

My eyes snap open. Shit. I completely forgot about my hidden
stash. "Those are your brother's. I forgot to bring my coat with me
when we went out, so he let me borrow his."

"You forgot to bring your coat... five times?"

"Uh-huh."

A playful smirk lights up her face. "You two really do like each
other."

My eyebrows shoot up. "Ah, why are you saying that... like
that?"

"Well, I'll be honest. At first, I was a little skeptical. You and
Arturo are very different. Like two separate species that were
never meant to occupy the same habitat, never mind have other
involvement."

"Couldn't agree more," I say under my breath.

"But you've been dating for weeks now. He's taken you over to
his place, and he's never brought a woman there before. And you,
you agreed to go with him to this fundraiser, and I know exactly
how much you hate these kinds of events."

Of course I agreed. When I initially refused to go, DeVille threatened to send his IRS buddies back to Naos!

"Also, every time he calls, you get this look on your face," she
continues, smiling delightedly. "It's like you're bursting with excit-
ing news but are trying to be all cool about it. As if you're too embarrassed to show your enthusiasm, so you try to hide it. But the
twinkle in your eyes can't be suppressed or hidden."

She thinks I'm excited when I'm actually trying to hide my torment? If my eyes sparkle with anything, it's with the ire that man stirs in me. Although I must admit, I do get perverse pleasure from discovering which buttons of his I can push when we go out. It's fun to watch as he tries to appear all lovey-dovey in front of everyone, even though I can totally tell he's fuming. I love seeing that left eye of his start twitching.

Still, he's not a bad actor. He's got practically everyone convinced that he's my perfect boyfriend. Not me. I'd rather suffer never-ending heartburn than date Satan DeVille for real. The only decent thing about him is that he's a good kisser. Amazing kisser. But I'd never admit that out loud. It's enough that our kiss keeps playing on repeat in my thoughts, and I can't seem to shut down the channel. Or forget the achy throbbing in my clit when he crushed me against his chest that day, all while he—

"But I think the jackets are a dead giveaway." Sienna's voice brings me back to reality. "You probably already know about his OCD when it comes to his suits. I bet you're just testing Arturo's boundaries. And he's letting you! So there... It's like an Animal Planet-worthy mating dance. *Soooo* cute."

My sister-in-law is delusional. A *mating dance*? WTF?! Maybe I should tell her how I want to slit her brother's throat in hopes that it would save me from being forced to marry the bastard. But I can't. I'm sure that whatever I tell Sienna about this situation, she'll relay it all to Drago.

As for the jackets... I can't help that I'm always cold. Or that I'm slightly forgetful. It's not like I've been stealing his suit jackets on purpose. Yeah, they are exquisite. Incredible quality. And they smell nice. I love that, when DeVille wraps his jacket around me, there's always that lingering bit of body heat. And I do appreciate his willingness to lend me his rather than making me go back to the car to get my own coat. So what if it happened the last five times? That just proves that I'm a bit absent-minded. Nothing new.

Okay. I am doing it on purpose. But only so I can piss Satan off.

"You should definitely go with this one." Sienna takes a simple gray silk gown off the hanger and throws it at me. "Pair it with that designer-cut cashmere coat I bought for you. Unless you'd rather have Arturo's jacket?"

"I'll make sure to bring my coat," I mumble.

Arturo

"Just admit it. You're doing this deliberately, aren't you?"

"You got here ten minutes early!" Tara snaps as she slides her arms into the sleeves of my Armani jacket. "I barely had time to finish my makeup and avoid leaving with only my left eye lined like some crazy pirate, never mind remembering my coat."

A shrill ring explodes from my phone. I fish it out of my pocket and bring it to my ear while watching Tara adjust the front of her dress. Tito's voice comes through the line, but the meaning of his words is lost to me because I'm preoccupied with the way the gray silk hugs her gorgeous breasts.

"Say that again," I grumble into the phone.

"They're shutting us down. This guy says he's from the DOB, but won't give me any other details."

Fucking great. What's crawled up the Department of Buildings' ass this time?

"Make sure he stays put. I'll be there in twenty." I hang up and meet Riggo's stare in the rearview mirror. "We need to reroute, Riggo. Head to the Brooklyn construction site. And floor it."

"Hmm. I didn't know the fundraiser was being held at a

construction site." Tara's now slouched so far she's practically melting into the buttery-soft leather of the car's back seat. Her eyes are trained on a pocket paperback in her hands. Where did she pull that out from?

"I have to deal with an emergency."

"Works for me."

She licks the pad of her finger and turns the page. It's a common enough action, albeit an impolite one in public. It shouldn't be as sensual as it was. The tip of her tongue peeking out from between her decadent lips has my mind warping, and I'm immediately catapulted back to our "fake" kiss.

A blast wave of sensations hits me all at once.

"A business matter, I presume?" she continues, still focused on the page in her book.

"Yes. You know it's rude to read while speaking with someone?"

"Sure. But I'm certain that Barbara's problems are way more serious than yours, so she needs my attention more than you."

"Barbara?"

"Uh-huh. She's been hired as a housekeeper for an evil and extremely obnoxious marquess who's trying to blackmail her into a marriage of convenience. It's the only way he can get his hands on the inheritance, along with the title of duke, from his older brother."

My eyes are glued to her mouth as she licks her finger again.

"I can totally relate to poor Barbara, considering the circumstances," she adds with a smirk.

She flipped that page just seconds ago. There's no way she can read that fast. Is she doing it on purpose? Teasing me? Flicking her tongue between her beguiling lips?

"Are you skimming?" I ask.

"Yup. It's my fourth reread. I'm skipping ahead to the good part."

"Which is?"

"The marquess tries to force himself on her. But Barbara gets saved by this introverted gardener, who recently returned home from a war. Later, she finds out that he's actually the duke's long-lost son. The legitimate heir to the duke's estate and title." A small smile pulls at her lips. "The true hero kills the evil marquess and then marries Barbara."

I make myself look away from Tara's lips and focus on the book in her hands. The colorful cover has a Regency-era woman in a fancy dress clinging to a bare-chested guy, whose ruffled white shirt is somehow pooled at his waistline. It looks like the kind of thing Sienna likes to read. She used to leave her paperbacks lying all over the house. I must have wondered at least a hundred times about what sort of satisfaction a woman as smart as her could get out of such trashy literature.

Shaking my head, I glance at my Rolex, eager to get the new shitshow at the construction site over with. But like a magnet, my eyes drift back to Tara's mouth. To those... Cushiony. Soft. Lustrous. Lips.

Lips that are still smirking.

"Well, sorry to spoil your fantasy, Tara, but there is no duke in shining armor who'll save you from marrying me."

"I know." She shrugs as if she doesn't care, but I notice her smile dim for half a heartbeat. "That's okay, because I made sure it would be worth it in the end. Didn't I?"

That she did. What the fuck possessed me to agree to give her twelve million dollars in our divorce?

Lying on the seat beside me, my phone gives off another insistent shrill, and Ajello's name lights up the screen. Answering it, I launch right into my report on our most recent drug shipment delivery, all while my eyes remain glued to Tara's lips. By the time I finish updating the boss, Riggo is pulling up next to the cordoned-off site where the demolition and cleanup of the old structure have nearly been completed. We're ready to start excavation for the new foundations next week.

Before we come to a full stop, I'm out of the car and hurrying toward two men standing next to the marked-off area.

"What the fuck is going on here?" I bark.

"That's the owner?" a man in a cheap navy suit asks Tito.

"Yes," my foreman confirms. "Let me introduce you. This is Mr. Arturo DeVille, the CEO of Gateway Development Corp." He turns toward the city suit. "Samuel Daniels. He's with the DOB Enforcement Unit."

"All our compliance documentation and permits were approved months ago. You're costing me money, Mr. Daniels. I'd appreciate it if you'd get your ass off my property." I jerk my head toward the perimeter gate.

Daniels straightens and crosses his arms over his chest. "That may be, but we received information that requires further scrutiny. I'm here to advise you that all work on this site needs to cease immediately until this matter is handled."

"What information?"

"I'm not at liberty to share the pertinent details at the moment. However, if I can ask you to please—"

A chirpy voice rings out behind me. "That navy color looks good on you, Sammy."

I spin around a fraction of a second faster than the DOB guy, both of us finding Tara with a huge grin plastered across her face.

"Tara?" Daniels exclaims, his whole demeanor changing from cold and rigid to friendly and full of charm as he practically leaps toward her, engulfing her in his arms. "My God! How long has it been? What are you doing here, pumpkin?"

Sammy? Pumpkin?

What the fuck? The son of a bitch is lucky he let go of her before he drew his next breath. Otherwise, it might have been his last.

"Seven years, just about. You're looking spiffy, Sammy. How's Mama Daniels doing?"

I watch my future wife lift up onto her toes to give this motherfucker a peck on the cheek. My hands fist at my sides as I fight the impulse to snap his neck.

"She's doing well. And how have you been, little trickster?"

"Oh, you know. Same old with me. So! What's going on that got my buddy's panties in a twist? You're here to give him the gears?"

"You're with him?"

"Yes, she's with me!" I close the distance and wrap my arm around her waist.

Tara shrugs as if she's indifferent one way or the other. "Let's just say we recently struck a deal, but we're still ironing out the kinks."

Sammy sizes me up before turning his full attention back to Tara. "We received a complaint, claiming that this location contained a building of historical significance. Someone high up the chain sent me here to put a hold on things until the bigwigs figure out who's who and what's what."

"This is goddamned New York!" I snap. "You can't throw a stone without hitting something that someone has claimed as historically or architecturally significant to qualify for grants or tax breaks. But the heap of crap that stood here, wasn't it. Check your records. It was assessed as a hazardous structure, and that's why we were granted the demolition permit in the first place."

"If that's the case, Mr. DeVille, you have nothing to worry about," Daniels states as his gaze lingers on Tara. "You'll be able to resume work as soon as we've made the necessary confirmation."

The urge to take this guy down and dig his eyes out floods me.

Why is he looking at my woman like that? They're definitely familiar and comfortable with each other. Friends, or something more?

So what? What if they were? Why the fuck do I even care? She'll be my wife in name only. I need to remember that.

Grinding my molars, I swallow the need to punch the idiot.

"How long will that take?" I ask.

"No more than a month. Maybe two, since this is a bit of an unusual matter."

"What?"

"Oh, come on, Sammy." Tara laughs, patting him on his chest. "Can't you push it a bit? I know you've got that magic. How about by the end of the week? For old times' sake. Otherwise, I'm afraid DeVille might have a coronary."

Daniels gives me a quick look before his attention is once more consumed by Tara. He seems to be swallowing her with his eyes. They have to be more than just old friends. Ex-lovers. I'm certain of it.

That realization is like a gut punch, knocking the wind out of me without any fucking warning.

"Sure, pumpkin." He nods. "I'll see what I can do."

"Thanks, Sammy. Really appreciate it. Please say hi to Mama Daniels for me, alright?"

Flash after flash of various ways I can maim the fucker occupy my mind while I glare at *Sammy* as he and Tara say their goodbyes and promise to stay in touch. Oh, there won't be any touches, literal or metaphorical. That, I can guarantee. Just before Daniels slides behind the wheel of his car, he glances back and gives Tara a wink. The direction of my thoughts turns to drawn-out torture and killing, so I step in front of Tara to block his view of her.

"Who was that man to you?" I somehow manage to sound like a human being rather than a snarling bull.

"An old friend." Her strawberry scent hits me as she flips her hair over her shoulder. "You're welcome, by the way."

Choosing to ignore her latter comment, I ask, "Just a friend?"

She arches an eyebrow and then simply walks around me, heading back to the BMW. We're playing tit for tat, apparently.

"Mr. DeVille?" Tito asks, coming up to stand next to me. "This will significantly impact our timelines. We may need to—"

"Tito, I don't want to discuss goddamned timelines right now," I snap and trail after Tara.

Inside the spacious car, Tara has tucked herself back into her seat, nose once more stuck in her lady porn. I slide in beside her and signal to Riggo to get us moving again.

"Were you two lovers back in the day?" I ask.

"Who?"

"You and Sammy-boy."

"That's none of your business."

"It is my business since you asked him to do me a favor. Favors require repayment, and I need to know to whom I'm indebted," I insist, trying my damnedest to believe that's the actual reason for my question.

"You don't owe Sam anything. I simply allowed him to reciprocate something I did for him years ago. He gets this done, and we're even."

"What did you do?"

Her damn book is hiding most of her face, but I still notice her rolling her eyes at me. "We went to high school together. Sammy's dad had a terminal illness, and none of the available medications helped with his pain. So I… um… brought something back for him from my trip to the Netherlands."

I snatch the book out of her hand. "You smuggled drugs across the border for some guy? Are you fucking insane?"

"It was medicine, not cocaine!" She grabs the book from me and pulls it to her chest. "I did what I thought was right, helping a friend. And you, you're being an enormous hypocrite right now, considering you run the most extensive drug trafficking operation in this part of the country!"

"What if you had gotten caught?"

"Thanks to those meds, for the first time in months, Mr. Daniels was pain-free and died peacefully in his sleep. He was surrounded by his family, who didn't have to helplessly watch him suffer in agony. To me, that was worth it. Besides, I was still a minor, with no prior offenses. I would have gotten off with maybe a fine. The benefits outweighed the risk."

"You were a minor. Great." I squeeze my temples with the heels of my hands. That organ transplant allegory Popov used makes so much more sense now.

"Oh, save me from your patronizing attitude, DeVille. I won't be judged by someone who couldn't recognize a good deed if it bit him in the ass." She positions her book between us, blocking my line of sight.

We spend the remainder of the ride in absolute silence. Aside from the vehicle noise and the world outside still spinning as it naturally does, the tranquility is only broken by the occasional sound of a turning page. Tara keeps herself slightly angled, hiding behind her book. But with my height advantage, I have no problem seeing her eyes as they quickly flit across the lines of text as she reads her stupid romance novel. Until she gets down to the bottom of the page, that is. Then, she lowers the book and gives me a full view of those bewitching lips. And the tip of that velvety tongue as she licks her finger. Every. Fucking. Time.

And my damn cock just gets harder and harder.

Fuck.

I need to get laid. And soon. It's been… months?… and my dick doesn't understand that we don't like this infuriating woman. Just as I'm reaching for my phone to text one of my casual lays, she does it again.

Her lips take on a slightly pouty appearance just before she brings her thumb to the bottom one. She keeps it there for a heartbeat, hovering over the tiny divot at the center. And then… that tongue. Rosy. Glistening. Fucking tempting.

Phone and intended text forgotten, my attention stays glued to that mouth until we reach the Williamsburg venue where the fundraiser is taking place. The entire time, I feel like one of Pavlov's dogs, waiting for the next turn of the page. Salivating at the metaphorical bell she's wielding. Growing more frustrated with every iteration.

Getting more and more turned on with every lick.

Chapter eight

 Tara

17:11 Satan: I'm fifteen minutes out.

A SHUDDER RUNS DOWN MY SPINE AS I stare at the phone screen.

Yesterday, as Satan was bringing me home after yet another "dinner date," my future husband informed me that, the next time he comes over, he'll be officially asking my brother for my hand in marriage. Which means, that's happening today.

"Oh my God, I think the black-dotted one is pregnant," Sienna yelps. Her nose is pressed to the side of the tank, and her eyes follow the fish in question as it jets among the various plants and structures that make up the aquascape. I have no idea how she managed to convince Drago to let her move the fish tank into their bedroom.

"See? Her belly looks swollen. We're going to have little fish babies!"

"I'm pretty sure the eggs happen first," I mumble. "And the big fish will probably eat the young."

"Oh, no! We need to separate the mommy from—"

"Your brother and I are getting married," I blurt out.

"—the other fish so they—" Sienna turns around, her eyes wide as saucers. "You what?"

"He's on his way here now. We'll be letting Drago know today."

"But… but I thought the two of you were just, you know, seeing each other." Her eyes search mine like she's expecting me to yell *Sike!* or *Just kidding, girl!* "Wow, Tara. Are you sure? It's only been a matter of weeks. A month. A bit more, maybe? Um… don't take this the wrong way… I love the idea of you two being together, but… marriage? So soon?"

I bite the inside of my cheek hard enough to make myself wince. Keeping this farce up for weeks, not being able to say a word to anyone, is excruciating. There's no one to talk to. No one to ask for advice. No one to even just complain to about how frustrating my life has become. I want to spit it all out, but I know I can't tell Sienna a thing. I mustn't.

"Maybe you should think about that for a while, Tara. Date for at least a few more months and—"

"There's no time," I blurt out. "We need to be married by the end of next month. That's Ajello's orders."

"Excuse me?"

Shit. I drop onto the edge of the bed and bury my face in my hands. "Yeah. Apparently, your don wants the ties between the New York Cosa Nostra and Drago's group to be even stronger. And he figures your brother and me getting hitched is the perfect way to do that."

"You… you're not in love with Arturo?" Sienna looks at me with sad puppy dog eyes, as if the whole world has just crashed down around her. "But… but… the flowers? All your dates? The cute mating dance you're doing with the jackets? You've been seeing each other practically every single day."

"All that was nothing but a pretense for Drago's sake. The last thing I want is for him to get into a confrontation with Ajello over me."

"Fuck Ajello! He's a scheming, pompous asshole! How dare he pull this shit again? Let's go to Drago, and you can tell him everything."

"Really?" I look up, meeting Sienna's frantic gaze. "And then what? Drago gets pissed. Kills your brother? Goes to war with Cosa Nostra? Maybe tries to take out Ajello, too?"

"Yes. I mean, no. Shit. I'm calling Arturo and telling him to put a stop to this nonsense."

"Don't bother. He's made it very clear that he'd never go against the don's orders. It's a done deal."

Sienna's shoulders drop. She sits on the bed beside me and sighs. "So, where does that leave you? You two seem to have been getting along. Do you, at least, like Arturo?" When all I can do is shake my head, she continues, "Not even a little? I mean... I know he can be a handful, but..." Her eyes sparkle with faint hope as she asks.

The glass is always half-full with my sister-in-law. Even amid the most devastating situations, she looks for a silver lining. This time, unfortunately, there isn't one.

"I can't stand your brother, Sienna. And he definitely doesn't have any love for me."

She grabs my hand and squeezes. "You can't spend a lifetime tied to a man you don't love."

"Actually, we came to a compromise. It will only be for a year. Later today, we're signing a prenup. Twelve months of marriage, after which, he'll give me a quick, uncontested divorce"—I force a smile to break across my lips—"and twelve million dollars." I pause, gauging her reaction before continuing, "Mark your calendar, girl. This time next year, we're going on the most amazing shopping spree."

"You're serious?"

"Dead serious. But you can't tell Drago a word, Sienna."

Sienna leaps off the bed and starts pacing the length of the room. Her fingers rake through her hair while she wears out a path on the floor. Left to right. Right to left. She remains silent for several minutes, with only her rapid breathing and the muffled scrape of her orange faux fur slippers on the floorboards filling the space between us. Once in a while, she stops and throws a look in my direction. It brims with questions, concerns, and unhidden pain. Then, she continues her mad trek. Finally, Sienna stops and wraps her hands tightly around her middle. Pure devastation is written all over her face.

"I can't. I can't lie to Drago, Tara," she chokes out. "I promised him I'd never do that again. I... You can't ask that of me."

Guilt hits me square in the chest. Instead of dealing with my own shit like a grown-up, I ran my damn mouth and blabbed the truth. And look what that got me. An even bigger mess than before.

"You know Drago," I whisper. "You think he'd let this go without bloodshed? Without either your brother or mine ending up hurt or worse?"

Sienna slumps beside me on the bed, looking totally dejected. The two of us remain quiet for a long while, simply staring at the nearby wall as if the answers are written there. My vision slowly blurs, and my nose starts prickling. Taking a deep breath, I press my palms to my eyes, trying to stave off my tears.

"I'm so sorry for putting you in this position, Sienna," I say, sniffling. "I was feeling so lost and... and I just had to tell someone."

"It's okay." A slight sob escapes her. "I'm sure Drago will understand and forgive me when I eventually explain."

"You could destroy half of the human race or do something equally catastrophic, and my brother would still stand by you. He loves you so damn much, it's fucking scary."

Sienna leans her head on my shoulder. "Someday, you'll meet someone who'll love you just as much. Initially, he'll be a stubborn grump, of course, because you don't like men who give in too easily. Maybe he'll be a moody marquess. Or an alpha wolf shifter. Or even better, a ruthless wolf shifter who is a marquess, and he'll love you so much he'll risk his life to save you."

I can't help but smile. "You're back in your shape-shifter era, I see."

"Yeah." She shrugs sheepishly. "Oh God, Drago is going to flip out when Arturo actually asks for your hand today."

"Yeah." My gaze slides to the fish tank where the plump little fish happily zigzags among her friends. "What if I tell Drago that your brother got me pregnant?"

"You think *that* would make the situation better?"

I try imagining my brother's reaction to hearing that a guy he can't stand knocked me up. "Nope. Definitely not."

The loud rumble of an engine sounds outside. Sienna and I exchange looks, then dash toward the window. A massive stretched car pulls up and parks in the driveway. With both of us half-hidden behind the curtains, we watch as my soon-to-be fiancé (officially) steps out of the vehicle and heads toward the mansion's front door.

"Do you think he came armed?" I whisper.

"Arturo is always armed," Sienna answers back in a barely audible voice. "Should we go downstairs? Or we could wait until we hear the furniture being smashed?"

"For sure we should go downstairs."

I dash across the room with Sienna on my heels.

As has become their habit, my brother's dogs are sleeping in front of Sienna and Drago's bedroom door, but the moment she and I exit the room, the three of them spring up and trot behind us down three flights of stairs. We reach the ground level just in time to see Drago's office door shut. Shit. We're too late.

"Now what?" I ask. "Should I go in there?"

"Yes, that's a good strategy. Less of a chance they'll kill each other if you're with them."

"Okay." Drawing a deep breath, I set off across the hall.

Until today, it was easy enough to pretend this whole clusterfuck wasn't really happening. *What's one year, anyway? Twelve months. It'll pass quickly, right?* With my feet practically dragging on the marble floor, I approach my brother's office. *Three hundred sixty-five days tied to Arturo Fucking DeVille. Oh God.*

I twist the doorknob and step inside, just in time to witness Drago and the scourge from hell having a standoff in the middle of the room, guns pointed at one another.

"You are not marrying my sister, DeVille." Drago's furious voice reverberates through the room.

Great. The happy news has obviously been shared.

"I'm not really looking for your permission, Drago. I asked because some of us still respect old traditions, even in this day and age. But I'm marrying Tara regardless of how you feel about it," Satan replies in an identical, pissed-off tone.

"Okay, guys." I take a step toward them, holding my hands out like I'm approaching two snarling predators. Moving slowly, I circle until I stop at DeVille's side. It might look like I'm supporting my man, but in reality, I need my brother to be able to see me and read my lips. "Could you two please put the weapons away so we can discuss this in a civil manner?"

"No," Drago growls. "Get out of here, Tara. And stay away from the door."

"Listen to your brother, Tara," the devil tacks on. "Leave."

Right, the two alphaholes have spoken.

I shift, drawing both men's attention to me even while they continue to point their guns at each other. With my heart in my throat, my eyes frantically flit from my brother to my future husband. *Fuck. Fuck! FUCK!!* What do I do now? Think, damn it, think!

"I'm pregnant!"

"WHAT?!" both men bellow in unison.

Drago's nostrils flare, and his murderous glare slashes DeVille. "You got my sister pregnant, you son of a bitch?"

Oh, shit! *Wrong move, Tara.* Bad, bad decision.

I wedge myself between them, facing Drago. "He didn't," I blurt, an instant too late to realize how *that* sounds, so I quickly add, "I mean… *maybe*. But… I might be pregnant. We had sex. Lots and lots of sex. So much sex that I might be carrying twins. Even triplets."

I chance a look over my shoulder at DeVille. He's watching me with raised eyebrows. His eyes look like they're glowing, but I can't be sure if it's because he's laughing or getting ready to shoot me next. His gun is still aimed at Drago's head, but it wouldn't take much for him to switch his target.

Well, fuck that! I've had enough.

"Lower your weapon," I snap at DeVille, then turn back to my brother. "You too, Drago, put down your gun. I'm sick of this macho bullshit between the two of you. I'm a big girl and I can decide for myself."

"And you've decided to marry this guy?"

"Yes."

"By your own free will?" He narrows his eyes at me. "No one is making you do this? And this isn't some sort of game where you two are just fucking with me?"

"Of course not!"

"You're actually in love with this jerk and want to spend your life with him?"

Stepping back, I lean against Satan's chest and grab his free hand, wrapping his arm around me. Immediately, I feel the heat of his body and the hardness of his taut muscles at my back, his warm breath upon my neck, and the flex of his splayed fingers on my stomach as he tightens his hold on me. His spicy cologne invades my senses, the hint of sweet smoke sending shivers racing along my spine. My pulse speeds up, and I hope my smile looks genuine as I say, "I am totally and completely in love with this jerk."

Exhaling audibly, Drago lowers his gun and slides it back into its holster. He stretches his hand out to me while a strange expression crosses his face. There's a mix of concern and resignation in his gaze. I take a step toward my brother, but the arm around my waist tightens even more. When I glance over my shoulder, my gaze collides with a dark, smoldering glare.

Before I can say anything, DeVille's hand falls away. The loss of that contact chills me.

Confused by the myriad of emotions overwhelming me, I turn back to face Drago. As my brother pulls me into his arms, an all-consuming warmth, something I've always connected with safety and home, envelops me.

"Okay, sis," he whispers as he drops a kiss on the top of my head.

I pull back, searching his eyes. What am I looking for?

"Okay?" I choke out. That's all he has to say?

"You're right. You can make your own decisions, Tara. That's what you want, isn't it?"

"Um... yes?" Why did that come out like a question?

Warm lips graze my forehead this time. "I hope you won't regret your choice."

Panic and sheer terror at what I've done turn my stomach as my brother takes a step back. He's letting me go. Allowing me to marry

DeVille. Despite everything I said, I guess I figured he'd still "save me" from this mess somehow. Just as he's always done.

Has Drago finally decided I'm beyond saving?

Drago

Twenty-four hours earlier
Naos

"You're looking good, Ajello," I say while bringing a glass of whiskey up to my mouth to hide my grin.

Three long, freshly made scratches mar his jaw. Based on the shape and spacing of the thin red lines, I'd say the markings were done by a small animal. My guess, the endless war between the don and his wife's demonic cat has reached new heights. At this rate, the feud is turning into an urban legend, leaving some of us eager to see who'll come out on top. There might even be a pool happening. In certain circles.

"Life treating you well, I assume?"

"Perfect, actually," he replies, his gaze intensely focused on my forehead. "Love what you've done with your eyebrow. A new trend among the bikers, perhaps?"

I run my hand over my brow, and my palm comes away smeared in pink goo glinting with tiny gold sparkles. Sienna's latest purchase: the *Super Sparkling, Long-lasting Lip Gloss*. They got that one right.

Awesome.

"Yeah. It's the newest craze." I grin.

This idle chitchat isn't fooling me for a minute, and I can't help but wonder what the hell the Italian don's scheme is this time. And why exactly is he sitting in my club?

If my memory serves me right, Salvatore Ajello has set foot in

Naos only once. A year ago. To discuss the renewal of our collaboration. That's when he offered Sienna DeVille to me as a wife, to sweeten the deal. Having him across from me again, while we sit in the same booth, gets my mind spinning over what devious plan he's cooked up now. Especially since he insisted on meeting face-to-face. Just the two of us.

"What brings you here, Ajello?"

"A delicate family matter, if you must know. One that I need you to hear me out on. Don't go off the rails and start killing the parties involved, as I expect you might be tempted to do. Listen to the reasons for what I'm about to tell you, and I'm certain you'll understand that there are benefits for both sides."

I narrow my eyes. "Stop your cajoling, Ajello, and just spit it out."

"I'm concerned about a friend of mine, so I suggested that he should get married."

I shake my head. What's with Ajello and his recent obsession with getting everyone around him hitched? Is arranging marriages a new hobby of his, or is he just bored? A man like Salvatore Ajello, with nothing productive to do, is a serious threat to society. God only knows what crazy ideas might pop into his head. But if he has developed a sudden interest in matchmaking, I can get Adam to contact a buddy of his who runs a local radio station. Maybe Ajello could get his own show? Mm-hmm. Nightly dating advice from the Cosa Nostra don. Live, on air. I snicker inwardly, imagining it.

"You free on Thursday evenings?" I ask.

"No. Why do you ask?"

"No reason." I shrug. "So, why come to me? You want to book Naos to hold the celebration? Looking for a friends and family discount for these poor souls getting blissfully wed? Who are they, by the way?"

"Arturo and your sister."

My forehead furrows. I must have misread his lips. "Say that again."

"Surely you've noticed the two of them are dating."

"Bullshit. It's a stupid farce DeVille put Tara up to somehow. I haven't yet figured out his endgame, but I don't believe for a moment that shit between the two of them is genuine."

"That's unfortunate." Ajello spreads his arms along the back of the sofa. "Because it is serious. In fact, Arturo will be coming to see you tomorrow to formally ask you for your sister's hand. He greatly values traditions."

"He can ask." I grin. "And I will maim him."

"What you should do, Drago, is ask yourself why your sister agreed to marry Arturo in the first place."

Rage clouds my vision. I stand up and lean over the table, getting in Ajello's face. "What did you do, you asshole? Did you threaten her like you threatened Sienna? Because if you did, I'm going to—"

"I did absolutely nothing beyond offering the name of a bride," he interrupts. "Whatever made Tara go along with the idea of marriage is something between Arturo and her. If your sister wanted you to intercede in that situation in any way, she would have come to you."

The anger pulsing in my head morphs into confusion. A moment later, a shocking revelation sends me reeling. There's no way Tara is in love with Arturo. Which means she's been faking with that bastard, probably for my sake. The question is, why? What did she get herself into this time? And why the fuck didn't she come to me for help?

"Where the fuck is my brother-in-law? I'm going to put a stop to this insanity immediately," I bark. "Whatever she did, I'll fix it."

"Like you always do?"

"Yes!"

"You'll just keep on saving her over and over? Robbing her of every opportunity to solve her own problems? To own up to the mistakes she's made and feel pride when she finally has a chance to overcome them? " He cocks his head to the side while his gaze drills into mine. "Are you really that selfish? Or maybe… you're simply afraid."

My throat burns with the acid rising up from my gut, and I want nothing more than to punch this motherfucker. Because he's right. And I hate him for it.

"You can't expect me to just sit back and watch Tara ruin her happiness. Regardless of how they act, I know she hates him. Trying to prevent my baby sister from being miserable for the rest of her life," I rasp, "is *that* your view of selfishness?"

"Actually, it will only be a year."

"What?"

Something resembling a slight smirk dances on Ajello's lips. It must be a trick of the light because the man never smiles.

"A little birdie told me they made a deal. Arturo and Tara. He'll give her a divorce once their year of marriage is through." A corner of his mouth edges upward. "And she'll receive a million dollars for every month they're together. That was her demand, which Arturo had no choice but to comply with. Very clever, that sister of yours."

"*Isuse.*" I snatch the tumbler of whiskey off the table and down the contents in a single gulp.

"I know you love Tara. She's the only blood you have left. But she desperately needs to learn how to deal with the repercussions of her actions. Alone. And this particular lesson is best learned when it's lived. Despite this useless animosity between you and Arturo, you must know that he would never do anything to hurt your sister. So why not let this marriage play out and see what happens?" He shrugs. "Besides, there's that little fact that you owe Cosa Nostra for saving your life after your skirmish with the Romanians. Surely, indulging me by not standing in the way of this union is reasonable in terms of repaying that debt?"

"What do you get out of it?" I snap. "This… this foolish marriage experiment or whatever you want to call it? And what's in it for DeVille?"

"I want Arturo to be happy. And you undoubtedly want the same for your sister. I'm confident that he and Tara are actually a perfect match. Neither of them thinks so, but I'm certain this little ordeal will prove it to them. For it to be a success, though, I need you to do your part."

"Meaning, just sit back, watch, and pretend I'm buying their charade?"

"Exactly." Ajello rises and adjusts his jacket. "Trust me. I have a good feeling about this."

With his hands in his pants pockets, the Italian don strides across the empty dance floor. Despite a slightly uneven gait, he looks as if he's taking a casual stroll. Not a worry in the world rests upon him.

"A fucking brain disorder," I mutter. "That's what you have, you scheming lunatic."

Next to my empty glass on the table, my phone vibrates with an incoming text. I ignore it, still too preoccupied by that conversation. The man is obviously nuts. But he is also right. I've been squeezing Tara too tightly, trying to keep her safe. From everything. Even her own choices.

Maybe… Maybe it's time to let her save herself.

But, if things go south… If that smug, pretty-boy bastard hurts my sister… That gold cross around his neck won't be the only one he's wearing. And he won't survive my brand of faith.

CHAPTER
nine

 Tara

"**A**BSOLUTELY NOT." I PUSH THE STACK OF PAPERS that comprise an extremely detailed prenup agreement across the desk so forcefully that the folder it resides in slides off the polished surface and lands in DeVille's lap.

"You seem to be under the impression that these terms are negotiable," he growls. "They are not."

"The deal we made was that I'd marry you. We did not discuss anything about me not being allowed to work at Naos. Nor needing to accompany you to every single one of your fancy Italian events, or playing hostess during dinners for you and all your Cosa Nostra cronies. And there was definitely no mention of having to live in your house!"

Satan's eyes bore into mine as he slowly rises from his executive chair. Gripping the folder in his hand, he rounds the desk and comes to stand right beside me.

"I don't know how marriages work where you come from, and I don't care." He sets the agreement in front of me again. "I'll be paying you a million dollars per month, and I'm going to see that you *earn* every single cent, Tara. So yes, for the next year, you're going to be the dutiful, docile, and modest wife who'll act as is expected of her. As is expected of her position... The spouse of the second-highest-ranked man in the New York Family."

"Oh, so you all treat your wives as if they're your well-trained pets?" I snap the folder open and leaf through the pages listing all of this bastard's requirements. *"Will not contradict her husband in front of Family members or other influential witnesses,"* I read out loud.

"We hold the trait of a supportive spouse in high regard."

"You mean you expect blind obedience! And what about this? Do all Italians dictate how their wives should dress?" I point to the list of not-allowed items. *"Jeans or other casual or indecently revealing attire (athleisure wear and pajamas with bathrobe, in particular); see-through shirts and miniskirts that would be viewed as inappropriate at high-class functions. Unsuitable footwear, like sneakers and flip-flops, during social events. Improper hair accessories (specifically, hair curlers and towels)."*

"I don't give a fuck how you dress in private, but in public, yes. I expect you to look the part. So far, when we've gone out, you've worn the most ridiculously infelicitous things. My guess is you've done it all simply to piss me off." He grabs the back of my chair and spins me around to face him. His eyes almost glow with the anger blazing in their depths as he leans over, bringing our faces to the same level. "That stops right now, Tara."

"Do you expect me to warm your bed every night, too?" I snarl. "Is that a requirement of being your wife? Since you're paying me, you want me to be your whore?"

Arturo's nostrils flare. He draws closer still until our faces are barely an inch apart, until we are practically sharing the same air.

"*Warm* my bed? Oh, I'm fairly certain that you would make it as glacial as the Arctic."

Asshole! I lift my chin. "Then you wouldn't mind if I choose to occupy another man's bed instead?"

"As long as you're discreet, I don't fucking care."

With my gaze locked on his, I grab the folder off the desk and slam it against his chest. "I want my own room, maybe Sienna's old bedroom, since she told me she liked it. And I want the payment section revised. The full amount due is to be deposited into my bank account. No cash."

His expression morphs into a mask of indifference as he continues to stare at me, but I don't miss the slight twitching in his left eye. He's got to be furious and trying not to lose his shit. Well, too fucking bad! Did he really expect to pay me with his dirty cash? I'm not that stupid.

He reaches into his pocket to take out his phone, then dials someone. I'm guessing his lawyer. DeVille's eyes never leave mine as he speaks, asking for revisions to the prenup document.

"Done. I'll get the updated version in a moment." As he puts his phone away, a hint of a smile tugs a corner of his lips. "You did notice the clause specifying that if you don't follow these rules, you won't get anything, didn't you?"

"Yes," I grumble. Jerk.

"Good. In that case, we can sign once it comes through."

That barely-there curl of his lips turns into a full-blown smirk. A smug grin belonging to a man who is accustomed to winning his battles.

He must figure that the document, with its nearly ten-page attachment that outlines Satan's demands for how I am to behave and appear as his wife, all so I can get paid at the dissolution of our marriage, will ensure he maintains his carefully crafted image within the New York Cosa Nostra. That it will ensure his dear friends will never doubt his choice of a bride. That I will measure up to their idiotic standards without question. That I'll present as perfect in every single way.

The problem with someone so egocentric is that, after a while, they get sucked into their own delusions. That "I'm always right" view they have of themselves blinds them to the truth. They won't ever grasp the possibility of anyone below their social standing besting them at their own game.

Leaning back in the chair, I cross one knee over the other and my arms over my chest, letting a smile break across my lips. I'm well aware that I'm entirely on the opposite end of the "perfect" spectrum. But the one thing I am good at, where my strength truly lies, is finding the overlooked details. I've had plenty of practice spotting inconsistencies and ambiguities in a written text. And that prenup agreement of his has quite a few parameters that could be explored as potential loopholes that I've already noticed.

He wants to play dirty?

Game on.

"By all means. Get the pen ready," I say with glee.

The revised prenup arrives just minutes later. His lawyer must have been hovering, waiting for DeVille's call. As soon as the document comes off the printer, Satan approaches my side of the desk and slams the stack of papers in front of me.

"I almost forgot." He pulls a small square red velvet box from his pocket. Then, he opens it and sets it on top of our prenup. "For you. *Darling.*"

A beautiful gold ring, with the most exquisite round emerald at the center, and flanked by several shining marquise-cut diamonds along the tapered band, lies on the silky cushion.

The brilliance of it is like a punch straight to my chest.

I stare at the pretty trinket that represents everything I've ever dreamed of. A promise of forever. Joy and happiness. A vow of endless love.

So many times I've imagined a day when the man I love would lower himself down on one knee. Would pledge to cherish me. Protect me. Would ask me to be his wife. Every fantasy I dreamed up was more romantic than the one before. None included a pretentious asshole presenting an engagement ring on a stack of papers containing the terms for the end of our marriage.

Goddamned Arturo DeVille has managed to ruin even this special moment for me. It might have hurt less if he had buried a dagger in my heart.

"Let's see if it fits," Satan says, picking up the ring.

My soul weeps in despair as he takes my right hand, not my left. Wraps his warm palm around mine. It doesn't matter that this marriage is a sham. Temporary. This isn't how it's supposed to be!

The ring slides onto my finger as if it were meant to be mine.

The stupid jerk even knew that Serbs wear their rings on the opposite hand from the Western tradition. A small part of me hoped he'd screw up and place the ring on my left hand, just so the disappointment would remind me this isn't real. But the bastard obviously did his research.

"Perfect." My fiancé nods. "Do handle it with care. It was a custom order from Rome."

Really?

In that case, I can't wait to do the dishes with this damn rock on my hand.

Pulling my gaze from the glittering emerald, I look my future husband right in the eye. "I'll do my best, *darling*."

And I'll do everything I can to make sure Satan rues the day he chose to marry me.

Arturo

Something isn't right.

I grab my laptop, pulling up my emails so I can do some work, but my eyes keep darting to Tara. Ever since we got into the car, she's been serenely curled up on her seat beside me, reading yet another of her books with a bare-chested dude on the cover. Her face is lit by a pleased smile, and sparkles dance in her eyes. The glint in those green depths almost matches the luster of the engagement ring on her finger. Almost.

What the hell was I thinking? Why did I drop a small fortune on that thing? I knew she'd need a ring once we got officially engaged, but I figured I'd just get something locally. Anything from Tiffany's would have met societal expectations, so why did I end up making a request for a bespoke-designed ring from the most exclusive jeweler in Italy? Why did I insist it should contain a natural Heirloom-grade emerald in the richest shade of green at its center? Why not a diamond or a ruby? Christ. And why… why do I feel nearly feverish with excitement seeing that rock on Tara's hand? I need my head examined, that's why.

Does she like it? She didn't really say anything about it. I couldn't read her expression either. She just seemed withdrawn. Maybe she was too distracted by our discussion over the prenup to appreciate the ring? Or maybe I should have waited for another time to give it to her?

That conversation wasn't exactly easy, but I honestly expected more of an argument from her about the prenup. Not about the properties or assets she won't be entitled to, but about the specifics of how she should act and dress that I insisted on including.

But there were no protests whatsoever. Not even regarding

the behavior expected of her at high-profile events. I thought for sure she'd go for my balls when I pointed out that there is to be no talking unless she's directly asked for her opinion, no drinking more than a glass of wine, and no cussing. But nope.

I know, all that makes me sound like a chauvinist tool. That's not who I am. But where Tara's concerned, I can't take any chances. She's too wild. Too unpredictable. Too beautiful. And sometimes, too naive. Too inexperienced in dealing with Cosa Nostra.

As a society that clings to traditions, there are so many who put a great deal of stock in public image. They can be ruthless toward anyone who deviates from the norm. The thought of some underhanded bastard looking down his nose at Tara, or worse, using her to get to me, turns my stomach. But I'll be damned before I ever let *her* know that.

Her track record speaks for itself. I mean, what self-respecting woman would want to go to dinner with curlers in her hair and wearing something hardly a step above a ripped workout outfit? One time, she actually did dress in yoga pants and a sports bra, complete with an athletic bag flung over her shoulder. When I pressed her on what the hell she was thinking, she informed me of a Zumba class she was headed to after our date. On another occasion, she got into the car in her pajamas and a bathrobe. Her explanation: I arrived early, and she didn't want to keep me waiting.

Honestly, that was better than her next chosen outfit. I had reservations at a fine dining establishment in Tribeca, and she showed up in a see-through mesh top and a skirt so short it could have been used as a belt. Riggo was bringing the car around just as Tara walked out the front door, and he almost ran into a tree.

And then, yesterday... Surprisingly, she was dressed appropriately in a nice wool jumpsuit. Except she had a bath towel around her head. Apparently, the special leave-in conditioner treatment she used needed another hour under the wrap. Luckily, the drive from Drago's to our destination was lengthy, and she discarded the towel before exiting the car.

Each time, Tara's actions are deliberate, delivered for the purpose of riling me up. I'd admire that daring streak in her if I weren't worried she'd pull a similar stunt in front of my business partners or subordinates. Their vicious gossip might not bother me, but it would make her life infinitely more difficult. They'd smile in her face but tear her to shreds behind her back. She'd never fit into our world because respect is everything in Cosa Nostra.

I know that her absurd hijinks are just to piss me off. Payback for forcing her into this marriage deal. It should make me furious on all accounts. The problem is, though, I've actually started to enjoy her little antics. And I can't have that. So that tyrannical and condescending document I made Tara Popov sign is as much for her protection as it is for mine.

So why the fuck is she smiling? And why do I find it both aggravating and alluring?

"Is that another one of Barbara's steamy escapades?" I ask. "Who's it with now? A stranded sailor? Another rich duke, perhaps?"

"Don't be ridiculous. Romance novel characters are like swans. They mate for life."

"Oh, I'm sorry. I didn't mean to voice such blasphemous questions."

"It's okay. I wouldn't expect someone like you to comprehend the dream of finding a loving lifelong partner."

"Someone like *me*?"

She doesn't answer, just continues reading.

"And? Why not?"

"Because you're already married to your precious Cosa

Nostra, DeVille. And anyway, it's not as if any reasonable woman could fall in love with a jerk who outlines in a ten-page manifesto how she's expected to behave while married to him."

"That agreement was drafted specifically for you, Tara. It's not something I would have done for someone else."

"Oh, aren't I lucky?" She tilts her chin, pursing her lips in the process. "A special contract for a special wife. That's so nice. I've never felt so uniquely singled out before."

"You know exactly why I had to do it."

"Nope, not really."

"Our first 'date,' when I wanted to take you to a nice dinner at a fine establishment, you showed up in a cropped sweatshirt with those plastic things in your hair. A lot of affluent and powerful people, people like the owners and CEOs of reputable and influential companies, many of which the Family collaborates with, dine at the place we were headed."

"And you were afraid your dignity would take a hit if you arrived with a date dressed in an old sweatshirt? I had no idea that your ego was so fragile."

"Perception is reality when it comes to these people. And the Family cannot afford to be perceived as weak. Anyone can be made or broken based on their image and reputation, which is true in the Mafia just as much as within the corporate world. That's why you won't ever see a CEO going out in a polo shirt or a CFO wearing flip-flops. And since my job is to represent the Family, I won't ever be caught in anything that disgraceful. My date won't be either. And most especially, neither will my wife."

"God, you must be a Virgo."

"A what?"

"It's a zodiac sign. When's your birthday?"

"September ninth. And I don't believe in astrology."

"Yup, Virgo. Knew it right away. Jesus, I've never met a man with such a large stick up his ass."

My lips twitch, and I barely contain my smile. I've clearly lost all my marbles because instead of being royally infuriated by her audacity to speak to me in this manner, I'm actually amused. Her constant needling irritates me to no end, but at the same time, I've found myself eager to see what she'll think of next.

My reactions to Tara Popov are becoming more than a mere inconvenience. I can't believe I still haven't made that call to Miranda like I've been intending to for weeks. My ex-lover could have helped me exorcise this unhealthy attraction I seem to have developed toward my future wife. Why haven't I contacted the buxom blonde already? Oh right. Because every time I reached for my phone, Tara's likeness popped into my thoughts. A picture of her, naked and pressed under my body, gasping for her next breath as she bites retort after snarky retort at me. While I fuck her senseless.

I shake my head and reach for my phone. "One of Gateway's business partners is celebrating a company anniversary on Friday. You'll accompany me."

"Can't. Our *Slava* is on Friday."

"*Slava*? What's that?"

"A big cultural celebration to honor our patron saint. All our friends and family are coming over for lunch." She licks her thumb before turning the page. "Also, I can't go on any fake dates until after. We're expecting about three hundred guests, so Keva has recruited the entire household to help prepare *sarma*. She'll kill me if I try to ditch."

Three hundred people?

"Alright. What time should I be there on Friday, then?"

Tara shuts her book with a loud snap and scrunches her nose at me. "Family and friends, DeVille. And you're neither."

In all my dealings with the Serbs over the years, I've gotten a glimpse of how flirty their guys get. There's no way I'm letting Tara attend that damn *Slava* unsupervised. "I'll bring the wine..., my darling future *wife*."

CHAPTER
Ten

Tara

"HE JUST INVITED HIMSELF," I grumble as I arrange the ham sausage and slices of cheese on the large oval platter. "You can't just invite yourself to someone else's family celebration."

Sienna picks up a sprig of flat parsley and starts arranging it on top of the bowl of tuna salad, creating an artistic flower design. "Drago told me that no invitations are needed for *Slava*. Isn't everyone welcome?"

"Technically… yes. But—"

"You two are officially engaged now. It'll be weird if he doesn't come, won't it?"

"Yes, but—"

"And Drago, along with everyone else, would most certainly get suspicious if your fiancé doesn't show up." She lifts the salad bowl, admiring the intricate garnish she created with parsley and cherry tomatoes. "So actually, this is a good thing."

I furrow my forehead. Maybe it is. My brother's behavior has been exceptionally strange lately. Ever since DeVille came by to ask for my hand in marriage, Drago hasn't questioned our relationship at all. No acidic remarks. No threats directed at DeVille. He's been acting as if everything is perfectly normal and even asked if I needed any help with wedding planning. Knowing the animosity Drago feels toward Sienna's brother, I'm entirely dumbfounded by his actions. It's like he's done a complete about-face.

Oh my God! What if he found out the truth? Then this change of behavior would totally make sense! And it might mean—Shit! Drago believes strongly that "revenge is a dish best served cold." What if he's pretending to be okay with everything now, but is actually biding his time to take DeVille out when he'll least expect it? During the wedding ceremony, perhaps?

"Sienna," I choke out. "Have you told Drago... anything?"

"What?" She stills, briefly glancing at me. "Of course not."

"Are you sure?"

"I promise you, Tara," she says, suddenly overly preoccupied with adjusting the placement of the cherry tomatoes. "I haven't said anything to Drago"—her voice drops to just above a whisper—"that he didn't already know."

"What do you me—"

"Tara!" Keva yells from somewhere outside the kitchen. "Your Italian is here. Since he's early, put him to work. The chairs won't unload themselves, and Jovan needs help at the pits."

"You better go," Sienna says. "I'll finish up here."

As she practically pushes me out of the kitchen, I give her a leery look. "Okay, I'm going. But I'm fairly certain your brother won't be interested in helping. God forbid he get a crease or a stain on his fancy suit."

"Well, he got you into this marriage fiasco. Let him reap what he's sown. That's only fair, right?" she scoffs.

A grin breaks out across my face. She's absolutely right. Why not take this opportunity to humble his arrogant ass.

"No."

I give my fiancé my most sugary smile. "You'll be a part of this family soon, darling. It's very important for you to be involved." I wrap my hands around DeVille's upper arm and lean my head on his shoulder. "You wouldn't want my brother to get suspicious and think something is wrong between us, would you?"

DeVille gives me a look that might just burn the ground under my feet to ash. The hard lines of his face and the dangerous glint in his eyes make him appear infinitely more menacing on this beautiful, bright, sunny day. And quite handsome.

He glances at the part of the backyard where five plump, whole pigs are skewered on spits above the fire pits. I struggle to hold my laughter at bay, even as nerves tingle my nape from being remotely close to the open flame. The expression on his face, though, is one of utter bewilderment over what he's seeing.

"You people are completely nuts." He shakes his head. "Roasting pigs in your yard as if we're back in the Middle Ages. Isn't there an ordinance about this or something?"

"And with you being such a law-abiding citizen, I can see how that would make you uncomfortable."

"You don't really expect me to sit by the fire and spend hours rotating pigs over the coals?"

I grin. If smoke from the roasting pits gets into his clothes, I'm afraid DeVille might have a heart attack. "An hour at most. Maybe two. As you can see, Jovan needs a break. He's been out there nearly three hours already. But you're a newbie, so if your delicate sensibilities can't handle it, I'll understand."

Something that sounds like an animalistic growl leaves DeVille's throat. It's deep, and rumbly, and sexy. My guess is the sound means he's frustrated as hell. The slight twitch in his left eye supports that theory. I smile. Mission half accomplished. This new task should nudge him completely over the edge. But there's no way he'll do it. Unloading ten dozen chairs off the delivery truck and then carrying them over to where the massive tent will be set up behind the house has already made its mark. His typically swept-back hair looks slightly more tousled than intended by his style. He's abandoned his tie and suit jacket somewhere. His pristine white shirt is now marred by several creases, the least of which are on the sleeves he's rolled up. I've spent most of the last hour ogling the corded muscles in his forearms, watching them flex and ripple as he carried the chairs toward the tent. Satan has damn fine forearms. And his back... Fuck. His back... Wide and sculpted, creating a perfect triangle with his narrow waist.

My gawking had nothing to do with his beautiful physique, of course. I was just making sure that he didn't end up in another argument with Drago or some of the other guys. And the fluttering feeling in the pit of my stomach? The one that I can't seem to shake? Yeah, that has nothing to do with him either. It's just my usual anxiety that something might go wrong. That's all.

His eyes bore into mine, and then he dips his head, bringing his mouth to my ear. "This is some sort of payback, isn't it? *Darling*?"

"Of course not," I whisper in reply. "What would I have to retaliate for? It's not as if you threatened to pin a murder on me should I not do your bidding."

"I seem to be out of options." His lips brush my earlobe with every word. "Especially with your brother lurking behind that stack of chairs, believing he's invisible. We can't give him cause to be suspicious."

"Indeed." I nod quickly. The tone of his voice is making me nervous.

"I'm so glad you agree."

A yelp leaves my lips as DeVille seizes my waist. In an instantaneous move, our chests slam together as he brings us into contact nearly from head to toe. Satan's palm on the small of my back sends waves of heat racing across my skin, spreading the warmth to every cell of my being. He cups the back of my head with his other hand, and my nerve endings light up as if scorched. His strong fingers tunnel through my hair while he tilts me back.

Feeling precariously off-balance, I grab his shoulders for support. "What are you doing?" I choke out, caught in the depths of his sexy, dark eyes as his mouth lingers a mere inch above mine.

"Making sure your brother has no doubts," he growls and captures my lips.

His mouth claims mine, and everything within me turns into molten lava. The drag of his fingertips over my scalp sends waves of heat racing down my spine. His scent leaves me spiraling, burning up with need. To hold him close. Closer. Feel the press of his hard chest against my aching breasts. To stay trapped in his searing clutches, while DeVille sets everything around me on fire.

I feel him. His essence. Radiating through my body and mind until he's everywhere. In every molecule. Spreading. Like a disease. And it feels so damn good to be infected, consumed by the destruction that devastating mouth of his brings.

Loud cheers and laughter explode all around us, breaking the spell. Pulling me out of the abyss. My eyes snap open, only to be confronted with a smoldering gaze. He might have freed my lips, but his dark depths continue to hold me captive.

A light breeze blows across my heated features, whipping my hair across my face. I swallow and quickly untangle my arms from around his neck.

"You've made your point…, DeVille."

"I agree." He nods and straightens up, but his arm stays tightly wrapped around my waist. "Don't you think we should be on a first-name basis at this point?"

Breath catches in my lungs. I *did* almost use his name, but managed to stop myself in time.

"Nope." I step away, shaking off his hold. "I have work to do. See ya later."

His eyes follow me as I rush toward the house. Fleeing but feeling the weight of his burning gaze with every step.

After that kiss, I'm too weak to face the issue of his name. Too damaged to resist the temptation. Too frayed to admit the truth. How long has it been since he noticed? How long has he waited to confront me on this? I've been very careful. Never call him by his given name. Not even in my thoughts.

I have my reasons.

But at the moment, I'm not willing to risk my fate and let the devil win.

Arturo

"Wow! That's a lot of people, Mr. DeVille. Looks fun, though."

"Debatable." I toss my bundled-up shirt, reeking of smoke and barbecued meat, onto the passenger seat next to Riggo. "Take this to get dry-cleaned right away. The suit, too."

"Sure thing. In case they ask, what happened to it? Did you spill wine or—"

"I spent two fucking hours roasting a fucking pig. That's what happened." I slide my arms into the fresh shirt Riggo brought me and start buttoning it up.

Damn that woman! And her crazy family. I could also kick my

own ass for being a dumb fuck. If I bothered to ask the time this grand lunch was supposed to happen (six in the evening, apparently) instead of assuming a noon-hour meal like every normal person out there, I would have avoided being dragged into this madness. I could have done some of the actual work that keeps piling up on my desk instead of being treated like one of the clowns in the Popov circus.

There I was, in my custom-made Tom Ford, carrying stacks of foldable chairs. Spit-roasting a goddamned pig over the fire, while surrounded by four more. Chasing one of Drago's dogs that got loose and tried to take a bite of that slow-cooked meat. And then, I got recruited to help set up a tent the size of a small country. A fucking tent!

Thank God that monkey business is done now. With all the prep finished just in time, the guests have been arriving for the past half hour, taking their seats at long tables arranged beneath the canopy of the open-sided tent. Their chatter is competing with the music blaring from enormous speakers in all four corners of the canvas palace.

I wonder if these new arrivals will have stupid death threats for me, as well. Most of Drago's men have tossed theirs out already. That was fun. Nothing says "Welcome to the family" like, *We're gonna fry your ass.* That was the message from Jovan, the guy I relieved at the fire pit. Before he went off, he felt the need to tell me that skewering a person like a pig was a common practice in the past. Then, he congratulated me on my engagement. Later, as I was helping chase the dog, Drago's second-in-command, Filip, mentioned that with only a word from my brother-in-law, his beasts would tear me to pieces. Then, he asked if Tara and I had created a gift registry somewhere. Even Keva, their housekeeper and de facto mother, from what I've been told, didn't hold back. She approached me with large meat shears when I went into the kitchen to get something to drink. Snapping the blades right in front of my face in a not-so-subtle show of force, she told me just how much she loves Tara. That bullshit kept happening the whole afternoon. A veiled threat, followed by happy wishes for my upcoming marriage.

"Oh. There's your fiancée, Mr. DeVille." Riggo pushes his arm through the car window, pointing somewhere between the tent and the house.

I follow the direction of his finger, trying to locate the woman in washed-out jeans and a cropped top, with a mass of tangled dark-brown hair piled haphazardly at the crown of her head. No luck. Only a crowd of men and women in elegant attire, heading toward the buffet tables.

"She's not—" My gaze freezes on a woman in a long pale-blue gown. She's talking with a guy near the edge of the tent. The side of her wrap dress flutters in a slight breeze, once in a while lifting to bare her entire leg. If she hadn't just moved her hand to hold it down, I bet she'd be flashing everyone her underwear. As much as the view of a hot chick gets my blood pumping, I'd never let my woman—

Wait!

I know that dress. The last time I saw it, its wearer doused me with punch.

My eyes snap up, zeroing in on Tara's face. Her smile is wide and friendly as she chats with the guy at her side.

Are they flirting?

I grind my teeth.

Doesn't matter. She can flirt with whoever she wants for all I care.

The guy's hand rises to Tara's upper arm.

"Hey, Mr. DeVille!" Riggo shouts behind me. "Should I wait for you or..."

My feet eat the distance to the tent while my eyes stay glued on the scumbag's hand on Tara. How dare he—

I stop in my tracks halfway to my destination. Nope. I will not act like some jealous oaf and make a scene in front of all these people. Just because—

The asshole's hand slides down to her forearm.

A red haze fills my vision.

I close the distance to the schmuck in ten seconds flat. Snaking my right arm around Tara's waist, I lift her out of the way while burying my left fist in the guy's solar plexus. The man stumbles back, his foot catching on the speaker's power cable. The giant electronic device, mounted on a tripod stand, tilts when its wire is yanked by the falling man. For a brief second, it hovers in place, but then the whole thing crashes down on the end of the buffet table. Several bowls and platters of food launch like projectiles in the opposite direction.

"What the fuck!" Tara wriggles in my hold. "What's the matter with you? Why the hell did you knock out my cousin?"

Cousin? "You don't have any cousins."

"Of course I do. Baki is my great-grandmother's second husband's daughter's nephew."

I glance at the guy lying unconscious on the ground, then at the woman in my arms. "He looked…" *Like he was flirting with you.* "He looked suspicious."

"Suspicious?"

He was caressing your arm! I clear my throat. "He has a gun."

"Of course he has a gun, DeVille! He's working security, for crying out loud. But in case you didn't notice, every man here has a gun! Now let me down so I can check on h—" She takes my chin and tilts my head to the side. "Um… there's something on your forehead."

"What?"

"I think it's…" She reaches out, swiping her thumb over my skin. It comes away smeared with something white and gooey. Squinting her eyes, she brings that finger to her lips and licks. "Yup. It's tuna salad. Sienna spent tons of time arranging the garnish on it. She's gonna kill you when she hears you demolished it. Put me down so I can help clean up this mess."

I don't want to set her down. The way her front is crushed against mine makes me aware of every inch of contact between our bodies. It feels so good. And her lips. So, so close. God, I want to ravage her lips again. I want to—

"Mm-hmm." I quickly lower her to the ground and take a step back. "Right."

Still, I can't make myself look away from her, watching as if bewitched as she crouches and starts collecting overturned serving bowls and platters off the grass. She hollers something in Serbian, and several guests join her in straightening everything out. The rest don't appear overly perturbed by what just happened. Most remain at their tables, drinking and laughing, and not even glancing this way. The band keeps playing on the far side of the tent. Come to think of it, the music didn't even pause while I caused that scene. Everyone is acting like nothing at all happened. If anything like this occurred at one of our Family gatherings, people would be in an uproar. Shocked. Outraged. Indignant. Hell, at the moment, even I'm appalled by my own behavior.

"Hey, you. Italian boy."

I look over at an old man in denim overalls who somehow materialized next to me out of thin air. He's got a shaggy head of white hair and a long, scruffy-looking beard covering half his face. Deepset, wrinkle-lined eyes glower at me from beneath his bushy brows.

"Can I help you?" I ask.

"You hurt our Tara"—he leans toward me—"we kill you."

My eyebrows shoot up.

"And it will hurt. A lot." He lifts his hand and makes a slicing motion across his throat. "Chop, chop head. Closed casket funeral. Capisce?"

I blink. *Who the fuck is this guy?*

"Very good. Good Italian." He slaps me on the back and thrusts a beer bottle into my hand. "Cheers."

I watch as the wacky grandpa walks away, headed toward the garden shed a few yards from the kitchen loading doors. He grabs a rake from where it leans against the structure and lumbers over to a flower bed that's still covered in last season's leaves. Great. Even Popov's gardener is now dishing out death threats.

Squeezing my temples, I sigh. This marriage is an idiotic idea. A fucking mistake. If anything deserves that label, it's this. What alternate reality did I land in? I'm just thankful that Tara and I agreed to set an expiration date for this disaster. Otherwise, if I were forced to associate with this family for the rest of my life, I might go completely bonkers.

Turning away, I let my gaze sweep the crowd around me, looking for a particular pale-blue dress. A moment later, I locate Tara squatting next to the fallen speaker, a platter of ruined salad in her hands. A scrawny black cat is beside her, licking the offering as my fiancée runs her fingers along the feline's back.

Suddenly, everything around me seems to fade. The people and their clamor. The dreadful music that is way too loud to be ignored. That damn black cat, which looks identical to the one I've run into on several occasions in the past few months. All that's left is the dark-haired woman in an outrageously sexy blue dress. She becomes the focal point of my attention. The only thing I see.

When did her lips become so rosy and soft-looking? Are they to blame for the overpowering urge I feel to kiss her?

Nah, it must be just a trick of the light. And I only kissed her to play my part in this unhinged escapade. There's no other reason. There never could be. Thinking otherwise would surely mean I need to see a shrink.

As if hypnotized, though, I keep staring at Tara as she pets the cat. Her slender fingers comb through the animal's silky fur, and I all too vividly recall how it felt to have them rake through my hair while I devoured her lips. The very air around us felt heated, and each of my nerve receptors pulsed with raw, fervent voltage. I wanted to be somewhere else. Somewhere without other people. Just me and her. Alone. So I could do much more than merely kiss her. So I could slide my hand beneath that dre—

Enough!

I lift the bottle of beer to my mouth and throw back the contents. Exhaustion and lack of sleep are obviously taking their toll on me. That's the only explanation for me losing my fucking mind. Tossing the empty bottle into the trash can, I set off toward Tara.

"The wedding's in two weeks. Have you started packing?" I bark when I come up to her.

"No. Why?"

"Get started. But don't bother with this getup or anything like it that makes you look like a common tramp. No one wants to see you flashing your ass in civilized society."

I believe my words have momentarily stunned her. But she recovers quickly and juts out her chin. Her green eyes harden into clear crystals. Cold. Narrowed. Shooting daggers at me.

That did it. Reset us to how we were before.

Loathing everything about each other.

As we should.

Good.

CHAPTER
eleven

 Tara

"**S**O?" I ADJUST MY VEIL AND DO A QUICK PIROUETTE IN front of the wall mirror. "What do you think?"

The horrified look on Sienna's face is outright comical. She's frozen in the middle of my room, her frantic eyes roving up and down as she gapes at my wedding dress.

"Arturo is going to lose his shit," she whispers.

"I don't see why. I've followed each of his specified parameters."

My dress is floor-length, covering me from my neck to the tips of my pointy shoes. The matte satin skirt falls in a graceful A-line. An empire waist and modest chapel train exude timeless sophistication and create a flattering silhouette. The fitted long sleeves and body-hugging bodice are a fusion of draped panel detail and lacy fabric, and a delicate belt and a beautiful pearl-encrusted brooch cinch just below the bust. A stunning blooming motif adds a hint of intrigue to the hidden décolletage. For additional drama, a waterfall sash flows from the raised waistline down the front of the gown. I smile at my reflection in the mirror. The dress is elegant and a thousand times better than I ever imagined it could be.

"It's *black*, Tara!"

"It's not my fault your brother didn't specify the color in the prenup. That meant I was free to choose whichever shade I wanted on my own. He set the rules, and I merely exploited a loophole, so he doesn't have anyone but himself to blame. At least the dress isn't as depressing as what I initially requested. Originally, I just asked Zahara Spada for something suitable to wear to a funeral. This is gorgeous, no?" My cleavage is not on display. The regal high neckline completely takes care of that, actually. Granted, there is a little peekaboo action happening through the elaborate three-dimensional floral pattern. But that's lace! No slits means no one is in danger of seeing my unmentionables. 'Cause God forbid an old Italian man gets a glimpse of my backside. Jeez! "And look, it comes with a vintage-inspired beaded fishnet headpiece." I slide the headband on and arrange the edge of the short veil over the upper part of my face. "Perfect."

"You can't show up to your wedding dressed in black! It will cause an epic scandal."

"Oh, I'm counting on it."

Sienna grabs my shoulders, spinning me around to face her, and pulls the hair band with the veil off my head.

"Listen, I get it. You want to stick it to Arturo for making you marry him. But, the two of you did come to an understanding, didn't you? It's just for a year. Why not try to make it as painless as possible, for both your sakes?"

"I wasn't given a choice, Sienna. He backed me into a corner, and I can't let him get away with it. I might have agreed, but I'll never be who he expects me to be. So yeah, I intend to exploit every loophole, every ambiguity in that prenup filled with insulting clauses that he made me sign. I'll be more than happy to deal with your brother's wrath if it means I get my own chance to fuck with him."

"Arturo would never hurt you. I know him."

148

"The man you know is your brother. Arturo. The man who raised you, cared for you, loved you above all else. But he is *that* man for you and your sister alone. To everyone else, he is Arturo DeVille, Salvatore Ajello's right hand. The underboss of the New York Cosa Nostra. Ruthless. Cruel. Incapable of unselfish feelings, just as his boss is. Trust me on that." I put my veil back in place, then grab my black clutch off the bed. "And I'll make sure that for the rest of his life, he curses the day he decided to mess with mine."

The sharp tap of my heels on the wooden floor breaks the abnormal silence in the mansion. As I rush down the wide stairwell, an echo from Sienna's shimmering yellow pumps follows close behind. Almost everyone is already at the wedding venue, with only Drago and Keva remaining in the house. Both are waiting by the front door, with their faces tilted up, gaping at me as I descend.

"Tara!" Keva exclaims when I stop before them. "What in hell is this?"

"Artie and I wanted to match our outfits for our big day." I grin. "So cute, isn't it?"

"That's hardly appropriate. Black is for mourning, girl, not something to be married in. Drago, please knock some sense into her and make her go change this instant."

I steal a look at my brother, expecting him to start questioning my choice of outfit. Or, more specifically, my reasons behind it. Until this moment, I didn't even consider that it might clue him in that something isn't as it seems. Shit.

Drago looks me over through narrowed eyes for what feels like an eternity, then dips his head until we're face-to-face. "Do you have something you want to tell me, sis?"

"Well"—I bite my lower lip—"I asked the guys to disassemble and pack my bookshelves, and have them moved to my new home. I hope that's okay?"

"Of course. Anything else you want to share?" The look in his eyes grows more intense as his gaze focuses on my black veil.

"Um… I think I might have killed Norbert."

One of his thick eyebrows shoots up.

"The peace lily you gave me. He's down to only a handful of leaves, but I'm taking him with me anyway. With everything going on, I forgot to water him regularly. And, you know, plants need water. But I'm sure he'll bounce back real quick. A new beginning, for the both of us." I'm babbling like an idiot, but Drago makes me nervous as hell when he looks at me like that. As if he sees through each of my lies.

"Mm-hmm. I hope both you and the plant enjoy the change of scenery. Love the dress, by the way." He straightens and opens the front door. "Time to go, then. Can't have *Artie* worried that you're not coming, can we?"

"Yeah. Sure." I force a smile and quickly dash past him.

"Oh, just one thing, Tara."

I stop in my tracks. "Yes?"

Gravel crunches under the soles of his shoes as Drago comes up behind me. His gait is unhurried and measured. He stops right next to me and leans over to whisper in my ear.

"I love you, Tara. And I will always be here for you. No matter what happens, I'll listen and help if you need it. Even if it's something really bad. I know you want to do things on your own, but hopefully, you realize that you don't have to. All you need to do is ask. Never be afraid to do that. Okay?"

"Yes."

"Good. Also… If I ever find out that Italian schmuck has hurt you in any way… any way at all… I'm going to kill him."

A cold shudder races down my spine. That. That's the exact thing I was afraid of. Gathering every ounce of resolve left within me, I turn on my heel and tilt my chin up.

"Thank you. I'll keep that in mind. But rest assured, what I feel toward him, I've never felt for any other man. Trust me on that."

The car door swings open.

"We're here."

I stare at my brother's extended hand, unable to move. It started raining when we were halfway to the wedding venue. The sound of raindrops smashing on the roof of the car echoed inside my head, making it feel as if someone was banging a hammer against my temple. Or maybe that was just my heartbeat. My pulse skyrocketed with every mile we drew nearer.

"Tara?"

"Sorry." I grab Drago's hand, imagining it as a lifeline, and step out of the vehicle. "Just um… excited. And… ah… nervous, too."

"Hey. I know there'll be a ton of people there you won't know. If you don't think you can handle that, say the word. I'll get rid of them faster than you can blink, and we can have a more intimate ceremony."

"I'm fine, Drago. But thank you. You're the best brother a girl could have."

The tightness in my chest increases as I approach the building, and it feels as if something huge and heavy is pressing on me, making breathing almost impossible. My legs have turned to stone, weighing me down while I climb the slippery granite steps. Would the wedding be delayed if I accidentally slipped and broke a leg? Probably not. Satan would likely demand we complete the ceremony before he'd consider rushing me to the ER.

At the top of the grand stairs, two valets in red and gold uniforms are holding open the glass double doors. The lobby of the luxury resort chosen as the location for the nuptials is overflowing with white and sage flowers. They are everywhere. Along the walls, suspended from the high ceiling, arrayed in tall overflowing pots set up at the base of the chiffon-draped pergola. More arrangements create a tunnel-like structure of beautiful blooms that leads toward another set of doors. Beyond them, the conference hall that's been turned into a wedding venue.

An epic, flower-framed aisle bisects row upon row of white seats, where at least five hundred people have gathered.

All of them, staring at me.

If I weren't holding on to Drago's arm, I'd have undoubtedly stumbled walking in. I school my features to hide the panic threatening to consume me and take careful steps toward the altar and the table covered in white satin on the far wall.

Every set of wide eyes I meet is gawking at me in curiosity, disbelief, and outrage.

All of them, except one.

Dressed in an impeccable black suit, Arturo DeVille is waiting for me at the end of my path. His dark gaze follows my every step. Despite appearing to be a dignified groom, I recognize the tightly controlled expression on his face. There's no surprise, no shock concealed in his features. It's pure, savage rage. Hidden behind the mask of a polite smile meant to fool all these people.

Murmurs trail behind me from both sides of the aisle, whispered *tsk-tsks* dog me from the right. The groom's side, where the Cosa Nostra members are seated. None of that makes the fine hairs on my nape rise as does the look in the devil's eyes. I've come to recognize the carefully hidden hatred lingering in his chocolate-colored depths whenever his gaze turns to me.

That wrathful stare has been my constant companion over the

past two weeks. Ever since that staged kiss Arturo laid on me at *Slava*. The kiss that, for me, didn't feel fake at all. Up to that point, things between us were moving in a cordial direction. We even managed to have fun at times. But then, everything changed.

Since that day, DeVille has reverted to being Satan. He's been acting annoyed, and occasionally, outright mean. We went out five more times to keep up appearances, and each of our interactions got progressively worse. His recent animosity rivals his behavior on the night he tried to pin Stavros's murder on me.

I've asked myself, what the hell happened? What pushed him over the edge? I'm drawing a blank trying to rationalize his altered attitude, and frankly, the fact that I care is pissing me off. He wants to be an asshole, he can be my guest. All it's doing is making me feel less guilty over my choice of wedding dress.

With every step I take toward my groom, I see his fury. And a vow of retaliation. I want to look away, but can't. It's as if he's somehow ensnared me, forcing my eyes to lock with his. It's the same hypnotic feeling as when he kissed me. What is this power that DeVille wields?

His kisses have burrowed into my consciousness, dug so deep that I can't erase the memories or the sensations they stirred. And now he holds me captive, trapping me within his bottomless gaze. Why can't I tear myself away from that dangerous glint in his dark depths that burn like the fires of hell are raging within them?

Maybe he really is Satan personified.

"DeVille," Drago says beside me as we close the distance to the altar. "Don't make me kill you."

"Tara will never be the reason you try." DeVille's smile lights up his face.

Drago kisses my cheek and turns away, taking a seat in the first row on the bride's side. Leaving me standing next to my soon-to-be husband. A man who's barely holding it together, narrowly restraining his urge to wipe me off this earth.

"Well played." The velvety timbre of his voice makes me shudder. A menacing smirk pulls at his lips as he reaches out and grasps my hand in his. "But you'll soon realize that not all victories are sweet, *gattina nera*."

My throat feels so dry, it's as if I've swallowed a wad of cotton balls. I force myself to look away, to focus on the wedding officiant. Luckily, he doesn't appear to have heard my groom's words. Those were for me only. Was it a threat? It didn't actually sound like one. More like… like a promise.

Oh God, what have I done? I allowed a few crooked smiles and two shattering kisses to make me forget who he really is. Went too far in a game I'm not sure I can win. Did I truly believe I could fuck with the second-in-command of the New York Italian Mafia? Did I expect to get away with it? Based on his steel grip on my hand, running is no longer an option.

My damn anxiety spikes to another level. Nothing I try seems to shake it off. It crawls up my spine like some multilegged creature, making me shudder and break out in a cold sweat.

I should have confided in my brother. If I had told Drago the truth, he would have found a way to get me out of this disaster, and we might have managed to resolve it without bloodshed. But I was too stubborn to ask him for help. Too proud to admit that I fucked up yet again. And too terrified of the possibility that my latest screwup would lead to his death.

And now, it's too late. With so many Cosa Nostra members present, calling everything off would be akin to a slap in the face. A blatant and very public sign of disrespect. And a potential cause for an open war between our two organizations.

The officiant has started speaking, but his words just wash over me, without any of their meaning penetrating. I stare at his moving lips as panic builds and builds within me. It's getting harder and harder to draw a breath.

"I do." Arturo's voice thunders next to me, nearly making me flinch. Everything inside me tenses. This is real. I am getting married. To Arturo DeVille.

Switching his attention to me, the officiant slashes me with his reproachful gaze, as if I've committed an unspeakable crime. He speaks, but his words continue to elude me. Everything sounds muffled, like it's coming from deep beneath the sea.

"Tara." A whispered rumble on my right, followed by a squeeze of my hand. "Say it."

Say what? Oh. Right. I gulp a lungful of air.

Just like when I was a kid, about to do or say something I damn well knew I shouldn't, I cross my fingers. I'm lucky one of my hands is hidden in the folds of my skirt, which allows me this little bit of superstition. An act of atavistic defiance from deep in my foggy brain.

"I do." That didn't sound like my voice, but I know I said it.

DeVille slipping the wedding ring on my finger barely registers with me. It's a thick band of yellow gold that weighs a ton. Or at least it feels like it does. Like a shackle. Gleaming bright right next to the engagement ring.

Feeling all kinds of anxious and confused, I look up to find him scowling at me, his brows furrowed.

"Your turn," he says without moving his lips, gesturing discreetly with his eyes and a slight incline of his head to the little girl standing beside us. She's cute in a ruffly princess dress, holding a white velvet cushion. Upon the tiny pillow rests a larger wedding band. How did I not notice the girl in the first place?

Trembling, I pick up the ring. As if in slow motion, I lift DeVille's left hand and start sliding the band onto his finger. The damn thing gets stuck around his knuckle. *Shit.* I feel the scrutiny of hundreds of eyes staring at me and my inability to slip the ring on my groom. The silence around us is deafening.

"Do not drop it," Arturo whispers so only I can hear. "It's bad luck."

"Can't get worse than this," I say under my breath, biting my lip as I push the gold band as hard as I can. It finally slides into place. *Thank fuck.*

My ears suddenly feel like they're plugged, so I try to swallow. Is the room beginning to spin? The only thing that seems to be keeping me steady at this point is the heat from Arturo's hand spreading into mine. No. Not Arturo. Satan. Satan DeVille. I need to remember that.

I look around, spotting the ornate pen and documents on the signing table, and automatically take a step toward it. The pressure on my hand makes me stop. Only for a fraction of a second, because my groom is quick to lead me there himself. He picks up the pen and adds his signature to the wedding license.

My turn is next, and I almost drop the pen. Why do I feel kind of lightheaded? I concentrate on the dotted line at the bottom of the page and somehow manage to sign my name. The surname looks a bit askew. Likely because my fingers are shaking. It hit me while I was signing. I'm not a Popov anymore. I had to write DeVille.

I'm Tara DeVille now.

Mrs. Arturo DeVille.

I am officially the devil's bride.

We return to the altar after our witnesses sign, too, and stand before the officiant. I close my eyes, unwilling to face the truth.

"I now pronounce you husband and wife."

Did he say something else after that? I'm not certain. Thunderous applause descends on the room, threatening to suffocate me like the nightmare I often had as a child. One where I was stuck alone in a dark room, and a cacophony of voices suddenly erupted around me. From deep beneath my feet, from behind the hidden walls… all calling out to me, urging me to join them. I never knew where they wanted me to go, and no matter how hard I pressed my hands to my ears, I could not drown out the voices. Back then, the only escape was the bright light of day. Now, unfortunately, there's no way to awake from this nightmare.

My eyes pop open, and I blink, trying to clear the blur that has taken over my vision. Turning, I face my groom, while my heart pounds against my ribcage, and a pulsating whoosh echoes in my ears. It's loud enough to block out the roaring cheers in the room. I shiver as icy chills crash like wave upon wave upon me. Am I getting sick? It's so cold in here. Why is it so fucking cold all of a sudden? And why is my husband's face starting to sway in front of mine?

His thick arm suddenly wraps around my waist. My feet leave the ground as he lifts me against him.

"Don't you dare faint on me, Tara." I feel his words vibrate through his chest, pressed flush with my own. "The entire Family is here, watching."

"Both you and your Family can go to hell, Satan," I pant. There doesn't seem to be enough oxygen in this room. "I need to get out of here. Now."

His hold on my waist tightens. He grasps my chin with his free hand and tilts my face up, scrutinizing me with narrowed eyes. I see the exact moment he realizes what's happening.

Arturo

I should have noticed it sooner.

Shortness of breath. Unfocused gaze. The way her hands tremble while she squeezes mine tightly. Typically, I'm a lot more observant of my surroundings. If this were anyone else, I likely would've spotted it immediately. But Tara has always had an uncanny ability to push my buttons. She does it like no one else. Around her, my entire mental capacity is split between fighting my attraction and trying to curtail just how furious she makes me feel. I've been seething since the instant the hall doors opened, and my fiancée, clad in black, appeared on the doorstep. But looking at her now, so fragile all of a sudden and falling apart in my arms, my fury evaporates, transforming into grave concern.

"Breathe," I whisper.

"I'm... trying." She sounds terrified. Her voice is shaky.

Fuck.

My gaze falls on her slightly parted lips. Everyone is waiting for the kiss while we look like we're exchanging words of love. I wasn't going to kiss her. I couldn't let myself get close to that bewitching mouth again. I had no idea how I was going to weasel out of it without making a scene or drawing attention, but right now it no longer matters.

She's having a panic attack.

Without a better idea of what to do, I take the only possible action.

One that I promised myself I would never repeat.

I slam my mouth to hers.

Fire flashes to life inside my veins, scorching every cell in my body. It consumes me so completely that the cheers exploding around us are insignificant blips on my radar. Nothing matters. Nothing but the delectable woman clinging to me.

I devour her lips like a starving man. For weeks, I've imagined doing this, needing to know if my next taste of her would rival the previous two. It's more. So much more. Sweeter. Intoxicating. Invigorating.

A jolt of pure power zips straight into my gut.

Or maybe a bit lower.

After a beat of hesitation, she returns the kiss with a vigor equal to mine and buries her fingers in my hair. Squeezing the strands, scraping her nails against my scalp. Dainty, sharp teeth sink into my lower lip. The wild little kitten bit me.

I bite her back.

Wanting to deepen the kiss, I tilt my head and feel something odd brush against my cheek. Somewhere in the recesses of my mind, I realize it's her veil. Without breaking our lip-lock, I slide my hand to the top of her head, pull off the stupid band with that netty-looking thing, and throw it behind me. As if a black wedding dress wasn't enough, she added a mourning veil to her attire.

"No one has ever defied me as you'd done today," I murmur into her mouth.

"Good," she mumbles back. "It's imperative to keep your enormous ego in check."

My lips twitch with silent laughter. She seems to be back to her old self again.

The raucous applause and cheers have died down, and only polite clapping remains. We probably have gone beyond the acceptable wedding kiss, but I don't care about any of that right now. Tara's flavor has become ambrosia to me. With every taste, my craving for her grows.

I slide my palms to her butt, lifting her higher, closer, settling her pelvis to rest over my crotch. She immediately wraps her legs around my waist, with only the layers of our clothing between us. Hopefully, that skirt of hers will hide just how hard my dick is. It's been ready to break through my zipper since the instant our lips connected.

Pain shoots across the back of my head as she tugs on my hair, all the while her mouth keeps attacking my lips. Wild little kitten. As she lets go of my strands, her palms glide along my neck to settle on my tie. And then, she starts loosening the knot. I growl deep in my throat and seize her chin with my fingers.

"Your crisis management stunt is top-notch." I smile, drinking in the sight of her. Flushed cheeks, hair in complete disarray, makeup smeared all over her complexion, and she's panting like she's suddenly been cut off from her life support. "After this, nobody will even remember your wedding dress."

Two brilliant green pools, framed by the longest dark lashes, gaze at me in confusion. "What?"

"You trying to rip my clothes off at the altar, in front of all of our guests, may have shocked everyone into forgetting your black gown."

She blinks, then slowly looks toward the gathered assembly, at the hundreds of people staring back at us, dumbfounded. The room is deathly quiet. The crowd is holding its collective breath.

Tara's focus snaps to me. Instead of confusion, that panicked look is back in her eyes, and her lower lip is quivering.

"I...." The grip of her legs around my middle tightens. "I... Can we please leave?"

"That's the plan. The reception has been set up in the banquet hall next door."

Whatever color remained on her skin before, drains. As if unexpectedly exhausted, she wraps her arms around my neck and buries her face in the hollow of my throat. "I don't think I can handle the crowd anymore today."

My nostrils tingle with the fragrance of her strawberry shampoo. The sweet and slightly tart aroma of freshness, summer, and just her. I inhale it, soak it in. Revel in her essence. I should insist we attend our reception, make her suffer through hours of uncomfortable toasts and grand posturing. It would be a fitting punishment for what she pulled today. She needs to know from the beginning that my tolerance for disrespectful behavior is less than zero. Even when it comes to my wife.

But as I hold Tara's trembling body in my arms, instead of a defiant wildcat, she seems like a neglected kitten, shivering in the rain. I'm instantly flooded with an urge to protect her, keep her away from harm. I want my arms to shield her from this day forward. I want to be the one she turns to for warmth.

Which is beyond idiotic, considering most of the time I can't be in the same room as her without losing my fucking mind.

Not to mention, this kitten is more than capable of scratching my eyes out with her tiny claws.

But not today. She's given up the fight.

My eyes scan the room, taking in the guests still seated in rows, waiting with visible confusion for us to make our recessional down the aisle. We should have exited by now, not continued to stand at the altar for minutes on end.

"There's no way in hell we're going to incite an even grander scandal by not showing up to our own wedding banquet, Tara."

"My teeth are at your carotid artery, Satan." Her lips feather along my skin as she whispers into my neck. "Wanna make this a blood-drenched wedding?"

I can't help but laugh. Her voice is weak and shaky. She's still reeling, but she's not letting it stop her from delivering the threat. My feisty wildcat.

Shifting my hold beneath her ass, I fish my phone from my jacket and dial my driver.

"Riggo. I need the car at the back entrance."

"So? Now what?" Tara asks, lifting the train of her dress off the car floor.

I ignore the incoming call from Cosimo and focus on my *sweet* bride. The moment we got out of the venue, she all but leaped from my arms and rushed into our awaiting ride. Since then, she's been brooding in her seat beside me. These are the first words she's spoken in the past twenty minutes.

"Now, we get you settled in your new home. Your things should have arrived already."

"I only have one home. And you made me leave it behind, along with everything else. Family. Friends. My freedom."

"Are we really going to rehash this again? We made a deal. Stop whining about everything like it's the end of the world."

"I'm not whining! How can you expect me to be thrilled about being forced to spend a year of my life living with a man I hardly know?"

"I think we've gotten to know each other well enough." My phone is ringing again, so I reach for it and glance at the screen. Nino Gambini. Probably calling to find out where the hell we are. "I have a packed schedule over the next few weeks. Aside from regular business shit, there are several social engagements that I'm expected to attend. I'll send you the link to my calendar."

"Why do you think I give a crap about your social life?"

"As outlined in our agreement, you will accompany me to each one, Tara. Make sure your attire is suitable."

"Aye, aye, Satan." She shoots me a condescending grin. "Any further instructions?"

"Yes. Stop addressing me like that."

"And how would you like to be addressed? Your Highness? Mr. DeVille, maybe?"

"Arturo would suffice. Or, there's always 'darling.'"

"Absolutely, *darling*."

The car slows down, making a turn toward the gate, and beyond it, the house.

"Do you have something against my name?" I ask.

"Why?"

"Because you haven't used it. Not once. It's always *DeVille*."

Tara looks away. "Seems like my stuff has arrived."

The car rolls to a stop next to a sizable moving truck parked at the front entrance of my house. A mountain of bags and boxes is piled on the porch, almost completely blocking the door.

"You sure you packed everything?" I ask, stepping out of the car and holding my hand out to help Tara as she follows.

"I think so," she singsongs, completely ignoring my gesture, "but Drago will drop off anything I may have left behind."

"I was being sarcastic, Tara. What the hell do you have in those things?"

"Books. Clothes. Books. My favorite recliner. Bookshelves. More books."

I shake my head. *Christ*. "That won't all fit in Sienna's old room."

"Hmm, that's too bad. I suppose, then, I'll need the biggest room you have."

"That would be the primary bedroom. And as it happens, that belongs to me." I lean down to whisper in her ear. "Are you offering to share the bedroom with me?"

"God forbid. Any other room that's large enough to fit all my stuff, and is also as far as possible from your lair, will do. Please and thank you."

A smirk tugs at my lips. Not like I ever intended to allow her the use of Sienna's room. "As you wish."

Tara's eyes turn into slits as she stares at me with suspicion. But then, she raises her chin and heads to the front door.

Nope, that's not happening. Catching up, I quickly scoop her into my arms.

"Hey!"

"Appearances, *gattina*. It's tradition for the groom to carry his bride over the threshold."

"No one from your precious Family is around, so there's no need for this pretense. Put me down."

"My housekeeper is here, and she loves to gossip. Bailing on our wedding reception is as far as I'm willing to bend traditions for you. And I've only done it because you had a panic attack and nearly passed out at the altar."

"I did not have a panic attack! And I don't faint. You must have confused me with one of your delicate Italian girls."

"I'd never make a mistake like that. You're about as different as could be from an Italian woman." I let her feet touch the ground and nod at my wide-eyed housekeeper, who's watching us from the foot of the stairs. "Greta will show you the way. Your things will be brought up shortly."

"Great." Tara tries to shake my hand off her hip. "Do you mind?"

"I think you forgot something." I pull her closer. "Plenty of witnesses with all the moving guys around and Greta here. I'm sure they expect the newlyweds to engage in romantic displays of affection. A kiss would assure them that everything is as it should be."

"I can't stand you. The three previous incidents of kissing you in front of our families for the sake of appearances were dreadful enough. I have no interest in repeating the experience. Like, ever. So what would make you think I'd kiss you for the sake of your hired staff?"

"My feelings for you are not that different, Tara. Having my mouth on yours is like letting myself be burned alive. But personal sacrifices must be made for the greater good." I haul her flush with my chest. "Make sure it looks genuine."

Tara's lips break into a sugary smile. She takes my face between her palms and lightly brushes my lips with hers. "Certainly. Let me show you how much I love being your wife, *darling.*"

Absolute bliss. That's what it feels like to have her mouth on mine again. Her scent… her softness… the sweet, sweet—PAIN!

"Oops." The little hellcat smiles innocently as she licks a drop of my blood off her bottom lip. "Apologies, darling. Got a bit carried away. But you insisted I show you the depth of my feelings."

My nostrils flare. Fury explodes inside my chest, but it has nothing to do with her stunt. I'm furious with myself, with my body's and my mind's reactions. Because each time we kiss, I feel like I'm plugged directly into a raw power source that makes my heart race and every neuron I have catch fire. Every one of my senses heightens the moment we touch. She does that to me. Only her. Wakes me up from whatever zombieland I've been trapped in. I never even realized I was drowning in that hell. And now, I'm pissed beyond measure that she's the one who has this effect on me.

"Greta is waiting," I grind out through my teeth. "You should go. Start unpacking."

She marches past me without another word, her head high, and climbs the stairs to the upper level. Poor, confused Greta trots in Tara's wake.

As soon as Tara disappears from sight, I audibly exhale,

allowing myself to relax finally. Releasing the tension in my muscles doesn't help relieve the pressure in my cock, though. I've been as hard as rock for over an hour. Since the moment my mouth connected with hers. I'm glad that, for once, she actually listened. If she hadn't and stayed, my hands and my mouth would have been all over her body, and then I'd have thrown her down and fucked her through the floor right here.

Tara

"The truffle bruschetta is amazing. You're really missing out," Sienna mumbles into the phone, her mouth obviously full of the delectable appetizer. "And the wine! Sweet and crisp all at once, and it hits the taste buds just right. Works great with the pork ribs, too."

"Glad you're enjoying yourself." I let myself fall face-first onto the big four-poster bed.

"I sure am. The two of you caused quite a stir, disappearing like that. But I guess it's not that surprising, after that kiss and all. It's all anyone's been talking about. I heard someone mention that you must have been in a hurry to… consummate the marriage." She giggles.

"Yeah, sure. Has Drago said anything?"

"Nope. Nothing at all."

I furrow my brow. That doesn't sound like my brother. Even if he bought the farce of me marrying DeVille for love, I expected him to do… *something.*

"Maybe you convinced him that you're in love. I mean, that kiss looked fucking real to me. The two of you practically tried to devour each other. It was hotter than hell. Are you sure you don't like Arturo?"

Closing my eyes, I let my mind drift back to the altar. A tremor runs down my spine as I recall my husband's strong arms around me. Being crushed to his hard chest while he ravaged my mouth before hundreds of astounded eyes. That fucking kiss! It was… it was everything, least of all a rescue from my panic attack.

It's been a long time since full-blown anxiety overwhelmed me in public. Last time, I had to hide somewhere out of sight. Wait it out alone until it finally passed, an hour later. But today… Well, I never would have imagined emerging from my tailspin so fast. And all because of how that devil kissed me. It must have been the shock. My reaction. Just out of shock. I probably would have acted the same had he slapped me.

"Trust me, I'm sure." I flip over and stare at the ceiling. "Anything else interesting happening at my wedding reception?"

"Well… The don and his wife also disappeared shortly after the ceremony. Honestly, I was surprised they showed up at all, considering their baby girl is barely a year old. I still find it hard to wrap my mind around the idea that Ajello has a child. Oh! There's grilled salmon here! You guys really should have stayed."

"Yeah, no thanks. If I had to spend even a minute longer with your brother, I would have gone postal."

"It can't be that bad. Maybe he'll grow on you? I mean, Drago and I didn't know each other at all when we got married, and look at us now."

True. But everyone could tell right away that my brother fell crazy in love with Sienna the moment he set his eyes on her. He was a total goner who wouldn't let other men so much as look at her, never mind touch her. To this day, he worships the ground she walks on.

"Drago and Arturo are nothing alike, Sienna," I croak.

"I know, but—"

"Listen, I'm dead tired and I have a bunch of boxes to unpack. I'll call you tomorrow, okay? Bye."

I hang up and pull the extra pillow over my face. Maybe I would've had the kind of love Sienna and Drago have, too, if I'd actually tried making it work in one of my previous relationships. Maybe I could've had a man ready to step in front of a bullet for me, just as my brother did for his wife. But I don't. Instead, I'm stuck with an arrogant asshole with a short fuse, who would rather throw me to the wolves than save me.

As I'm wallowing in my misery, a whisper-quiet knock sounds at my door.

"Mrs. DeVille, it's Greta," a chirpy voice calls out. "The movers have all your things organized. May we bring them inside?"

"Sure. Just a sec."

I drag myself out of bed and shuffle to open the oak double doors. Four guys in matching blue denim work shirts saunter in, all huffing as they carry large cardboard boxes.

"Just stack them there, in front of the fireplace." I motion toward the left side of the room.

"Perhaps you'd like to have them on the other side, by the window, Mrs. DeVille, in case it gets chilly? You might want to light a fire," suggests one of the movers.

I shudder at the thought. I'd rather freeze to death than go anywhere near a flame. "By the fireplace is fine, thanks."

As the guys transfer all of my belongings, I take a quick tour of my new bedroom.

It's more of a spacious studio with two distinct living areas. On one side, there's an open sitting nook nestled into a circular bay created by tall French windows. The other end is dominated by a king-size bed. Separating the two is a floor-to-ceiling, fully rotatable, wooden slat partition that allows for either an open, see-through concept or additional privacy when the slats are shut. The overall design is modern, but it feels warm and inviting, not barren like many such places are. It also looks like no one has ever occupied the room before.

The peach carpet under my feet must be the plushest, thickest in existence. It feels like it's made from the softest wool imaginable. I revel in the sensation as I cross to the glass wall that faces the front yard. Even at this time of year, the grounds are pretty, and I can picture myself curled up with a book in the shade of a massive birch tree. My tranquil moment, however, is broken by the rumble of an engine coming to life outside.

I pull back one side of the buttery smooth white satin drapes just in time to see my husband rushing down the front steps toward his usual swanky stretched BMW. He's putting on his suit jacket while speaking on his phone. Must be in a helluva hurry. As he reaches the car's back door, he pauses and throws a look over his shoulder. Gazing directly up at me.

I drop the curtain like it's bitten me, letting it fall back into place. When I brave a peek out a minute later, both the vehicle and Arturo are gone.

"Mr. DeVille has been called away on an urgent matter," Greta says as she sets my pot of peace lilies on the coffee table. "He mentioned that he likely won't be back before morning."

"As if I care," I say, though not loud enough for her to actually hear me.

My dear husband obviously couldn't bother to take even his wedding day off. It's not that I want him here with me or anything, but it proves that he lives and breathes for his precious Cosa Nostra. The man just dumped me at his house with barely a word.

Couldn't even show me around himself. And I'm just supposed to live here?

Whatever.

"Okay, I think that's everything." Greta nods toward the mountain of boxes. "Would you like help unpacking, Mrs. DeVille?"

"I think I'll leave it for tomorrow. Thanks."

"Can I get you something to eat?"

"No, thank you." My stomach is feeling so tight, I don't think I'll ever be able to eat again.

"Okay. If you change your mind, there are a few things in the fridge."

I wait until she walks out, then rifle around in one of the boxes labeled *Books*. It takes a bit of effort before I can finally pull out my favorite romantasy. It might be my wedding night, but it seems that I'll be spending it in a nice, warm bath.

Pathetic. But nothing new.

Arturo

"No, no one has been able to reach Mendoza for months. After his compound was blown up, he went to ground." I throw my jacket over the back of the couch and sink into the cushions. "Hernandez isn't answering either."

"How much product are we short?" Ajello asks. I can practically see him scowling into the phone.

"Our guys are still checking all the crates and measuring everything out. But we're missing a quarter of a ton, at least." Aggressive morning sunlight punches through my living room's unshuttered window, hitting me straight on. I squeeze my eyes shut, trying to escape the brightness and also lessen the piercing pressure at my temples. Slumping deeper into the couch, I throw my forearm over my face. "I left Pietro at the warehouse. He'll call me back as soon as he has the final tally."

"You left your bride alone on your wedding night so you could oversee our men unloading a truck? Were they not capable of doing it on their own?"

"This delivery was delayed. And now, the number of crates doesn't match what we were expecting. The buyers were already breathing down my neck, have been for days. They'll be even more unhappy with this latest turn of events. Of course I had to go and check out the shipment myself. I need to know what the fuck is happening. It's in my job description, boss."

"Your role requires you to be at the top of your game, not play mother hen and babysit shit that you have competent people to handle. Did you even sleep?"

"No. I just got in." I glance at my wristwatch. It's a little after seven-thirty. "I'll wait an hour or so, then call Spada. He might have an extra quantity of coke he'd be willing to off-load. Enough that it might pacify our buyers until the next shipment arrives."

"I'll reach out to Massimo. You go to sleep. That's an order, Arturo." The line goes dead without preamble.

Fucking great. I toss the phone on the coffee table and sigh, but a sudden coughing fit comes over me. I lean forward, trying to clear my airway. It feels like several minutes pass before I can draw a deep breath. My chest aches from the pressure. Goddamned chain-smoking Pietro and his stupid cigarettes. Next time he lights up around me, I'll shove his smokes down his throat.

Once I manage to drag myself into the kitchen, I take a bottle of water from the fridge, then climb the stairs to the second floor. Off the landing to the right is a hallway that leads to Sienna's and Asya's old bedrooms, as well as a couple of guest rooms that face the backyard. Turning left, I head toward two sets of doors.

After I saved up enough money, I purchased this house for my sisters and me. I wanted a fresh start for us and believed a new home could give us that. Maybe I was wrong. Maybe we should have stayed in our old house, where memories of our parents filled every room. But I couldn't do it any longer. Couldn't handle being between those walls anymore. Because amid the happy memories of our family, there was another. One that got louder and louder with every passing year, drowning out all the rest. The memory of me in that house, telling my five-year-old sisters that their mom and dad were never coming home.

It was the hardest fucking thing I've had to do in my life.

Stopping before the first set of oak double doors, I stare at their white surface as if they'll tell me their secrets, what's hidden behind their solid bulk. But I already know what room lies beyond them. And who it belongs to. The mere possibility seemed like a far-off future when I purchased this place.

The realtor went on and on about how this property had two sizable primary bedrooms. The largest on the market in this neighborhood, he said. As if I gave a fuck about that at that moment. The most important factor for me was that it had a big yard for my sisters to play in, and that the house was in the suburbs, away from the hustle and bustle of the city. Once I bought it, I occupied the room at the end, while the one behind these doors remained empty. Designed as a secondary suite for the lady of the house, the space sat bare and barren, unable to fulfill its true purpose for years. I figured it would stay that way, until, that is, business needs won out and I got tapped as an ideal candidate for an arranged marriage.

Seems that time is here.

But my wife, who is asleep behind these doors, is nothing at all like the kind of woman I figured I'd have to wed.

The turn of the knob doesn't create the slightest sound, so I open the door and step inside. My footsteps are muffled by the thick carpet that covers the sitting nook. Just weeks ago, this room was completely devoid of furniture and other accessories. It was a bleak, unfinished space. I decided to have it renovated and outfitted after returning home from one of my visits with the Popovs.

People love to gossip. Idle words travel faster than a New York rat up a drainpipe, and the information that Arturo DeVille's wife is sleeping in his sister's room would have spread through the Cosa Nostra grapevine like a firestorm. And where would that have left us? Deep in the fucking shit.

We never tried to pass this off as an arranged marriage, where a scenario like that could have been explained. But even if we did, once the deal was made, it would be expected of us to present as another happy couple. Never air our dirty laundry for everyone to see. That's the way of the Cosa Nostra. And as Ajello has so beautifully put it, as his underboss, it's my job to set an example in our social circle. Promote those family values he spoke of.

That was my only motivation for getting this second primary ready for Tara. The fact that I made that decision after the first time we kissed is nothing but a pure coincidence.

That kiss meant nothing. Just a means to an end. Like all the others.

Silently stopping next to the partition separating the two parts of the room, I lean my shoulder on the wooden frame. A beam of light streams through the narrow gap between the drapes covering the window, illuminating the delicate female form curled up in the tangled sheets.

Her tiny sleeping shorts don't hide her long, beautiful legs. I let my gaze travel upward to where her tee has ridden up, baring her midriff. A glint shines off the piercing in her belly button, casting sparkling sunbursts in the dim space. I can't take my eyes off it. And not because of my usual belief that navel piercings are unbecoming of a refined lady. More than once I've woken up with a hard dick after dreaming of licking that bedazzling jewel.

Finally breaking out of the hypnotic state induced by that shining temptation, I continue my fervent perusal of my sleeping wife. My hungry gaze eats up the swaths of her smooth skin, the swell of her breasts beneath her T-shirt, and the elegance of her neck until they land on her slightly parted lips. It's the only part of her face visible to me. The rest is hidden by the blanket of her shiny, dark locks lying across her eyes and nose.

The pounding in my temples ratchets up, and I nearly wince from the crushing pressure. The inside of my throat feels so raw, as if it's been scratched to shreds. I unscrew the bottle cap and gulp the water, cringing with every painful swallow. It doesn't dampen my enjoyment of watching my little kitten sleep. I have no doubts that she'll give me hell the instant she wakes up, so I take the time to appreciate her like this. In precious peace. Her present tranquil state is the grossest misrepresentation of her true hazardous nature. Somehow, though, I admire the wild side of her that urges her to defy me at every turn. It leaves me so fucking randy.

Soundlessly, I make my way to her bed and pull up a corner of the blanket, freeing it from the tangles around her feet. Tara constantly grumbles about being cold, so much so that half my wardrobe is missing. My suit jackets better be among the stuff she brought with her, or this kitten might find herself in another bout of trouble.

With the blanket tucked under Tara's chin, I head for the set of sliding doors across from the windows. Another meaningless feature in this home. But I can't wait to see my wife's reaction when she discovers it.

The connecting doors between our rooms.

 Tara

"Finally." I sweep the hair off my face and take in my work.

All four hundred and seventeen of my paperbacks are arranged on the shelves in the sitting area of my room. It took a while to organize them by subgenre. The only thing left for me to do is unbox my special editions. Those I'll be setting up on my cherished book-case that I brought from home. But before that, I need to deal with my clothes.

Last night, I only had enough energy to dig out my pajamas and a change of clothes for today. Everything else is still in the suitcases and boxes lined up near the bed. After slicing through the packing tape of the wardrobe box labeled *Dresses,* I flip open the flaps and start pulling out my stash.

The bulk of my dresses are casual, everyday-wear numbers. I do have a few that could be considered fancy, elegant gowns. But mostly, I'm a pants girl. In my book, a good pair of pumps can elevate any pants outfit to a classy ensemble. However, that won't cut it with my darling husband. The unique terms of our prenup agreement clearly outline that he expects floor-length designer dresses for his damn social engagements. And according to the schedule he was so kind to share with me, there will be three of those this month alone. I'm thankful I was able to raid Sienna's closet and borrow some of her more muted pieces. They'll do in the short term, but an unavoid-able shopping trip is definitely in my future.

Holding a handful of the nonslip hangers and their accompany-ing dresses, I head across the room to the walk-in closet. It's conve-niently located near the bed, with oak double doors that match in style to the ornate room entrance. There's a freestanding armoire sectional on the other side as well, but that thing is too small for all the clothes I had to bring. Not to mention my stash of Arturo's "borrowed" jackets that are still hidden among my unpacked things.

Shifting the hangers to my left hand, I grab the handle and slide the door to the side. It moves smoothly and silently, without much effort, to reveal—

"What the—" I choke out.

My eyes bounce across the spacious room, eventually landing on the massive bed at the far end and a muscular male body sprawled face down upon it.

A naked male body.

My jaw hits the floor. This isn't a walk-in closet. My asshole husband put me in a room that connects to his own! And the man sleeps naked! Naked!

I spin around, wanting to slam the door shut. No matter how gorgeous he is, he doesn't deserve any attention from me. The bastard's ego is big enough. But an overwhelming sense of curiosity gets the better of me. Biting my lower lip, I glance over my shoulder.

It's undeniable that Arturo DeVille is a handsome devil, especially in those bespoke three-piece suits of his. But I never expected him to be this well-built. I'd be lying if I didn't admit my heartbeat picks up speed as I ogle the mass of impeccably defined muscles laid out before my eyes. Every part of him looks like it's carved from marble. Every sharp plane, ridge, and valley is chiseled to perfection. Including his ass. Especially his ass. I'm pretty sure I could bounce a coin off that thing.

Ugh! I hate myself for looking!

Stupid dickhead! Why does he have to be so goddamn beautiful?

Tearing my gaze off his glorious behind, I stare at his thick, inked forearm as he clutches the pillow to his face. The memory of that strong arm holding me up during our wedding ceremony floods me. The way his presence, just being held by him, managed to pull me out of my spiral into an inevitable panic attack was simply unreal. Incredible. Unlikely. But true nevertheless. It's as if Arturo DeVille is a force of nature, stronger than anything in his path.

Aside from my family or very close friends, I've never felt safe around people. But at that moment, the arms of my archenemy were the most sheltered place on earth. I would have done anything to stay within their secure embrace. Just the idea that he might let me go spiked greater anxiety.

I craved more of that heat he carries within him. The bastard's skin is always hot to the touch. I went for his tie, trying to get closer to his warmth. Needing more skin-to-skin contact. But he assumed I simply wanted to fuck him. Whatever. Satan DeVille can imagine whatever fantasy he likes.

However, the truth… the truth I can't deny, is that in his arms I felt protected. As if having him with me would somehow make everything right. That, even after everything he's done, the way he's treated me… something inside me still recognized Arturo DeVille as safe.

Could it be because he already knows what a disaster I usually am? He read that background check on me, so I can't possibly disappoint him. Is that what made him a refuge in my spiraling mind? It must be. It can't possibly be anything else.

Can it?

This line of thinking is getting me nowhere. Arturo DeVille *might* have done me a solid, but that's it. Who says he won't demand something in return? Well, he won't if I just don't admit to anything. As of this instant, all stupid thoughts about him need to be gone.

After discarding the stack of dresses on the nearby chair and tiptoeing my way to his bed, I yank on the corner of the pillow, ripping it out of his hold.

"Wakey, wakey, darling. Care to explain what happened to my room being as far from yours as possible?"

Arturo cracks an eye open, squinting at me. "What time is it?"

I blink, momentarily bewildered by how… how boyish he looks. There isn't a trace of his usual flawless swept-back style. His hair is all tousled from sleep, sticking up in every direction and falling across his eyes. That constant scowl he wears is also missing from his face. His morning voice is raspy, more than it typically is.

"Um… almost noon."

"Fuck," he sighs, moving his big hand to cover the half of his face not smashed into a pillow. "I need to get back to the office. Meant to catch a couple of hours at mo…"

Silence. I wait for him to continue, but instead of words, his deep rhythmic breaths fill the room. He's asleep again. Should I wake him?

I poke his bulging biceps. "DeVille."

"*Ma lasciami dormire,*" he mumbles into his pillow.

Holy shit. His voice is even more seductive when he speaks Italian. Husky, spellbinding, like a purr. I'm certain whatever he said wasn't an invitation to join him but, damn it, it sure sounded like that to me.

I poke him again, but he doesn't even stir. Is he dead? No, I wouldn't be that lucky.

My eyes glide along his trunk-like arm, cataloging the shapes inked into his skin. A thin gray snake is coiled twice around his wrist before it winds its way among the depicted foliage. Part of its body disappears behind a wicked-looking human skull on DeVille's upper forearm. The wings of some sort of mythical creature hug his massive biceps and triceps, and above it all, a dagger with a ribbon attached to the hilt. A word I can't quite make out is etched upon the wavy strip. I tilt my head, trying to get a better look, but all I can make out is *l'On.*

I shouldn't be so eager to inspect the tattoos on my husband. Actually, nothing about Arturo DeVille should hold my interest, but I still find myself leaning closer, stretching to decipher the inked script. Ha! The first word is *l'Onore,* but there's more. I brace on one leg, holding my arms out for balance to get to a better angle. If I stretch just a bit more, I could—

My foot slips.

I throw my hand in front of me to regain my equilibrium, only to end up sprawled on top of my husband. "Shi—"

He moves faster than a damn ninja. One second, I'm flopped over him, and the next, I'm on my back, pinned under a fuming mountain of hard muscle. My wrists are secured above my head in Arturo's hands, and he's glaring down at me.

"Tara?" He blinks as his expression morphs from a murderous snarl into a perplexed frown. "What the fuck?"

"Exactly!" I try to wriggle free. "Let me go!"

"What are you doing in my bed?"

"I'm not in your bed!"

He lifts an eyebrow.

"It was an accident, okay? I was trying to get a better look at your tat, and I slipped. Now, release me."

"I think this is the first time a woman has ended up in my bed *by accident.*"

My mouth falls open, preparing to deftly send him to hell, only for me to be completely ensnared by the wicked glint in his eyes. Eyes that are entirely focused on my lips. His hair is somehow even more tousled, making him look a little wild and all kinds of sexy. It's like he's suddenly become a totally different man than the uptight jerk I've come to know and hate. The sleek, decorous, and exacting Arturo DeVille has always been a sight to behold, albeit an extremely irritating one. But this... I never could have imagined him like this. Disheveled. Slightly feral-looking. Smelling of clean soap and shampoo, without any trace of that rich blend of exotic spices and earthy sensuality of the cologne he always wears.

The rumpled Arturo DeVille is a thousand times hotter.

My breath hitches in my lungs. And I can't seem to make my limbs move. Or maybe I just don't want to. Having Arturo DeVille—a very naked Arturo DeVille—crushing me into the mattress beneath him is intoxicating. An experience that sets off an ache deep in my core and makes my clit throb.

Desire. Desire floods me, spreading tingles over every part of my body.

My throat goes dry at the memory of those sinister lips on mine. My fingers itch to reach out and muss that hair, all so I can revel in knowing that it was I, and not sleep, that left him this way. The cross dangling off his chain draws my eyes to his collarbone. It's an undeniably sexy collarbone. I want to reach out and stroke it with the tip of my finger. Or maybe my tongue. What would it feel like to—

No!

Stop.

I shut my eyes, trying to force the mental images of him fucking me, hard, right here and now, out of my head.

"Are you sure it wasn't intentional?" His gravelly, deep whisper rolls over me as his warm breath feathers the shell of my ear. He sounds like sin personified, like the devil he is. Tempting me into his villainous lair, to do dark, lustful deeds that I should, but I'm not sure I would, regret. "If you want to broaden the articles covered in our prenup, *gattina*, all you have to do is ask."

"Keep dreaming, Satan." Channeling as much strength as I can, I yank my arms out of his hold and shove his chest, pushing him off me. The instant I'm free, I scramble off the bed. "I'd rather screw a toaster."

Sweeping my hair over my shoulder, I turn on my heel and swiftly flee back to my room. And I make sure to send the door sliding hard against its twin as I shut it. Anticipating a loud bang, I'm a bit disappointed when it connects with a soft thud. *Damn modern conveniences!*

"What a jerk," I mumble as I cross my room and then head downstairs in search of some food.

Most days, I don't eat breakfast, but today, there's a gaping hole in my stomach that demands to be filled. It has nothing to do with hunger, though. I'm a stress eater, and getting unexpectedly turned on by my *husband* requires gastronomic intervention. Stat.

As soon as the thought of food enters my mind, a loud rumbling erupts from my gut. Despite my level of dread going through the roof yesterday as the wedding drew closer, I couldn't stomach a thing. Associating with Arturo DeVille seems to have turned even my own quirks against me. I shudder to think what other new hell actually living with him will bring. Whatever it might be, it will have to wait until I can get some decent grub. Something tells me I'm going to need to keep up my strength.

There's no one in the kitchen, so I decide to help myself, going straight to the fridge. It's one of those enormous French door refrigerators, promising an assortment of tasty and comforting things within its chilly interior. Is there a chance that some of the leftovers from our banquet were sent over? My mouth is already watering as I imagine the truffle bruschetta Sienna mentioned. It sounded divine. Or maybe there's cake. Surely someone delivered at least a few slices of our wedding cake!

Eager, I pull the fridge door open and feel my enthusiasm drop like a lead balloon.

Tomatoes. Cucumbers. Bell peppers. Zucchini. A bunch of chives, dill, parsley, and a ton of other rabbit food. I move things about, hoping to find something other than salad ingredients to pick on. Nope. A carton of eggs. Lots of meat, but it's all raw, stacked neatly in plastic packaging. Some white button mushrooms, as well as another container of weird-looking purple things. And cheese. A big wheel of pale-yellow cheese. There are also several packages of different types of grated cheese and a container of five other varieties cut into small cubes. *Holy shit!* The slide-out tray looks like a dairy farm threw up in there.

"Eggs it is, I guess."

I grab three eggs and a piece of hard cheese out of the fridge, setting them on the counter. Just a few steps away and directly across from the breakfast bar is a double oven and a multi-burner stove. The massive appliance is set under a sleek stainless steel range hood. I bet a professional chef would be jealous of this kitchen. I'm reaching into the side cabinet to get a frying pan when my eyes fall on the cooktop surface.

Gas burners.

My throat gets tight, closing up.

Chills break out and run through my body.

With my eyes glued to the stove, I slowly back away. Every shaky step backward is preceded by a rapid exhale of breath. I keep retreating until I bump into a wall.

"You're making us breakfast?" the wall whispers in that deep, gravelly voice right next to my ear.

I shriek, nearly jumping out of my skin.

"The fuck, DeVille? Want me to have a heart attack?"

"Didn't figure you for being so skittish."

I huff and quickly slip by him, pretending to be super busy starting the coffee maker.

"What about our breakfast?" Arturo nods toward the eggs and cheese I left on the counter.

"It's not *our* breakfast. It was meant to be mine, but I changed my mind. Do you have deli meat or something I can use to make a sandwich?"

"I try to avoid processed food. There's some ribeye you can grill."

My gaze jumps to the burners again. "Nope. Don't really feel like cooking."

"Do you want me to grill the steak for you?"

"And give you a chance to poison me, get rid of me altogether? Not happening."

"Suit yourself." He shrugs nonchalantly.

Once my coffee is brewed, I carry it to the breakfast bar and perch on the stool on the far side. The location allows me a full view of the kitchen, including an unimpeded line of sight to Arturo, who's rummaging in the fridge and pulling a bunch of ingredients out. He's dressed in pressed black pants and a dove-gray shirt with the top two buttons undone. His ever-present gold cross hangs around his neck. Each time he moves and the sunlight streaming through the window falls on the jewelry, I flash back to Arturo's bedroom. His bed, more specifically.

I mean DeVille's. Satan's bedroom. Not Arturo's!

Sipping my coffee, I feign complete disinterest in what he's doing while secretly watching him. He moves around the kitchen with effortless precision. His every action is methodical, and the expression on his face shows deep concentration. The steak is already sizzling on the side grill. The bell peppers are sliced into strips, and the zucchini is cut up into small cubes before he throws everything into the pan. Next, he grabs a slim, dark bottle of cooking oil and pours a little splash on the veggies.

As he sets the oil aside, a flash of blue flame surges from the burner. My coffee cup nearly slips out of my hand. I grit my teeth and look away, forcing myself to remain seated. Breathing deeply to calm my heart rate.

"I'm having dinner with a business associate on Tuesday," he says as he tosses in cherry tomatoes and then stirs the food, seasoning it at the same time. Whatever spices he's using are blending with the aroma of grilled beef and sautéed veggies, and the kitchen smells divine. "He's coming down from Boston. Unfortunately, due to some personal obligations, he couldn't make it to our wedding."

"What does that have to do with me?"

"You'll be accompanying me. And, you'll be on your best behavior. Understood?"

"Define 'best behavior.' Should I just keep my mouth shut and look classy? Or would you like me to also fetch a ball when you throw it? You know, to show your important business associate what a well-trained wifey I am?"

"Very funny. Adriano Ruffo is from the upper echelon of Italian society, Tara. He's also just become our main contact with the Boston Cosa Nostra on the joint construction project we're working on."

"Oh? Is he a prince or something? Should I curtsy when I meet him? Kiss his hand or—"

"You're not kissing his anything!" Arturo snaps.

A noisy sizzle and pop sounds from the range, probably from the splash of oil or a bit of rendered fat hitting the burner. Despite knowing the likely cause, my eyes still dart to the stove, anxiously searching for the giant orange tendrils of an inferno reaching toward me. But there's nothing there except the tiny blue flame.

"Damn wet tomatoes," Arturo grumbles, focusing back on the pan. "And no, Adriano is not a prince. But his great-grandfather was a duke. Adriano owns one of the largest transport companies in the US. We're considering proposing an additional collaboration, centering on his fleet of trucks. Another tie between New York and Boston."

"Fancy that! Is he married?"

"Why?"

"You really need to ask?" I tilt my coffee cup, trying to get the last few drops. "A duke. And a crazy rich one at that. It's as if a hero from one of my novels has sprung to life. Hopefully, he'll still be available a year from now, once I'm a happily divorced woman, that is."

Bang!

I flinch.

"Adriano is a widower," Arturo barks as he slams a cupboard door closed. "His wife died tragically only a few months ago. So, make sure you keep any such comments to yourself when you meet him. Do you understand, Tara?"

"Woof, woof." I grin.

Hubby slashes me with an angry stare while plating the food. Then, he brings the dishes to the breakfast bar and forcefully sets them on the wooden surface between us. "Eat. Or would you like me to get you some kibble? Just let me know if you prefer a particular brand."

I lean over the bartop, invading his space. "I'd rather eat dog chow than anything you've prepared, darling."

"Well, in that case…" With a self-satisfied smirk lighting up his face, he takes the plate that was meant for me and transfers the scrumptious-looking fare onto his own.

The divine aroma invades my senses. Sautéed veggies. Grilled steak. Something spicy and sweet. Saliva pools in my mouth, and every inhale is practically torture. My last decent meal was yesterday morning. And after that goddamned wedding, food was the last thing on my mind. I did wander downstairs around midnight and grab a banana from a bowl of fruit in the living room, but that was it.

"You sure you don't want some?" Satan asks as he spears a piece of juicy steak and lifts the fork to his mouth. His movements are slow and deliberate. Taunting. He's baiting me on purpose.

"I'm not hungry, DeVille, for anything you have to offer." I slam my empty coffee cup on the breakfast bar and leave the asshole to his amazing meal, retreating on principle while my stomach churns in protest.

CHAPTER
Thirteen

Tara

"H EY, GRETA?"

The housekeeper stops fluffing the throw pillows on the couch and glances at me over her shoulder. A muted rendition of a French chanson sounds from one of the earbuds dangling from the band around her neck. "Mrs. DeVille. Can I help you with something?"

"Um, yeah." I clasp my hands behind my back. "I was wondering… would you be so kind as to make me lunch?"

She blinks at me in confusion. "Well, of course. What would you like to eat?"

"Anything home-cooked would be great. I'm not picky." I give her a sheepish smile.

For the past two days, I've been living on bananas and cheese. I guess I could have ordered a delivery or asked Riggo to drive somewhere I could get a proper meal, but I didn't want DeVille finding out about it and asking questions. The last thing I want is to have to explain to that dick that I'm scared shitless of the fire. Any kind of fire, really, but especially the sort associated with gas stoves. I don't need him to think I'm a total basket case.

"I can make a simple pasta dish for you in no time. Or, would you like to have meat with it, too? It would take a bit longer to prepare, but—"

"Pasta sounds amazing. Thank you."

I follow Greta into the kitchen, then perch in my favorite spot at the breakfast bar. Someone moved the bowl of fruit from the living room, leaving it on the counter right next to the coffee machine. As soon as that fact registers, I glance away from the bunch of fresh bananas. If I don't see any in the next decade, it will be too soon.

"Oh. Mr. DeVille must have read your mind," Greta chirps while peeking under the tinfoil covering a deep baking pan left on the stove. "Beef lasagna. And it's still warm. I'll plate some of this for you."

"Absolutely not," I growl, then quickly clear my throat. "I mean… no, thank you. I'm not a fan of the combination of two sauces. Could you make me something else?"

Lies! I love lasagna. The layers of noodles, and meat, and cheese… Jesus, I can feel myself drooling.

"Oh, that's a shame. You should share that with Mr. DeVille. He's very passionate when it comes to food, you know? Frankly, I've never known a man who enjoys cooking as much as he does. Other than on special occasions, when catering is more convenient, he always prepares his own meals. No processed foods, of course. No artificial flavors. Only fresh and organic ingredients. You won't find any junky snacks or anything like that in his kitchen, that's for sure."

"I've noticed," I grunt. *Damn psycho.*

"One time, when he was hosting a business dinner here, he refused to serve an entire order of a dozen lobsters, all because they weren't prepared well. So he had one of the men drive an hour away, to a place Mr. DeVille approves of, and bring back fresh shellfish, which he proceeded to cook himself."

"Sounds exactly like him." An anal-retentive perfectionist. "And where is the master chef now?"

"Oh, he was up at six sharp and headed to the office shortly after. Something about some permits that needed to be renewed ASAP. He did return a couple of hours ago, but just before you came down, I saw him get back into that big car of his and drive off with Riggo." She *tsks* like a fretting mother instead of an employee talking about her boss. "I'm worried about Mr. DeVille. He's been working so much these past few months. Always on the go. It's unhealthy. He's always been tireless in his dedication to his work, but not even he can function on so little sleep. And I told him this morning that he needs to see a doctor about that cough of his. But you know what he said? He hasn't got the time." Greta shakes her head like all this is some grave tragedy, and hands me a cup of coffee.

After staying up way too late last night, editing Sienna's latest manuscript, I definitely need it. Oversleeping isn't my norm, but it worked out great because I didn't need to fake it for once. My brain, though, was still fairly groggy when I finally got up. When I thought I heard some muffled bark-like and wheezing sounds, I dismissed them as imagined or random noises. Hmm, must have been Satan, coughing up a lung. Whatever. He can drop dead, as far as I'm concerned.

"Men are known to be bullheaded." I shrug, not having a better response for her.

"Maybe you could talk to him? With you here now, he's bound to spend more quality time at home, right? You guys could go to the movies. Or a Broadway show, even. A picnic in the park is always nice."

I lift an eyebrow. A picnic. With Satan DeVille?

"Or... maybe not a picnic. Mr. DeVille doesn't like those, actually."

I roll my eyes. Is there anything Mr. DeVille does like? "I'll keep that in mind."

"Here you go. *Cacio e pepe*." Greta sets a plate in front of me. "It's my *nonna's* recipe. Spaghetti with black pepper and Pecorino Romano. I hope you like it."

"Thanks so much, Greta. You're an angel."

"Oh, it's nothing. I hardly ever get to cook here since Mr. DeVille takes care of that himself. If you'd like, I can show you how to make it next time."

My eyes dart to the stove, but I quickly avert them. "Um... I'm not a very good cook. A bit of a disaster, actually. So, would you be able to fix something for me tomorrow, too?"

"Absolutely. No worries at all."

Greta stuffs her earbuds in place and disappears around the corner. As soon as she's out of sight, I start shoveling forkful after forkful into my mouth. The simple spaghetti tossed in a buttery pepper and cheese sauce is... different. Not *entirely* unpleasant. There's just something off with it. I don't really care, though. After two days of limited options, I'm greatly thankful for some "real" food. But my gaze keeps straying to the pan of Arturo's lasagna, and my nose is tempted by the heavenly aroma of the dish.

It doesn't matter! I'm not touching it, wouldn't even if it was the last thing on earth left to eat. I can't! Knowing Satan made it... for me... that's unthinkable! Way too intimate, in my view.

Being a part of a couple that cooks for each other is one of the romantic notions I've always wanted to experience. It'd mean we both took the time to get to know each other's likes and dislikes. That we shared a deep and meaningful connection, infinitely more intense than I ever intended to have with DeVille. So I won't let that man rob me of yet another special moment—having my *real* husband prepare food for me. That, I will treasure and save for my *real* marriage, not this sham that I'm currently forced to live.

I will not allow Arturo DeVille to destroy yet another precious dream of mine. Won't let him take it away from me. Giving in is not an option. Because some things taste too bitter while promising to be sweet.

"Crap." I lower the drill and take stock of the results of my labor. There are exactly twelve shallow holes in the wall, all within an inch of each other, but none are deep enough to get a screw into.

After lunch, once I finished up with my editing project, I decided to tackle my next challenge. Setting up the bookcase for displaying my collection of special editions. It was moved here from my room at Drago's but remained shoved in the corner of my new bedroom for the past two days, awaiting me finding an ideal spot for it. And I have. The stretch of wall between the two French windows is perfect. However, since the bookcase is over six feet tall, it needs to be anchored so it won't topple. No problem. I asked Greta to find me a drill.

"This damn wall must be made of concrete," I gripe and press the trigger of the power tool again. "But I've faced more vile enemies in my life and prevailed."

Attempt number thirteen proves to be as unlucky as I should have expected. The drill bit encounters something just below the surface, and due to an unexpected kickback, I end up making a gash along the drywall. The tool slips from my hand, falling to the floor with a loud thud. And, because I engaged the trigger lock when my hand started getting tired, the drill keeps vibrating across the carpet like some convulsing creature.

"What in hell are you doing, woman?" a male voice booms behind me.

"Isn't it obvious, DeVille?" I twist around so I can face the intruder.

I move too quickly, and the step stool I'm using wobbles beneath me. I shriek and grab onto the nearby drapery panel to steady myself. Immediately, a brief creak, and then a sharp snap emanates somewhere above me. It occurs a split second before the entire curtain rod dislodges from the wall and flies toward my head. I flinch and yelp, shutting my eyes. Bracing for the inevitable. Before the thought of self-preservation even enters my mind, two strong arms wrap around me and whisk me away.

"You," the deep, irritated voice hisses next to my ear, "are a walking disaster, Tara. A hazard to yourself!"

Gingerly squinting my lids open, I come face-to-face with my fuming husband. He's cradling me in his arms and glaring down at me. There's a big red welt on his forehead, right above his brow. Worry for his well-being suddenly floods me. *He got hit with that damn rod!* But it almost immediately dissipates as his words finally sink in.

A walking disaster.

It's not as if I haven't been called names worse than that throughout my various relationships. *Dumb. Clueless. Melodramatic. Unhinged.* To name just a few. So I'm not sure why Arturo calling me by one more hits me so hard. *DeVille.* I meant DeVille.

"Well, thank you, darling. I'm glad you hold me in such high regard!" I scramble out of his embrace and get down to search for the fucking drill among the mound of wrecked white drapes. The blasted thing is still vibrating. "Fuck!"

"Tara," Satan growls.

"Just… leave me alone."

"You'll hurt yourself. Let me—" He breaks out into a coughing fit, sounding genuinely awful.

I drop the edge of the drape and narrow my eyes at him. "You should listen to Greta and get yourself checked out."

"Afraid you'll end up as a young widow, *gattina*?" Another bout of coughing overtakes him. He buries his face in the crook of his elbow until he's able to draw a deep breath. "I'm fine."

Locating the drill under the piled material, he walks up to inspect my masterpiece. "Were you trying to bust a hole for another window here or something?"

"The drill bit kept hitting… whatever"—I flip my hand at the wall—"and wouldn't go through."

"So you tried a dozen times?"

"Actually, it was thirteen."

DeVille shakes his head. A crooked smile plays on his lips as he moves the step stool out of the way. It takes him mere seconds to drill the hole I've been struggling to make for nearly an hour. It takes him even less time to create another over the other marked X.

"There." He extends his hand. "Anchors?"

"What?"

"The plastic things that get fitted into the holes. They keep the screws in."

"Oh." I kneel next to the toolbox Greta gave me and rummage through it. "I didn't expect you to know how to do this manual, home reno sort of stuff."

"Why not?"

I raise one of my eyebrows while looking him over. Even with his shirt sleeves rolled up and while holding a drill, he still somehow manages to look sophisticated.

"You just don't seem like the type," I say, returning my attention to finding what I need in the toolbox. Finally, I spot the orange plastic thingies and grab a couple. "Here."

DeVille stretches his hand toward me, but instead of taking my offering, his arm snakes around my waist, and he pulls me to him. My chest collides with his, knocking the air from my lungs.

"And what type do I seem like, Tara?" he asks, leaning in.

"An overly arrogant one. One who'd never stoop to hands-on, hard work."

"Mmm. I can assure you that I enjoy *hard* work, and I've never shied away from anything that requires *hands-on* effort. I'm also very adept at a variety of techniques. Especially the carnal kind."

There's a wicked glint in his eyes as he delivers his claim. Is he insinuating...?

OMG, he is!

A shudder works its way through my body, and a deep, throbbing need settles in my core. I bite the inside of my cheek, trying to dispel mental images of Arturo putting his *hands-on efforts* to use. Specifically, his fingers on my pussy. My clit pulses with anticipation, and I can't help it... A sigh escapes me.

His molten gaze instantly falls on my lips. Without thinking about what I'm doing, I find myself leaning closer. Closer to that sensual mouth of his. Magnetically drawn nearer, as if his eyes have the power to summon me. I suck in a breath, inhaling his scent. Exhilarating. Alluring. Addictive. His lower lip ghosts over the edge of mine, and every one of my rational thoughts flies straight out of the window.

I wrap my arm around his neck and pull him to me, capturing that enticing lip of his with my own.

He kisses me back. Hot breath fans my face as he crushes me to him. As he ravages my mouth. As he devours me like a starving man at a long-awaited feast. The spicy fragrance of his cologne plays with my senses as I counter him kiss for kiss.

His hand trails downward, squeezing my ass, making my mindless need skyrocket into a—

The heat of his palm stills over my butt cheek. And, somehow, that sudden lack of motion is a splash of cold water on my overheated flesh. My eyes fly open. Colliding with chocolate-colored depths. We stare at each other, both trying to catch our breath.

Split second.

Then, as if zapped, he and I jerk apart. Forcing several feet between us.

"Umm…" I look away, unwilling to face him. Reluctant to meet his gaze again. "I need to find that wall anchor I dropped."

"Yeah. Okay. Good."

Arturo nods, avoiding my eyes when I pass him the little thingy after spotting it on the floor. My own gaze won't venture anywhere near his, but probably not for the same reason.

What the hell was I thinking? Kissing him?

Shit. He's never going to let me forget that.

"That's perfect," he says, slipping the anchor into place.

He continues to work utterly unperturbed. Not about what just happened between us. Not about getting drywall dust on his fancy suit. As if his sleek business attire is simply a part of who he is and not what he wears, the man speedily progresses through sinking the anchors into their holes. Then, he slides the heavy bookcase into position, and finally secures the shelf brackets to the wall with screws. He makes it all look easy and effortless. Banging out manual tasks without breaking a sweat.

"There. All done." He gestures toward the shelf and, collecting the toolbox, heads across the room as if we hadn't kissed only moments ago.

Reaching the door, he throws a swift look over his shoulder. "I hope you haven't forgotten our plans for this evening."

"What plans?" I breathe out.

"Our first public appearance as husband and wife. As I told you, we're heading to meet Adriano Ruffo, so please make sure you review every clause of our agreement for specific instructions on how to present as my spouse. And don't forget to smile."

Arturo

"Yes, the first phase is proceeding on schedule. The slight setback due to the city's mix-up with our paperwork was on an unrelated project." I bring the wine glass to my lips and down the entire contents.

Adriano Ruffo leans back in his chair, observing me with hawkish eyes. This is the first time I've met the man in person, although I've been hearing various things about him for years. Mostly through the rumor mill that runs rampant within Cosa Nostra.

Having met Spada, I expected his point person to have a similar air. Rough around the edges. Explosive, bordering on nuts.

Ruffo is none of those things. Actually, he's the polar opposite of his don. Calm. Cultured. Civilized. Nothing about him is overstated, and yet, he looks like a man who wears power like a second skin. Early forties. Black hair, with a touch of gray at the temples. His height might be the only similarity between Ruffo and Spada. In fact, the Boston point man may even have an inch or two on his boss. Overall, although all outward appearances peg him as a corporate type, he's got a build that says he'd be able to hold his own in a fight. And with that, he probably has his pick of the ladies, despite carrying around a few extra pounds.

Nothing about the man seated before me would ever hint at his high status within the Boston Family. As far as I can tell, he's not armed. There's no visible ink anywhere on him. He's also not into the flashy jewelry that so many of my Italian peers tend to prefer. Anyone looking at him would peg him as just another wealthy but ordinary businessman. And, I have a feeling that's exactly what he wants to project. The black-framed glasses he wears reinforce that image.

"I'm happy to hear that, DeVille." He does that gentle head nod to convey he's paying attention. "As you're aware, this particular venture is very important to our *Famiglia*, and we sincerely hope that everything will proceed smoothly. Just as you had previously assured Don Spada it would during your meeting with him."

"I'm glad both our organizations recognize this endeavor is crucial, not only because of its value but also for its significance for our ongoing collaboration. As I've already stated, you'll continue to receive regular updates."

"Excellent." Ruffo's gaze slides to Tara, who is sitting on my right. "Would your wife like something else, perhaps? She hasn't even touched her meal."

"Tara?" It takes everything in me to keep my face expressionless. The effort is colossal, matching the restraint I've held myself with for the past twenty minutes. One slip, and I'm going to throttle her to death! "Is something wrong with your food, *gattina*?"

Her smile is as big as the Cheshire Cat's. And her eyes are so wide, they're practically bulging out from a face that's entirely frozen in a state of cartoonish happiness. She looks demented. Tilting her head, she beams that crazy grin at me. She's been wearing this idiotic expression since the moment we stepped foot in this dining lounge. It hasn't slipped even for a second throughout the entire fucking evening!

"It looks amazing, darling," she says without moving her teeth. That damn smile remains in place. "I'm just not hungry."

"Let's summon the chef. Maybe he can whip up something more

to Mrs. DeVille's liking." Ruffo gives a barely perceptible wave, and within seconds, four waiters, a maitre d', and the chef materialize at our tableside. They line up like soldiers waiting for inspection, hands clasped behind their backs. "Please, order whatever comes to mind, Mrs. DeVille."

Tara glances at the assembled staff, then turns her attention to Ruffo. Her already impossibly wide smile grows even more. "I wouldn't want to impose. Maybe there are other patrons who are waiting for their meals."

"No imposition at all. Staying at hotels isn't my thing, so I bought the entire resort in anticipation of this meeting. We're the only ones here, as you can see. Feel free to ask for anything you want."

"Oh, that's very kind of you."

Her voice is like a bird's song. Sweet. Charming. Playful. She's never once used that tone with me.

My jaw aches from how hard I've got it clenched. The jealousy is raging like an inferno inside me.

"I've never met a gentleman like you, Mr. Ruffo," she adds.

That's it! I rise so abruptly that my chair nearly topples over. "Apologies for cutting this short. We have a previous engagement we must attend tonight."

"Of course." Ruffo stands and offers me his hand. "Looking forward to our next meeting. Hopefully, we'll get a chance to discuss that additional opportunity for collaboration you mentioned. I'm eager to learn how my transportation network could strengthen the ties between our Families."

"I'm confident that we will." He can shove his trucking business up his ass, for all I care right now.

I wrap my arm around Tara's waist and practically drag her out of the place.

A few throaty grunts and a menacing-looking club, and I'd pass for a Neanderthal in a heartbeat.

"You were exceptionally rude," Tara chirps as we head across the nearly empty parking lot, occupied only by two essentially identical vehicles. Mine and Ruffo's, I suppose. "And there I was, doing my absolute best to appear as dutiful and docile as I could muster," she continues.

"Yeah, sure."

"Obviously, nothing satisfies you, DeVille. I followed every instruction you set out. Down to the tiniest detail. I'm wearing a fashionable ankle-length dress. Minimal makeup. I didn't utter a word until I was spoken to directly. And when I did, not a single cuss left my lips. Speaking of which… I maintained the mandatory ever-present smile."

"I'm certain your facial muscles will cramp from all that fake grinning." I open the back door of the BMW for her, allowing her to slide in behind the driver. "You looked ridiculous, by the way."

"I'm glad." She smiles at me then. It's not a fake one this time. This smile is genuine and makes clear what she left unsaid. *Go fuck yourself, DeVille.*

I slam the door shut once she's in and head to the other side of the vehicle with my blood boiling in my veins. Somehow, my darling wife has found the blueprints to everything that makes me tick. She knows just which nerve of mine to poke to make me lose my fucking shit. In more ways than one.

What the hell possessed me to kiss her earlier? Or did she kiss me? I don't fucking remember. There was no one around for whom we had to perform. No one we needed to fool with our kissing. Still, my brain must have short-circuited. The only thing I recall is the incessant hunger. For her. I wanted to devour her. Consume her. I wanted to indulge. Indulge. Indulge.

The fuck?

Settling into my seat, I immediately reach inside the door pocket to fetch the bottle of ibuprofen I stashed there yesterday. This entire week I've felt like crap, and this morning, a gripping tightness and soreness settled in my chest. Maybe it's these pills that are causing my behavior? I must have taken too many in the last twenty-four hours. Yeah, that's got to be it.

I grab a bottle of water out of the cup holder and pop two more pills.

"You're doing drugs now?" Tara grumbles next to me.

"Yes. A man needs to be completely stoned to spend time in your charming presence."

Tara's eyes flare in surprise, and maybe a little hurt, before she quickly looks away, focusing on something beyond the window. Although she's trying to hide her reaction, I don't miss the slight quiver of her lower lip. *Shit.* Each time I allow myself to feel this insane attraction to my wife, my self-preservation instinct kicks in, and I become the worst kind of asshole. The kind that needs to spew crap from my mouth to deflect and get myself back in line.

I squeeze my temples, feeling like the absolute dick that I am. "It's only over-the-counter painkillers, for Christ's sake. I just—"

"I don't really care," she huffs.

"Tara—"

"Can we please just drive the rest of the way in silence?" She sighs. "Please."

"Fine. Whatever."

I pull out my phone to check how long it will take us to get home. Nearly an hour, according to the GPS. With Ajello controlling New York City, this golf resort and country club for the elite has frequently been chosen as a venue for meetings. Since it lies outside the borders of our territory, it's as close as a member of another Family could get without our don's express permission. But its remote location is also the reason why Adriano Ruffo must have been able to purchase the establishment in the first place without incurring Ajello's wrath.

Grabbing my laptop off the side console, I set it on my lap to start going through emails that arrived in the last few hours. There are more than a dozen that need my immediate attention. I answer the one from Ajello first, responding with a report on next month's drug shipments, then move on to reviewing the concept sketches submitted by our architectural firm. Sometimes this damn job feels like I'm a Fortune 500 CEO instead of the underboss of a New York crime family.

I work for almost half an hour, making notes on changes I'd like to see. The pills have finally kicked in, lessening the ache in my chest and the throbbing at my temples. However, even feeling marginally better, I'm still having a hard time concentrating on what I'm doing. And that's all because of Tara. My wife, who's been silently moping on the seat beside me.

For the umpteenth time, my eyes dart toward her. "Why didn't you eat anything?" I close the laptop and slide the device back onto the console. "That steak was actually decent."

"Can't keep smiling while I eat. And you were adamant about that requirement for social functions in our agreement."

"Jesus. I'll fix you dinner when we get home. Did you enjoy the lasagna?"

"Haven't touched it. Greta was kind enough to make something else for me."

"What? Why?"

"I already told you, DeVille. I won't eat anything you prepare, on principle."

My nostrils flare. I don't understand why this pisses me off so much. What do I care if she'd rather wolf down takeout or processed crap? But it does. It irritates me a great deal. Instead of getting some much-needed shut-eye after my early meeting this morning, I spent over an hour making homemade lasagna for her. And I wanted her to like it, damn it.

"Do you intend to starve, then? Because from what I gather, you don't know how to cook."

"I cook. I just won't do it in a kitchen where the feng shui is all wrong. Your stove is close to the northwest corner. Do you have any idea how unlucky that is? I refuse to touch it." She crosses her arms over her chest. "Greta said she doesn't mind making my meals. But if she's unavailable, there's always takeout."

Yeah? We'll see about that.

We've just made a turn onto a wider road when the car jerks violently to the side, and the tires screech as Riggo slams on the brakes. The sharp movements send Tara careening straight toward me. I catch her in time to prevent her from smashing her head into the window or being tossed toward the privacy partition between us and the front seat.

Sliding the screen down, Riggo glances at me over his shoulder. "Apologies, Mr. DeVille," he says. "That vehicle in front of us fishtailed and then made a sudden stop. They might have had a tire blowout. Should I see if they need help?"

I peer ahead, checking out the road conditions through the windshield. A guy in jeans and a black hoodie is crouched down next to the driver-side tire of his full-size black pickup. This might be an infrequently used side road, at least at this time of year, but the asphalt is new. No potholes or anything else that might cause sudden damage to a heavy-duty tire like the ones on this guy's rig. Especially to the extent that an abrupt stop would be necessary. He didn't even bother pulling over to the shoulder.

The man rises and kicks the tire with his boot, then turns toward us. With a casual shrug, he beckons Riggo to come over, as if he does need help after all. I keep my attention on the nimrod as I reach into my jacket and pull out my gun.

"Really?" Tara grumbles next to my ear. I didn't realize that I was still holding her tightly pressed to my side. "Are you seriously going to get out, guns blazing, because some poor guy got a flat?"

"Riggo. When I tell you to, hit the gas." I turn to face my stubborn wife, bumping my nose with hers in the process. "Get down on the floor."

"Why?"

"Because the doors can block more bullets than the windows. Down. Now!"

"Bullets?" She blinks at me twice in confusion, then quickly untangles her legs from mine and crouches on the floor between the seats. "Fucking great."

Considering she experienced a panic attack during our wedding vows, I'm expecting her to lose her shit any second. In fact, I kinda expected she'd be halfway there by now, right after bullets were mentioned. But instead of drowning in hysterics, my wife simply adjusts her skirt and flashes me an angry scowl. Unbelievable.

I cock my gun. "Floor it, Riggo."

The car launches forward.

The *poor guy with a flat* reaches behind his back, pulling out a weapon. At the same time, the passenger door as well as two back doors fly open, and three other guys leap out of the pickup just as our car rushes past them.

Rhythmic pings pepper the back of the car as the shooters spray us with gunfire. One of the rounds ricochets off the rear windshield, leaving an indent in the bulletproof glass. The bastards are using armor-piercing shit. I lower my window and return fire.

"I should have married Conrad," Tara mutters from her spot on the floor. "I could be having a great time somewhere in Europe, enjoying a shrimp cocktail right now. Not getting shot at in the middle of nowhere."

"Who the fuck is Conrad?" I bark while aiming at the pursuing truck. A couple of guys have their heads out of the side windows, while another pops up through the sunroof. I should probably be thankful their driver is too busy to also shoot at us right now.

"Someone I dated in college. We were such a good match. His dad is an oil tycoon, so Conrad used to spoil me rotten. But we'd only been seeing each other for a short time before he proposed. I panicked and broke up with him. He still calls me occasionally, though."

I grit my teeth and send another round at the pickup that's dogging our every move. "Well, tell your oil tycoon brat that if he calls my wife again, the next call you'll be getting is an invite to his funeral."

"You can't forbid me from speaking with my friends!"

My head snaps toward her. "Of course, I—"

A bullet whizzes past my face, missing by mere inches. This damn woman will get me killed! I return my attention to the assholes chasing us, but the pickup has steered toward the middle of the road, escaping my line of fire. *Shit.* I change the gun's magazine, then slide to the opposite window, opening it to resume shooting.

"I thought you were left-handed," Tara continues mumbling. "It fits with your personality. Left-handed people are known to be domineering."

"Will. You. Stop. Talking?!"

"And easily distracted. Looks like the bad guys are gaining on us. You're not doing a very good job here, you know?"

"There are three of them and"—out of the corner of my eye I notice her peeking over the edge of the back seat—"GET THE FUCK DOWN!"

I grab the back of her dress, pulling her away just as the car careens to the left. The force of the motion sends us both sprawling on the floor of the car, with me landing over her.

"What the fuck is wrong with you, woman?" I bark. "Want to get your pretty head blown off?"

"I'm worried about our situation!"

More bullets bombard us as Riggo changes lanes, trying to shake off the gunmen. I need to get back to laying down cover fire, but I can't look away from Tara's pouting lips. They're luring me in again.

"Our situation is quite fine," I grit out.

"No shit?" she bites back, her eyes glinting with defiance.

She's so fucking sexy when she's angry. I sweep away a strand of hair that's fallen across her face, trying to fight this gravitational pull toward her. That resistance lasts all of two heartbeats before I surrender to the urge.

I slam my mouth to hers, seizing her tempting lips. Maybe it's our ordeal, or it could be just the taste of her, but my mind takes an unexpected trip off a cliff. Nothing else seems to matter except having my wife pinned under me as she kisses me back. The sounds of gunfire, the screech of tires, Riggo's worried shouts... Everything gets drowned out by Tara's soft moans.

A piercing crack explodes above us. I immediately wrap my arms around Tara's head as pieces of shattered glass from the rear window rain down. The car swerves to the left, sending us both bumping into the seats.

"We're hit. Lost the driver-side back tire," Riggo shouts. "I need to pull over before we spin out."

Fucking great. I flick the lever beneath the seat to release the hidden compartment under the extendable footrest and grab an Uzi out of my reserve weapons stash.

"Do not leave the vehicle until I say so," I growl while snapping the magazine into the Uzi. "You got that, Tara?"

"Yup," she chokes out.

"Good." Grabbing the back of her neck, I pull her toward me, pressing my mouth to hers for another quick kiss. Then, scrambling to my feet, I shove open the door and climb outside.

The pickup has stopped at an angle several car lengths behind us, and three assailants are gathered on the far side of the truck bed, spraying bullets in our direction. The fourth man is slumped, unmoving, in the front passenger seat.

I take cover beside the rear wheel and unleash burst after semi-automatic burst over the trunk of the car, aiming for the dicks' heads poking up above the rim of their vehicle. The morons didn't have enough sense to make sure their ambush wouldn't happen under the damn full moon, and now we're engaged in a fucked-up game of a Whac-A-Mole. My bullet finds the guy who is the furthest from me, and he jerks backward. The other two quickly duck down. I keep firing as I spring up and run toward the pickup.

I'm halfway to my target, shooting at the guy hunched by the back bumper, when the other goon rounds the hood of the truck, his gun aimed at me. A burning sensation explodes in my arm as the bullet catches me just below my shoulder. Without breaking stride, I shift the Uzi to my right hand and face the shooter, just as he stumbles and falls to the ground.

Halle-fucking-lujah. Riggo finally came to his senses and decided to join the firefight.

I veer and continue toward the pickup while steady shots ring out at my back as Riggo provides cover fire. Another goddamned miracle. The kid must have practiced because he usually can't shoot for shit. His technique would give a hysterical woman a run for her money, 'cause he typically sends bullets flying every which way. As if quantity rather than accuracy is more important. I *tsk*. Fucking kids nowadays.

The last remaining shooter is crouching behind the truck when I round the front of the vehicle. It's the driver, clutching a gun. With me raining bullets down on one side and Riggo doing the same on the other, the bastard's got pinned with nowhere to flee.

"Throw down your weapon," I bark, aiming at the center of his head. "Then come up. Slowly."

The man doesn't move, just glares at me with his brows scrunched into a deep V. I don't think he understands what I said. Or maybe I'm not who he expected?

"The gun," I repeat, pointing with my muzzle. "Throw it."

His eyes dart to my right, where one of his dead comrades is splayed out on the ground. The faint click of a cocking gun echoes on my blind side. I pull the trigger, hitting the driver between his eyes, and spin around just as another gunshot pierces the early night. The guy whom I assumed was dead is instead half-upright, clutching his bleeding neck with both his hands. Blood is gushing like a geyser. A discarded gun is lying on the asphalt next to him.

Son of a bitch. An hour ago, the thought of Riggo saving my life would have been laughable.

"Nice shot," I holler behind me, aiming at the dying man. The kid has definitely gotten better.

"Why, thank you, darling."

My head snaps toward the truck's rear end. Where my wife is standing in the middle of the road, pointing a gun at the now-dead shooter.

CHAPTER
fourteen

Tara

"**W**ILL YOU STOP FIDGETING?" I SNAP.

A low grunt is the only response I get.

Rolling my eyes, I resume disinfecting Satan's shoulder. Luckily, the bullet just nicked him, and the wound won't need more than a couple of stitches. What a shame.

"Still can't get over that a *walking disaster* saved your life, huh?" I look up, meeting Arturo's narrowed stare.

The lighting in his bathroom is great, illuminating every angle of his handsome face. I have a thing for men with sharp cheekbones, and his look as if they were carved from a jagged stone. And those are not the only parts of him that appear sculpted. With his shirt completely unbuttoned and the sides hanging loose and open, his chiseled pecs are on full display. Mere inches from my face. Close enough for me to feel the warmth of his skin.

As if that wasn't enough, the guy is sporting a fucking eight-pack. An eight-pack! I thought that was only a myth. Leave it to the devil himself to warp my reality. It truly is a shame that someone so drop-dead gorgeous is such an irritable prick.

"Well?" I prod. "Is that why you've been grouchy for the past hour? I totally get it. Must be a terrible hit to your massive ego, darling."

Another grunt, followed by a huff. Maybe his throat is raw after all the yelling. While we were waiting for the cavalry to arrive, I had to endure his vehement tirade. Right there, in the middle of the desolate road.

It went as well as I might have expected, with an odd curveball thrown in. A lot of, *Are you out of your fucking mind?* A few, *What the hell possessed you?* Followed by the surprising, *You could have gotten hurt!* I seriously doubt that last one was out of any real concern for my well-being. Satan was probably just pissed over a close call where he might've had to explain to Drago my sudden imitation of Swiss cheese. *If* it came down to it. But it didn't, so now I get to deal with the petulant bear instead.

He did relent and give me his jacket when he noticed me shivering in the cold. That was sort of astonishing, considering the timing. I figured that since he was on a roll, he'd also ream me out for once again forgetting to bring my coat. He didn't. But he did tell me in no uncertain terms that, from that moment on, he was placing the Family on "high alert," and that I wouldn't be allowed to go anywhere without a security detail. Then, he clammed up and didn't say another word. Not while his men descended on us, nor during our entire ride home. It was a bit unnerving, actually.

I look away and tug the fabric of his shirt. "You need to bend down. I can't reach the—"

Arturo wraps his uninjured arm around my waist, hoisting me onto the bathroom countertop.

"I guess that works, too." Armed with a needle and thread from the first aid kit, I focus on the tear in his flesh. "You sure you don't have any local anesthetics?"

Instead of answering, he snatches the bottle of whiskey that he left next to the sink earlier and takes a long drink straight out of the bottle. That explains the kitchen detour before we came upstairs, I guess.

Taking a deep breath, I pinch the sides of the wound and insert the needle into his flesh. He doesn't even flinch.

"Did your brother teach you to shoot?" His deep voice in the confines of the bathroom almost startles me.

"Oh, so you're talking to me now?" I lift an eyebrow. "Yes, Drago taught me. Did you teach your sisters?"

"Of course not. Women shouldn't handle firearms."

"'Women shouldn't handle firearms,'" I say in my best impression of his voice. "Jesus, listen to you."

He grunts again, and the muscles of his jaw tense.

I can hardly contain my laughter. What would he think if he knew that Sienna is almost as good with a gun as me? Should I tell him? Just to pester him a little more?

My eyes wander to Arturo's right forearm. The sleeve of his shirt is torn in several places and saturated with blood. He got hurt while shielding me with his arms when the rear windshield was blasted away. No one I know, other than my brother, would have been willing to do that. For me. Put themselves in harm's way to save *me*. Certainly not the losers I've dated before.

"This is done." I tie the thread just like Keva taught me and nod toward his right arm. "Let's look at those cuts now."

"It's fine."

I shrug. "Whatever. If it gets infected and you end up with gangrene, the doctors will just chop off your arm. But I guess that's not an issue since you're ambidextrous, right?"

His eyes turn into slits as he stares at me. That devilish gaze holds me hypnotized as he slowly shrugs off his shirt and throws it onto the floor. Then, he extends his arm, placing his palm on the mirror behind me.

My throat suddenly feels dry, but I try to swallow, feeling nearly intoxicated by his proximity. The urge to wrap my arms around him and lean my forehead on his chest is crushing. I need that contact. Need to feel his heartbeat. Need to be sure he… isn't dead.

The danger to me during that chase and shootout was practically nothing compared to the peril he willingly put himself in. Taking on four armed men. Alone! Away from the cover of our vehicle. Idiot!

I almost had a fucking heart attack watching Arturo sprint toward the assailants. Does he think he's indestructible? A goddamned superhero? Riggo's shouts for me to get down were pointless. I couldn't take my eyes off the fearless fool. Couldn't move, couldn't draw a breath. Too fucking terrified that a bullet would find him. He sprinted through a hailstorm of them. And then I saw it. The impact and his slight jerk as one pierced him.

That's when my heart stopped beating. When air abandoned my lungs. When a silent scream ripped through my head until it finally registered that he was still moving. Still advancing. Still shooting. Was still alive.

Shaking my head to get rid of this ridiculous desire to nuzzle his warm, broad chest, I force my focus to his arm.

"Jesus fuck, Arturo," I choke out, staring at the bloody mess that is his forearm.

"Just spray it with a disinfectant and wrap it up. The cuts aren't deep."

"I have to check if there's any glass in the wounds first."

"Just can't wait to start digging into my flesh, huh, *gattina*?" His lips curve into a crooked smile.

"Yup, nailed it."

His smile widens. He takes another big swig of his whiskey and nods. "Carry on."

With all the dried blood and the ink underneath, I can't see shit. I grab a towel hanging on the wall beside me and soak it under the spray of warm water. It takes me at least ten minutes to manage to clean up his arm. It must hurt like hell, but Arturo doesn't let out a sound. He does, though, take a few more swigs and sets down the now half-empty bottle.

Annoyingly, he was also right. The cuts seem shallow. It looked much worse with all that smeared blood. There aren't any glass shards in the wounds, either, thank goodness. I cover the cuts with disinfectant spray, then take a roll of bandage and start wrapping it around his forearm.

As I do, my eyes keep darting to his biceps. To the wings of a creature and the dagger overhead.

To the words inked across his skin.

l'Onore ... Rispetto.

I want to know what they mean. Why are they important? To him.

If there's anything I've learned, it's that my husband doesn't do anything half-assed.

And, fuck. Those muscles! The bathroom is large, but from here, squashed between the mirror and Arturo's body, the space seems minuscule. This close, I can feel his warm breath fanning my cheek.

"Is this what it takes for you to finally say my name?" he whispers right next to my ear.

"What are you talking about?" I mumble while rummaging through the first aid kit in search of medical tape to secure the bandage.

"I quite like the sound of it on your lips. Maybe I'll make it a habit to bleed more often, just to hear you say it again."

"I have no idea what you're rambling about, DeVille."

"No?" He places his hand over mine, right where I'm holding the end of the bandage pressed to his forearm to keep it from unraveling. "But I think you do."

That wicked smirk dances on his lips again. He holds my gaze captive as he applies pressure to the back of my hand.

"What the..." I try pulling away, without success. "Stop. Stop it right now."

He just keeps pressing harder, until bright red stains start seeping through the sterile white gauze, spreading under my palm.

"The fuck, Arturo! Stop doing that!"

That devilish grin on his face transforms into an unnervingly devastating smile. "I was right."

"You're absolutely unhinged."

"Hmm, maybe." He grasps my chin between his fingers and leans forward until his lips hover just an inch from mine. "But only around you, it seems."

"You're drunk," I whisper.

"I certainly hope so."

His mouth slams against mine with such force that breath gets trapped in my lungs. The kiss is hard and angry. And it immediately sends me into a blissful state. Someplace where all rational thought ceases to exist.

All that remains is the ability to feel.

My arms wrap around Arturo's neck of their own volition. My tongue duels with his as if this kiss will never be enough. My God! His lips... Trailing along my chin, down the column of my neck, across my collarbone, they are the embodiment of sinfulness itself. I can't escape them. I don't want to! All I can do is hold on for dear life.

I spear my fingers through the soft locks of his hair, arching my back to offer more of myself to him. More for that deviant mouth of his to explore as it continues on its downward path, trailing those tantalizing lips toward my breasts.

"You damn witch."

His low growl is followed by the sound of ripping fabric. Cool air hits my overheated skin as the two parts of my ruined dress hang off me, held in place only by the thin spaghetti straps. The gap he's torn exposes me right down the middle, almost entirely baring me to the waist.

"No bra," he rasps, devouring my bare breasts with his eyes. "Wicked, wicked woman."

Rough palms seize my flesh. His touch is firm but also incredibly gentle as he squeezes the tender globes. It makes no sense. How can he be such a contradiction? How can his touch set me on fire and, at the same time, soothe all the burning aches? But that's exactly what he does.

He lowers his head and draws my left nipple into his mouth, rolling the peak between his lips as he flicks it with his tongue. A moan explodes from my throat when his teeth graze that sensitive flesh. Goose bumps break out all over my body while a jolt of adrenaline shoots straight through my veins. Everything, everything tingles. Spasm after spasm runs down my spine.

Just as when the sensation starts to ebb, he switches his attention to my right nipple.

My eyes roll into the back of my head. "Oh, God!" I scream in ecstasy.

"It didn't take long to elevate me in your opinion."

His palms slide up my thighs, caressing, dragging the skirt of my dress along with.

I should be throwing back a snarky comment, but every capable brain cell I have is focused on his lips again. How can they be this soft? How can they be this sinful? How can I keep them fused to mine like this? Devouring. Claiming. Giving.

Somewhere in the recesses of my mind, a shrill alarm is blaring. Urging me to put a stop to this. To flee from this insane onslaught of dangerous emotions. Feelings I can't even begin to comprehend. Instead, I tighten my arms around Arturo's neck, lifting myself off the counter as I try to get closer to him.

Rough hands slide under my ass, pulling my skirt upward an inch at a time. Leaving it bundled around my waist. As those hands retreat, exploring the curve of my hips, my thighs, they drag my lacy thong along with them. Gliding it down my trembling legs while Arturo's mouth stays busy ravaging me.

"Feisty little cat… thawing under my touch." Sharp teeth sink into my lower lip. "Not so much of an ice princess now, are you, *gattina*?"

"Go to hell, Satan." I seize his lips in a brutal kiss.

"Aw, I've been demoted once more."

His hands trail up my legs again, pushing them apart, inching closer. Closer to my center that's weeping with need. The tips of his fingers graze my pussy, and I almost shatter.

"Say my name." A growl. A whisper. A reverent plea.

My core throbs, begging for… something. Something I refuse to acknowledge but can't suppress. An absolute urgency to have Arturo DeVille possess my body, in every possible carnal way.

With one more nibble to his lips, I lean back. Putting physical distance between us. His devilish eyes bore into mine. Steady. Waiting. Unblinking.

Waiting in vain, because I won't be saying his name out loud again. Ever.

To use a person's first name is to give them power. Power over you.

Something I've believed since I was a little girl. Something the fairy tales taught me. Something that still scares the shit out of me to this day.

Utter a monster's name and you're left in ruin. And he gets to walk away with a piece of you.

"No," I choke out. *You've always been and will always be a villain in my story, DeVille. There's no way I'll allow you to steal from me. Not my soul. And definitely not my heart.*

Arturo

Anger. Frustration. Torment.

Anger sweeps through me with yet another bout of her defiance. She's being obstinate, stubborn without any logical reason to be.

Frustration grips me upon the realization that I'd do just about fucking anything to hear Tara say my name again. I nearly goddamn combusted the first time it left her lips. I want—no, need—her to speak it. I'm sick to death of this "DeVille" bullshit.

And the torment of the pure agony of viselike pressure in my dick. The poor bastard is harder than fucking steel, ready to burst because of the insatiable need to be buried inside my wife's heat.

Fucking awesome. All three emotions are raging within me. I try to remain calm, to keep my careful composure intact. All while cursing her once more for scrambling my brain. Turning me into a stark raving lunatic. The more she denies me, the more I want whatever she's withholding. But the truly nutty thing about this is that I fucking enjoy the yearning. Crave the longing for what I can't have.

"I promise that you will." Smiling, I lean closer, licking the edge of her earlobe. "You'll scream it for me, *gattina.*"

I plunge my finger into her pussy on her next breath.

The sharp inhale, and then the moan that leaves her… Oh fuck, I could come just from hearing that soft, plaintive sound. My thumb finds her clit, and I start rubbing that sweet bud in slow circles, all while soaking up the sight of her.

Tara's head is thrown back, her lids half-closed. That gorgeous hair of hers cascades down her back. Her strawberry scent completely engulfs me, driving me utterly insane.

I must possess her.

Must make her mine.

I need… I need to see her unravel.

For me. Only for me.

Her breasts rise and fall with shallow breaths, rapidly increasing in tempo as I press harder on her clit. I push my finger deeper inside her pussy, gently caressing those inner walls. She's so damn tight. So damn beautiful in her rapture. I'm holding on by a most fragile thread.

My entire hand is already drenched in her tempting juices. I want to taste them, but I can't. Not yet. I need to torture her a bit more, just as she's been tormenting me. For weeks. Months, really. This woman has a talent for getting under my skin.

I move my free hand to her delicate neck, wrapping my palm around her throat. I don't squeeze, just hold her lightly, letting her ride my finger like a woman possessed. I can feel every quick draw of her breath and her racing pulse beneath my fingers. It's fast. So fucking fast. And her pussy is quivering.

With her eyes half-open, she's glaring at me. A blend of fury and elation gripping her features. It's clear as day, she detests that I'm the one who's bringing her this pleasure, but neither can she deny wanting more of it.

"My name," I growl, pulling my finger out, only to push it hard and deep inside her again. "Say it, Tara."

"Satan." The word gets muffled by her moan as I thrust my finger as far as I can.

Stubborn, willful little creature.

Too damn pigheaded to admit to whom she belongs.

"I'm going to make you come... so hard"—my hold on her neck tightens—"that everyone within a mile of us will hear your scream." Grasping her chin, I tilt her head so she can fully look at me. "And I'll do it using just one hand."

"Not happening."

There is so much annoyance in those green depths as she glares at me, our faces only inches apart.

"Watch me." I smile, feeling the telltale tremble of her walls around my still-buried finger.

With my gaze locked on hers, I press right over the epicenter of her clit, right over where she's the most sensitive. Simultaneously, I let my finger curve inside her pussy, finding that other special spot of hers.

A shrill mewl of pleasure explodes from her throat. The sound is almost my undoing. My cock is weeping in my pants. I'm so hard, it's fucking painful.

I slide my thumb just a little lower, adding more pressure to her clit while her pussy continues to spasm around my finger. The satisfaction of seeing my wife fall apart in my hands because of the pleasure I gave her is only rivaled by the feel of her warm cum all over my palm. She can deny it, but the proof is indisputable. And watching her lost in rapture almost makes me blow my load. Holy shit, I'm so turned on and my dick isn't even in her.

I lower my head and bite her lip. "You were saying?"

No words leave her. She's shaking so much that I move my hand to the back of her head, worried she'll bang it on the damn mirror.

Slowly, I slide my other hand out and bring it to my lips.

"If you behave as you should"—I lick her nectar off my finger—"next time, I'll eat your pussy until you pass out."

The look she levels me with is filled with disdain. Grasping the shreds of her ruined dress, she clutches them at her breasts as she slips off the counter.

"Thank you for the offer," she says amid labored breaths. "But there won't be a next time."

"Why not?"

She squeezes between me and the vanity to gather her shoes off the floor. When she straightens, there isn't even an inkling of the blissed out contentment on her face that I'd expect after what just transpired. Only unwavering determination.

"Because, DeVille, I learned to never repeat my mistakes."

Turning on her heel, she walks out of the bathroom, leaving me surrounded by the most exhilarating aroma on earth. The scent of strawberries and my wife's orgasm.

My mouth waters.

Fucking hell! As the door shuts in her wake, I barely have enough strength to stifle the urge to storm after her. To catch her and fuck her, properly this time. But I let her run.

Because this is madness.

All of this is goddamned madness!

Swiping my hand across the counter, I send the bottle of whiskey flying. It hits the door with a loud *crack* and shatters into a gazillion pieces.

Just as my mind did a moment ago.

Damn that woman.

CHAPTER

fifteen

📖 Tara 📚

"**M**Y SINCEREST APOLOGIES, MRS. DEVILLE, BUT I DO not know where your car is."

I squint at the blond guy in a blue-gray suit. "You're Tony, right?"

"That's correct."

"Well, Tony..." I take a menacing step toward him. "My friend Jovan dropped my car off here last night. He said that he left it with a guy named... Can you guess?" I take another step. "Yup. *Tony.* Are there several Tonys around here?"

"Umm..." He throws a fleeting look toward the ground-level window. "I think you should ask Mr. DeVille."

Figures. I grit my teeth and turn on my heel to march back inside the house. What the hell did that asshole husband of mine do with my car?

It's been three days since that disastrous scene in DeVille's bathroom. And every damn day since then I've been trying to wipe it from my mind, to forget how easily and thoroughly he undid me, leaving me panting on his counter. Every moan, every hitched breath, they all blare through my mind like an air siren. My thoughts are riddled with how wantonly I behaved. All because of Arturo DeVille. Because it was *he* who made me that way. But I can't. Can't think about it anymore. I refuse to acknowledge those earth-shattering minutes of my life. They never happened.

Too bad that my treacherous body can't seem to forget them. As soon as DeVille enters my field of vision, everything within me instantly vibrates. Every cell, every nerve ending, rings with the echo of his touch. My lower lip, which he so tantalizingly bit that night, immediately starts to tingle, as if it's ready and waiting for yet another kiss.

The situation between my legs is even more drastic. My pussy weeps, craving his wicked caress. The muscles in my core clench each time a memory of his hands on me surfaces. The throbbing achiness is almost too much to bear. The need he stirred up is so overpowering, I can hardly sleep at night.

I hate myself for my body's reaction. I'm pissed that I can't erase Arturo from my thoughts. But more than anything, I detest my stupid heart for its betrayal. For every time that man steps into the room, each time my eyes find him anywhere, my treacherous heart takes flight. As if it's happy to see the bastard. As if it's racing to get closer to him. As if it thinks it's somehow wanted. What a dumb, ignorant heart.

Thank fuck the gorgeous devil must agree with me that what happened between us in his bathroom was a massive mistake. The following day, he wouldn't even look at me. I saw more of his back and heard more of his grunts than at any prior point of our acquaintance. And he hasn't tried to maneuver us into a similar circumstance again. Not that I would allow that to happen! No, no way!

Lately, DeVille has been treating me almost like I don't exist. He leaves the room as soon as he spots me in it. He says nothing at all when we happen to occupy the same space. Which has been very rare, actually. He's been gone for long hours every day.

Most times, I get up in the morning, and he's left the house already. He returns, more often than not, after I've gone to bed. But, somewhere between those times, he still makes the most scrumptious dishes for me, leaving them on the kitchen counter to drive me bonkers with their heavenly aroma. Carbonara. Grilled sausages with stir-fried veggies on the side. A delicious-looking veal dish in white sauce. Even a homemade pizza! I've started dreaming about these blasted things, imagining scarfing them down. That is, when I'm not dreaming about Arturo doing the eating. Of my pussy.

I don't touch the food he prepares, of course, holding true to my convictions about that. However, the past couple of days have been really trying, and my resolve is starting to crack. There's only so much temptation a person can withstand. I'm also so sick of eating nothing but cheese, salads, and fruit. I did order delivery once, and had Greta make me another of her tasteless meals, but that was as much as I was willing to risk. I'm still determined to make sure DeVille doesn't find out about my irrational fear. I can't give him more ammunition to use against me.

That's why I got so excited when Jovan messaged me that my car had finally been fixed. It needed a new fuel pump, which had to be sourced and specially ordered for Old Betsy, so it took a long time. Jovan had my ride delivered to DeVille's front gate, and I'm super pumped (pun intended) to get to use it right away. Now I can head off to a bunch of places, get whatever food I like, and Satan will never know!

Except... my car is missing, apparently.

"Where's my car, DeVille?" I snap as soon as I storm into the living room.

My husband is lazing on the couch, a laptop propped up against

222

his knees. A steaming mug of tea and a bottle of ibuprofen are within arm's reach on the coffee table, right next to his mouse.

He doesn't even grace me with a look, just continues pounding on the keyboard. "Your car?"

"Don't play dumb with me. Jovan texted me that he dropped it off at the gate last night. Left it with a guy named Tony."

"Oh, you mean that fifteen-year-old piece of junk with a crack across the windshield and rust all over the body and chassis?" He slams the laptop closed. "I had someone deliver it to one of the local charities. We even got a tax receipt."

"You *what*?"

"My wife won't be seen driving that ancient heap, Tara. It's disgraceful and humiliating. Riggo will take you to a dealership to pick out something new. Something more becoming of your new status. Here."

Completely dumbfounded, I watch as he takes out his wallet and throws his Black Amex on the coffee table.

"You had no right!"

"I had every right. I'm your husband. My word is the law for the next year, or did you forget that?"

"As if I could."

"Good." He pops two painkillers. "I'm glad we've sorted that out."

Dickhead.

"And what might be 'more becoming of my new status,' oh Your Snobbish Highness? A supercar? Gold-leafed, perhaps?"

"Whatever will make people turn their heads in awe."

"Is that so?" I grin and snatch the credit card off the table. "See ya later."

I tap my chin with my finger as I size up the shiny red Bentley in the middle of the dealership showroom. According to the little placard beside the vehicle, it comes fully stocked with all the gizmos and whatchamacallits, luxury knickknacks, and hand-stitched genuine leather seats.

"Nope," I declare.

"But… this is the most high-end vehicle we have in stock, ma'am," the salesman says. "And it's a limited edition, to guarantee exclusivity. I can assure you, you will not find a better state-of-the-art car in New York."

"The car isn't the problem. It's the price."

"Oh. I understand. Well, how about we take a look at some of our more affordable—"

"It's too cheap," I add.

The sales guy's eyes bug out. "It's… It's four hundred thousand, ma'am."

"Exactly." With my hands on my hips, I take a look around the showroom.

This is the third place I've visited, and none have had anything for over half a million available on the lot. The most expensive cars are all custom orders, with months and months of waiting time. I, however, want to make sure I follow my husband's directions today, preferably by spending at least a million dollars of his money.

I'm pondering whether to just cut my losses and go with the red monstrosity on my right when my gaze catches on the billboard across the street. It's an ad for a new blockbuster. But it's not the dude in a spandex suit that snags my eye. It's what's in the sky above him.

My lips pull into a smile.

Bingo.

 Arturo

"I'm in a meeting, Tony," I bark into the phone and then immediately start coughing. Fuck, it feels like I'm gonna spit up a lung. I rummage in my pocket, grabbing another lozenge and popping it into my mouth. "Unless it's urgent, it can wait," I finally manage to add.

"It's not urgent, sir, but I thought you might wanna know that… um, your wife… the vehicle she purchased has arrived. It's—"

"Tony, that's definitely not anything I need to know right now." I cut the call and toss the phone to the massive desktop. "Where was I?"

"Projected increase in revenue and other benefits of switching from our current provider to Adriano Ruffo's freight company for distribution," Ajello says from his executive chair behind his office desk. "Is he open to discussing a potential partnership on that front?"

"Yes. On our video call this morning, after we discussed the latest on the project in Manhattan, I brought up the idea again. Ruffo insisted that it should be discussed in person, so we didn't get into the details. But he's undoubtedly interested." I shift in my seat. Despite the way I've been swallowing cough drops like fucking candy, the scratching in my throat persists. "I've looked into the numbers a bit. Ruffo's fleet consists of more than fifteen thousand trucks and nearly four times as many trailers. They move freight for over fifty companies across the US, exclusively. We're talking big names here, multiyear contracts. Everything from home furniture and appliances to refrigerated goods to construction materials."

"What's their annual revenue?"

I look at my notes. "Financial reports put TTM at six point two billion. Mind you, that's the trailing twelve months figures from his trucking side alone. That doesn't include all the other stuff Ruffo is into, like the logistics services his company provides."

"Commendable." Ajello nods. "But here's what I don't get. Working with major corporations, the logistics processes must be vigorous, not to mention all the regulations and inspections that they face. And, I would imagine, the cargo is sealed for transport well in advance of being picked up. That means chances to mess with it or opportunities to use routes as a front to smuggle product have to be limited. So, how does he manage to distribute tons of drugs with that setup?"

The sharp, stabbing pain each time I draw a deep breath rears its ugly head. My throat clogs with a burning pressure, and I erupt into a gut-squeezing cough. Once the fit finally passes, I snatch the bottle of water off the table. "I have no idea."

"You don't look well, Arturo." Ajello slashes me with a disapproving glare while watching me swallow another painkiller. "You should take a few days off. It's Friday. Go home, get some rest."

"Out of the question, boss. The annual Best In Business Gala is tomorrow night. We can't—" Another bout of hacking overtakes me. "We can't miss this opportunity to network, not to mention to schmooze with potential business partners out in the open. On Monday, I'm sitting down with Wang regarding that clusterfuck in Chinatown. And the following day, I'm meeting with the lead architect for the condo complex. Also, have I mentioned the arrival of our next shipment in just a few days?"

"Right. That gala would give you a chance to spend quality time with your wife." His head bobs like he's weighed my words and seen the error of his earlier remark. "But otherwise, you're on sick leave, starting now. I'll let security know not to allow you in the building until I inform them differently."

"I do not need sick leave. And I don't have the time to be sick, particularly now, since Nino isn't available to fill in."

There's still no intel on the guys who jumped us on the road earlier this week. None of the stiffs had any ID. The truck they used was reported stolen two days before they ambushed us. With the number of people or groups with a grudge against the Family, or me personally, being endless, I can't even guess who might have been behind the attack. Nino has spent the past week casing every dive bar and strip joint where lowlifes from other shady orgs hang out, trying to see if there's any chatter. All without success.

Ajello pins me with his gaze. "Yes, you do. You're dismissed, Arturo."

Indignation courses through my veins as I snatch my laptop and file folders off the desk and storm out of the don's office. Ginger, Ajello's administrative assistant, rushes toward me, blabbering on about the Princeton warehouse and the lease that's expiring next week. I grit my teeth and continue down the hallway toward the elevator. Although I'm virtually ignoring her, she keeps trotting after me.

"You know what, Ginger?" I hit the elevator button with way too much force. Shoving the laptop under my arm, I hand her the file folders. "Take this to the don and tell him that I hope he has fun with the paperwork."

The elevator dings. I step inside and slam my finger on the button for the parking level. As the doors close, Ginger's dumbfounded face gets blocked from my view.

Fucking great. I can't believe Ajello put me on forced medical leave. Especially when the shit I've got to take care of is piling up sky-high. Over the past year, I took exactly one day off. One! The day Sienna got married. No one can argue that I don't carry out my duties to the don and this Family with utmost proficiency. And this is the thanks I get? All because of a little cough?

Said cough picks this exact moment to remind me that it's whopping my ass. I bend over, coughing up a storm big enough to start wondering if my organs are going to come out. I do feel like hell warmed over, but I'm not going to let that stop me. Even though my lungs feel like they'll implode from the pressure squeezing my chest, and every muscle in my body aches. Damn it, I need to kick this bug already. I dig out another throat lozenge and pop it into my mouth.

By the time the elevator stops at the underground garage, I once again feel like I can survive on the shallow breaths I've been reduced to. I finally got my driver's license back this morning, so I head straight for my Land Rover. Sliding behind the wheel of the SUV, I sigh and lean my head back for just a minute.

What car did my hellion purchase? I got a call a few hours ago to confirm that my credit card hadn't been stolen. Apparently, my wife was trying to put through a transaction of one point two million on the Amex. That's what I get for telling Tara that she could buy whatever she wants. I own up to my mistakes, so I allowed the purchase. Hopefully, she didn't get an ugly-ass convertible. I detest those.

As soon as I saw her junker parked on the driveway, the memory of Tara in that dark alley flashed in my mind. I don't care how well her car was fixed; I don't trust it. Can't be convinced that rust bucket won't let her down again. And what if I'm not there next time? What if she's alone and gets stranded in the middle of nowhere? What if the brakes fail and my wife ends up in a crash? Nope. I couldn't do it. Couldn't allow even the slightest possibility of that to exist. So I made it disappear. Sent it to car heaven, or wherever. Made sure she'd never get into that thing again.

I also doubled her security detail, assigning another team of bodyguards to trail her. Always. She'll never be left unprotected again. And

I know the new car will have all the safety features. I'll also make certain we install all the custom upgrades. Tracking. Bulletproof glass. The works. I just need to know what vehicle she selected.

Maybe Tara would have reacted better to my move with her old car if I had simply admitted the truth. But instead, I came up with that asinine explanation, making it sound like she needed to drive something flashy, something more becoming of my wife. Like I'm a stuck-up snob, or something.

Stupid, I know. But it works better for the situation we're in.

The dashboard clock lets me know that it's just after six, still early evening. Plenty of time to get more work done. I'll pay a visit to Wang and try to solve whatever issues his people have with our crew's schedule. That damn storage location needs to be finished ASAP. Hell, it needed to be done weeks ago. Then, I can make a quick call to our lead architect and go over the new renderings he sent for the next phase of our construction project. Some of the details are not coming out the way I've pictured them. That means I'll start my sick leave as of tomorrow. Tonight, keeping busy will distract me from thinking about my wife. And her tight little pussy.

Not that there's even a remote chance I'll be able to fully get the image of her flushed face out of my mind. For days, I've been walking around with the biggest hard-on, constantly thinking of how she looked as she orgasmed on my hand. Shit, this past week, running into her around the house was fucking torture. Every time I saw her, I was instantly back in that bathroom with her. So I've stayed away. Worked as much as possible. Hell, I've put a hundred miles on the treadmill at the gym just so I wouldn't go sniffing her strawberry shampoo. But every time I close my eyes, there she is. Beautiful. Aroused. Euphoric.

And there goes my dick again.

Every.

Fucking.

Time.

It's almost midnight when I arrive home. As I drive up to the house, heading for the garage out back, I catch a glimpse of a huge shadow in the middle of the backyard lawn.

What in the world…?

I hit the brakes and get out of the SUV.

Not possible.

Not even *she* would be this insane. Right?

"Um… I tried to tell you, sir," Tony mumbles as he comes up beside me.

"How the fuck did that thing get here?"

"It was dropped off by a flatbed truck, courtesy of the seller. The delivery guys apologized for ruining the grounds, but this was the only space large enough to leave it."

I take a step closer, still unable to believe what I'm seeing.

My impertinent wife bought a damn helicopter!

That audacious… ballsy… recklessly clever, crafty woman!

An explosive laugh builds in my throat. I press my fist over my mouth, trying to swallow it down.

"Sir?" Tony gives me a concerned look. "Are… are you okay?"

The deep, guttural guffaw bursts out of me and explodes into the night. My throat and lungs scream in protest, and another coughing fit overcomes me. None of that is enough to make me stop fucking laughing.

"Um… sir? Should I try to return it?"

Finally, I manage to get my breathing under control. "No. Just leave it where it is."

Shaking my head, I head toward the house.

"Greta," I call, stepping through the front door. "Where's my wife?"

My housekeeper peeks around the corner. "She's upstairs, asleep. You saw the helicopter, I take it?"

"Hard to miss it."

"Are you angry with Mrs. DeVille?"

I'm not sure why, but I'm not. I can't bring myself to be even a little mad at Tara. Actually, she just made my day, completely wiping the last few shitty hours from my mind. Fuck me, I don't even remember the last time I laughed this hard.

"Nope. Not mad at all, Greta."

Two graying eyebrows hit her likewise gray hairline. "Huh. Well, I'm glad. But, I get it, Mr. DeVille. It's difficult to stay mad at the person you're in love with."

I stop in my tracks.

How in the world did my housekeeper get the preposterous idea that I'm in love with my wife? That's ridiculous. No, wait. I guess it makes sense. We have been pretending to be a happy couple whenever there are other people around. Our little act must be convincing.

"Has she eaten the stew I made her?"

"Oh… um… no. No, she didn't. Mrs. DeVille ordered burgers instead."

The muscle in my jaw ticks. My wife would still rather eat crappy takout than a homemade meal.

"I'm sure she wasn't trying to hurt your feelings, sir. Mrs. DeVille probably just doesn't like lamb. She doesn't seem to be a fan of the carbonara either, because she didn't eat the pasta you left for her yesterday. I uh, served her a grilled cheese sandwich instead, and she practically licked the plate."

Suddenly feeling none of my earlier mirth, I cross the living room until I'm standing arm's length from Greta. "As of tomorrow, you are not to prepare any more food for my wife. Is that clear?"

"Oh. If you say so, Mr. DeVille."

"I do say so. And let the gate guards know that all food deliveries are strictly forbidden. If the delivery person loiters in place, tell security to shoot like the bastard is trespassing. Is that clear?"

"Crystal clear, sir. No food deliveries whatsoever."

"Good," I bark as I head up the stairs.

"Oh, Mr. DeVille," Greta calls from the front door. "I forgot to tell you… It's a bit chilly tonight, so I lit Mrs. DeVille's fireplace. I hope she enjoys waking up to a toasty room and the pleasant sounds of a crackling fire."

Uh-huh. I don't give a fuck about what Mrs. DeVille enjoys.

My ass is dragging. It's a struggle to muster the strength to take a shower and slap a new dressing on my shoulder wound. Even though I'm completely wrecked, I feel the need to steal a quick look at Tara before I hit the sheets. After sliding open the connecting door between our rooms, I prop my good shoulder on the doorjamb and simply watch my wife sleep, bathed in the warm, flickering glow of the fireplace.

If Tara and I agree on anything, it's that what happened the other night was a mistake. But hers wasn't the same as mine. I don't know what came over me. Why I couldn't keep my desire at bay. Maybe I did have too much to drink when she took care of my wounds. Actually, there's no fucking "maybe" about it. That shit stung like hell. I drank more than enough to get wasted, and that's what made me lose my grip on my control.

The maniacal urge to taste my little hellcat swept through me like a fiery storm. My blood boiled with the need to possess her. Lungs burned with the desire to steal her breath. I haven't touched a drop of alcohol since that evening, and yet my head is still spinning from the half a bottle of whiskey I put away. Better than whiskey dick, I guess.

No such problem in that department. My cock is fucking aching. Jacking off hasn't helped. I want to taste her. Want to feel her tremble in my arms again. I'm craving her moans, her mewls, her whimpers. The hitch in her breath. Dying to know if I could make her scream my name.

My madness, apparently, runs deeper than sexual yearning. What's driving me wild goes beyond getting my wife into my bed. There's this need for me to conquer. To claim her in every possible way. To make sure everybody knows she's fucking mine, and not just because of some flimsy piece of paper. Not because of the deal we made. She is mine. Mine to hold. Mine to keep. Mine. Even if she doesn't know it. Doesn't want it. She's still mine.

And that's the shit that's been running through my mind for days. Jesus. The woman drives me nuts. I really don't know what the fuck is wrong with me. Staring at Tara from across the room, I seriously doubt I'll get my answers.

One of her shapely legs has escaped the confines of her duvet, and I can't help but ogle the milky soft expanse of her skin. I want to explore every single inch of her. With my hands. With my tongue. With my dick. Want to hear her breathy sounds as I pound that tight, soaking-wet pussy of hers. Watch her face while I make her come.

Yeah, touching her was undoubtedly a colossal mistake. Now I know exactly what I'm missing. I should never have let my hands venture anywhere near her pussy. So why, instead of agreeing with her on the "mistake" issue, did it piss me off that she called it that?

Stepping as quietly as I can, I cross the distance to her bed. As usual, she's tangled up in the blanket, but most of it has slipped down to her waist. How does she manage to get herself so twisted every night? I grab one of the edges and straighten it so it covers her up to her neck. She likes the warmth.

"You're fucking with my mind, *gattina*," I whisper into the darkness and silently leave my wife's room. My head is killing me, so as soon as it hits the pillow, I fall into a deep, dreamless sleep.

Tara

The smell of burning wood. Smoke. So, so much of it that it's becoming impossible to breathe. I scream. The door bursts open, and Drago stumbles into the room. With him, an onslaught of heat and a thick, dark cloud.

"Tara!" he shouts as he grabs me off the bed. Even safely in his arms, I can't stop screaming.

My tiny hands wave madly in front of my face.

My eyes are burning from the smoke, welling up with tears. Somehow, though, I can still see my twin sister. She's cowering on the other side of the room, her back pressed to a wall. With her little body shaking and horror etched on her sweet baby face, she's simply standing there. Unmoving. Quiet, as always.

Drago keeps yelling, reaching out for her, but my own wailing is making it hard to hear what he's saying.

I blink, and everything around me dissolves. We aren't in our bedroom anymore. And Dina is nowhere I can see her.

"Dina!" I cry out, but only a broken croak escapes my aching throat.

My lungs can no longer function. There's no air. The putrid smoke singes my nose, scorches my eyes. I've wrapped my arms around Drago's neck as he carries me through a tunnel of fire. It's closing in on us from every side, getting ready to swallow us without mercy. We are going to die. We are—

My lids fly open. Breath wheezes out of me. A goddamned nightmare. One I haven't had in quite a while.

No, not a ghastly dream.

A memory.

I was barely four, but that night has forever burrowed into my mind. I keep reliving it, over and over. Feeling the devastating helplessness of a child, but seeing it twisted by my adult thoughts. In the two decades since, its grip on me has never waned. Even now, I can feel the heat on my skin. Taste the smoke in the air. My throat is scraped raw, making swallowing hard. It's as if I'm still there. In the middle of an inferno, reliving that hell all over again.

There's no way I'll get any more sleep tonight. It usually takes me a while to shake off a nightmare, and this latest one is worse than any before. More real somehow. Almost as if I can still smell the charred scent in the room. It's invading all my senses, wrapping around me like a deadly shroud.

Throwing my legs over the edge of the bed, I sit up. It takes me a moment to realize that the darkness in the room isn't total. An odd light flickers somewhere behind me, casting my shadow onto the door connecting my bedroom with Arturo's. I look over my shoulder, searching for the source, when my eyes latch onto the fire.

A terrified cry erupts from my lips. I leap off the bed and scramble backward, plastering myself to the sliding door, my eyes still locked on the orange flame across the room. Has it followed me from my grisly nightmare into this awful reality? Tremors shake my whole body. Icy fear slides down my back. My legs turn to jelly, wobbling as they struggle to support my weight. And all I can do is stare at the raging blaze dancing over stacked logs in the fireplace.

"No!" I grit out, beginning to fall.

My mind can't process what's happening. The flames that looked contained just a moment ago have seemingly grown, completely filling my vision. A haze descends around me. The room fills up with smoke. So much smoke. It's stinging my eyes. My nose. I'm choking on its bitter stench.

"No. No. No." I'm shaking my head, trying to flee on quaking legs from the inferno surging toward me. The cool surface at my back reminds me there's nowhere to go, and something intrinsic tells me not to trust my eyes. The thought has barely formed when the door behind me slides to the side.

"Tara." A large tattooed arm wraps around my waist, preventing me from hitting the floor. "What—"

Twisting around, I throw my arms around Arturo's neck and clamber halfway up his body. "Out," I whisper into his chest. Holding on as if my life depends on the refuge only he can give me, I hang on to him with all my might. A whimper escapes me. "Please, get me out of here."

"I will, baby." His hand lands at the back of my head, caressing me as if I'm a wounded animal. "Just tell me where you want to go."

Tears threaten to choke me, but I somehow form the words. "Away from… bad dreams."

The door slides shut, and then I'm being carried. Where to, I don't know. Don't care. I just know I'm safe. I bury my fingers in Arturo's hair, clutching the soft strands in my grip. Musky shampoo, lemongrass soap, and clean male. His scent wraps around me, and I take my first deep breath since waking up, thrilled to the bone that I can no longer smell charred wood and smoke.

The bedframe creaks as Arturo climbs onto the mattress. Keeping me pressed to his chest, he lies down on white sheets. I don't dare move a muscle as I end up sprawled on top of my husband, listening to the rhythmic sound of his heartbeat. The melody lulls me, and along with his scent, chases away my ugly thoughts of fire and destruction.

"Tara?" His warm palm glides down my back. "Do you want to talk about it?"

I shake my head and nuzzle into the soft spot where his neck and shoulder meet, just above his clavicle.

"You sure? I know a thing or two about bad dreams." His tone is gentle, soothing. Like nothing I've heard from him, but everything I need right now.

"No, thank you," I whisper.

"Okay." Still keeping his arm tightly wrapped around me, he tugs the blanket up, covering us both. As I finally let myself relax, my breathing evens out, and I drift into a tranquil state as his palm continues to glide along my back. His strokes are slow and light. Tender. Something I never would have expected from Arturo. Especially after my latest act of defiance. Maybe he hasn't seen the helicopter yet?

"Did you see my addition to your… fleet?" I press the question into his neck.

"Yes."

Oh…

I wait for him to say more, but our steady breaths are the only sounds in the room. Whatever his reasons, I appreciate him choosing to wait till tomorrow to rip me a new one for the stunt I pulled. Tonight, I can't handle any more "excitement."

My eyes flutter closed, and I surrender to sleep. Rocked to dreamland by the comforting rise and fall of his chest beneath me. Protected by the steady, hypnotic beat.

CHAPTER
sixteen

Tara

"Y ou bought a helicopter?" Sienna's screech echoes through the dining room.

"Yup." I dig my fork into the Tupperware container and stuff another bite of delicious pork chop into my mouth. "Your brother insisted that I get something that would make a statement."

"Uh-huh. But a helicopter?"

"Can't make a grander entrance than arriving in a—Ouch!" I jerk away and snatch the brush out of her hand. "Could you please be more gentle? I'd like to have some hair left after all of this."

"Well, *that* hairstyle requires volume with a capital V." She points to the image on my phone that I have propped up against the water bottle, then snatches the brush back and continues to tease the strands at the top of my head. "What did Arturo say about the chopper? I'm betting he lost his shit, right?"

I lick the fork clean, then dive into another bowl and scoop up some rice. "Well, that's the thing. He didn't."

I woke up in my husband's bed this morning. Thankfully, its rightful occupant was long gone. The cool sheets told me he had been for hours. It took my muddled brain nearly a minute to remember how I ended up in DeVille's room, in his bed, in the first place.

My initial thought was that we had sex. All things considered, that might have been the lesser evil. If I could choose, I would pick getting dirty with Satan DeVille over having him witness my meltdown. And if that wasn't enough, I'm pretty sure I spent the remainder of the night sleeping on top of him. The feel of his arms wrapped around me lingers even now like a ghostly caress. If I had woken up still tangled in his embrace, I would have been mortified and ready to kill myself.

"I was already asleep when he got home last night, and he was gone well before I woke up this morning. So, we haven't talked about it yet." I shrug, deciding I neither want to discuss with Sienna nor ponder on my own, the events that happened in between. "He just texted me a bunch of links to various regulations, and to the training and certification programs. Then, the contact info for his insurance agent. And finally, the name of a guy who's apparently a pilot and already works for him. Not at all the reaction I expected."

"That's strange. Maybe Arturo is just in shock. But, girl, what in the hell are you going to do with a helicopter?"

"No idea," I mumble through another forkful of pork chop. "Especially now, with a team of bodyguards trailing me wherever I go." As I talk with my mouth full of delicious food, I feel like a total pig, but don't care. I was fucking starving when I showed up at Drago's today. "God, I miss Keva's cooking. Do you think there are more leftovers in the fridge that I can take home with me?"

"Um… sure. You know there are usually tons. But are you sure you're going to have room for them at your place? How do you like Arturo's cooking, anyway? Pass me the hairpin."

"Haven't tried it. It's a statement. I won't eat anything he makes," I say, handing her a tiny U-shaped wire. The words have barely left my mouth before I flinch as the metallic ends dig into my skull. "Christ, Sienna."

"Okay, fair. But I'm not used to playing hairdresser in the dining room. Let's go upstairs. The lighting is so much better there."

"We can't! We're spilling tea, and the unwritten Serbian rule is that all gossiping happens in the dining room."

"*Whyyyy?*"

"I don't know. It just is." I shrug right when Sienna pulls on another strand of my hair so hard that it feels as if she'll yank it out. *Ouch!*

"You know, I really hoped this animosity between you and Arturo would fade."

"Not happening anytime soon," I bite out. My tone is hard, but deep inside, I feel my resolve wavering a bit. Arturo didn't push me to explain my behavior last night. Neither did he call me a hysterical basket case, which I kind of figured he would. He just… held me. And it felt so damn good.

"You might change your mind if you give his lamb stew a try. What are you eating anyway? Just getting delivery?" Sienna asks while plunging more pins into the massive bun at the crown of my head. "I know Greta is a terrible cook. She might be even worse than you."

"I was doing a bit of both, ordering in and putting up with a few of her meals. Until this morning, that is. Apparently, your brother banned all food deliveries to the house, and he gave Greta a direct order not to cook for me anymore. I think he's making his own statement. I can either eat what he makes or starve." Taking a deep breath, I continue, "I see a lot of sandwiches, cereal, and instant ramen in my life over the next year. Just think—one week down, another fifty-one to go. Yay, me."

"Oh, for the love of God! You two are unbelievable." She shakes her head. "But... why don't you just—"

"Make something for myself?" I raise an eyebrow. "Sienna... Gas stove. Remember?"

"Oh."

"Yeah. *Oh*," I sigh. "I get chills down my spine whenever I look at that thing." After last night, I think I might just stay away from the kitchen altogether. At least for the foreseeable future.

"I'll explain it to Arturo. He'll have it exchanged for an electric range."

"You won't say a word to him. This is my personal shit, and I don't want it broadcast to everyone. Especially your brother." *No more than I already have.*

"Tara—"

"Are we about done?" I interrupt.

"Yeah, all finished. Just need to add hair spray. Close your eyes."

"Don't forget the feathers," I say as the fine mist rains down on me from every direction. Sienna seems determined to use up an entire bottle on my head.

"Okay, but don't lose them." My skull gets pricked again when she sticks a peacock feather into the mass of my locks. "These are my favorite."

"I'll keep that in mind."

Once Sienna steps away, I pick up the handheld mirror off the table, lifting it in front of my face. She's done an amazing job. My hair looks nearly identical to the image I showed her as a reference. "Outstanding. Do you think it'll stay put all night?"

"Absolutely. Where the heck are you going, a masquerade or something?" she chirps, adjusting one of the ringlets behind my ear. "I had no idea Arturo would be into something like that."

I smile.

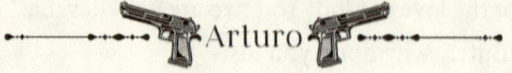

Arturo

I cross my arms over my chest, watching my sisters fidget in their seats on the other side of the table. "Alright. Let's hear it."

"Hear what?" Sienna chirps.

"This oh-so-urgent matter that needed to be discussed. In person. Right away. And couldn't wait a moment longer."

"Can't we just want to have coffee with our dear brother because we miss him?"

"It's the second Saturday of the month. Which means that your favorite shoe store is having a half-off sale that starts"—I glance at my watch—"right about now. I don't see you skipping it in favor of coffee with me."

"I love you more than I love pretty, discounted shoes!"

"Uh-huh. And Asya, you just decided on an impromptu trip to New York just so you can join us for an overpriced drink?"

"The pakhan's private plane is always on standby, and Pasha and I liked the idea of a quick trip. This deli has the best pastrami on rye sandwiches," Asya mutters.

"Mm-hmm." I set my palms on the table and lean over. "Are you pregnant, Asya?"

"What? No."

My gaze slides to Sienna. "Are *you* pregnant?"

"I'm not. And stop this nonsense. We just wanted to have a tiny little chat with you."

"So, there is a hidden agenda after all. What is this? An intervention?"

"Maybe." Her grin is perfectly innocent.

"Right. I'm all ears."

They look at each other. Then, Sienna nudges Asya with her elbow, nodding in my direction. Asya shakes her head, nudging back.

"Okay, Okay. I'll say it." Sienna mimics my earlier pose and crosses her arms over her chest. "We're concerned about you, Arturo."

I snort. "What about me that troubles you so much?"

"Your wife," Asya deadpans.

"Excuse me?"

"We both like Tara. A lot. But the way you've treated her sounds like the absolute pits. Sienna's been keeping me in the loop, and I gotta tell you... I'm completely shocked. Did you really make Tara sign a prenup with a bunch of rules about how she's allowed to dress and act?"

My head snaps to Sienna. "So, Tara told you the truth, I take it?"

"Yes. Every terrible bit. Including you threatening to frame her for murder. I have to say, I'm appalled, Arturo."

"Appalled." Asya nods at the same time. "You're lucky she hasn't told Drago. I mentioned to her that she should. I'm so disappointed in you, big brother."

"My marriage is none of your business," I bark. "Or yours, Sienna."

"Since you're doing your utmost to sabotage your happiness, I'd say it is," Sienna throws in.

"Happiness? I didn't choose Tara for my bride. I was ordered to marry her. If she were the last woman on earth, I wouldn't have picked her."

"Right," she continues. "Because she isn't Italian. Doesn't give a crap about our social traditions. Isn't afraid to challenge you or say what she really thinks. She's basically the polar opposite of the ideal wife you created in your head."

"Couldn't have said it better myself."

"Yup. Must be a real bitch to have fallen for your unwanted wife, then."

"That's the craziest crap I've heard in quite a while," I chuckle.

"Is it?"

"Listen, sis. I understand that you have these cute delusions about how the world revolves around love and all that mushy shit. I blame those books you like to read for that nonsense. But life isn't a romance novel, Sienna. And certainly not the life I've chosen to lead. It's tough, and daunting, and the only way to get through it is by following reason, not flights of fancy."

"So, having feelings for Tara is unreasonable?"

"Exactly. I won't lie and say that I'm not attracted to her in some bewildering way. She is a very beautiful woman after all. But that's just basic chemistry. There's nothing else to it."

Sienna leans toward her twin. "Told you. He slept with her."

"I haven't."

"But you want to!"

"Yes, I do. That doesn't mean I'm in love with her." I take a sip of the coffee our waiter delivered. "She has made my life complete hell, Sienna. Tara is entirely unpredictable. And she's got a real talent for pissing me off. The woman gets under my skin like no other. How could I ever be interested in someone like that for more than a good fuck?"

"Mm-hmm," Sienna smirks, then tilts her head toward Asya again. "That's why he made her sign that stupid-ass prenup."

I narrow my eyes at her. "I made her sign that prenup to protect my interests and to make sure she doesn't make a fool of me, especially in public."

"Oh, please. Your ego is the size of a small planet. As if your wife's choice of clothes or little theatrics could ever come close to hurting it."

"Okay, since you're such a psychoanalyst, why don't you explain my real motivations, then?"

"It's simple." She shrugs. "You've liked her from the very beginning, theatrics and all. That made her an anomaly that's threatened to crush your carefully constructed idea of how things should be. Which would equate to failure in your book. So your solution was to neutralize those exact traits that attracted you to her in the first place by making her act like everyone else. Because God forbid you actually develop any sort of deep feelings toward your wife and not just have her around to fulfill a social role."

"Didn't you hear me? I don't have any feelings for Tara, damn it! She's rude. Half-wild. Bullheaded. And she doesn't give a fuck—"

"About you." My sister smiles. "Yeah. That's got to be a bummer. Unrequited love is the worst. No wonder you're going out of your mind."

I rake my hands through my hair and pull at the roots, glaring blankly at the table before me. "She demanded a million dollars for every month she's married to me."

"Arturo, you threatened to frame her for murder," Asya says softly.

"Indeed," Sienna adds. "If I were her, I would've insisted on at least double of that! You would have deserved it just for being an asshole to her."

"In that case, she should have asked for triple." This is from my gentle-souled Asya.

I stare at both of my sisters. "Shouldn't you two be on my side?"

"Not this time," they say in unison.

"Great," I sigh.

"Talk to her." Asya takes over now. "Stop being a jerk and admit you like her."

"There's nothing for us to talk about." I throw back what's left of my coffee and rise. "Sorry to cut this get-together short, but I need to head home to change for the gala tonight."

"Be careful, brother," Asya says in that soft way of hers. "Or it might be too late."

I reach for my wallet. "Too late for what?"

"For you to come to your senses. There are many prominent men out there, and one might end up snatching Tara away from you."

"Yeah? Well, good riddance."

CHAPTER
eighteen

 Tara

I PRESS MY PURSE TO MY STOMACH AND INHALE, STARING AT Satan's door. He arrived home about twenty minutes ago while I was putting the final touches on my makeup. I heard him coughing out in the hallway, and he sounded much worse than yesterday. Stubborn idiot. I'm tattling to Sienna first thing tomorrow morning. Maybe she can knock some sense into her boneheaded brother.

Not that I'm worried about his health or anything. God knows, if DeVille dropped dead, it would solve a lot of my problems and… My stomach hits the floor. That cough really did sound serious. What if he's actually sick?

Reaching into my purse, I take out my phone and shoot Sienna a quick text. Okay. There. I did my good deed. Now, someone else can worry about Arturo, and I can go back to not caring about him at all. It's just… Ugh. Alright, maybe I do care. But only a little. Perhaps I should suggest we skip this stupid shindig? But even if I do, I doubt he'd consider it.

My fingers shake slightly as I lift my hand to knock. I'm not sure why I'm so nervous to face him. I do know it's not because of the reaction I'll surely get as soon as he opens his door. Am I anxious to see him because of what happened last night?

I can't quell the hurricane of emotions that's been brewing in me. Can't dismiss the feel of his arms around me. The way he held me... Gently. With his palm stroking soothingly along my back, all while I frantically clung to him. The peace I felt in his embrace. The safety. For that brief moment in time, I finally felt like nothing on this earth could harm me. I wish I could forget it, but I can't.

Something shifted between us, there in the dead of night, and I'm not sure if it was a *bad* something or a *good* something. As it is, one of the many barriers between us has disappeared. It's like... like I don't hate him as much as I did before. And, I don't like it. Don't like it at all. Don't enjoy this feeling in the slightest. Especially because it's directed at the man who chose to turn my life upside down. Ripped me away from my family, not giving it a single thought or harboring a moment's regret. As if I'm some kind of toy for him to play with. So I refuse to feel anything for him other than disdain.

I came into this house with the intention of keeping Arturo DeVille away from me. Both physically and emotionally. That was my plan, my safety net. I've failed at one condition; I don't intend to fail with the other.

Steeling my spine, I knock. Twice. On the other side, fast, measured steps. Approaching. The door slides open, revealing my annoying husband, who's in the process of closing the clasp on his wristwatch. How can he make such a simple act look so sexy?

"You ready?" he asks while fumbling with the golden band. "We need to hurry if—"

The words die on his lips the moment he looks up. An outright hunger shines in his eyes as he stares at me. That look of desire, however, quickly morphs into shock as soon as he notices my hair.

"Are you fucking kidding me?" he growls.

I grin. "What do you mean, darling?"

Arturo grits his teeth and takes a menacing step toward me. My self-preservation instinct has me retreating from him.

"You're going back to your room"—another step closer—"and I don't care how, but you're going to fix that… that"—the final step makes me bump into a wall—"monstrosity and make yourself look normal."

"No can do. There's so much hair spray, I'd need to wash my hair. And if I do that, we'll definitely be late."

He doesn't reply, but I see the muscle spasm in his stubble-covered jaw. Fury rises off him like a thick, dark cloud. Any moment now, he might strangle me. The gentle, caring man from last night is nowhere to be found.

Inside my chest, my heart feels like it's being squeezed. An invisible hand has got ahold of it. That's what I wanted, right? To bait him into being pissed off at me. If he is, it makes it so much easier to hate him. So much easier for me to forget… other things. So why am I not jumping for joy, having succeeded in my goal? Why do I feel like crying?

"I don't see what the problem is," I continue, digging my nails into my palm to make sure my voice won't break. "I have not breached any of the terms of our agreement. The hairstyle is elegant. Regal even. I used a painting of Marie Antoinette as inspiration. Her appearance has always symbolized wealth and power. 'The grander the hair, the higher the social status,' they said. So I thought this would be more than suitable for tonight's extravagant event."

"Maybe in the fifteenth century!" he snaps.

"Actually, she lived in the eighteenth."

Arturo's nostrils flare. He plants his palms on the wall on either side of me and dips his head. That ravenous look returns as his eyes focus on my lips. "Will you at least remove the damn feathers?"

"I'll consider it. *If* you ask nicely."

The lid of his left eye starts twitching. *Oh boy.* I appear to have hit dead center with that "ask nicely" comment.

He leans closer until our cheeks nearly touch. A pleasant quiver shimmers along my spine as his stubble ever so slightly brushes my skin.

"You seem to be very invested in finding ways to defy me, *gattina.*" His lips are right next to my ear as he whispers. Warm breath fans the delicate flesh of my earlobe. "I've been thinking about it a lot."

"Hmm?" His proximity is making my every fine hair stand on end. Inhaling the sweet aroma of woods and the exotic warm spice of his cologne, tempts me to turn my head and bury my nose in the crook of his neck. Just as I did last night. "And what have you concluded?"

"I think…" Those soft lips ghost across the side of my face, and every neuron in my body catches fire. "I think that it turns you on, Tara."

The air gets lodged in my throat. I open my mouth to deny it, to tell him how utterly idiotic his presumption is, but the words won't form on my tongue.

He dips his head lower until his lips press just below my ear while he continues in that sultry, raspy voice. "Ask me how I know."

"How?" I exhale.

"Because it has the same effect on me…, *gattina mia.*" His lips close around the pulse point on the column of my neck, sucking my skin between his grazing teeth.

An electric current zips through my veins, rattling my bones to the marrow. Every part of me tingles with charged energy. It's how I feel each time we kiss. As if I'm melting. Dissolving into the ether only to be held together by his heated touch. This man is going to be my ruin. I just know it.

A faint moan escapes me, betraying my steadfast resolve to resist Arturo's seduction. I grab the lapels of his suit jacket and tilt my head to the side, giving him greater access. His lips trail a painfully slow path to the juncture between my neck and shoulder. It's a searingly hot kiss. Suddenly, he seems to be everywhere, even though it's only his mouth that's touching me. I can feel the power of that contact all the way between my legs, where my core clenches in desperate need.

No. This can't be happening. Not again. I am not attracted to Arturo DeVille. And never will be.

His mouth continues the assault on all my senses, lighting me up from the inside. I'm teetering between begging for more and searching for the strength to stop this. No matter what I do, I lose.

But it doesn't feel like a defeat when his teeth gently scrape my shoulder. When the silky fabric of my skirt starts to drift upward along my bare legs. My calves. My inner thighs. Wait… Those are calloused fingers. Lightly touching my hypersensitive flesh. Up. Trailing upward. Pulling my thong to the side…

The sudden pressure on my aching clit sends a jolt of heat through me, sparking to life the flame that's now burning me alive. A low moan escapes my throat as air rushes from my lungs.

"I love the way you purr when I tease your pussy."

My ability to shoot back a snarky response is nonexistent. All because of the way he's now rubbing my clit. His slow but forceful motions are driving me insane. I squeeze the lapels of his jacket, holding on for dear life. Holding on to him.

His rhythm oscillates, switching from slow to fast, fast to slow. It's as if he knows exactly what it will take for me to lose my mind completely. I throw my head back, panting, getting wetter by the second. Coming closer and closer to the edge.

Holy shit!

He can do that with nothing but his hand. No one else has ever made me orgasm just by letting their fingers play with my clit. Yet here I am. On the cusp of once again falling over the edge, guided by Arturo goddamn DeVille.

I hate myself for every moan of pleasure, every second of surrender, every shuddering breath. Everything he's making me feel. And still, I never want him to stop.

His lips fall to my neck again, claiming my flesh with a force that straddles the line between pleasure and pain. The teasing of my pussy halts, and I'm just about to protest when he suddenly pinches my clit. *Hello, cosmos!* I explode. Reduced to stardust in a fucking supernova.

"See? I was right after all, little cat."

The satisfaction in his voice is unmistakable. He pulls his hand away and brings his fingers to his lips. With his gaze locked on mine, he licks them clean. Just as he did the other night. And just as before, it has exactly the same effect on me. I nearly come again simply from seeing him do it.

"You taste so damn sweet." A devilish smirk tugs up the corner of his lips. He slips the tip of his thumb into his mouth, sucking off the remaining cum. "Not even the slightest hint of that bitterness you so enjoy spewing. Which makes me think. All of that... Your venom... It's nothing but an act."

"Enough." I plant my palms on his chest to push him away, but end up just leaving them there. Too weak to force even a smidge of distance between us. Still shaking after coming down from on high. "Move."

He takes an unhurried step back while his gaze drifts to the side of my neck, right to where my skin still tingles from his kiss.

Slowly, I raise my hand, touching the tender spot just below my ear. "You... you left a hickey on me?"

"I guess I did."

I open my mouth. Then snap it shut and storm past him as fast as my heels allow. Satan DeVille has left a fucking hickey on me. Marking me where anyone could see as if I'm... I'm... his possession or something. And... and I like it.

Shit.

Arturo

Beneath the soaring eighteen-foot ceilings, the massive crystal chandeliers cast shimmering light on the milling attendees. This ballroom is something else. An opulent space that brings to mind the grandeur of historic European hotels. It's decked out with a glossy dance floor, majestic skylight, stately columns, and countless French doors that in warmer months would allow guests to explore the venue's other areas.

It's almost ironic that in this neoclassical banquet hall, everybody is staring. At us. Not surprising, considering the monstrosity gracing the top of my wife's head is at least six inches tall. I'm not even sure how to describe her "hairstyle." A three-story-wedding-cake-inspired bun? A leaning hair tower of feathered disaster? Who knows. But no one could ever say that Tara lacks creativity, that's for certain.

But not every look of astonishment is because of her centuries-old royal updo. Despite her outrageous hair, my wife looks divine in her elegant navy-blue formal dress. It hugs her body, wrapping around her slight but mouthwatering curves before gently flaring near mid-thigh, highlighting her figure. The off-shoulder neckline adds a touch of sophistication without revealing too much of that milky skin I can't stay away from. She's beautiful. Ravishing. And *mine*. But she remains tempting to all these assholes. They can't hide what they're thinking, and I'm seized anew by volcanic rage whenever I spot another man glancing at my wife, devouring her with his eyes.

I've been unprepared for the eruption of hot jealousy and have no idea what to do with it. What I do know, though, is the more I get my hands on this beguiling woman, the more I crave her. The scent and taste of her arousal are forever infused within me. Even now, among the crowd of the best and brightest, the glitter and glam of high society, the only thing I can focus on is her.

Her smile is bright, but it doesn't reach her eyes. And her fingers feel clammy in my hand. Something about that nudges the far fringes of my mind. She must be nervous, stepping out at such a public event for the first time as my wife.

I pull her close, mostly because I can't help myself, but it also appears to give her some comfort. She sags against me slightly without seeming to be aware of it at all.

"Is that…" Tara murmurs next to me. "That guy, in the brown suit… It's—"

"Nope." I wrap my arm around her waist and steer her in the opposite direction. There's no way I'm allowing Adriano Ruffo to be anywhere near her again.

What the fuck is he still doing in New York? And is Ajello aware of it? Whatever, I don't have the time or inclination to deal with Mafia politics tonight.

"You didn't even let me finish."

"You don't know him." I gesture toward a man peering at a floor vase overflowing with an enormous flower arrangement. "There. That's Senator Larson. His family owns several vineyards in California. Would you like to meet him?"

"Why would I want to meet an old boar who looks like he's already wasted?"

Because *he is* an old boar, interested only in golf and wine. Not a recently single billionaire whom she thinks of as a *gentleman*.

The grip around my lungs tightens, and I start to cough. *Fuck.* Before we left home, I swallowed a couple of pills to help with this goddamned cold, but nothing seems to be working. My sore throat and the throbbing in my head have me in a constantly irritable state. And with the way I'm feeling, I don't have the patience to keep ignoring the lustful looks my wife has been garnering since the minute we arrived at the gala.

"Good point." I step aside to snatch a tumbler off the tray being passed around by the closest server and throw back the contents without another thought. Whiskey burns the back of my throat, soothing the uncomfortable scratchiness.

"Why am I here, anyway?" Tara asks. "This isn't a Family event, so I don't see why I need to be present."

"I didn't want to rob you of an opportunity to showcase your defiance of the explicit directives we agreed to."

"Oh. You could have spared me three hours trapped in a chair while your sister created the symbol of my rebellion." She points to her hair. "Three hours. It hurt. A lot. And now my scalp itches from all the hair spray."

"The lengths to which you're willing to go in your efforts are praiseworthy."

"Well, I'm glad you can acknowledge my hard work, darling." She beams that ridiculous fake grin at me and nods to the left. "Friends of yours?"

The direction of her gaze takes me to an approaching elderly couple wearing matching outfits. The man's blue suit is the exact same shade as his companion's dress. The gold buttons on the sleeves of his jacket complement the decorative brooch on the woman's shoulder.

"There are no 'friends' in this social circle, Tara. Those are the

Wrights. Several steps removed, but still related to the British royal family. Being considered 'very distant relations' doesn't dissuade them from their high opinion of themselves, though. They still think they're better than everyone else. The Wrights happen to own one of the largest cosmetics companies in the world."

"Really? Maybe I could ask the aristocratic lady for some samples. That is, if I'm allowed to speak." Her fake grin widens.

"You are," I grumble. Not that she needs any of that nano-whatever-crap the Wrights have been trying to jam down everyone's throats. I doubt there's anything that could make Tara more beautiful than she already is.

"Mr. DeVille!" Lord Wright exclaims, shaking my hand. "I'm positively delighted to see you here tonight. Especially in such charming company."

He turns to Tara, his palm already halfway extended toward her. Not happening. I casually swat his hand away. A sixty-year-old man, married or not, is not touching my woman.

"This is Tara. My wife." I snake my arm around her waist and give Wright a pointed look. One that says, *Keep your paws to yourself, or you won't like the consequences.*

"Oh yes, I see." The man laughs nervously. "Of course. I had no idea. It is a pleasure to meet you, Mrs. DeVille."

Tara smiles even more widely. "It's an honor to meet you, Lord Wright." Somehow, she manages to say that through her teeth, not allowing her grin to slip even for a moment.

Christ. I lightly squeeze her waist in warning.

Tilting her head to the side, she bats her long lashes at me, giving me her most innocent look.

Okay. I give up. She can suffer facial cramps, for all I care.

"And this is my lovely wife, Loretta," Wright continues, then faces me. "Loretta has been urging me to ring you about that wonderful investment opportunity we discussed last year. Tell me, have you had a chance to consider it?"

"Exfoliation creams and pore-minimizing products are hardly a good fit for Gateway Development Corp. We'll have to pass."

"That's a shame," Loretta comments, her calculating gaze fixed on Tara. "But perhaps your beautiful wife would be interested in becoming our brand ambassador? You have a wonderful complexion, my dear. I can already see the billboard in Times Square and—"

"No," I bark. Just the thought of my wife's image plastered every-goddamn-where for men to drool and jerk off to has the murderous wrath within me flaring.

"But why not?" Loretta insists. "She would be a worldwide sensation within twenty-four hours of her debut. Without the atrocious hair, of course."

My head snaps toward the nasty woman. "Care to repeat that?" I growl, pinning the shrew with a look I typically reserve for degenerates I catch talking shit about the Family. It's usually followed by the sound of their breaking bones.

"Um… I-I," she stutters, casting a fleeting glance at her husband. "I meant the avant-garde style your wife obviously prefers."

"I must have misheard you then." I turn my glare on her husband.

"Undoubtedly. Avant-garde. Haute couture. She's simply striking." Wright nods, grabbing Loretta's elbow. "But… ah, we should be heading out. Good evening to you both." They are gone from view in mere seconds, lost among the crowd.

And not a moment too soon.

I'm glad I've mostly managed to lead Tara away from the remainder of the horde. With my occasional bout of fighting not to lose a lung, I can't imagine anyone wanting to get too close anyhow. Still, there are a few who look like they might want to give it a try. And I can't have that. Despite her bravado, my wife definitely isn't at ease with all these eyes on her. While pressed to me, she keeps fidgeting with the side of her dress without seeming to realize that as she does, her hand rubs against me. Dangerously close to my already half-hard cock. She's not even trying, but her propensity for stirring up hazards is top-notch.

"I thought you said my hair is ridiculous. You said as much when you called it a 'monstrosity,'" Tara whispers next to me as she watches the crowd gathered around the champagne tower warily.

I take a step behind her and tighten my hold on her waist, dipping my head to speak softly into her ear. "Regardless of the reasons that forced us into this marriage, you are my wife. And you will be treated with respect. I won't allow anyone to be rude or belligerent to you, especially in public. What you and I say to each other in private, that stays between us." I blow on the peacock feather stuck in the side of her bun as it tickles my nose. "And *ridiculous* doesn't even come close to describing this abomination, *gattina*."

Tara tilts her head, giving me a sideways look while something that sounds like a muffled moan leaves her tightly pressed lips. She appears as if she's struggling not to laugh. For a couple of heartbeats, victory is nearly in her grasp. Until she fails. Her eyes sparkle with mischief while her lips pull into a radiant smile.

"I have to agree with you on that one, Satan." A low, sensual chuckle slips from her, the sound mixing with the chatter of people and the occasional clinking of glass.

Her smile lights up her entire face. It's not the fake grin this time, either. It's real. And warm. And directed at me. Her anxiety seems to have also faded; she's not pulling on her skirt anymore. I must have been able to distract her enough to allow her to forget her troubles. Realizing that makes me feel like a fucking superhero or whatever. It's a damn good feeling to know that I was able to make her laugh, make her happy. And make her feel safe. When was the last time a tiny thing like that made my heart beat faster? Made me pause to enjoy a small, simple moment? I don't even remember.

"Is the crowd tonight typical?" she asks. "There seems to be quite a menagerie of guests."

"Yeah." Somehow, I manage to pull myself together. "Lots of prospective business opportunities await. Let's mingle."

The chairman of the board, representing a well-known venture capitalist firm, is sipping a flute of champagne next to the hors d'oeuvres table at the center of the room. I've been trying to arrange a meeting with him for the past two months. But instead of heading directly to him and using tonight's opportunity to back him into a corner until he accepts, I find myself steering us in the opposite direction.

One of the owners of a country-wide retail chain is lingering by the open bar on the far left side of the ballroom, swaying slightly as if he's already had a few too many. This would be a great time to schmooze the man, try to see if I can dig up some inside information. Just last week, Ajello and I were debating whether we should buy some of their stock. I direct our path to the right instead.

For nearly half an hour, we walk aimlessly around the room, all while I do my best to avoid being dragged into a conversation by whomever we pass. What the fuck am I doing? Business was the only reason I wanted to come here tonight. I should be networking, making connections with the big fish in the room and trying to determine whether there's a way for us to exploit them, not strolling casually with my arm around my wife.

But that's all I seem to be interested in. I wish all these people would just magically disappear, leaving me alone with the gorgeous woman at my side. My wife. My wife, who I just want to take home and find some mundane, meaningless crap to argue about. All so I can enjoy her blatant attempt to defy me. To give me a reason to whisk her into my bed. Carry her off like some kind of caveman, then fuck her senseless, turning my bedroom into a sex den.

The thought stops me in my tracks. Have I completely lost my fucking marbles?

"Are you alright, DeVille?" Tara arches her perfect brow at me.

No. I don't think I am.

And fuck! I hate, *hate*, *haaaate* her not using my name!

"Arturo DeVille," a guttural, slightly accented voice calls out. "And little Tara Popov. What an unexpected surprise to see you here."

I turn around, spearing the interloper with my glare. Katrakis Senior. He wobbles toward us on unsteady feet, looking slightly disheveled and obviously drunk.

"Heard you had issues with some paperwork recently. So awkward," he slurs.

Motherfucker. I knew he was behind that fiasco with the permits.

"No sweat. It's been resolved. A misplaced item is easily found when you have capable people working for you." I tighten my hold on Tara's waist, discreetly waving my security guys off when I see them approaching. "But I hear you're still looking for yours. Any luck locating your missing son?"

Tara's spine stiffens, and she leans into me. Maybe I shouldn't have brought that up, all things considered.

"You know something about my boy's whereabouts?" the Greek sneers through his teeth.

"I don't bother with small fish, Katrakis. Perhaps you should look for your spawn in Atlantic City. As I've heard, he tends to frequent the casinos there quite regularly. Maybe that's how he ended up losing the deed to the property that's now mine?"

"You scumbag," he hisses. "Always too full of yourself. You think you're better than everyone else? Well, you're not! See"—his angry gaze slides to Tara—"you're screwing my son's scraps. How does—"

For more than a decade now, one simple rule has been my credo. *Do not lose your shit in front of prospective business associates.* That means I've had to control my temper more often than this fucknut's shit-for-brains offspring jerked off to his own reflection. Along with biting my tongue, I've had to curb every impulse for violence. Any deviation would tarnish the carefully crafted reputation our Family has been trying to maintain. To outside society, I've done everything possible to appear as nothing but a savvy businessman. One who would never engage in a physical confrontation with someone amid a crowd of witnesses. Never.

My fist connects with Katrakis's face before the son of a bitch utters his next syllable. He flies backward, landing on his ass several feet away.

Screams erupt across the room as guests notice the commotion and the blood gushing from Katrakis's broken nose. He doesn't try to rise, just keeps lying between two tall tables and moaning like the fucking sissy he is.

"This is the one and only time you will disrespect my wife," I growl. "Say another word about her, and I'll rip out your tongue and shove it up your ass. Mark my words."

A collective gasp rises from the crowd that have gathered around the Greek. But no one is even trying to help him because everyone is staring at me. I've met almost all of them at one time or another, and they probably thought they knew me. I thought I knew myself, too. I was wrong. I didn't spare a single breath thinking about that credo of mine or the ramifications of my actions. All I thought of was my wife. And how I will never allow anyone to hurt her.

"Let's head out." Putting my hand on the small of Tara's back, I urge her toward the exit, silently telling my guys with a look to stay put and deal with the fallout here instead.

"That was subtle," Tara murmurs next to me as we walk away.

"Whatever happened to that 'make no scenes' and 'cause no scandals' decree you plastered all over the terms of our agreement?"

"I'm"—*cough*—"in a bad mood," I grumble while trying to squelch the scratchy pressure in the back of my throat.

"No shit."

We've picked up our coats and are heading down the hallway that leads to the main doors when the sound of someone calling my wife's name behind us stops me. I glance over my shoulder and spot a twentysomething man in a form-fitting suit running toward us.

"Tara!" he yells again. "Is that really you?"

My wife turns around, and my hand falls from her back.

"Conrad? Oh my God! When did you get back?!"

Conrad? I search my memory. Did she mention *a Conrad* to me? The ache in my head is ramping up, and I can't remember. *Fuck.* I really need to get some serious sleep.

As the guy reaches us, it hits me. The brat of an oil tycoon. The one who *still* calls her. The one she *could have* married. And probably wishes she did.

"I can't believe this! It *is* you," the guy exclaims and pulls *my wife* into an embrace.

That's the final straw. The tipping point. The last drop that sends my brimming jealousy over the edge. I wrap my arm around Tara's middle from behind, lifting her out of his reach while I fist the front of the idiot's jacket with my other hand. "Step. Away."

"The fuck, DeVille?" Tara thrashes in my hold, her feet kicking several inches above the floor. "What's wrong with you?"

"*Arturo* DeVille?" The pissant backs up a step. Surprise flashes in his eyes as they dart from me to Tara and back again.

"Correct." With my glare locked on the handsy little fuck, I dip my head until my stubbly cheek rests against the smooth expanse of Tara's. "Is that your ex-fiancé?"

"What? No… I mean, yes. No. No! It wasn't official—Would you let me go already?"

A *fiancé*. I crush Tara harder to my chest and touch my lips to the shell of her ear. "You should tell the boy to leave."

"I won't. We haven't seen each other in years. Put me down, damn it." She tries to kick my shin.

The brat must have a couple of working brain cells in his head after all because he appears to have grasped the situation, and he takes another step back. Good. His chances of escaping alive have marginally improved. Considering I've already gone off the deep end tonight, at the moment, I'm close to ripping him limb from limb.

"Put your hands on my wife again, and I'll fucking end you," I growl.

His eyes shoot to Tara's hand, which is wrapped around my wrist. With my palm splayed across her stomach, her right hand and my left are nearly side-by-side. Our matching wedding bands glisten front and center. His gaze lingers on the rings for a brief second before sliding away.

"I see… Tara, we'll catch up some other time, okay? I'll call you—"

"No, you won't." I avoid another of Tara's attempts to inflict bodily harm upon me. "Now, get lost."

"And you called *me* a savage, DeVille?" Tara snaps while trying to wriggle free. "Where are those civilized manners of yours, that impeccable behavior you take so much pride in?"

"I'm wondering about that, too." A glance down the hall confirms that the oil brat is out of sight, so I lower my wife to the ground.

"Get bent, DeVille!"

The moment her feet touch the marble tile, she dashes toward the exit as fast as her heels can carry her, furiously click-click-clacking through the vacant corridor. The cakey-hair-tower on her head hasn't held up to all the commotion, and it's sagging, slightly askew.

One of the iridescent peacock feathers appears to have been lost somewhere along the way.

A doorman in a flashy uniform stands back as far as he can, holding the heavy door open and watching her march past him. I bet he's seen a lot of furious women storm out of the venue before.

"Wishing you the best of luck, sir." He tips his head at me with a look of solidarity in his eyes. A fellow sufferer, it seems.

I step out of the building just in time to see Tara with her hand on the door of a taxi, ready to slip into the car. The elegantly dressed couple who must have just arrived in that cab is already climbing the hotel stairs.

"Tara," I warn her, allowing my voice to carry over the hum of the city and across the half a dozen or so yards separating us.

She lifts her free hand, offering me her perfectly manicured middle finger.

I rush down the stone steps as panic surges inside me. We still don't know who's behind that attack on the road or the reason for it in the first place. Even now, culprits could be lying in wait, waiting for another opportunity to strike. And my wife is getting into an unknown fucking taxi! I am less than ten feet from her when she slams the car door practically in my face. The next second, the vehicle pulls away from the curb with a loud rumble.

"Tara!" I yell, but the taxi is already weaving through the New York traffic.

Damn that woman! I stand in the middle of the sidewalk, enraged and terrified all at the same time, glaring at the cab's receding lights. My car is parked in an underground garage, about a block from here. By the time I get it, who knows where that hellion will be. That's also assuming the cab driver isn't some psychotic killer. *Fuck!*

The blast of a horn behind me jars me from my spiraling thoughts. I look over, finding that another taxi has pulled up. That'll do.

I sprint to the driver's side and throw open the door. "Out!"

A man in his midfifties gapes at me as his hands tighten on the wheel. "What?"

Oh, for the love of God. I grab the front of his shirt and pull him out of the car. Buddy even proves himself helpful by unbuckling the seatbelt.

Damn, damn that woman.

As soon as I slide behind the wheel, I hit the gas.

I'm thankful the gala this year was held at a hotel in the Financial District and not in Midtown. But even at this late hour, traffic is still a bitch. I switch lanes, trying to close the gap with Tara's taxi, but my efforts might be futile. As the street light changes before me, I cut off a shiny town car to get ahead, and the driver lays on the horn before flipping me off.

That's two tonight, but it's not the birds I'm chasing. I need to catch up to my wildcat before she completely disappears from sight.

"Oh, dear. Did we miss the turn?" a high-pitched voice chirps behind me.

Slowly, I look into the rearview mirror. An elderly lady in a thick brown fur coat and with a dead fox wrapped around her neck stretches in the back seat.

"I must have dozed off. It's so difficult to stay awake this late into the night at my age, you know?" She gives me a motherly smile. "But that's alright, my boy, you can just go around the block."

Fucking great. Not only did I steal a fucking cab, but apparently, I've also kidnapped someone's grandma in the process.

"We're taking a shortcut." I step on the gas.

The taxi my wife used to make her escape is only a couple of vehicles ahead. I remember that big dent on the rear bumper.

"It must be stressful working as a cab driver here in New York," the old lady continues. "Especially for a foreigner. Have you been here long, Bjorn?"

What?

"Is that a Danish name? Or Swedish? You don't look very Swedish to me. Did you dye your hair black, maybe? It suits you much better. But you should update the photo on your driver's license."

I glance at the ID card pinned to the dashboard. The picture is of the fiftysomething blond guy I pulled out of the car. "Yeah. It also makes me look about twenty years younger. Could you please stop talking now?"

"How rude!"

I briefly shut my eyes and take a deep breath. The stabbing pain in my chest chooses that moment to reappear, along with a weird wheezing sound whenever I inhale.

The traffic seems to ease up a bit—thank fuck—so I press harder on the gas only to slam on the brake a second later. A flash mob has suddenly filled the street, blocking the intersection in every direction. Tara's taxi managed to slip past them just in time.

Of course it did.

"Fuck!" I hit the steering wheel with my fist and lay on the horn.

Tara

"Thank you so much." I hand the money to the taxi driver while one of Arturo's security guys holds open the cab door. Just my luck. It's that weasel, Tony.

"Mrs. DeVille." He looks at me with confusion. "Did something happen?"

"Yeah. Your maniac boss happened," I mumble as I get out and rush toward the front door.

Jackass. How dare he?

For a while there tonight, I actually had a good time with Arturo. It was kinda fun mingling with some of those snooty people and seeing their reactions to my hair. And Satan surprised the hell out of me when he stared down that aristocratic crone and called her out on her comments. It was sweet of him to come to my rescue, even though I didn't need his help. I could have handled her on my own, but it was still a very gentlemanly move on his part. A pretty sexy one, too.

He spent the rest of the evening with his hand on my lower back or wrapped around my middle, guiding me to make certain no one bumped into me. I pretended not to notice, of course, but I appreciated his thoughtfulness. Not that I'd admit it to him. And I'd rather eat my own foot than acknowledge that I enjoyed Arturo DeVille's company. But I did. I really did.

His touch also had a surprisingly calming effect on me, easing my anxiety about being among so many unfamiliar people to a manageable simmer. I'm not sure if my husband has figured me out, or if his choosing to keep us mostly away from everyone was just a coincidence. Either way, this was the first time I've ever felt comfortable in a crowd.

That stunt with Stavros's old man was overkill, but I can't be mad at Arturo for that. The guy essentially called me his son's leftovers, and it kind of hit the mark. Not in the sense that he obviously meant it, but because I often felt worthless after my terrible relationships. So, although I don't like seeing anyone in pain, I'd be lying if I didn't admit that seeing Arturo lay him out to defend my honor, like a true knight from one of my books, was hot as hell.

Until Arturo turned irrational and possessive and ruined everything.

I'm just through the threshold when the roar of an approaching vehicle stops me. I glance over my shoulder to see another cab pulling up. When the driver's door opens, my dear husband steps out, looking furious as fuck.

Why was he driving the taxi? Where's the actual driver? And who in the lord's name is the bewildered old woman in a fur coat who just got out of the back?

"Did you decide to change careers, darling?" I holler at him.

Arturo doesn't seem to find my question funny, because he slams the vehicle door shut with enough force that it sounds like a gunshot in the dead of night. His focus is locked on me as he draws nearer with a homicidal expression on his face.

Time to flee.

"Okay then. I'll see you in the morning." I blow him a kiss and immediately run inside.

Sprinting in four-inch heels isn't for the faint of heart, but I manage somehow. I cross the entry hall with lightning speed, then, hiking up my dress, climb the stairs two at a time. As soon as I reach the landing, I dash toward my room, not taking even a split second to look back.

I head straight for the en suite bathroom, taking off my clothes along the way and dropping them on the floor. The space is enormous, easily the size of my entire bedroom back home. The white marble vanity with its rectangular basin sink spans the length of a wall. Across from it is the massive, glass-walled shower that could accommodate five people, at least. The cabinetry is wood, matching the tones in the bedroom, and there are peach accents everywhere. I love it. Can practically feel my stress dissolve in the spa-like luxury.

I don't even bother removing the hairpins before entering the shower and turning the water on. With all the hair spray Sienna doused me with, my hair will need to be soaked before I can even attempt to remove them. I tilt my face toward the ceiling-mounted rainfall shower head, closing my eyes while I let the warm water soothe me. Damn, this feels good.

"What part of *we're on high alert* didn't you understand, Tara?"

I scream. Heart beating in my throat, I look over at the source of that growled demand.

Arturo stands in the open doorway of the shower stall, gripping the glass panels on either side.

"Get. The fuck. Out! Right this second, DeVille!"

"Did I not say it clearly?" He takes a step into the enclosure. "Or did you simply choose to ignore me? Defying me again for shits and giggles."

The cascade of water beats down on me, plastering my hair to the sides of my face. As the drops hit, the backsplash sprays onto Arturo's clothes, but he doesn't bother moving out of reach. His angry eyes are totally locked in on mine. Not even my fully-exposed boobs and pussy distract him.

"I just decided that I'd had enough of your erratic behavior," I bark. "Forcing me to adhere to the bullshit rules you insisted on including in the prenup is one thing. Threatening my friend is where I draw the line. You don't get to do that, asshole!"

"Friend?" He takes another step closer. "You were engaged."

"We weren't! He asked; I said *no*. And why would my past even matter to you?"

Another step. This one brings him right under the water. It soaks through his fancy suit pants, his white dress shirt. He towers over me, partially blocking the spray. His hair is sopping wet, turning his already inky black strands as dark as midnight. The rivulets flow over the planes of his face, dripping onto mine. He takes my chin between his fingers, tilting my head up. Despite us both being drenched, the look in his eyes nearly incinerates me on the spot.

"No other man gets to ask you to marry him, *gattina*. Not in the past. Not in the future. Just me."

The breath stalls in my lungs and then escapes me in short bursts. Just moments ago, the water was pleasantly warm. Now, however, it feels scorching.

"No one…" He dips his head lower, barely brushing his lips over mine. "No other man gets to put his hands on *my wife*. Just me."

Heat rushes straight to my core, and my ravenous pussy feels like it's on fire. I fist the front of his wet shirt and slam my mouth to his. Holding back wasn't even an option. A second longer and we'd both burn to ash.

The kiss is blissful torment. Heaven and hell, all rolled into one. I hate myself for failing to resist the intense pull I feel toward this domineering man. But at the same time, I can't go on without having his lips devour mine. His kisses… The best fucking sensation in the world.

Still holding on to my chin, he reaches down with his other hand and grabs my ass, squeezing my flesh tightly. Frenzied, driven by desperate need, I tug on his shirt, pulling it out of his pants and unbuttoning it.

"For the record," I say against his lips while basically tearing his shirt off. The zipper of his pants is next. My hands are shaking as if I'm an addict on the verge of another fix. An instant later, I yank down his pants, along with his boxer briefs, leaving them to pool around his ankles. "You never *asked* me to marry you."

"I also never asked to have my head fucked with," he growls in response. "But here you are, doing a bang-up job of it."

Arturo's thick cock nudges my stomach as he towers over me, his downturned face a mere breath from mine as water streams off him onto me. We stand there, under the overhead spray, like we're in some weird, silent standoff. Two enemies who can't seem to decide whether they'd rather kill or fuck each other.

"Are you just going to stand there or what?" I snap.

A dangerous, low growling sound erupts from Arturo's throat. His piercing gaze doesn't leave me as he grabs me under my thighs, hoists me up, and wallpapers my back to the shower wall. Shivers race across my skin when the tip of his cock slips through my folds.

"What I'm going to do"—he pushes inside me, slowly, and a strangled gasp escapes my lips—"is fuck you hard. Hard enough you forget every guy you've ever been with. Every last one."

My inner walls stretch as he presses deeper, rubs those hidden pleasure nerves with every inch of his advance. Oh God, he's so big the intrusion is almost painful while, at the same time, it feels like pure bliss. I draw in a shaky breath, welcoming the feeling, reveling in the tremors that spread from my core to my outer limits. A wave of heat rolls through me while the torrent of water cools my electrified body.

"And then, I'll fuck you again. And again. And again." His teeth graze my lips, producing quivers, both inside my pussy and across the surface of my flesh. "Until the thought of future men becomes unthinkable."

He keeps sliding deeper, deeper into me. Once he's entirely in, I'm overcome with the feeling of complete fullness, so encompassing that I can't distinguish where my form ends and his begins. It's the ultimate fit. As if our bodies were made specifically for each other. As if our joining was an eventuality we couldn't escape. Every nerve, every cell within me, vibrates with pleasure after yearning for so long to have Arturo inside me. This... carnal clash between us feels predestined. Unavoidable. Idyllic.

I hate him.

I hate him for making me feel like this.

"Slightly overconfident, aren't ya?" I blurt, meeting his slashing gaze.

Arturo's eyes narrow, and he drops his forehead to mine. "We'll see."

For just a moment, we remain silent. Motionless. Lost in the deafening cascade.

"You're on the pill?"

"Yes."

Squeezing my hips, he pulls out completely, only to plunge back in so forcefully that I choke on my breath. A moan rips from my throat as he withdraws again. But then, I'm panting, gasping, mewling as he thrusts back in, again and again.

A brutal, quick kiss, and he straightens. Shifts. Puts more vigor into his ramming hips.

My back slides up and down along the tiled wall as Arturo pounds into me over and over. With each hard thrust, he seems to get further, deeper, relentlessly gratifying and punishing me at the same time. As the tremors racking me intensify, I'm left soaring higher and higher. Sated, yet wanting more. Needing more.

Our bodies collide. I'm left in ruin. This shouldn't feel so damn good, but it does.

Digging my nails into his shoulders, I throw my head back. My world tilts on its axis as I'm left breathless in the arms of this man.

"Look at me!" he growls, filling the room with his deep baritone.

I open my eyes, and my throat swells with emotion. Arturo's gaze instantly captures me. His lust-filled depths are glowing with fire. And even under the steady stream of water, I feel the heat. His jaw is clenched, lips are pressed hard together as he continues his earth-shattering onslaught.

"Good. I want to witness every fucking second of you breaking apart for me," he bites out as he slams into me again. "Want to see your eyes roll back as you come on my cock. And when your pussy is filled with my cum, I want you to memorize exactly who has been fucking you. You got that, Tara darling?"

I can't utter a word. He's pounding into me so hard and fast that all I can do is gasp for air. Every time he pulls almost completely out feels like a monumental loss, an aching absence. Each returning plunge is a welcome relief. But it's not just my treacherous, treacherous body that receives him gleefully. My stupid heart, too, thunders a surrendering beat.

Damn him!

"Go to hell, darling!" I snarl back.

My response seems to send him into a frenzy. Adjusting his hold, he angles his thrusts so each ram of his pelvis hits my clit and his cock reaches that elusive spot inside me, sending me climbing to new heights.

All rational thoughts flee. I'm reduced to nothing but instinct. A collection of raw nerve endings, sensitized flesh, and overwhelming need. Shivers race down my body, convulsions shake me from the inside. I barely have enough strength to cling to Arturo while being fucked out of my mind. A scream forms deep in my chest, and I can't keep it in. Can't suppress it. It detonates, ripping out of me. Every cell in my body lights up like fireworks as I come harder than ever before in my life.

I think I might have momentarily blacked out. Spiraled down into an euphoric abyss. Arturo's wild roar as he comes jolts me back while his arms tighten around me. My vision is blurry as I barely have enough strength to meet his eyes. But true to his word, Arturo watches me, heaving out hard breath after hard breath. His dark gaze piercing me like a sword. Slashing through my remaining armor. Obliterating the last of my walls.

What the hell was that? It was epic. Way beyond anything I've ever experienced before. And I have a feeling, never will again… unless… unless it's with Arturo. Because, I'd bet my life that he can deliver again and again.

This man… He has destroyed my foundations. He has also given me what no one else could.

He has robbed me of an imagined future but delivered a better-than-fantasy reality.

The jerk was right. There's no way any other man could make me feel like he has.

Yet another thing Arturo DeVille denied me.

And there's no way I could ever hate him for that.

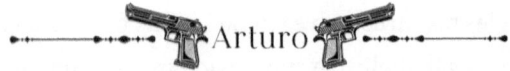

Arturo

Sorceress. Enchantress. I don't know what kind of voodoo this woman wields, but it must be some serious witchcraft.

"You're slipping." Pushing open the shower door, I step over the pile of my soaked clothes that we flung out earlier.

"You're too wet," Tara says into the crook of my neck, but tightens her legs around my waist.

She clings to me like a baby koala as I head to the built-in towel cabinet on the far wall near the tub. The steam in the room is so thick it makes the entire space look almost mythic.

As I pass the mirror over the vanity, I can't help but stop for a moment. Our shapes are blurry since the glassy surface is completely covered with condensation, so much so that I can only make out our vague outline. Reaching out, I wipe off the moisture, revealing our reflection. Tara's face is turned away, putting her glorious dark hair front and center. The wet mass of slight waves cascades down her back, nearly reaching her naked ass. With her arms and legs wrapped around me, we appear as if we're interlocked. I can't look away from the sight. Damn, it feels so good to have her in my arms like this.

"I'm freezing over here, DeVille."

My blood pressure skyrockets each time she calls me that. I wish I could figure out her deal. What the fuck does she have against my name? I've heard her call me Arturo. My name on her lips has become almost as great an obsession as the taste, the smell, and the feel of this woman in my arms. The only times she seems to slip, though, are when I'm bleeding. I wonder if I'll have to lose every drop of blood in my veins before she'll use only my first name.

Grabbing a towel from the shelf, I drape it over her shoulders and step out of the bathroom.

The lights in the room are off, all except for the floor lamp near the window. Its soft glow casts a spotlight directly on the unmade bed. Of course the bed was left in disarray. It's what my wife is good at. It's as if she purposefully leaves proof of her existence everywhere.

Sweaters and hoodies are frequently scattered around the living room. Left on the back of the couch like her calling card. A trail of random books scattered across every available surface. In the den, on the breakfast counter, and even in the laundry room. The milk jug is always shoved onto the wrong shelf in the fridge. In the antique bowl on the downstairs bookshelf, a pair of earrings she wore on one of our dates.

When I look around, it's as if I can track my wife through the house. If it was anyone else's shit, my obsessive-compulsive personality would have forced me to immediately tidy up. Everything has its place. Except Tara. And her stuff, apparently. My wife doesn't just "fit" into a specific slot in my life. She has taken it over completely. And it never even crossed my mind to do away with her things. It's almost like… like I *like* seeing her crap everywhere. In the house. Our home.

My gaze is drawn back to the tangled sheets and to the pile of chaotic pillows near the headboard. Did she have a restless sleep? Was she tossing and turning last night, dreaming about me fucking her? Because I did. I've been dreaming of sinking into her every single night. Since the moment she entered this house. And if I'm honest with myself, since way before then.

I'd hoped this bizarre obsession with a woman who tempts me to claim her as mine at every turn would end once we finally fucked. Considering the rock-hard state of my dick mere minutes after I just had her, my hope was a foolish dream.

"You need to dry your hair before going to sleep," I say as I lower her next to the messy bed.

Tara tilts her chin up, looking at me through the wet strands covering her still-flushed face. "Is that an order?"

"Yes."

Those brilliantly green eyes squint in defiance. "You don't get to give me orders, DeVille."

I stare back at her, soaking in the sight of this bewitching creature. Every single detail about her leaps out at me. Her neck, reddened by the scrape of my scruff and still sporting my hickey. The mark I was more than thrilled to brand her with. That pillowy lower lip of hers, blood-red and swollen from my bruising kisses. Her breasts, with mouthwatering nipples, peeking through the wet strands of her mane.

It's like we're back in the shower because she's glaring at me so intensely she could burn me alive. Her eyes are roving down my chest, scanning my torso. Is she cataloging the marks she left on me? I'm certain there are trails upon trails of her fingernail scratches across my back. It's not hard to picture, considering the shredded appearance of my front.

The room around us is completely silent, save for our breaths, which are becoming more rapid while we eye each other in our second stare down of the night. The air between us grows thicker, charged to a point where a tiny spark could make it combust. *Fuuuuck*, I want to fuck her. Again. Tonight. Right now.

But I won't.

Once was risky enough. I can't let this absurd addiction consume me.

"I'm gonna head to bed," I say through gritted teeth.

"Terrific idea."

"Fine." I nod.

"Okay," she bites back.

My breath comes out in quick bursts like I just ran a fucking marathon, all because this woman and everything about her is driving me out of my skin. I fist my hands, hoping that'll be enough to stop me from reaching for her. My palms sweat and itch with need. With every second, every heartbeat, the frustration, the want inside me builds and builds, and there's nothing I can tell myself that'll make me turn around and leave.

The freckled nymph before me might be having a similar problem. Her body is leaning toward me while desire and reticence battle for supremacy across her face.

I dip my head and whisper, "You really need to get into that bed, *gattina*. Right the fuck now."

With her kiss-bruised lips slightly parted and her own breaths ragged, she takes a step closer to me instead. The head of my painfully hard cock presses against her stomach, just above her jewel-studded belly button. That slight contact is almost enough to bring me to my knees. Black spots appear in my peripheral vision as unbridled lust grips me by the balls.

"Go to hell, DeVille."

Whatever thread of self-control held me together, snaps.

Dissolves. Melts into oblivion. Whatever mental capacity I had, is gone. I swing her into my arms and toss her to the center of the bed. In the next breath, I'm bracing myself over her.

"So fucking soft," I mumble as I drag my lips toward her navel, toward that damn piercing that's been taunting me for so long. "How can anything be so damn soft?"

A shaky puff of air leaves her as I suck the little trinket between my lips. The tip of my tongue traces around and around it, while I glide my palms along her inner thighs, spreading her legs wider, inching closer to her heat.

A moan, loud and needy, explodes from her when I slide my thumb through her wet folds, seeking her clit. I start with a small amount of pressure, then increase it as I rub tight circles around that sensitive nub. I keep my rhythm steady, matching the motion of my tongue over her piercing.

Her breathing grows more uneven, her moans pick up and echo off the bedroom walls. I feel her trembling beneath my touch, edging ever closer to that precipice, and I've barely begun.

Pain shoots through the back of my head as Tara fists my hair, pulling me closer and pushing my mouth to where she wants it more. As if I need an implicit invitation.

This girl. *My* girl.

"Impatient little cat," I growl, licking her belly button one more time.

But I'm more eager to bury my face in her pussy than to take my next breath.

Her scent… Sweet and seductive. My own personal brand of cocaine. I breathe her in, deeply, keeping that scent captive in my lungs as I push my tongue into her opening. *Lord in Heaven.* That initial taste of her is an overdose. But if I die now, I die a happy man.

Pushing her knees further apart, I attack her decadent honey, fucking her core with slow, methodical strokes of my tongue. Lapping her nectar to get every single drop. Kissing her lower lips, her silky folds. Sucking her clit just to hear her purr. Indulging in my wife like I'm a ravenous, famished man.

Tara's panting fills the space around us, all while she vibrates like the strings of a priceless violin in my hands. And I'm enjoying every second of making her bow as I play, her mewls music to my ears. Before this night is through, I'll touch, lick, and kiss every inch of her body. I'll make her fall apart on my tongue, my fingers, my cock. I'll drive the memory of other men from her mind. I'll ruin her for all others. The only one she'll feel, she'll crave, is me.

"If this is hell, *gattina*"—I blow a warm breath over her sensitive flesh, making her quiver all over again—"I'm never coming back. Ever. I'll happily spend eternity inside your pussy."

Flattening my tongue, I give her slit another long lick, from her back hole to the edge of her smooth mound. Then, I seal my lips over her swollen clit and suck. Hard. Harder.

A shrill scream of *YES, OH GOD, YES!* explodes from her. She comes, almost yanking my hair out by the roots. And I nearly topple over the edge along with Tara. That tingling at the base of my spine tells me I won't last much longer. But I continue to feast on my wife, stroking and sucking, letting her ride the high. Her body trembles beneath me, shaking so hard that if I didn't know better, I'd worry over the cause.

Yes… This is now my mission. To learn everything about her body, find each of her erogenous zones. Make her feel the most sinful things. Give her the most exquisite pleasure. Ensure no one else could ever live up to what she can experience with me. She can continue to despise me. God knows I deserve that and more. But she won't be able to live without my touch. She'll never stop craving our carnal mating. The only man for her is me. Any others who even think of stealing her, I'll destroy before they ever get the chance.

I trail a line of kisses from her pussy toward her chest, pausing to circle her sparkling jewel with the tip of my tongue again. I suck and gently bite her nipples. Draw one delicate breast into my mouth. Then the next. Nip those fine collarbones. Lick my way up the column of her neck. And finally capture her mouth.

"See how sinful you taste," I rasp against her quivering lips.

Her shuddering exhale is my only answer.

She musses my hair while she kisses me back. Slipping her tongue into my mouth, sucking my own. I glide my hands up her arms. Pull them over her head. Capture her wrists.

"I didn't expect to leave you speechless, *gattina*. It's a bit surreal, if you ask me."

"Fuck you." Huffed words uttered between scorching kisses.

"You will. We're nowhere near done, Tara darling." Lifting my hips to let my cock nudge her entrance, I plunge inside with one powerful thrust.

Heaven. Feeling her warm, wet heat clamp down on me. The welcoming embrace of her pussy is the ultimate gratification. Like coming home. Time stops. Maybe ceases to exist altogether. Everything around me disappears. Everything other than my wife. Shaking under me. A look of pure rapture on her face. I watch her. Mesmerized. Watch her lips part with every moan. Notice the rapid rise and fall of her beautiful breasts with every shallow breath she takes. The fluttering of her long, dark lashes as her glassy green eyes hold tight to mine.

I keep slamming my body into hers, hard and fast, trying to fool myself into believing that the warmth spreading through my chest, the jackhammering of my heart, and the sudden inability to swallow are all simply the effects of great, intense sex. The kind of sex that leaves you feeling wild. Still, though, it's nothing more than a biological reaction. Magnetic chemistry between her and me. None of it is based on an emotion. Certainly nothing that would shake the ground under me. And the need to claim her, possess her, chain my wife to me and throw away the key, that's just the delusional ramblings of my sex-drunk mind. Too many pheromones, not enough sleep.

That's all it is. All it ever could be. It can't be anything else.

I won't let it.

CHAPTER
eighteen

Arturo

THE ALLEY IS DARK, AND THE BUILDINGS ON EITHER SIDE OF me are closing in. *Every window is blacked out. Every shadow is cold and threatening. The moon is no help as I continue searching for—*

I come to a sudden stop. Where am I? And why is it so fucking cold? My teeth are chattering.

Pulling my jacket tighter around me, I let my eyes glide over the unfamiliar neighborhood. How the fuck did I end up here? I don't remember. I'm...

I'm searching for someone.

Yes. I'm searching for someone I lost.

Who? Who is it I can't find?

Asya?

Yes, she must be the one I'm searching for. My baby sister disappeared.

I peer left down the street, then to the right. No one is there. Doesn't matter. I resume my run. That's what I have to do. Keep going. Keep searching for someone important to me. Someone who is mine. I need to find them. To protect what's mine. To watch over them like a damn hawk.

A lone street lamp comes into view. Far down the block, just before the intersection. A silhouette. A lone woman, standing right under the light.

"Asya?" *I call out.*

"I'm fine, Arturo," *the woman responds in Asya's voice.*

A sigh of relief escapes me. She is fine. Yes. Happily married to that damn Russian.

"I was looking for you," *I say.*

My sister smiles. I can't really see it because she's too far away, but I'm certain it's true. "It's not me you're searching for."

She's right. I've been trying to find someone else. But who?

"You already found her. The one you've been looking for all along. You just haven't realized it, yet."

"Found who?" *I step closer.* "Tell me!"

"Salvation comes in many forms, Arturo."

"Salvation?" *I reel back while despair overwhelms me.* "I'm incapable of saving anyone, sis. I couldn't save you! I searched and searched, but in the end, someone else ended up rescuing you. I failed. Failed both my sisters. Almost lost Sienna, too, because of my mistakes. I won't fail anyone else."

The cold wind blows, sending dust and debris into my face. The temperature must have dropped even further.

My sister cants her head, watching me like she finds my words amusing.

"She is not the one who needs saving." *Soft words drift toward me.* "It's you."

Me? What do I need to be saved from?

"From yourself, Arturo."

The streetlight fades, casting the alley into darkness, the silhouette of my sister dissolving into thin air. Only her words are left behind. Carried by the freezing wind. Echoing off the walls. Ringing inside my head like a piercing Klaxon.

"Arturo!... Arturo!... Arturo!"

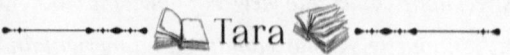

Tara

"Arturo!" I yell, shaking his shoulders. "Wake up!"

Sweat is clinging to his scorching-hot skin as he thrashes from side to side. I've been trying to wake him up for several minutes. This isn't normal, and I'm starting to freak the hell out. I shake him again, harder this time, while trying to ignore the panic that's threatening to overwhelm me.

Finally, his body stills. His eyelids slowly flutter open. *Thank God!*

"You must have had a night—"

Wait. Something isn't right. He's looking at me, but his eyes are unfocused. I take his face between my hands. Beneath my palms, he's burning up.

Fever.

"It's... cold. So cold here," he drawls while tremors rack his body. His gaze is aimed in my general direction, but it's as if he's looking through me.

"Arturo?" I shake him. Lightly this time. "Look at me."

An odd, barely-there smile pulls at his lips. "Sure. I always enjoy looking at you, *gattina*. Even when you're throwing canapés at me."

I gape at him. Crazy man. "You have a fever."

"Mm-hmm... Can I have a kiss, too? That wild kind where you bite my tongue?" His lips form into a pout. The movement is slow as if he's tempting me to take him up on his offer.

He's delirious. And definitely running a fever. A bad one, it seems.

"Great," I mutter to myself.

What do I do? How does one deal with such a high temperature?

Drago has never been sick, not with any serious illness. And I've only ever had sore throats and the stomach flu. What the fuck do I do?

I was prepared to deal with many unpleasant things when I came to live in this house, but not this. Not this gut-wrenching fear that's settled in me as I watch my husband with no idea how to help him. Hell, give me another long lecture or a shouting match on my utter ineptitude at being a proper wife, I'd rather endure that. Not this.

Not this.

Scrambling down from the bed, I run to find my purse. Sienna will know how to take care of her brother. As soon as my fingers wrap around the phone, I hit her number.

She answers on the seventh ring.

"It's two in the morning, Tara. What—"

"Arturo is sick," I say as I climb back into the bed beside him. "He's burning up. And he's babbling nonsense. What do I do?"

"What's his temp?"

"I... I don't know. I don't know where the thermometer is. But his skin is hot to the touch. And the gibberish he's spewing makes him sound like his damn brain is fried."

"Yeah, alright. I've seen that before. It happened when his fever spiked above a hundred and four."

"A hundred and four?" I choke out as my stomach tumbles to my feet.

"Yeah. You need to bring it down. Fast. Get him into the shower. Lukewarm water, though. Not cold."

"How? He's twice my size, Sienna. And he's barely coherent, " I cry out. "Would meds help? He's been carrying a bottle of ibuprofen with him for days, popping that shit like fucking candy. I could try to find it."

"It won't be fast enough. The pills, I mean. They'll take too long to work. At least get some wet towels and cover him from head to toe. I'll call Ilaria and ask her to come see him. Best not to give him any meds until then."

"Ilaria?"

"The don's mother."

"Ajello has a mother?" I thought that man was spawned. By something dark and unnatural.

"I know, it's hard to believe. But she's a nice lady and a great doctor, so don't worry. I'm gonna hang up now and call her. Keep me posted on how things go, alright?"

"Sure. Wet towels. Ilaria. Keep you posted." I press my palm to Arturo's scalding forehead. "Tell her to hurry."

I toss the phone away and rush into the bathroom to get the towels.

Fifteen minutes later, I'm staring at the pile of half-dry towels next to the bed. I've been changing them almost as fast as I place them, but it hasn't done anything. Arturo's skin feels just as hot as before. Maybe even hotter. *Fuck.*

"Arturo." I push the strands of his soaked hair off his face. "We need to get you into the shower."

He blinks, slowly. His still dazed-looking eyes finally meet mine. "Mm-hmm… Love showering with you. Will you let me eat your pussy again?"

"No!" My cheeks warm. I can feel myself getting red all over. "You have a fever, and we need to bring it down."

"So no pussy? I'm not going then."

"I wasn't asking." I grab his wrists and pull, trying to get him up and out of bed. "A little help here, please."

"Nope. No pussy, no help." He drops back onto the pillow.

Jesus! "Okay. Fine. Whatever you want." He can't even sit up, much less go down on me.

With effort, I manage to get him on his feet, but both of us almost end up on the floor when he loses his balance. Catching him just in time, I swing his arm around my neck, and supporting him by his waist, lead him toward the bathroom.

"I love your smell," Arturo says, burying his nose in my hair.

"Um... thank you."

"I haven't let Greta change my sheets since you spent the night in my bed. They smell like you, and I wanna keep them like that forever."

"That's gross."

"*Noooo.* But if you don't like, I can get new ones," he says, straightening out. "But only if you move in. Into my bedroom, my bed. If you always sleep with me. On top of me. I loved that. Love many things about you, actually."

"I think you might be losing it. Watch your step!"

"Oh, bossy! I like that, too. But you know what I absolutely adore?" He chuckles. "Neck snuggles."

"The what?"

"This!" He grabs me around the waist and lifts me, squeezing me to him so that my face gets crushed into the hollow between his shoulder and neck. "Yeah, just like that."

"Are you nuts? Put me down or both our asses will be on the floor."

"Mm-hmm... that'll be fun, too." He lowers me to the ground, swaying.

Shit. I wrap my arms around him, keeping him upright. "Come on. Just a few more steps."

The last five feet to the bathroom feel like fifty. We shuffle the entire way. Once I finally get him into the stall, I prop him against the wall and turn on the shower.

"This might feel cold to you with how high your fever is. But I promise, the water is actually lukewarm." I extend my hand toward him. "Come on, Arturo."

A crooked grin spreads across his face. "I'd tread icy waters or walk through the fires of hell for you, wildcat." Locking his fingers around mine, he pulls me to him and steps under the cascading stream.

It's only been a few hours since we were in this exact position, with water sluicing over us. Yet, nothing seems quite the same. The look in Arturo's eyes is missing the dangerous edge that's usually there. Right now, the way he's staring at me is unlike any other time he's looked at me before. His eyes are soft. Unguarded. That fever and delirium must really be messing with his head.

A pang of longing hits me dead in the chest. What would it be like to have Arturo DeVille look at me like this always?

"You came into the freezing shower for me," he whispers, stroking my cheek with the back of his hand.

"It's not freezing." I lift onto my tiptoes and brush his lips with mine. Even they seem softer somehow. Maybe it's the water trailing over both our faces. "Just seems that way to you."

"And you said my name"—his fingers caress along my jaw—"several times."

"I was under duress. It slipped."

His other hand slides to my back, stroking the length of my spine under my wet T-shirt. It's the only piece of clothing on me. My husband, though, isn't wearing anything. And still, our touching doesn't feel sexual.

My palms glide over his rock-hard chest, then circle to his back, slowly exploring his glorious body. Everything in me tingles with awareness. My pussy is still tender from our unrestrained, frenzied sex earlier tonight, yet I'm aching for more. Throbbing with the need to feel him. One circle over my clit, and I'm sure I would explode. Crumble like only he can make me.

But that's not what I want right now. I want this. The slow movement of his fingers along my chin. His tongue, probing my mouth. That pleasant sensation at the base of my skull as he tunnels his way through my hair. That's what I want. All those wonderful things. From him.

The need for this basic affection is strange, considering the volatile game of tug-of-war we've played since day one. Nothing between the two of us has been easy. Nothing except the undeniable pull both he and I feel. There's just no way to resist that kind of chemistry for long. No matter how many times my mind tried to deny it, my heart recognized the lie. I knew that eventually Arturo and I would end up in bed. His or mine, it wouldn't have made a difference. We both would have surrendered to that intense physical magnetism. But this, this moment right here, it doesn't feel like plain sexual attraction. It's something else entirely. And I have no idea what.

Or maybe I do.

Going along with this farce of a marriage, I thought I was doing the right thing. Sacrificing a year of my life for my family. Fixing yet another of my endless fuckups. Accepting a man who doesn't love me. A dangerous man who blackmailed me. A man who, outside of fucking, finds me lacking in every way that matters. Just like all the previous men in my life have.

I thought I could do it. Could temporarily shove my dreams, my happiness aside. Twelve months. Should hardly be an effort after a lifetime of not having what I crave. A man who will treasure me above all others. Love me more than himself. Despite my being a *walking disaster*, as Satan DeVille so eloquently labeled me. But that's my life. And regardless of the messes I've made in it, there's

one thing I've always been adamant about. One thing that I promised myself. The one thing I would never screw up.

I'd only fall in love with a man who loves me back.

Stupid, stupid, stupid. Because I managed to fuck that up, too.

"Hopefully, that's enough." The tip of my nose stings as I step
out of Arturo's embrace and shut off the water. "Let's get you back
to bed. The doctor should be here soon."

"Good thinking, getting him into the shower."

Blonde, sophisticated, and completely confident in herself, Ilaria
sets down her stethoscope.

I look at Arturo, sprawled face down in my bed. He collapsed
as soon as we got back from the bathroom, instantly falling asleep.
It took me nearly ten minutes to wrangle his overgrown limbs into
a T-shirt and a pair of pajama pants, so he wouldn't be "meeting"
the doctor naked.

"What's wrong with him?" I ask, biting my thumbnail.

"Pneumonia. Most likely viral, but we'll know for sure once I get
the results of the lab tests. I am detecting symptomatic wheezing in
his breathing. That's a good indication of inflammation in his lungs."

"Is that... bad?"

"Less bad than bacterial pneumonia. How long has he been
coughing?"

"Um... about a week. Maybe two."

"The antipyretic I injected him with will bring down his fever.
I'll send someone over in the morning with antiviral meds. They'll
help speed up his recovery."

"Alright... What else?"

"Typically, with this type of pneumonia, the flu-like symptoms resolve on their own. He just needs rest, plenty of fluids, and good nutrition. Give him warm tea with lemon and honey for his throat. Homemade soup. And keep him in bed for the rest of the week, minimum. Don't let him do any work."

"I'm not sure that's possible."

"He got himself into this because he was irresponsible. He ignored his symptoms, then stuffed himself with over-the-counter drugs that did nothing but mask his condition until the infection escalated." She shuts her medical bag with more force than she probably intended. "Men are idiots," she adds.

I snort, then slam my palm over my mouth. It's hard to believe that someone so... normal... mothered a merciless bastard like Salvatore Ajello.

"So, that's it?" I ask. "He'll be fine? What if his fever spikes again?"

"He can continue with ibuprofen for his aches and fever, if it returns. Have him take it every four to six hours. Cold shower, but only if absolutely necessary. Also, you should distance yourself for a few days. Staff, too. With viral pneumonia, Arturo will still be contagious until he starts feeling better and is fever-free."

Yeah. Considering our carnal encounters, it's far too late for me to play it safe. "Well, if I haven't gotten sick by now, I'm probably okay."

"If you do start experiencing symptoms, call me immediately." Ilaria rises and collects her cashmere coat from the recliner. "I'll see myself out." On the other side of the room, she pauses at the door. "You know, when I got the call just after two in the morning, I was certain I'd be digging a bullet out of someone. Pneumonia, though... I'd take that over a gunshot wound any day."

The moment she leaves, I climb onto the bed next to Arturo. He looks much better than he did an hour ago. Which means I could probably get some sleep. Lying down next to him, I press my lips to his forehead. Still hot. But not as bad. Snuggling into his side, I sigh.

Keva once told me that secrets whispered into the darkness stayed there forever. Locked away where no one could get to them. Dawn is still a couple of hours away, yet soon enough, the first rays of the morning sun will be breaking. Their light will spill through the window into the room. Now, though, now it's still dark. And based on Arturo's even breaths, he's deep in the land of slumber. Too far away to hear my confessions.

"Would it make me a bad person if I admit that I wish you'd stay delirious?" I whisper next to his ear. "Or maybe I could pretend you weren't when you said you'd walk through fire and tread icy water for me? Would that make me too pathetic?" A lock of his hair has fallen over his face, so I reach out to sweep it away. "Yeah, I think so, too. But that's okay, you know? I'm known for doing stupid stuff like that. So, I'll let myself pretend. Just until morning. And then, we'll both go back to hating each other. What do you think?"

Silence and rhythmic breaths are my only answer.

"I curse the day I met you, Arturo DeVille," I whisper. Then, drop a kiss on his shoulder and close my eyes.

In a few hours, the sunrise will scatter the stillness of the night. Will burn away my secrets—the truth—that I can't face in the light of day. Chase away my silly dreams, and usher me back into the grim reality. Wiping out his sweet words from my memory. Once I wake up, I'll go back to keeping Arturo DeVille at arm's length. Because that's the only way I can save myself.

From heartbreak.

From wanting something that I know could never be.

From craving forever with my husband.

CHAPTER
nineteen

Arturo

I LEAN MY HIP ON THE BREAKFAST BAR AND WATCH MY WIFE as she tries to disassemble the coffee machine. At least, I assume that's what she's trying to do. In her efforts, instead of using one of the screwdrivers I keep in the drawer just to the left of her, she's wielding a butter knife, attempting to unfasten the tiny screw.

"Damn you, you little fucker," she grumbles. "I will not be bested by a piece of aluminum."

"That's stainless steel, actually," I say.

Tara spins around so fast she knocks the bag of coffee beans off the counter. "What are you doing here?"

"This is my house." I nod at the coffee maker. "And that thing you're trying to kill is my favorite kitchen appliance."

"Get back upstairs. Ilaria put you on strict bed rest."

My forehead furrows. "Ilaria was here? When?"

"You don't remember?"

"No."

An emotion flashes in her eyes so fast that if I weren't watching her closely, I would have missed it. But she refocused her attention on the coffee maker too fast for me to get a grasp on it. And although I'm not entirely positive, it looked like hurt shining in her eyes.

"That means you don't remember her sticking a huge needle into your naked ass. Shame."

"Sorry to disappoint, but the last thing I recall is fucking you senseless in the shower, and then making you scream my name while we burned up the sheets in your bed." Pushing off the breakfast bar, I come up behind her and lay my hand on her hip. "And I'd love a repeat. Watching you come on my hand, my tongue, my dick, will help me forget all the aches my body is currently feeling."

She swats me away without bothering to turn around.

"You have pneumonia. Get back in bed."

I drag my nails through my stubble, feeling a bit confused. Did I do something last night to upset her? She can't still be mad about our spat at the gala, because I know we moved passed that when she begged me for more after she came on my tongue. The melody of her sweet little mewls, while I was balls-deep in her, is still playing in my head. I mean, she *might* still be mad. My woman sure knows how to hold a grudge. And she's never shied away from being snarky. But whenever she's had something to say to me, she's always done it to my face. Now, though, she is avoiding all eye contact. In fact, she's doing everything she can to look anywhere but at me.

"Screwdrivers are here." Opening the drawer next to her, I pull out a red-handled flathead and set it on the countertop. "Can I ask what you're doing?"

"This thing won't work properly. There's so much limescale buildup."

"Did you try cleaning it with vinegar first?"

"Who are you? Martha Stewart?" She grabs the edge of the counter, hanging her head as if in defeat.

Something isn't right, I just know it. I reach for her arm, but she leans away from my touch. Her movements are swift and immediate, like I've got the plague or something.

"What the hell is wrong with you?" I snap. "Why are you acting like this? You won't even let me touch you!"

"Because I don't want you to."

"What the fuck? Since when?" I growl, sick to death of this constant push-and-pull. "You can't just pretend like this thing between us isn't happening."

"There is no *thing*!" She turns around and meets my gaze for the first time. "It was just sex, DeVille. You scratched my itch, I scratched yours. Nothing else has happened," she huffs. "What? Do you think your cock is magical or something? That a few rounds of hate fucking would somehow make me forget that neither of us are in this marriage by choice? That you literally blackmailed me into it?"

"It certainly seemed that my wife found my cock magical while I was railing her through the mattress earlier." I lay my hands on the counter on either side of her. Caging her in, because she looks ready to flee. "So let me get this straight. We fucked, and we'll do it again. Soon. And often. But it changes nothing?"

"Exactly. Now, please go back upstairs, DeVille. You were running a high fever all night, and Ilaria mentioned that you might be contagious. I have no desire to catch what you've got."

"Fine. Whatever." I grab a bottle of water from the fridge and storm out of the kitchen, fuming.

Did I expect things to be different between us? Nah. And I don't want anything to change. She and I are just as we were when we started. Dealing with the shit situation that landed at our feet.

She still hates me, and I don't like her, either. And it should stay that way.

Besides, that woman is obviously incapable of forming a healthy relationship. If for a minute there, I thought we might try, it must have just been my raging fever talking. Clearheaded, I know better than that. I knew from the start that the two of us were a big mistake. One that I tried to contain with all the rules I made her agree to. Rules she's found a way to defy again and again. Pulling stunt after stunt until I lost my shit.

I never lose my shit. Ever. And especially not over a woman. Certainly not over a woman who fights me every step of the way. Or demands a fucking million dollars for every month of our marriage, as if proximity to me warrants hazard pay! And buys a goddamned helicopter when I offer her a new car.

A stupid grin takes over my face. Fighting it is futile. My little hellion.

I chuckle, but on my inhale, a nasty bout of coughing catches me at the foot of the stairs. *Fuck.* I grab the railing to keep myself upright. A minute ago, I was fine, now I feel like I've been run over by a bus.

That fever must have been a doozy because I don't remember shit from last night. Nothing after Tara and I rattled the glass walls of the shower and then repeated the performance in her bed before collapsing, exhausted. I know I didn't have the strength to get dressed before falling asleep, so how in the hell did I wake up in a T-shirt and a pair of pajama pants?

Halfway up the stairs, my tired ass stumbles 'cause I don't have the strength to pick up my feet. In that instant, a blurry image flashes through my mind. Tara laying a cool towel over my forehead. It's there one moment and gone the next. I shake my head. Perfect. I've started conjuring up delusions now. Imagining things that never could be. Seeing as my wife made her feelings toward me clear downstairs, she would have sooner left me for dead than nursed me to health.

Once I've finally dragged myself into my room, I rummage around, searching for my phone. By now, I must have dozens of emails and missed calls, but the damn thing is nowhere in sight. Maybe it's in Tara's room somewhere? I toss the jacket I just searched to the side and head for the door connecting our bedrooms.

The bed is unmade. Just as I left it. The sheets are tangled into a big mess. Both pillows have indents on them. Did she sleep next to me? The other side of the bed was empty when I woke up, so she must have gone to another room to sleep, fearful she'd "catch what I've got." I reach over and grab the pillow. The pillow that I know I did not use. I turn it around. Study it carefully. Then, with a look over my shoulder to make sure I'm alone, I bring it to my nose. It smells like her. That sugary strawberry scent. I bury my face in its softness and take a deep whiff.

Lips. Gentle and sensual, delicately trailing along the edge of my mouth. My hands slowly raking through wet, dark strands. Waterfall of silk over my fingertips. Whispered words and cold, cold water. Soothing promises and icy, biting pain. And then, the most delicious smoothness beneath my lips as they drag across the column of her neck. Hard spray pounding my shoulders. But in the echo of a shower, my name on a soft exhale of her breath.

I throw the pillow back on the bed. Definitely imagining things. Because I sure as fuck don't remember any encounter with my wife being anything other than explosive. There's never been a tender moment between us. She only ever calls me Satan or DeVille. Unless I'm bleeding.

Jesus, I'm so goddamned tired. And cold. So fucking cold. I let myself fall forward onto the bed, burying my face in the pillow I just discarded.

"Shit. You're burning up again…"

Hands. Stroking my face. Something wet and cool on my forehead. I swat it away.

"Damn it, Arturo."

I'd rather feel those palms. They're soft and warm. Jesus, it's fucking freezing. I capture one of the hands and press it to my cheek. Ah, much better.

"Open your mouth. Drink."

No. No, I just wanna sleep.

"Shit. If you don't take the pill, we'll need to have another cool shower, and I'm not sure I can get you in there by myself." Velvety voice. Cajoling. But desperate at the same time. "Please, Arturo."

I don't want a pill, don't want to drink, but I can't resist that sensual voice. I couldn't deny it anything it asks. So I cave. My throat feels raw as cold fluid rushes down.

"I'm going to soak more towels."

No! Don't go! I reach out blindly, grabbing the owner of that voice. Crushing the siren to my chest. Keeping her close. So close. So warm. So with me.

"Let me go. I have to—"

I shake my head. No! Not happening. Never letting you go. "You stay," I rasp. "No arguments."

"Your manners don't change even when you're delirious, DeVille."

I hate that. Hate when she does it. Puts distance between us by using my last name. I won't allow it. Want her close. Throwing my leg over, I drag her to me. Tangling our limbs together. Fusing us into one.

"I adore the way you smell," I mumble into her hair, inhaling the fresh, berry scent. It's sweet and tart, and so yummy. Sweet and tart like her.

"Yeah, you already said that. Please get your tentacles off me. I can't breathe."

"When I was little, strawberries were my favorite. They are fruity and sweet, and sometimes slightly sour. Perfectly balanced, which is what makes them great. Like you. Fucking perfect."

"You called me a walking disaster."

"You are. In an adorable, irresistible way. " I squeeze her tighter and sigh. "I'm so sleepy. Promise me you won't leave. Stay... with me."

"Okay."

 Tara

"It's just a stupid stove," I grumble as I stare at the range. I'm a hair's breadth from hysteria. "Just light the thing, set the pot down, and boil the damn water."

Rationally, I know the chances of this contraption going up in flames out of the blue are next to zero. Gas or not, appliances don't simply combust. But fear isn't rational. What I know and what I feel are two different things. And that's what isn't letting my feet lift to move me forward. Keeping me from taking that final step. The chopped-up ingredients for the veggie noodle soup are on the counter, right next to the pot I've already filled up with water. Everything's waiting on me to get a grip.

The health nut doesn't have a microwave, of course. So my best option is nonexistent. And it figures the esteemed Chef DeVille would have something against electric kettles, too. Because I checked everywhere in this fucking kitchen, searched every cupboard. Twice. Nada. With that, the last of my hopes failed.

Reaching into the back pocket of my jeans, I pull out my phone and dial Sienna.

"Tara! I've been calling you for hours. How's Arturo?"

"Fine," I croak. "Sleeping like a log."

"No fever?"

"Nope. Not in the last three hours." *Ahem.* I clear my throat. "Listen, can I make soup using hot tap water? Like really, really hot water?"

"Um... *noooo.*"

I lean against the breakfast bar and close my eyes, sighing. "That's what I thought."

"Tara? Are you okay?"

Am I? The last thing I ate was lunch. Yesterday. And excluding the brief stretch of shut-eye last night, I've been awake for more than twenty-four hours. "Fine. I'm fine."

"Do you want me to come over and help?"

Hmm, asking my sister-in-law to drive over an hour to help me make fucking soup would be a new low. "No need. I'll call you if anything changes. Say hi to Drago for me."

Setting the phone down, I resume glaring at the stove. Telling Greta not to show up today was a mistake, but I didn't want her to risk exposure to pneumonia. I did consider asking one of Arturo's guys patrolling the grounds to come and boil the water for me.

But that idea died a quick death when I pictured my darling husband laughing his ass off after hearing about it. Maybe I could just ignore Ilaria's advice and bring him juice?

"Shit."

My throat closes up, making it hard to swallow, as I take a step toward my doom. With shaking fingers, I reach toward the closest knob and turn it clockwise. Rapid clicking breaks the silence in the room, just as the faint but putrid odor of gas fills the air. A circle of blue flame rises from the burner. It takes everything in me not to turn tail and flee.

Instantly, I'm transported twenty years back in time as images of fire clawing at the walls of my childhood home flare before my eyes. A scream swells inside my chest. No! I can't do it. Can't let myself be sucked back there again.

I blink, banishing the mental fog and the scene of destruction, shifting my focus to setting the pot on the stove.

"Damn you, DeVille," I rasp as the pot nearly slips from my shaking hands. "Damn you, and your soup, and your goddamned kitchen."

As soon as the stainless steel container is squarely settled on the burner, I move several steps back and watch the tiny flame lick at the bottom of the pot. *I did it.* If someone told me I'd willingly go anywhere near a fire like this, I'd call them nuts and laugh all the way to the bank.

I'm gloating internally, feeling proud of myself and my triumph, but that happy buzz pops faster than a balloon meeting a porcupine. I can't believe it. I did it... for *him.*

Fuck.

Shoving my fingers into my hair, I grip the roots. I *am* a fucking disaster. But this is different. This is mercy. He's sick!

Arturo's temperature hasn't spiked in hours, so I'm hopeful

the worst of it has passed. That should mean no more sweet delusional ramblings. No more tender words that mess with my head. Nothing that blurs my perception of who Arturo DeVille actually is.

I have to stay true to my agenda. Keep him outside my walls and away from my silly heart.

I can't let myself fall for Satan DeVille.

Can't let myself fall... deeper.

CHAPTER
Twenty

Tara

"**G**INGER WAS ADAMANT THAT THIS CAN'T WAIT." THE man currently occupying my doorstep shakes his head. "As the CEO, Mr. DeVille is the only one who can sign this document."

I take a deep breath, trying to resist the overwhelming urge to punch this guy in the head. "He can't sign anything without reading it, and he's in no shape to do that right now."

Arturo's temperature has remained below the danger zone for the past two days, hovering just below one hundred. Worried that his fever might return, I've been sneaking into his room when he's asleep and using a noncontact thermometer to take regular readings. This illness has really wiped him out. That man has been sleeping a lot!

"These need to be signed right away, Mrs. DeVille. It's the don's orders. Something about tomorrow being the deadline."

"Fine. Come back at seven." I snatch the envelope out of his hands and slam the door in his face.

"'*It's the don's orders,*'" I mimic as I trudge to the living room and drop down onto the couch cushions.

When Ilaria came by to check up on Arturo yesterday, she

reiterated that light, home-cooked meals and plenty of warm fluids are crucial for a speedy recovery, along with plenty of bed rest. I
sure appreciate her care, but I wanted to scream, *I'm trying, damn it!*
I've spent hours watching videos on how to cook all kinds of comfort soups and quick one-pot meals.

Between waking up every two hours to take Arturo's temperature, racing to finish proofing Sienna's latest manuscript that's due
for submission tomorrow, and having a minor freakout every time
I'm forced to approach the gas stove, I'm dead on my feet. I'm also
spiraling a little. With paranoia about the gas and a fire setting in,
I called Greta and ended up spilling everything about what happened to Dina and how fucked up I've been since then. She helped
talk me off the ledge and, after, gave me a few tips on the soup I was
attempting. All that, somehow, left me feeling even more drained.
Now, though, I need to add reviewing this contract to my plate since
Satan is obviously still out of commission and will likely stay that
way for at least another day or two.

"I should just go bang on his door and throw it at him," I mutter
as I leaf through a couple of trees' worth of paper. How many pages
is this stupid contract? A fucking hundred?

"There's no way I'm spending the whole afternoon reading this
crap for him." Pages and pages of general provisions outlining administrative and legal clauses, then schedule after schedule with specifics on the scope of services, timelines, costs, and finally, payment
terms. A supply and purchase agreement. I reviewed a few of these
while working for Drago, and with all their fine print, they tend to
be a royal pain in the ass.

"Why should I care if he's too sick to work? This is his job
after all. He should be the one dealing with all this brain-numbing
mumbo jumbo." I grab a pen off the coffee table and settle into a

more comfortable position. "Yup, I'm gonna take this upstairs for him right away."

With my ballpoint skimming under the *Rules for Interpretation* section, I start to read:

If there is any inconsistency, ambiguity, or conflict between the wording of any Agreement documents listed below, the wording of the document that first appears on the list has priority over the wording of any subsequently listed document.

1) The articles of the Supply and Purchase Agreement...

Steam trails me as I leave the bathroom after my scorchingly hot shower. I haven't done much other than sleep for the past two days, but I still feel like I've pulled a few all-nighters in a row, and I look like death warmed over. At least that dreadful sore throat is gone, and I've mostly stopped coughing. Thank fuck.

I shuffle toward the bed, wanting nothing more than to collapse back onto the pillowy mattress, but knowing I need to make a few phone calls first. As I get closer, I spot a bowl of still-steaming soup on my nightstand. Hmm. Greta has been leaving my meals on the writing desk in the lounge area of my bedroom. Although cozy and surrounded by massive windows, the space happens to be in the far corner of the room. I figured she simply wasn't willing to risk getting sick, so she's been keeping her distance until now.

Next to the soup is a manila envelope. I ease onto the edge of the bed and pick up the package. Inside is a renewal contract from one of Gateway's suppliers, and it needs to be signed tomorrow, at the latest. I completely forgot about the blasted thing. Narrowing my eyes, I try to decipher the chicken scratch packed into the document's margins. When did Ginger's handwriting get so terrible? I'm assuming it was she who sent it over and left these notes.

As I try to concentrate on the pertinent sections, the pressure in my temples intensifies. Thank God Ginger has already identified the critical issues and added comments outlining the revisions that will need to be made. If I ignore her terrible handwriting, the notations she's left are rather good. Who knew Ajello's assistant had such a sharp eye for detail? Usually, it would take me an hour just to review the six pages of the pricing schedule, but with Ginger's notes, I'm able to finish my assessment in less than fifteen minutes, making only a few minor alterations to her proposed changes. Considering the time I've saved and the headaches I've been spared, I'm already planning to ask her to review all our contracts in the future.

Grabbing my phone off the charger, I notice more than a dozen missed calls and a shit ton of texts. I knew I was out hard, but so hard I didn't even hear it ringing? I swipe the screen down and notice that "Do Not Disturb" mode is on. Again. I never silence my phone, but for the past couple of days, each time I've woken up from a heavy slumber, I've found the setting active. Hell, I remember turning it off this morning!

I shove the envelope with the contract under my arm and dial my lawyer as I head downstairs.

"Atkinson, I'll have Tony drop off the contract with you. It needs some work," I rasp as I lumber off the final step. "Make sure they accept the proposed changes and send me the revised version for signing tomorrow morning."

"Sure," he replies. "If the changes are minor, it shouldn't be a problem at all. Oh, I tried to reach you earlier today about the zoning permits for the..."

He keeps talking, but I've lost the ability to form a coherent thought, all because my full focus has been captured by the sight before me.

Nestled on the couch, with her locks tangled around her head, my wife is sound asleep. The too-big T-shirt she's wearing has bunched above her waist, leaving her mile-long legs, the silky smooth skin of her slender hips, and a pair of black lace panties in plain view. The corner of a thick paperback with a pink cover is peeking out from beneath her cheek, partially hidden by her mussed curls.

"I'll call you back," I whisper into the phone and quickly cut the line. Then, just in case, I turn off the ringer.

As silently as possible, I cross the living room and crouch next to the couch, watching my little hellion sleep. Some of her dark tresses have fallen across her eyes and over the edge of the sofa, the ends reaching the floor.

I've always been attracted to women sporting short haircuts. Somehow, long hairstyles seemed less sophisticated to me. Now, though, the notion of my wife cutting that beautiful mane of hers makes me absolutely livid. If she knew that, she'd probably be in the hairdresser's chair within an hour, cutting her long locks off. Unthinkable! But if she ever gets the idea, I'll burn every hair salon in the city to the ground.

Two days. Two whole days I haven't set my eyes on her. Well... that's not entirely true. I woke up around three last night. And the night before. As if prodded awake by some demented internal alarm clock, I stared at the ceiling and fought the pull to go check on her. Something I've done almost every night since bringing Tara to my home. I lay in bed, trying to rationalize my need to make sure the woman who has been very clear about not giving a fuck about me was safe and comfortable. Nothing sensible popped into my mind. I was just being a dumbass. Over a woman. My wife. Still, I snuck into her room to make certain she hadn't thrown off her duvet as she tends to do in her sleep. I was simply being courteous. Unlike her. She hasn't bothered to look in on me these past two days.

Tossing the envelope with the contract on the floor, I carefully slide my arms under Tara's body and lift her. Greta must have already gone home, since I don't hear any other sounds in the house. It's silent except for my muffled steps as I carry my wife upstairs. She stirs, just a little, as I enter her room, and lets out a soft sigh before nudging her nose into the crook of my neck. My steps falter. I stop, freezing in place.

Her bed is mere feet away, but I can't make myself close that distance. I want this feeling. Having her this close, snuggled into me. I want it to last longer. Forever even. I stand, rooted in place, cradling my unwanted wife in my arms for what seems like an hour. When I finally make myself lay her down on the bed, instantaneously, a sense of profound loss hits me.

"Little witch," I whisper into the darkness as I pull the covers over her body. There's no other explanation; she must be a sorceress. Which would explain all the damn black cats! And only some sort of dark magic could have put a spell on me. A spell I'm powerless to escape. A spell I'm too feeble to flee.

Then again, when did I start to believe in magic?

Arturo

I ADJUST THE PHONE BETWEEN MY EAR AND SHOULDER TO prevent it from slipping and flip the thinly cut top sirloin in the pan. "Out of the question."

Pietro sighs on the other side of the line. He's getting too comfortable as one of my lieutenants. I'm gonna have to deal with his laissez-faire attitude, and soon.

"We've been dealing with the Vipers for more than a decade. Jackson is reliable. He'll pay," he protests.

"Full payment is always upon delivery. No exceptions. No money, no product."

"But—"

"No buts. We're not running a charity. If his gang can't come up with what they owe for the coke, the shipment will be offered to another party. He doesn't like the way I do things, he can go fuck himself."

"Shouldn't you be in a better mood, considering you've been off for a week?"

"Oh yeah, I'm out of commission for a measly five days and everything turns up unicorns and fucking rainbows. Like one of our trucks being stopped at the border when it should have sailed right through," I snap. "And us losing out on the warehouse lease deal because the goddamned contracts didn't get signed in time. Oh, and how about Carmelo managing to piss off Wang with one of his asinine jokes. Now the Triad is threatening to boot us out of Chinatown. That storage facility has been a pain in my ass for months, and now it seems we're back to where we started!" I throw the spatula into the sink, breaking a couple of glasses inside. "I'll be in the office in two hours to go over the latest contracts with the boss. First, I need to smooth out this fuckup with Wang."

Pietro clears his throat. "Uh, security has been informed that you're not allowed inside. Mandatory sick leave, per Don Ajello's orders."

"They can try keeping me out, but you might want to warn them that I'm not *in the mood*." I cut the call and toss my phone to the counter.

"You're not going anywhere."

I twist around to find Tara leaning on the breakfast bar, arms crossed over her chest.

"Decided to show your face at last, huh?" I bark.

This house is big, but I never considered it so large as to make it possible for my wife to dodge me for days on end. Especially since we're sleeping in bedrooms that share a fucking wall. She's been avoiding me, staying away like I'm a harbinger of death.

At least Greta had not deserted me. She made me meals and brought them up to my room several times a day, along with a newspaper for me every morning. But as much as I appreciate my housekeeper's efforts, there were times when I wasn't sure if it was pneumonia or her cooking that was doing me in. Somehow, her food was worse than ever. Her soups have been bland and flavorless.

Barely edible, actually. But regardless, I ate them whenever I woke up and found a steaming bowl on my writing table.

"Get back into your bed, DeVille." Tara jerks her head in the direction of the stairs.

"Worried I'll get you sick?" I lean my butt on the kitchen counter and take a big bite of my steak sandwich. "No need. According to Dr. Google, once the fever is gone, pneumonia is no longer contagious."

"Good to know. You're still not leaving. Your *actual* doctor said no work for at least a week."

"Concerned about my long-term health, *gattina*?" My eyebrow lifts. "No need to pretend. We both know where you stand. You've made yourself abundantly clear," I growl, slamming the plate with my half-eaten sandwich on the counter beside me. Whatever appetite I had is gone.

As I move past Tara on my way to the front door, I catch a faint strawberry scent. It knocks something loose inside me. A vision of my wife lifting a glass of water to my lips flashes through my mind for the briefest second. *Open your mouth. Drink.* I shake my head, pushing away the vagrant thought.

Imagine that, me vulnerable and needing someone's help. Depending on another person for life's basics, like food and water. It's almost laughable.

For almost half of my existence, I've been on my own. Not alone, but certainly self-sufficient. I had no choice and young sisters to care for. At barely twenty, I became their parent. Did I know what I was doing? Fuck no, but that didn't matter. They were my responsibility. My only family. My reason to stay alive, to keep going, when giving up would have been an easier task.

How many times have I heard someone say *I can't imagine how hard that must have been for you*? Hard? No one has a damn clue. It wasn't about looking after my sisters' needs. Providing food, shelter, and clothing. It wasn't about keeping them healthy and safe, about teaching them to be decent human beings. All those things I'd do again and again. Every day of my life, if I had to.

Tough? Yes. But hard?

Hard was living the life I was born into. Constantly fearing for the fate of my baby sisters should something happen to me. That terror was ever-present and bone-chilling. It hung above my head like the Sword of Damocles. I couldn't shake the dread. What if I ended up in jail? Or dead? Asya and Sienna might be sent to foster care, or a Cosa Nostra Family member who'd use them for their own selfish needs. Both options were equally horrific. Both plagued me nonstop.

That fear didn't lessen until Ajello took over. It never fully went away, but I knew... Knew without a doubt that Salvatore Ajello would keep my sisters safe if there ever came a day I no longer could. It didn't mean I gave up the fight. Didn't mean that, as they grew older, I didn't do everything in my power to take care of them. Often smothering them in the process. Or so both girls recently told me.

Yeah, I get it. I'm far from perfect. But life shapes us into who we are. In my case, an asshole with a type A personality. I function on rules, drive, and ambition. I value structure and stability because they allow me to reach my goals. I want everything done right and quickly, and often can't trust others to get that done for me.

Not even when I'm halfway dying of fucking pneumonia.

So no, I don't *need* anyone to look after me. Especially not a spoiled wannabe princess whose middle name should have been Chaos because I never know how she's going to react or what she'll say next. And my foolish desire for her to actually care about my welfare goes against the very fabric of my being. Which, truthfully, is driving me batshit crazy.

I cross the driveway, heading toward my SUV. It's parked in its usual spot, perfectly aligned with the front door in a way that taps into my inescapable need for efficiency. As I approach, my phone starts ringing in my pocket, but my attention zeros in on my vehicle instead. I cock my head, trying to figure out what's wrong with this picture.

The Land Rover is looking a bit tilted in place, sort of like the ground is uneven. But it's not. So why—

Son. Of. A. Fucking. Bitch!

Both of the tires facing me are flat. Picking up my pace, I walk around the vehicle, confirming that, in fact, all four of the tires are. Crouching next to the driver-side front wheel, I take in the red-handled screwdriver sticking out of the rubber sidewall.

She didn't!

"Tara!" I yell, spinning around. My gaze collides with my wife's as she casually leans against the jamb of the front entrance.

"I told you," she hollers back. "You're not going anywhere today, DeVille!"

That's it! I sprint across the driveway, straight to the house. Tara lets out a high-pitched squeal and dashes inside, slamming the door shut behind her. I reach it just in time to hear the deadbolt turn, locking me out.

"I'm gonna wring your neck!" I slam my fist on the wooden surface.

"All I'm trying to do is make sure you follow the doctor's orders." Her voice sounds muffled behind the barrier. "Chill out. I already made the arrangements for a tow truck. It will be here later today. And you'll get your SUV with brand-new tires back tomorrow, just in time for Ilaria's directive for bed rest to come to an end."

My forehead furrows. I thought she went stabby just for the sake of riling me up. "You mean, you couldn't think of another way to keep me in bed besides slashing my tires?"

"I… guess."

Squeezing my temples, I shake my head. A grin is fighting to come out, distorting my face despite my efforts to hold it at bay. "Tara… I own other cars. But even if I didn't, how do you think our security guys get to work?"

"I don't know. Bus?"

"Their cars are parked right beside the gatehouse."

"Oh," she sighs.

She sounds so defeated and glum, that I can't keep it together anymore. I stuff my fist into my mouth to keep my laugh from escaping.

"Yes. *Oh*," I snort, fighting to sound even-keeled. "Open the door."

"No, I don't think I should."

"Please."

Several beats pass in silence before I hear the unmistakable click of the lock. The door cracks open, but barely five inches.

"What?" Her freckled face peeks through the gap.

I lean down until our eyes are level and touch the tip of my nose to hers. "Don't fuck with the Land Rover again, Tara. You got me?"

"Don't expect me to nurse you back to health when your pneumonia returns. Got *that*, darling?"

"As if you would."

"Of course I wouldn't. Not even for an extra million in the bank."

Just as I thought.

My eyes drop to her lips, but the phone in my pocket starts ringing again. It's the fourth time in the last handful of minutes. I take it out and bring it to my ear. "What is it?"

"You need to get to the Brooklyn construction site," Nino says, sounding grave. "Like right fucking now."

"I'm on my way." I glance at my wife, who's staring at me with squinted eyes through the narrow gap. "I should be home for dinner, and I'll pick something up for us. Tell Greta to stay out of the kitchen from now on. Her cooking is even worse than I remembered."

Instead of a response, the door slams shut in my face.

 Tara

"That's for the booth at the far end." Jelena sets two White Russians on my serving tray. "So hey, not that I'm not happy to see ya, but how come you're here right now?"

I shrug in response.

"Did your sexy hubby finally let you out of the bedroom for a breath of fresh air? Wouldn't surprise me, if that's what actually happened." Leaning over the bar, she grins and wiggles her eyebrows at me. "Is it true that Italians are beasts in bed?"

"Definitely." Grabbing the tray laden with drinks, I quickly turn around and head across the dance floor.

I'm glad to be back at Naos. It's not that I suddenly enjoy waiting tables, but it's great to once again be on familiar ground. I need to feel in control of my own life, for at least a few short hours.

As usual at this early hour, just after four on a Sunday afternoon, most of the tables and booths are occupied, but the dance floor remains vacant. For most of the patrons present, this time is all about business, not about having a little fun. But things will pick up later. Around midnight, this place will be rocking, especially since Drago loosened some of the exclusive club rules over the last couple of months after the success of the biker bash. Now, on slower nights like Thursdays and Sundays, he lets Naos transform into a more conventional nightclub. A hotspot for the criminal underworld's young and restless, who appreciate the safe haven offered by my brother's club. Here, they can unwind or engage in executive dealings without fearing for their lives. Without having to capitulate or risk bloody engagements while meeting with rivals on hostile grounds.

Naos is a neutral territory where access is open to a variety of underground organizations in New York. As long as they follow Drago's rules, that is. And can afford the steep price tag. The safeguards that come with Naos's unique status aren't cheap, and Drago has made an enormous amount of money by offering this little sanctuary service. Security is always tight. At any given time, at least fifteen heavily armed men are scattered throughout the venue, making sure the neutrality of the place is maintained. That leaves everyone free to conduct their business, be it a truce between competing gangs or drug deals worth millions. Drago's protection ensures no throats get cut. And for the younger crowd, they can have a night on the town and not worry about a run-in with someone who might have a grudge against their side.

Crossing paths with one of the other serving girls, I head toward the furthest booth where two men seem to be engaged in a deep discussion. One, in a black suit, is sitting with his back to me. But the other, the guy facing me, I recognize right away. Although I don't know his affiliation, I've seen him around here plenty of times. It's also not hard to guess what type of business he's involved in. He's unassuming-looking, with tattoos peeking out from the collar of his simple white dress shirt. However, the files filled with headshots of people who often end up on the morning news are kind of a dead giveaway about his profession. In fact, he's got one with a mark in front of him now.

"Your drinks, gentlemen." I smile and set the cocktail glasses next to the yellow folder laid out on the low table. I don't mean to, but I catch a look at what's inside. A photograph of a man who seems familiar, even though I can't quite place where I might have seen him before.

"Mrs. DeVille," the suit-clad man says beside me. "What a pleasant surprise."

I look over, gaping at the owner of that cultured voice. "Mr. Ruffo. Didn't expect to see you here. Small world."

"Indeed. How are you? I'm glad to see you unharmed in the wake of the incident after our dinner meeting. Please pass along my sincere apologies to your husband."

My eyebrows furrow in confusion. "What do you mean?"

"The attack on your vehicle. I'm afraid it may have been meant for me."

"Oh. That's... I'm not sure what to say. I hope that sort of thing doesn't happen to you too often. People trying to kill you, I mean."

A smile spreads across his lips, but it doesn't appear the least bit genuine. "Of course not."

Yeah, sure. Especially considering what he's into. My gaze darts to the folder once again, but the photo of whom I assume is the target is no longer in view.

"So... I hope you both enjoy the rest of your day. If you need anything else, just wave," I chirp, quickly retreating to the bar.

This just proves it. People are never what they seem. Upon meeting him, I was completely certain that Adriano Ruffo was exactly who he presented himself to be. A gracious, sophisticated businessman with unfortunate ties to the Boston Cosa Nostra. I figured he got mixed up with them by chance, perhaps through a family connection. But here he is. Hiring a hitman to take out someone.

"Don't go into the back room," Jelena says as she approaches, carrying a full tray of drinks. "Some idiot pulled a knife, so our boys are reminding him of the house rules. It might take them a while to teach him the lesson. The guy had to be dumber than a post if he thought he'd get away with that shit."

I shrug. "Someone else will need to be on mop duty. I'm off in less than an hour, and I'm wearing my favorite pair of heels."

I lift the counter flap, slipping behind the bar. Although I'm still in the middle of all the hustle and bustle, crouching down by the cubby where I left my phone allows me a minute of peace. Sienna texted me, pretty much saying that Arturo and I are expected over for dinner tonight. *Soooo* not happening. I send a quick message back to her, letting her know I picked up an evening shift at Naos.

The less thrilling "fun fact" is the seventeen missed calls from my dearest husband. I bet he got home early and was pissed to discover that his trained wife-slash-pet wasn't there.

He should consider himself lucky. If I were home, I would likely be tempted to sprinkle rat poison on his food. While his sick ass was lying in bed, I've been going through hell and doing my damnedest not to have a full-blown panic attack. Each time I entered that kitchen and turned on the stove to make His Dickbag Highness food, I wasn't sure if I'd make it out. But I did it. And for what? For him to turn around and tell me his meals sucked?

Yeah, I know! I'm not the best cook, but I had no choice in the matter. Between me sending Greta and the other staff away and his orders not to allow food deliveries, I had to do something to feed the ungrateful germ-infested jackass! He's so fucking oblivious, too. He didn't even realize that it was just the two of us in the house since Monday. That it was I, not Greta, who took care of him. So, yeah... I couldn't slam that door in his face fast enough earlier today. I'm just thankful I managed to do it before he saw my tears.

I'm still hurt. And mad. Maybe I'll stay at Naos and do another shift so I don't have to go home and face him. I could even crash on the cot in the staff room tonight. My back is gonna kill me in the morning, but it would be better than the alternative. The one thing I won't allow myself anymore, though, is to feel concern for someone who obviously doesn't give a fuck about me. I won't ever let him hurt me again. Stupid bastard.

I swipe the screen, deleting every missed call notification. "Fuck you, Arturo DeVille."

Suddenly, the overhead lights go out, and the music dies.

What the—?

A resigned silence descends on the room. A few gasps sound here and there, but that's about it. The crowd here is not prone to falling into hysterics or raising alarms without good reason.

The emergency lighting along the baseboards comes to life.

"Everything is fine. Please stay calm." Jovan's voice echoes from somewhere to my right. "There may have been a short circuit in our electrical panel and—"

Automatic gunfire erupts in the air.

The mirrored wall and hundreds of liquor bottles above my head explode, unleashing a torrent of shards and liquid. I scream and cover my head with my arms.

Arturo

Six hours earlier

"I made the discovery when I arrived."

Taking off my sunglasses, I survey the scene of destruction before me. Even for a construction site, this place looks like an utter mess.

"Whoever hit us, did everything they could to not draw outside attention," Nino continues. "The exterior wall is intact, and I don't think there would have been much noise."

"How bad is it?"

"Bad. The generator power cables were cut, and most of the heavy machinery has been disabled. Hydraulic lines, circuit boards, distribution panels. You name it, they sabotaged it. Computers and other electronics in the site office were smashed to smithereens."

"Why didn't anyone report it sooner?"

"It's Sunday. The site has been shut down since about six on Friday night. We did have guards on duty. Both are dead."

I step over an electrical conduit that runs from the trailer serving as a mobile office. The container is located near the gateway, but well beyond the perimeter wall that's blocking access to the construction site. There's no sign of forced entry, and the door is unlocked. The smell of blood and stale food hits me as soon as I step inside the small space. The bodies of two security guards lie in puddles of blood. Both men have gaping holes in the middle of their foreheads. The message is clear. This was an execution-style hit. A bag from a local fast-food joint has been discarded a few feet over the threshold. Its contents are spilled across the floor, which explains the odor. The attacker likely gained entry by pretending to be a delivery guy.

"The shift changes at seven." Nino nods at the dead men. "If I didn't come today, we probably wouldn't have known about this until tonight."

"It's not a coincidence they picked the day the site is shut down. Killing our guys wasn't what they were after, but something else obviously was. This feels too precise, maybe even enough to require an insider's help. Any new hires?"

"I'll check."

"Do that. And send me the names." I approach a small conference table in the center of the trailer, glancing at the playing cards and a pile of chips scattered across its surface. "There were only two guards?"

"Yeah. I think so."

"There are three stacks of cards here, not two. So, who was the third player?" My eyes scan the room. There are boxes and filing cabinets crammed anywhere they'll fit. Extra chairs. A couple of desks with smashed computers and overturned phones. No third body. In the far corner, almost hidden by a fake ficus tree with a *Make Shit Happen* sign hanging off its branches, is a narrow door leading to the bathroom. "Have you checked in there?"

"No." Nino steps over one of the dead men's legs and opens the door. "Fuck."

"What you got?"

"Shot in the gut. Looks like—Arturo! He's got a pulse."

I reach into my jacket. "I'm calling Ilaria."

"Mr. DeVille?" Tony's eyes bug out at me at the sight of blood stains on my sleeves and shirt front. "Are you alright?"

"Peachy keen." I throw him the car keys. "Thanks for loaning me your car. It will need extensive detailing, especially the back seat. It's a bit of a mess. Have them put it on my account."

"Uh, sure. Oh! Your vehicle's back with new tires!" he calls after me.

I smile. My sweet little wife must be pretty disappointed about that.

As I step inside, the house seems unnaturally quiet. Other than the sounds Greta usually makes when she does the chores, it's been like that ever since Sienna moved out. Until this became Tara's home, too, that is.

I pause at the foot of the stairs, listening. No drill noises. None of the background music she likes to have on when she reads her smutty novels. Nothing. Not a peep. Maybe she's taking a nap? Even as that question rises in my mind, somehow I just know my wife isn't here. It's like the charge in the air is different. The house suddenly seems… numb. And I find myself missing the chaotic vibe that always surrounds her.

She must have already gone over to Drago's for dinner. My sister all but demanded our presence tonight. *Family dinner. The four of us. Get here as soon as possible.* She's such a little brat.

I grab my phone and hit Tara's number. The line rings once and then disconnects. Hopefully, she's just complaining to Sienna about how much it sucks to live with me or to deal with her "babysitters," as she calls the security guys I've assigned to her. But even if the two of them are making voodoo dolls or throwing darts at a picture of my face, I don't really care. I'm just thankful Tara understands we're on high alert and didn't fight me too much about having a protective detail.

Today's incident has me even more on edge, and I'd rather my wife were safe and sound at home right now. Do I wish she had waited for me instead of heading to her brother's on her own? Hell yeah, I do. I guess I'll just have to go fetch her as soon as I clean up. Unbuttoning my shirt along the way, I head up the stairs.

The man we found wounded in the bathroom ended up being another security guard. He survived the trip to our private hospital and is expected to pull through following his three-hour surgery. Ilaria seemed optimistic about his chances when I talked to her after she finished up in the OR. He hasn't yet regained consciousness, though, so I left Nino to wait around and question him as soon as he wakes up.

I need answers, and fast. And although I have my suspicions about who is behind the attack, I need to be completely sure before

I take action. Going after another criminal syndicate without proof would be foolish. But if I'm right, it means we're already at war and our retaliatory measures will be well justified.

Before jumping into the shower, I try calling Tara again. Still no answer. At this point, I'm getting annoyed. I'm sure she's not picking up on purpose. I should have included phone etiquette in the list of rules in our prenup. Live and learn, I guess.

As I'm putting on a fresh shirt after washing off the day's grime, my phone starts ringing. With my mind entirely on my wife and her irritating habit of needling me, I hit the green button then the speaker icon without checking the caller ID. "Ignoring my calls, *gattina*?"

Someone clears their throat. "The guard just woke up."

Disappointment hits like a punch to the gut. I wasn't expecting Nino. Closing my eyes, I try to get my head back in the game.

"Did you get anything out of him?"

"Not yet. He's still groggy. Might be another hour before he's coherent enough."

"Okay. I'll head back to the hospital in a few. If he tells you something before I get there, call me."

I grab my holster and jacket off the bed, then dial Tara once more on my way downstairs. The damn line rings and rings until her voicemail picks up. I call Sienna instead.

"Does my wife intend to answer my calls anytime in the near future?"

"I wouldn't know, Arturo. But if you take this tone with her, she should block you."

"Yeah, yeah. Put her on."

"Can't do that, sorry."

"Damn it, Sienna. I need to speak with her."

"What you need is to stop acting like an idiot and—" Her muted shriek cuts off whatever she was going to say next, and then she giggles in the background. "Stop it, Drago! I'm on the phone with Arturo."

"Hang up." That's Popov's gruff voice. "Unless you want your brother to hear your moans as I feast on your pretty pussy. For the record," he hollers, entirely for my benefit, "I'm totally okay with that, jackass."

Jesus! "Sienna! Is Tara there?" I yell, heading to my Land Rover.

"No, Arturo," she answers, returning to the line. "I'm afraid you'll need to look for your wife elsewhere. And I wouldn't be at all surprised if she decided to ditch your cranky ass. Bye."

Fuck. I get behind the wheel of my SUV and call Tara again while backing out. No answer. Where is that woman?

"Tony!" I shout when I reach the guardhouse at the gate. "Have you seen my wife?"

"She stormed out of here about an hour ago and got into a waiting Uber. I have no idea where she went. She mentioned that you pulled her security detail—"

"The fuck? I did no such thing! You note the plate on the car?"

"Umm… no. It parked a ways down and on the other side of the street."

Something she arranged on purpose, I'm certain. "I'm gonna head out and see if I can find her. Call me immediately if she gets back."

What if she went to meet with the silver-spooned oil brat? Curtis or Conan or whatever. Maybe the little shit decided to ignore my warning and reached out to my wife despite my threat? Or maybe Tara has just had enough, and as Sienna suggested, chose to leave me? Ditching her guards could certainly point to that.

The ringing of my phone interrupts my turbulent thoughts as

I'm flying down the road. For a split second, I hope it's my wife, but it's only Nino.

"What?"

"The guy started talking. It was the Greeks." That confirms what I already suspected.

"A raid on a mostly unmanned site because Katrakis is still pissed over losing the land? That's kinda pathetic, to be honest. If this property is so important to him, I would have expected the old fart to do something more drastic than fucking up our construction equipment."

"This was nothing but a prelude to the main act. Katrakis holds another party responsible for their loss and our gain, apparently," Nino says in a grim tone. "They are going after Drago."

"What?"

"Our guy overheard those fuckers flapping their gums while they were smashing up the office. They didn't know he was there at first cause he was in the john taking a piss prior to the attack. Seems that Katrakis believes Drago betrayed their trust by offloading the property deed to us before they got a chance to repay him."

That sneaky bastard. I should have guessed he was behind the offshore company that sold us the land. If my sister wasn't married to that dick, I'd enjoy letting Katrakis fuck him over real good.

"Have you let Drago know?" I ask.

"Just before I called you."

My phone beeps with another incoming call, and I glance at the screen to see that Sienna is trying to reach me. Quickly disconnecting with Nino, I switch lines.

"Sienna! Are you alright?"

"We're fine." Her slightly hysterical voice is nearly drowned out by the plethora of background noise. "Drago just put the house on lockdown in case of an attack here. But you need to get to Naos!"

"I have more important things to deal with right now than checking up on your husband's joint. And I'm sure his people are more than capable—"

"Tara is there, you idiot!" she shouts.

My heart stops beating. "What?"

"She just texted me a few minutes ago. I tried calling the club, but couldn't get ahold of anyone. No one is answering their phone!"

The tires screech as I do a one-eighty, hitting the gas and flying down the road like a bat out of hell.

CHAPTER
Twenty-Two

Tara

I N NORMAL PLACES LIKE BARS AND RESTAURANTS, WHEN thugs barge in with guns blazing, hysterical screams usually follow. Not at Naos, though. Other than pained gasps and quiet curses when someone gets hit, the rapid *rat-a-tat* and *bang bang* of gunfire are the only sounds.

"When are they going to turn the damn power back on?" Jelena grumbles beside me as she opens the hidden trapdoor in the floorboards. "What if we hit one of ours by mistake? Sig or Beretta?"

"Beretta, please. It'll take a few minutes to get the generator up and running." I grip the gun she holds out for me, then toss the other to Iliya, who's crouching a few feet to my left.

"You two don't move from here until this is over," Iliya barks as he catches the Sig. "Drago will have my hide if something happens to you. You hear me, Tara?"

"Got it," I lie.

There are only two emergency pod lights behind the bar, built in so close to the floor that I need to lean way down to be able to check the magazine. It's hard to know how many attackers there are because the raging firefight is all around us. It's like everyone present is shooting at the same time. If this were later at night, all firearms would have been securely stowed away upon entry into the club, but rules allow Naos patrons to keep their guns on them between opening hours and around nine at night.

"Is there a point to all this shooting when no one can see shit?" A few more bottles explode above me; glass and liquor rain down on my head. The stench of multiple spirits is more than pungent, irritating my eyes and nose. I press myself flatter to the back bar counter and cock my gun while my thigh muscles scream in protest. Crouching in heels is a real bitch, especially while trying not to slip in the puddle of spilled alcohol.

The overhead lights flicker to life just as a man armed with an Uzi leans over the bar counter right above Jelena. I react without a second thought, snapping my arm upward and shooting him in the head.

Jelena raises her shapely eyebrow. "That was fast. Are you sure he wasn't one of ours?"

"He's wearing a brown bandanna around his forehead."

My brother insists on a very strict dress code at Naos. No way anyone wearing a casual outfit, even as gang colors, would have been let inside.

Avoiding shattered bottles and shards of glass, I duckwalk to the edge of the bar and peek out into the main space. The booth dividers, which provide privacy but are actually bulletproof frosted glass obstacles that were installed specifically in case something like this happens, are still intact. Drago is adamant about having armored furniture around. Most of the guests and club staff have taken cover behind these barriers and are shooting in the direction of the main entrance.

One of the overhead speakers has crashed to the floor, breaking the stone tiles into a billion little pieces. Fuck, my brother is *soooo* going to lose his shit over that. He imported those tiles from Spain.

As far as I can see, there's only one casualty from *our* side. The body of the guy I suspect was a hitman is sprawled near the booth where he was seated. Adriano Ruffo is down on one knee next to him, firing at the attackers from a big-ass gun in a disturbingly casual manner.

The gang members, though, haven't fared as well. Three dead next to the entrance and another a little further inside, close to the edge of the dance floor. Only one appears to still be alive, hidden by a stone pillar a few feet away from the main doors. He's shooting randomly into the interior, trying to hit anyone in his sights. That means there are six assailants, including the man I offed just now. A rather small force for a raid of this kind. Perhaps they didn't expect much resistance?

"Tara!" Jelena grabs the hem of my shirt, yanking me backward. "There are more coming from the back!"

Shit. Keeping low and pointing my gun ahead, I follow Jelena to the other end of the bar where Iliya is slumped on the floor, pressing a hand to his bleeding side.

"Use this." I pass him a bar towel I grabbed from a cubby and crane my neck, taking a look through the narrow gap below the liquor shelves and just above the back bar counter. It serves as quick access to extra supplies lined up on the ledge that runs along the other side of the mirrored wall.

The club's back entrance is located in the storage room right behind that wall, tucked between the beer crates stacked on either side. Five more gang dudes in ratty jeans and oversized sweatshirts are pouring through the doorway. With how our bar is set up, there's no way for anyone up front to see the incoming hostiles. Jelena and I are the only ones aware of the new threat, and she's currently busy trying to stop Iliya from bleeding out. What are my chances of shooting all five thugs before they can kill me? Pretty slim, but I don't have a choice but to try. They're less than ten feet from us anyway.

I duck back down and take a deep breath. The wet cabinetry and my own sweat are starting to make me feel sticky. Here goes nothing. Gripping the gun in my hand, I spring up, aiming at the back door through the gap between two Johnnie Walker bottles.

The two guys closest to the entrance drop to the ground simultaneously.

What?

I blink, and two more collapse face down on the floor.

The last would-be attacker spins around just as another gunshot explodes through the air. The man's legs fold under him, and he slumps over, revealing a backlit figure in a black suit standing at the threshold. His arms bent at his sides; a gun at the ready in each hand.

I lower my weapon, staring at my husband, while Arturo steps over the dead guy and heads my way.

The shooting has stopped in the main part of the club. In the sudden stillness, the heavy fall of his soles on the tiled floor echoes like thunder in my ears. He slips his weapons into their holsters as his gaze fixes on me.

I follow him with my eyes until he reaches the edge of the dividing wall and then emerges in full view at the end of the bar counter. A couple more steps, and he stands right in front of me.

"Having too much fun to answer my calls, Tara darling?"

"You could say that. How was your day?"

Quiet chatter erupts from the people behind me, and I realize that our exchange has drawn attention from everyone left inside. The weight of dozens of eyes suddenly drops on me. I can feel them *all* watching us, and it's making me nervous as hell.

"Eventful." Arturo puts his hands in his pants pockets. "I was under the impression you understood we are still on high alert. So, what the fuck are you doing here? Without your guards, I might add."

"Naos is considered one of the safest places in town, DeVille."

"Oh really? My bad, then. I guess I just wasted a dozen goons to get to you for no goddamned good reason since you were, obviously, PERFECTLY SAFE! WHAT THE ACTUAL FUCK IS WRONG WITH YOU?"

"Don't yell at me, DeVille!" Something wet slides into the corner of my eye, and I quickly wipe it away while trying to keep my composure in front of this infuriating man. "I have a nearly full magazine in my Beretta, and I sure as hell know how to—"

"Is that BLOOD?"

I look at my hand. There's a red stain across my knuckles. I must have got nicked by a glass fragment and didn't notice with all the shit going down. Whatever. "Do not change the subj—"

His fingers seize my chin, tilting my head to the side. "Tara." A low rumbling growl leaves his throat.

"I'm fine." I brush his hand away. "Will you stop interrupting me? You're making a scene, by the way. And we both know how much you enjoy doing that in public. This place is a mess, and I need to—DeVille! Put me down!"

"No," he grunts as he carries me toward the storage room. "We're going home to have our scene in private."

"Are you nuts? The police are probably on their way, and Iliya needs medical care. I have to—"

"You are not a lawyer. Nor a doctor. What you are, is my wife. And currently, you're bleeding."

"It's just a fucking scratch, Arturo!"

"Mm-hmm. And that's definitely a conditioned reflex."

"What?"

He walks into the storage room and navigates around the racks of supplies near the back door. I spot two more dead bodies.

"You only say my name when one of us is bleeding." He kicks the door open, stepping outside. "Do you feel nauseated? Headache?"

"I don't have a damn concussion! Now, put me down."

"No."

"Why the hell not?"

He stops next to his SUV and pins me with a death stare. "Because, if I do, I might go back inside the club, where I'll kill every man in Drago's employ for failing to keep you safe. And unharmed. Because, my dearest wife, I'm still not over my panic that I wouldn't get here in time. That I'd arrive, and you'd be dead or dying. And now that I have my hands on you, there's no way I'm letting you go. But mostly, because if my hands were free, I might just strangle you myself for scaring me shitless."

My lips twitch upon hearing his words. "Let me get this straight. You were worried about me. Yet you want to kill me. Or, do you want to kill me because you were worried for me?"

"It's a toss-up," he growls and slams his mouth to mine.

Arturo

"I think"—I nip Tara's lower lip and kick the front door shut—"we need to check out your wound first."

"It's fine," she says while fumbling with the buckle of my belt.

Jesus fuck, I really hope that's true because I think I'll explode if I don't get my dick inside her *now*. I don't even know how I got us home in one piece. Or how we got from the vehicle into the house and didn't just end up fucking on the driveway. My jacket was lost shortly after we exited the SUV, and I haven't the slightest clue where the holster with my guns is. Probably out on the porch.

But this is as far as we're going. I'm sinking into her right here, right against the front door. Right this second. It's the only way for me to accept that she's safe and sound. To snap out of this dense fog of terror that took over my mind as soon as I pulled into Naos's parking lot. I feared I was too late. She was dead. I lost her. Proof. I need physical proof. I need her now, in my arms, to feel the life in her veins.

"Ah, but you're prone to being less than truthful." Seizing her chin with my fingers, I bring us face-to-face. "Let me see."

A small smirk breaks across her bruised lips. Tilting her head to the side, she gives me a better view of her temple, all while she continues to undo my pants. "So? Will I live?" she asks, taking out my rock-hard cock.

I try to focus on her cut. Nearly goddamn impossible with her hand stroking my length. Heaven. Her touch is pure heaven. The wound, though, does look superficial. The bleeding has already stopped. Nevertheless, the urge to strangle her for putting herself in harm's way doesn't leave me.

"You might, if I let you." I release her chin and pull up the hem of her miniskirt instead. "But your brother's security personnel definitely won't."

"You won't lay a hand on my friends, DeVille."

Instead of answering, I grab the band of her panties and rip them off in a single tug. She doesn't get to make such demands, especially since she could have been killed because of those people's incompetence. Grabbing her ass, I press her up against the door and bury myself in her wet heat with one powerful thrust.

She cries out, but I know I haven't hurt her. Her eyes roll back, and she mouths, *More.* Her loud moans fill our entranceway, echoing off the ceiling. The way she purrs all but makes me blow my load. Unacceptable. I'm nowhere near done with her.

Capturing her lips with mine, I slide my left palm along her spine, her neck, cradling the back of her head to protect it from the wooden surface. Then, I slowly drag my cock out only to slam inside her pussy again. Another loud moan erupts from my fierce bewitcher, reverberating through the room at levels approaching a scream. It nearly allows me to forget the roar of gunfire, and the endless cacophony of breaking glass and crashing debris that thundered in my ears as I shot my way into the interior of that damn club.

Slam.

Fearing I'd find her injured.

Slam.

Find her dead.

Slam. Slam. Slam.

Tara's fingers tunnel through my hair, her nails scraping the back of my head. It hurts, but this pain is good. A great reminder that she's here. She's alright. With me. My little hazard is okay.

"You're not leaving this house ever again," I growl while changing my angle, driving deeper into her welcoming warmth while my tongue invades her mouth just as fervently. "This door I'm fucking you against… It's the closest you'll be allowed to the outside world. I'll chain you to my bed if I have to, all to keep you from these disasters you draw to yourself like a magnet."

"You can try." The cunning witch smiles against my lips, just before chomping down on my tongue. Hard. Sending a jolt of electricity straight to my cock.

I withdraw, quickly, until only my tip remains sheathed inside her pussy. "Do not fuck with me, Tara."

"Why not?" She tightens her legs around my waist and wriggles her butt, trying to pull me closer. Her heels dig into my back as she attempts to force my cock deeper. When I don't move an inch, she slashes me with her frustrated stare; her hands slide down to my biceps, and nails dig into my skin through my shirt. "Fucking is the only thing that seems to work well between us, isn't it, Satan?"

I'm tempted to shake her and yell *You're wrong!* Sex isn't the only good thing between us. It's not the only thing I crave. But my dick wants to make me a liar. Whatever self-control I had remaining, cracks. Disintegrates as I get sucked in by her inescapable green gaze. Vaporizes under the force of her onslaught.

I squeeze her ass cheek and plunge my cock into her until I bottom out. "Do. Not. Call me that."

Her slick, tight pussy embraces me as it does each time, spasming around my length in a euphoric rhythm. Again, it's a battle for me to hold back, to continue rocking my hips and extend this moment. Wrapping her locks around my wrist, I fist her hair, tilting her head so I can consume that stubborn, snarky mouth of hers. I attack her lips with the same intensity as I slam into her pussy, claiming and punishing her all at once. Every moan that leaves her lips, every panting breath, I revel in each of those passionate sounds, thrusting harder and harder to wring more and more from her. We were made to be joined together. Our bodies fit so fucking perfectly.

This mind-blowing chemistry between us is so potent. My insatiable hunger for her makes me want to fuck her all the damn time. But that's not the only thing I want. It hasn't been for quite a while.

I want to watch as she does silly things like dismantle my coffee machine with a butter knife. Or as she drills useless holes in the drywall to add another bookshelf. Her crazy hair? Fuck, do I love it. Love seeing what insane updo she's going to coax it into. And all the absurd outfits she comes up with to surprise the shit out of me. Her teasing. Each of the times she tried to piss me off in the beginning... I want more of that. All of it.

For it's only now I understand the power of her spell. That unwavering tenacity of hers. I want to wake up every morning with her body draped over me. That was bliss. Absolute bliss. Having her sleep on top of me. That's what I want, every damn day. And if need be, I'd suffer unending pig roasts. Put up with obnoxious relatives. Drown in an ocean of unfamiliar food. If it meant she would stay.

Stay forever.

But she never would.

"Witch," I growl as I pick up my tempo.

Tara's moans grow into full-blown screams of ecstasy with every surge of my cock. Dear God! She is so beautiful. Flushed and unrestrained in my arms. Her entire body is shaking. Her nails sink like claws into my back. I've never seen a more magnificent sight than my wife teetering on the edge. Knowing that I brought her there.

"Has any man ever fucked you like this, made you choke on your own breath?" I demand. "Has anyone ever made you so wet that your cum runs down your legs to the floor? Have they?"

"No," she gasps out.

"And no one but me ever will. You might not like me, *gattina*, but know this. I'll cut off the dick of any man who dares to touch you. Or even simply comes close to you. You're mine."

Her nails dig into my shoulders, sending rivulets of blood sliding down my skin.

"Now, maybe. But not once our time is up."

"Now. Tomorrow. In a fucking year. A decade in the future. I don't give a shit! I'll make a eunuch out of any asshole who thinks he can have what belongs to me."

Adjusting my stance, I change our position, slanting her hips so I can reach even deeper inside. Closer. I want us much closer. More connected, even though it's impossible to be more physically close than we already are.

Her unrestrained cry breaks through the silence of the empty house. Rings off the walls as she oh so beautifully comes apart in my arms. I grit my teeth, urging myself not to let go, wanting to let her ride out her orgasm, wringing more of these sweet, sweet moans from her. Only after she starts coming down from her high do I submit to my own climax. Gripping that stubborn chin, I plunge inside my wife one more time and fuse my mouth to hers. She continues to tremble as I fill her with my seed. Mark her. Possess her. Claim her as mine. Revel in the pleasure that brings me.

She is *mine.*

Elation.

Mine.

Rapture.

Mine.

Bliss.

But only for a little while.

Rage. Despair. Agony.

With her silky mane fisted in my hand, I bury my face against her neck. Breathing in her essence. Soaking her in while I still have the chance.

I fought so hard against these feelings. Against my inextricable need for her. This fierce grip she has on me. I made it my mission to convince both of us that our union was a horrible match.

What a dumb, blind idiot I am!

While doing my best to make my wife despise me, I've managed to fall hopelessly in love with her.

CHAPTER
Twenty-Three

Tara

"**A**RTURO!" SIENNA'S SHRIEK CARRIES DOWN THE LINE. "Drago and I have both been trying to reach you and Tara for hours! I can't believe you'd let me worry—"

"It's me," I whisper into the phone. Leaning against the bathroom wall, I slide down until my naked ass hits the cold marble tiles.

"Tara? Well, how nice of you to call. Eventually! Drago has been going out of his mind, even though Jelena tried to reassure him that you were okay. He's been ready to storm Arturo's house for hours, and it took everything I had to keep him away. Why didn't you call us sooner?"

"Um… I'm not sure where my phone is. But I'm fine. We're both fine. Sorry for not reaching out right away. I was… busy."

"Busy? With what? What's more important than—"

"Busy being fucked senseless against the front door."

"Oh." There is a short pause. "Okay, well… In this case, you're forgiven."

"Thank you. How are things at Naos? Did anyone else get hurt?"

"It's a mess. There was one casualty among the customers; the rest are only flesh wounds. Aside from Iliya, but he'll be alright.

We're not changing the subject, though, chickie. Without going into too many details… because, ew, he's my brother… was it good?"

I close my eyes and sigh. "Sex with Arturo is always good. Better than good, actually. Sometimes, it feels like it's too good to be true."

"I knew it!" she shrieks with glee. "I told you you'd grow to like him! It's so great that we'll get to stay sisters-in-law on the double front. Drago is going to lose his shit, though, when he hears this. He keeps telling me you'll be dumping my brother any day now. I saw that video of Arturo going batty after you slashed his tires, and it was beyond funny—"

"What?" I whisper yell. "What video?"

"Oops. I shouldn't have said that."

"Sienna!"

"Well… My resourceful husband had Mirko hack into Arturo's security feed. Please don't be mad at him, he only did it to check up on you."

"Check up? WTF, he was spying—"

"Well, considering the circumstances, he was worried." Sienna's voice is barely audible. "You can't really blame him for it."

"What do you mean? What circumstances?"

"Um… Drago knows, Tara."

"Knows what?"

"That Arturo blackmailed you into marriage. He doesn't know the specifics, nothing beyond what Ajello told him. Which wasn't that much. Just that you and Arturo have an agreement, and that Drago should stay out of it."

"What?" My stomach drops to the floor. "Since when?"

"Just before your wedding."

I drop my face into my palm. Figures. I should've known there was something up with Drago. He was much too unconcerned after our engagement was announced.

"But that doesn't matter anymore, does it?" she continues in a light, chirpy tone. "With you two falling for each other, this is basically a real marriage now. Who would've guessed that Ajello's meddling would result in another love match?"

A love match. Yeah. I shake my head. What a half-baked idea.

"Nothing has changed, Sienna. Arturo and I are still trying to drive each other nuts, only now we end our arguments in bed."

"God, the race between you two to see who's more stubborn is a dead heat! Why won't you both stop acting foolishly and talk to each other? Just tell Arturo how you feel about him."

"I feel nothing toward him," I sniff, surly.

"Sure. Could have fooled me. If you feel nothing, you'd be sawing logs right now instead of crying in the middle of the night."

The phone case cracks in my hand from the force of my squeeze. "I refuse to feel anything for a man who is incapable of loving me back."

"Yeah, it doesn't work like that, girly. And for the record, Arturo is head over heels smitten with you."

"Mm-hmm. He has a weird way of showing it. I can really feel his love when he makes it absolutely clear how I'm the total opposite of what he considers a perfect partner. For crying out loud, he made me sign a prenup with clauses detailing how I'm allowed to dress! Does that sound like something a man who's *head over heels smitten* would do, Sienna?"

"When it comes to Arturo, yes. It's exactly what he would do," she sighs. "I know it's hard to understand, but that's just how he's wired. If the two of you would simply sit down and talk. Admit your feelings, then maybe—"

"I'm not confessing to that jerk that I'm in love with him!" My hand flies to my mouth, but it's too late to hold back the words. "Um... I gotta go. Bye."

Throwing the phone to the floor as if the fucking thing is poisonous, I scramble up and all but run out of the bathroom. Only to stop in my tracks, right there on the threshold.

My husband is sprawled face down on the bed, asleep with his right arm extended toward the empty space beside him. Next to him is the still-dented pillow I used when I lay motionless for nearly two hours, staring at nothing after we collapsed following our second round of hate fucking.

Hate fucking. Can I call it that anymore? Knowing I don't hate him?

How long can I continue to lie to myself?

How long will I pretend to believe it?

When I agreed to this stupid, stupid marriage, I thought I'd put my life on hold for a year, max. In the meantime, my Prince Charming… my knight in shining armor… and our happily ever after would be out there somewhere, waiting for me. The moment when I finally found him would simply be delayed, nothing more. But I'm afraid that's no longer true.

Whether I want it or not, I now know that I'll forever compare every other man to Arturo DeVille. And I'm fairly certain Satan wouldn't hold a candle to any of them. How could they not be better with all of his many faults? His idiotic devotion to silly traditions, like we're still in the nineteenth century, is truly ridiculous. It's also kind of funny, though, and I love calling him out on it every time. But… although he might be half-stuck in the past, his dedication to his convictions is actually endearing. And I'd be a hypocrite if I didn't admit that there's a place for chivalry in the modern world. I'd give him zero points for being gentlemanly, but I can't. Even though he brought me "funeral" flowers. And Arturo never hesitated to lend me his jacket, despite probably knowing that I was only messing with him.

Then, there's his grumpiness. When it comes to being moody, it'd be impossible to find anyone who scores higher on that scale than him. Still, even Arturo's cantankerous disposition is kinda sweet. He acts bossy, like an unmitigated tyrant, yet he does things no other overlord would do. I mean, the guy forbade Greta to make food for me and dictated that I couldn't even get delivery. But he keeps cooking all of my meals. Even knowing that I refuse to touch anything he prepares himself.

Still, he's all too quick to remind me that he's only with me because of his don's decree. As if without that frequent statement, I'd get the silly idea that he might actually like me. There's no need for him to go through all that effort; I'm completely clear on his feelings without him spelling them out for me. It's obvious since he never misses a chance to point out what a disaster I am. Although I must admit, he does it with that rather irritating smirk on his handsome face. And there's never any malice shining in his eyes, but something else... something different. It's almost as if he finds my constant screwups... amusing? I also have to give it to him—he's never brought up my shortcomings unless we've been alone.

And now, this latest. Arturo barged his way into an all-out firefight, killing who knows how many attackers, just to get to me. Who does that kind of shit? I mean, I know Drago would do it. He wouldn't even hesitate. But anyone else? Especially for me? I never imagined anyone but my knight doing something like that. And Satan DeVille's armor is certainly not *that* shiny. He probably did it just to show off.

Whatever. It doesn't change my feelings. Maybe I don't hate him, but I... will deny anything more.

With my footfalls muted by the thick carpet, I cross to the bed and climb in. As soon as the mattress dips, Arturo stirs and throws his trunk-like arm over me, pulling me into his side. I let him.

Actually, I snuggle closer until our bodies seem to fuse together, with my leg tangled with his and my cheek pressed to his shoulder.

Pure warm bliss.

Yup. A textbook example of a red flag. That's who Arturo DeVille is.

The man who ruined the fantasy in my life. Because I know... I fucking know! Once our year together is up, once my search for that perfect prince resumes... every man... every other man in the world, I'll somehow find lacking. There's no one out there who compares to Arturo DeVille.

It's dark. Perpetual midnight. No moon. No light of any kind.

Around me, a thunderous roaring. Whistling. Howling.

The wind.

I'm in the eye of a hurricane. Stuck inside a black abyss.

Far, far away, a drumbeat.

Heartbeat?

I know it's my only hope of finding a way out.

That sound becomes my beacon. Beckoning to me through the nothingness, through the relentless frenzy that I can feel, but cannot see. I follow the beat. It's important. It is everything to me.

I can't lose it. So I run. I don't know where I'm headed, but I need to get there before the drumming stops. Before that beat falls silent. I can't lose it.

Air rushes past me. Cold. Bitter. Biting. Blowing me off my feet.

I run, stumbling blindly, but I can't slow down. Can't falter. Can't quit.

Can't let anything stop me. I need to hurry, or I'll be lost.

Not because I fear the darkness, but because that rhythmic beating is my life.

Inside the void, inside the swirling vortex, I'm searching...

For the light of warm, green eyes.

My eyes snap open.

"Your snores are as loud as a freight train, DeVille," Tara mumbles beside me. Her hair has spilled across the pillow, strands tickling my nose.

I sigh. That was one weird as fuck dream. I lay my hand on the small of my wife's back and glide my palm upward along her spine. "I guess you should get used to it."

"Can I request a bonus?" She flips over, turning to face me. "A hundred grand for suffering due to hazardous sleep conditions that were not disclosed during our negotiations?"

I grit my teeth. She had to bring it up again. "Saving you from gun-wielding thugs wasn't in the contract either, yet I did it anyway."

"Please. Those idiots had more gusto than brains and had absolutely no training. We probably would have managed just fine without you."

"Yeah, sure." I gently sweep the hair off her forehead to have a better look at the cut she received.

"Were you really worried? At the club. You said you were scared for me."

A chill races down my spine. Saying that I was scared is putting it mildly. I was fucking terrified.

"Of course I was. Can you imagine the depth of the shit the Family would be in if something happened to you on my watch? Drago would have gone ballistic."

"I was at my brother's club when the attack happened. If anyone was going to be blamed, it would have been him."

Damn right, he'd be to blame! And is, actually. Something I won't forget anytime soon. But I can't admit that to her.

"You're my wife, and therefore, my responsibility. Having said that, from this point on, you won't leave our property unless your entire security detail and I am with you."

Anger flashes in her eyes. "You can't just lock me up!"

I can. And I will. I refuse to ever go through the kind of horrid shit I went through last night again. "You should put something on that cut."

"Don't change the fricking subject again!"

"It's not up for discussion, Tara. I'm willing to overlook the fact that you violated the terms of our agreement by working at your brother's club if you assure me that it won't happen again."

"Both you and your agreement can go to hell," she sneers and leaps out of bed.

My eyes track her as she rushes toward the door connecting our bedrooms, picking up her clothes from the floor along the way. She stops at the threshold and glares at me over her shoulder.

"By the way, what I agreed to is that I wouldn't *work* at the club." An impish smile breaks across her face. "Work implies payment for services rendered. Since I was simply helping out without the expectation of monetary compensation, there was no violation of the terms on my part. And there's nothing in that document that forbids me from doing it again. You really need to be more cognizant of the shit you sign, DeVille."

The door slides closed in my awestruck face.

I'm fuming the entire time I'm in the shower and while I get dressed for work. It's absolutely unthinkable that she'd risk her safety just to spite me! She's so damn stubborn! The fear that gripped me when I had no idea whether she was alive, hurt, or dead is still playing havoc with my head. The worst-case scenarios of my wife's body peppered with bullets or her being snatched away to God-only-knows-where are flashing through my mind, and there's nothing I can do to stop the crushing horror show. My guts twist, and the remnants of my last meal threaten to make a reappearance, sending me to double over at the thought of what could have happened if I'd been too late.

"Greta!" I holler as I hurry down the stairs while shrugging into my jacket.

"Yes, Mr. DeVille?" she calls back from the kitchen.

"I won't be back until late tonight, so consider your ban on cooking for my wife lifted. Could you please fix her something for lunch?"

She peeks around the corner. "Of course. Anything in particular?"

"Just see what she wants. But maybe forgo another soup. I'm sure she's sick and tired of those after a full week of eating them. By the way, thank you for going out of your way and cooking them for me. They were... quite nourishing."

"Oh no, that wasn't me. Did you like how the cream of potato turned out? Mrs. DeVille had a bit of trouble with it."

I jerk to a halt halfway to the front door. "You didn't make the soups while I was sick?"

"No, that was your wife. She was worried about you being contagious, so she gave me a week off and didn't let anyone else inside the house." She resumes wiping the countertop and then exhales a heavy sigh. "Poor thing. She was so nervous. Called me each time she thought the stove made a strange noise. Or whenever the smell of gas lingered in the kitchen longer than she expected it would. You might want to consider replacing it with an electric range, Mr. DeVille. This one must be a very painful reminder of what happened to her dear sister."

"Her sister died in a bomb blast."

"Actually, no. Mrs. DeVille said it was in the house fire that followed after the gas to their stove blew up. Honestly, if I were her, I'd probably never be able to go near another gas appliance or any kind of flame. But that girl—"

I don't hear what else Greta says. Instead, I take off sprinting up the stairs. Ignoring the ringing phone in my pocket. Not caring that it's probably the don on the line. What the fuck? Why didn't she tell me? I'm in front of her door in no time.

"Tara."

Knock. Knock.

"I'm sleeping!" An agitated, terse reply. "Go away."

I sigh, leaning my forehead against the white door. "Why did you lie? Why did you let me believe that it was Greta who was preparing my meals? And why... why the fuck didn't you just tell me about your issue with the stove?"

Her footsteps echo as she approaches the door and then opens it a crack. "I didn't lie, DeVille. You simply assumed. Just as you assumed many other things about me."

"I'm sorry, *gattina*. I... I thought you hated my guts."

"Save your apologies. Especially since, as you so eloquently implied, the food sucked a big one. I hope that, at least, the notes I left for you on that contract didn't disappoint you as much."

"Those were... amazing. But I figured it was Ginger who made them, not you."

"Hmm. Well... Perhaps, next time, *she* could nurse you while you run an insane fever, force-feed you meds, and drag your heavy ass into a cold shower to bring it down."

The door slams shut in my face for the second time today.

I stare at the slab of the door, at a loss for words, while a myriad of emotions rage inside me. Suffocating me. It wasn't a hallucination. All those flashes that I thought were a product of my fever were real. She was there the whole time. Jesus fuck, she could have gotten seriously sick because of me, all while I've been spewing shit at her like a stupid asshole.

And the gas stove... Fuck! I never even bothered to figure out the reason behind her reticence to cook. I simply assumed it was one of her bratty impulses. I never thought... Shit. She's been making me food for days. Dear God, my little hazard must have been scared out of her mind, and yet... she pushed past it. For me. For the ungrateful fucknut that I am.

Closing my eyes, I lean my forehead on the wooden surface. My palms, too, like I can shove the stupid thing away. Remove the damn barier between us. But it's not the door that's separating us. It's my idiotic behavior. From the very beginning of... us.

"Tara," I rasp.

"Leave me alone!" The words, muffled and a little broken, flow through the solid wood standing in my way. "And answer that bloody phone! It's annoying."

"Are you listening to me, Arturo?"

I drag my gaze up from my hands and look at Nino. We've spent the last hour in Ajello's office, briefing the don on our next steps for dealing with the Greek Syndicate. When Ajello's phone rang, and he got up and headed to the far corner to speak with his wife, my mind again drifted to the scene between me and Tara earlier. That's the only thing I seem to be capable of thinking of since leaving home.

"Not really." I shrug. My skin is crawling with the need to get home. To my Tara. I'm not sure I give a fuck about stategizing or generally doing my job right the fuck now.

"I said, it sucks that we can't simply kill the old Katrakis," Nino grumbles from the other side of the conference desk. "Politics, even Mafia politics, are such a pain in the ass."

I grunt. The two dead security guys at our Brooklyn construction site were Regular Joes, temps from a locally hired private security firm. A firm we've been looking at recruiting into our ranks. The deal isn't done yet, so we can't claim that it was our men who were killed. There's also ambiguity in terms of Katrakis's motive. Without any solid proof that it was a direct attack on our Family, we can't assert justifiable retaliation against the Greeks.

Navigating the criminal underbelly of the world is a tricky business. With so many players jam-packed into close quarters, one wrong move could seriously impact whether you live long enough to enjoy that elbow room you managed to carve out for yourself. Every action needs to be weighed against every possible outcome to ensure it won't endanger the Family's prosperity. I know that, too. And I've never had a problem with it. Until today.

"I'm going to crush that motherfucker's spine," I growl. The fear of what could have happened to Tara is still sitting like a boulder in my stomach. Just thinking about how close I came to losing her is driving me insane. "I'll be sure to do it one vertebra at a time. And then I'll hunt down the remnants of the Vipers gang and do the same to each man for going along with the attack on Naos."

"You know we can't get into it with them, Arturo. Or retaliate against Katrakis."

Yeah, I do. As it turns out, the Vipers owe quite a bit to the Greeks. Money that they got on loan to pay for their shipment of coke. Until this morning, we were unaware of that connection. Still, even knowing that Katrakis was pulling their strings, we're up against a code that allows the underworld to coexist without blowing itself to kingdom come. It dictates that only the wronged party may retaliate. Since it was the Serbian establishment that was assailed, only Drago can take action against the gang or the Greeks. Even though the Serb is our business partner, in this matter, Cosa Nostra's hands are tied.

"I don't fucking care."

"It's a pleasure to see you in such a great mood on a beautiful sunny day like today," Nino snickers. "Married life obviously agrees with you."

I raise an eyebrow. "Yeah? You want me to show you how overwhelmingly happy I am by giving you another split lip?"

"Oh, come on. It can't be that bad."

Yes, it can. The jury is still out on whether my ass wants to be home right now so I can strangle my wife for her audacity, or so I can fuck her senseless. "I told Tara, in no uncertain terms, that until this situation is resolved, she is not allowed to leave the property unless I'm with her. I wasn't gone five minutes before my security guy called to let me know that she tried to sneak out through the gate."

"You were no doubt tactful and very courteous when you informed her of that requirement." Nino's smirk widens as he crosses his arms behind his head. "And you surely assured her that you care for her deeply and that you're only worried for her safety. Right?"

"No." In fact, I did everything to make it sound as if I was only trying to avoid potential trouble between Cosa Nostra and the Serbs that would spring up should anything happen to her.

"Why not?"

"It's none of your business, Nino."

"You two need serious couples therapy, my friend."

I pinch the bridge of my nose. Yeah, I'm afraid no amount of relationship counseling will be enough to fix how badly I fucked up. Even if I ignore my pride and confess the truth... that I'm desperately in love with her, it wouldn't do any good. The woman absolutely detests me. And what would I tell her, really? *Forgive me for being a dumb fuck. I did what I did because I wanted to push you away. Because I couldn't stop myself from falling for you, and I didn't know how to deal with that.* Yeah, that'll certainly set everything right.

How do I make her understand the reason for my dumbass-edness? That, for years I've associated love with pain. With loss. Losing someone you love is the fate of everyone in this world, but when that love is ripped away from you in the most brutal fashion, it leaves a scar so deep, so jagged that it never heals. I lost my parents. Almost lost both my sisters, which opened that wound all over again. The last thing I ever wanted was to allow myself to love my wife. And then to lose her, too. That would destroy me. Decimate me completely. Annihilate my soul.

Tara's appearance in my life was a knockout punch I never saw coming. From the moment we met, I was a goner. For her. But I couldn't admit it. Couldn't accept it. Couldn't face the possibility of losing her. Deep down, I knew I would never survive it. So I've said and done horrible things to the woman I love to prevent my own destruction. To avoid love at all costs.

"Arturo." Ajello's voice booms across the room and startles me. "When was the last time you heard from Riggo?"

I look up, meeting his steely gaze. He's still on the phone.

"I'm... not sure." My forehead furrows as I try to remember. "Two, maybe three days ago. He was driving me nuts, wanting more responsibility. So I sent him over to Pietro's crew. Figured he could lend a hand while they tail Katrakis. Pietro sent me a text, though, saying he had plenty of people on it already. So I assumed he found another job for the kid. Why?"

"His sister told Milene that she hasn't been able to reach him."

"That's strange. The boy can be annoying as fuck, but he's always been reliable." I turn to Nino. "Has the surveillance team checked in?"

"Yeah, but as far as I know Riggo wasn't with them. Would he be dumb enough to try tailing Katrakis on his own?"

I groan. That definitely sounds like something Riggo might do. "Can you ask one of your boys to check the GPS locator on his car?"

"I can do it myself, from here."

Ajello nods and goes back to his phone call while Nino flips open his laptop. The rapid tapping of his fingers on the keyboard provides a subtle soundtrack to the boss's occasional groans. He's probably hearing another anecdote about Milene's demon cat. Ajello is about due for his weekly threat to "gut that scrawny little shit." No matter how much he grumbles, though, he ends up capitulating to his wife and her ever-growing collection of pets.

"Fuck." Nino's curse echoes through the room.

"What is it?"

"The main tag in Riggo's car has been disabled, so I ran the search through the secondary GPS. I had it installed as a failsafe on all vehicles used by our greenhorns." He turns the laptop around. "Check out the location of the pin."

I grab the laptop and pull it closer. On the screen, the map shows the red marker over a place in Queens, just outside the airport.

"A self-storage complex." I glance up. "One that belongs to the Greeks."

CHAPTER Twenty-four

 Arturo

"**H**AVE YOU HEARD BACK FROM OUR SOURCE AT THE precinct?" I ask as I check my guns.

"Yup." Nino nods as he makes a right turn. "No John Does matching Riggo's description have turned up in the past seventy-two hours. So, there's a chance the boy is still alive."

My jaw muscles clench. That chance is slim at best. But whether Riggo is alive or not, Katrakis is a dead man. He signed his own death warrant the instant he laid a hand on a Cosa Nostra member. Now, I don't even need to worry about pissing off Ajello by going after the Greek *stronzo*. Breaking his spine will be entirely justified.

We round another corner and turn into the parking lot of a local shipping and distribution company. There's a hive of activity, with plenty of delivery trucks constantly on the move. That should prove handy for masking our approach. And we can get close to Katrakis's building, which backs up to the shipping company's warehouse. Thank fuck for Nino's maniacal attention when it comes to security protocols. If he didn't have that secondary tracker installed on Riggo's car, it would have taken us much longer to narrow down this location.

"I still think we should wait for nightfall." Nino pulls the car to a stop. "Going in guns blazing at this hour is too risky. Too many eyes around, and we don't know how many guys Katrakis has inside."

"We've already lost too much time gathering our men. And it'll be dark soon enough. Besides, all these trucks give us plenty of cover, and the traffic noise from the Belt and the airport should drown out any gunshots."

Six more vehicles have been tucked in among the parked semis by the time I step out of the car. The sound of multiple car doors being shut gets drowned out by the cacophonous activity in the distance. I scrutinize the determined faces of nearly two dozen of our heavily armed men. If the full force of the Greek Syndicate is inside the storage complex, we'll be seriously outgunned. But that doesn't matter. We've been doing this for a long time.

"Remember, Katrakis is mine."

The men nod in understanding. Prior to coming over here, we went over every detail of our plan of attack. Everybody knows their role and position.

I take out both of my guns and head across the properties' divide.

Something doesn't add up.

I crouch next to the body lying face down on the concrete floor and flip him over. My bullet caught the bastard just above his left eye.

"Look familiar?" Nino asks next to me.

"Nope." I brace my elbows on my knees, looking up and down the long, narrow corridor flanked by endless metal doors to self-storage lockers. "I don't like this."

"Yeah. I expected greater resistance."

The front office, which we hit first, certainly showed evidence that a lot more men had recently been here. There was a pile of still-greasy pizza boxes and empty cans of beer littered around the room. Ashtrays overflowed with half-finished cigarettes, and smoke still hung in the air. All indications of a small army on the premises.

However, aside from the two security guards Pietro's team took care of at the front entrance and the one at the rear door that Nino dropped, we encountered fewer than a handful of guys along the corridors. Counting my dead buddy here, the total is actually six. I checked out each one of them, and none were old Katrakis. His inept bodyguard from the night they paid a visit to the construction site isn't among the dead, either.

"Any sign of Riggo?" I ask.

"His car was found behind one of the freestanding units, but there's no sign of him. Pietro took half our guys to the far end of the building. They're doing a sweep of every storage locker."

I glance down the long hallway to where our men are forcing open the metal doors. Some are using bolt cutters or drills they must have found in the office to break the locks, while others have opted to simply shoot out the things.

"You take the left side." I straighten and aim at the lock on the nearest unit on my right, sending the bullet flying.

Antique furniture. Boxes of crap covered in mold. Awful-smelling racks of ratty clothes. Every unit I open, I hold my breath, dreading and hoping to find Riggo. More often than not, the boy has been a pain in the ass, but I've got kind of a soft spot for him. His being here raises many questions. Some potential answers I refuse to entertain. My guess is Riggo was tailing Katrakis and got made. He was brought here to face the old man. But why risk holding a captive Cosa Nostra member? Why risk retribution for a fairly insignificant kid? Tobias Katrakis must be losing his touch.

"Nino?" I shout as I pull up yet another overhead door.

"Still nothing." His voice carries over the sound of the scraping metal. "I sent Pietro to check the outer buildings. Maybe they dumped—*Jesus fuck!*"

I spin around, catching Nino ducking under the half-opened door into a locker at the far end of the hallway.

"In here!"

When I reach the unit, the putrid stench of piss and blood hits me right in the face. The overhead bulb in the cramped space is out, but there's enough light spilling in from the corridor to illuminate the curled-up body on the dirty floor.

"They roughed him up pretty good," Nino barks into the phone pressed to his ear. His other hand is feeling the side of Riggo's neck. "Pulse is weak, but it's there. The kid is unconscious. We need to get him to the clinic, stat."

Crouching next to Riggo, I start checking him for other injuries while Nino gives Ilaria the rundown. The black-and-blue mess of the boy's face tells me that he sustained multiple blows to the head. Both of his eyes are swollen shut, and there are lacerations around his mouth and eyebrows. He's not wearing a shirt, and the expanse of his torso, especially his stomach and chest, is covered in more bruises. No bullet wounds, though, but there's definitely internal bleeding. He's also missing his right thumb. The bastards have beaten, tortured, and left the boy for dead.

"We're taking him in?" I ask.

"Yeah. Ilaria is on her way there. She says we can't wait for the ambulance to arrive."

Riggo doesn't react when I grab under his arms and Nino picks up his legs. We're nearly out of the building, on our way toward the car Pietro brought over to the rear entrance, when the kid starts to stir, groaning in pain.

"We've got you," I soothe. "You're safe, Riggo."

"Mr. DeVille?" he rasps.

"Yeah. Take it easy, we'll have you at the doc's soon. Don't talk."

"I'm... I'm so sorry... Mr. DeVille." The faint words trickle out of him. "The... the ring..."

Pietro holds the car door open as Nino and I gently lay Riggo on the back seat. "Now's not the best time to discuss jewelry, buddy."

His thumbless hand wraps around my wrist in a viselike grip; the force behind that hold is a helluva lot stronger than I would have expected from someone in his condition.

"They found it," he chokes out. "Stavros's ring. In my trunk. It must have fallen off when I... moved him. They... they wanted to know... how... how it got there."

I close my eyes. *Shit.*

"I didn't want to, Mr. DeVille, but... I think I told them... everything."

"It's okay, Riggo." I pat his hand. Nothing's changed. I just know that now Katrakis is gunning for me while I'm trying to find his ass so I can kill him. "You can let go of my wrist, and we'll take you to the clinic."

"They wouldn't... wouldn't hurt Miss Tara, would they?"

My blood suddenly runs cold. "What?"

"She killed the Greek heir. I... I told them I heard you say it..."

Terror, unlike anything I've ever known, engulfs me as I lean down, trying to catch every one of his words. Riggo's breaths are labored, and each uttered sound gets fainter and fainter.

"They all... they all went..."

"Where?" I shout, shaking his shoulders, trying to keep him awake. "Where did they go?"

"House... they went... to your home."

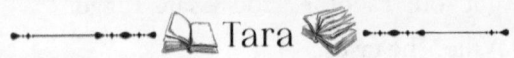

Tara

"I'm not in the mood for a movie tonight, Sienna. Maybe I can come over tomorrow?" I lodge the phone between my ear and shoulder so I can keep my hands free. "And anyway, Riggo is nowhere to be found, and I'm pretty sure there's no way I'll convince Tony to drive me over. He knows I'm under 'lock and key' as per His Highness's orders."

"You really should have bought a car, not a chopper," Sienna giggles. "And I'm on lockdown, too. Drago has gone nuts. He's been mobilizing his men, planning an attack on the Greeks since six this morning."

I hold the small hinged part of a metal hasp to the door panel and reach for the drill. "I knew he would. Those Spanish floor tiles were limited edition. He won't be able to get a replacement for them."

"It's not about the—Tara? You there? What's that noise?"

"I'm installing a lock!" I yell over the sound of the drill.

"What?"

"I found it in the storage room and—" A huge chunk breaks off the wooden surface. "Oops."

"Tara? What the fuck are you doing?"

I sigh and turn off the power tool. Leaning against the other side of the doorway, I slide down to the floor, stretching my feet before me. "I'm installing a padlock on the doors connecting my room to your brother's. Or trying to, at least."

"And you're doing that because…?"

"To make sure Arturo won't end up in my bed tonight. Or I in his. Take your pick."

"Because…?"

"Because then we'd fuck like rabbits. He'd make me feel like I've blasted off this earth. And after, I'd fall asleep in his arms and have the best goddamned sleep of my life."

"And that's… bad?"

"Very bad." I nod even though she can't see me.

"Um… why?"

"Oh my God! Will you stop?"

"As soon as you explain why sleeping with your husband and feeling good about it is *bad*."

"Because he's not what I imagined as a romantic hero! Not the knight in shining armor I was wishing for! That's who I was supposed to fall in love with, Sienna, not fucking Satan!" I dig my fingers into my hair, scraping my scalp. "Jesus. How do I manage to fuck up every single thing in my life? Even my own make-believe fairy tale?"

"Tara…"

"You wanna know what I did last night before I called you? I lay awake in bed, curled into Arturo's side as I imagined what it would be like if this thing between us were real. A happy marriage that started in a normal way. Maybe we'd have met and instantly bonded over how awfully lovey-dovey you and Drago always are. We would have gone on dates, real dates! Dates where we laughed and talked about everything and nothing. Books. His job. I would have teased him about reading his newspapers like an old man." A sad laugh escapes me. "We would have slowly gotten to know each other. I would have shown him how to edit manuscripts, and he'd teach me to cook. We would have just had fun together. At some point, Arturo would have saved me from some bad guys, of course. Maybe a thief who tried to steal my purse while we were out, but my gallant knight would have chased the bastard down." This time, the giggle that erupts breaks into a half sob that pushes its way out of my chest. "God, that's dumb. Outside my fantasies, I can't even imagine anything like that happening. All I can imagine is your brother standing on the sidewalk and laughing at my rotten luck."

"Arturo would never. He'd definitely chase the bad guy down the street," Sienna throws in. "And he'd likely break the guy's arms and legs once he caught him. Arturo loves you, too, Tara. I know it."

"Yeah, sure. Hang on to your baseless theories, and please don't interrupt my new daydream. Where was I? Oh, yes. One fine day, Arturo would pick a wonderfully romantic spot and get down on one knee. In front of witnesses! Many, many witnesses. He'd tell me that he loves me and that he can't live without me. And then, he'd ask me to marry him. To be his wife."

I close my eyes, picturing the scene in my mind. It's not that hard. I've always had a great imagination. Arturo kneeling on the ground in one of his fancy suits… doubtful, but it could happen. It is a tradition, after all. However, try as I might, I can't ever see him saying those words. To me. Even I am not that delusional.

"If that had really happened, would you have…?" Sienna's voice is almost a whisper on the other side of the line. "Said yes?"

"Yeah. I wou—"

The sound of automatic gunfire shatters the quiet outside the house.

I throw myself on the floor, face down, and cover my head with my hands. The shots seem to be coming from a distance, somewhere beyond the property gate. Still, a stray bullet could always find you if you don't take precautions.

"Um…" I say, reaching for my dropped phone. "Has your brother pissed anyone else off recently?" I pant as I crawl across the bedroom floor to a window.

"I don't think so. Why? And can you please turn off that damn drill? I can barely hear you!"

"That's not the drill." I slowly peek over the windowsill. Rapid flashes of light break between the tree branches and over the shrubs that line the perimeter fence, corresponding to the rhythmic burst of weapons fire. Four of Arturo's men, armed to the teeth, race across the driveway toward the gate. Their shouted commands echo into the night, and bring other security guys spilling into view. Some take off after their buddies, others assume defense positions around the house. I spot Tony crouching behind a stone column near the front doors, automatic rifle at the ready. "I think… we are under attack."

"What?!" Sienna's hysterical shriek explodes in my ear. "Get somewhere safe and lock yourself in. Call Arturo! I'll have Drago—"

Her frantic voice cuts off mid-sentence. *Shit.* I knew constantly forgetting to charge my phone would bite me in the ass eventually. Throwing the useless brick on the bed, I dash into Arturo's bedroom. He's got a couple of windows that face the backyard. Since he increased security at the house yesterday, there should be at least twenty men around here. More than enough to stop whoever is obviously trying to shoot their way through the main gate.

The stone walls that surround the estate make this place fairly impenetrable. The only other means of getting in is a heavily reinforced steel door located at the back of the property, along the expanse of the wall that runs behind the garage. It's hardly ever used, and according to Riggo, it can only be opened with a fingerprint.

When I reach the floor-to-ceiling window beside my husband's bed, however, my stomach plummets to the floor, and then the floor beneath my feet disappears. Just beyond the row of evergreen shrubs leading to the detached garage, several dark figures are sneaking toward the house. They've breached the perimeter.

I spin around, ready to hide somewhere they won't be able to find me, when the realization hits. Greta. Downstairs. She's working the late shift today. *Fuck!* I take off at a dead run across the room.

Arturo never showed me where he keeps his weapons, and I

don't have my own gun. I make a detour to the doors connecting our rooms and snatch the hammer out of the toolbox. It's not much of a weapon, but better than nothing, I guess. My heart is in my throat and pounding a mile a minute as I race toward the stairs while trying to keep my footfalls soft.

The entry hall is empty; the front doors are shut. Not that it helps much with all the windows on the ground level. I try not to think about the possibility of multiple attackers crashing through the glass as I rush along the hallway toward the kitchen.

I find Greta leaning over the sink, scrubbing an enormous pan, her hips swaying to music I can't hear. Her ever-present pink earbuds are firmly in place. A sigh of relief escapes me.

"Greta!" I snatch the wire, pulling the device from her left ear.

"Mrs. DeVille? What—"

Another round of gunfire erupts outside. This one sounds way closer than earlier. The slightly perplexed expression on Greta's face morphs into absolute panic. She pales, complexion instantly a shade that would rival a sheet of paper.

"We need to get upstairs, quietly. Don't worry. We'll be okay," I whisper, hoping what I'm saying is true. And that it sounds even mildly reassuring.

She nods, and even though she's trembling all over, she grabs my hand with a bone-crunching grip. My fist squeezes around the handle of the hammer as I lead Greta back toward the entry hall.

We are halfway to the stairwell when gunfire again explodes nearby. This time, it sounds like it's coming from the backyard. Loud shouts and clipped orders intermix with the incessant rattle of the weapons. I recognize Tony among the voices. The group of attackers must be larger than I initially thought, and they are advancing from multiple directions if Arturo's men haven't yet been able to stop them.

Greta seems to have frozen in place, her feet rooted to the floor. I have to basically drag her behind me as we climb the stairs to the upper level.

"Where the fuck is Arturo?" I mutter under my breath while urging Greta to keep up. "Still meeting with the don? Someone had to have called him by now. Wouldn't Tony or one of the other guys have told him about the shitstorm that has descended on us? He's got to be on his way back. Or maybe he already arrived and—"

I stop in my tracks. If my husband is here, that means he's probably at the gate, where the bulk of the firefight is happening. Oh, God!

"Greta!" I spin around to face her. "Take this," I say, shoving the hammer into her hand. "Go to one of the bedrooms and lock yourself in. Stay away from the windows. Understand?"

"Yes... But... what about you?"

"I'll be fine. Where's your phone?"

"My phone?"

"Yes. Where is it?"

"I... I left it in the kitchen. By the stove, I think."

"Okay. Now go." I all but push her up the stairs.

The instant she reaches the landing on the second floor, I race back to the kitchen. I have to get ahold of Arturo. I *need* to know that he's alright or I'm going to fucking lose whatever sanity I have left.

Greta's phone is right there where she said it would be. I grab it as if my life depends on it and punch in Arturo's number. I'm not even sure when I learned it by heart. The line rings. And rings. Then clicks over to his voicemail.

"Damn you, Arturo!" I hit the countertop with my palm and redial. If he got himself killed, I'm going to strangle him. "Pick up. Pick up. Please pick up!"

The gunfire and men's shouts sound as if they're right outside the kitchen walls, but I try to block all that out and concentrate solely on the ringing tone. Its familiar noise holds a promise, until it dumps me into voicemail again. Shit. Shit. Shit!

I redial.

Again.

And again.

Glass shatters somewhere behind me just as an enraged male voice yells down the line, "WHAT?"

Relief. Overwhelming, instant relief floods me. I've never felt such solace in my life.

"You're okay," I breathe.

Turning around, that blissful feeling snaps like a dry twig. Sheer terror puts me in a chokehold.

"Tara!" Arturo roars through the phone. "Where are you?"

I can't speak. Can't think. Not even sure if my heart is beating. I stare at the orange flames as they spread from the floor to the drapes.

"TARA!"

The fire moves like waves through water, spreading in every direction like ripples across a lake. More windows shatter as something flies into the living room through the glass. Small. Explosive. Bursting into an immediate fireball. Once the flash subsides, more flames spread around the area of impact.

The living room is now almost completely on fire. The carpet. The couch. The bookshelves.

It's coming. The arms of the fire are reaching for me.

Closer.

Closer.

Closer.

I can't look away. Can't move. Can't utter a sound.

My world has turned into an inferno.

"Fuck, baby, tell me where you are! I'm coming for you!"

I've lost the ability to breathe. My lungs seize up once the smoke and its putrid burned odor invade my senses. Regardless of the passage of time, that particular smell is permanently carved into my memory.

Crash.

More broken windows.

Crash.

Another on my right.

Crash.

That one was in the kitchen.

I wait for flames to spiral around my feet.

Nothing happens. Strange. What gives?

The gaping holes in the glass form a sort of mini wind tunnel. A burst of fresh air swooshes across me. It's brief and jarring, but not enough to shake off this paralysis.

Outside, night has fallen. The dark has swallowed everything beyond the fire's reach. Nothing moves. Nothing exists in that darkness. Nothing but the wind and the echo of my jackhammering heartbeat.

I stare. Stare while, lit by the flickering light of the blaze around me, the figure of a man fills the frame of a broken kitchen window.

Stavros's father.

Lifting a gun. Pointing it at me.

Smiling.

"Tara!" Arturo screams on the other end of the line. He sounds desperate. And so, so far away.

I should do something, right? Duck. Run. Magically teleport. Are there other options?

But I can't do anything. I can't even think clearly. I feel like an observer stuck outside my body. A spectator who is incapable of performing a single simple act. My body has frozen in this particular position, with the phone pressed tightly to my ear and my limbs unable to move an inch.

I don't even hear the gun go off. The only reason I know it has is because of the burning. Not the wall of heat at my back, but the gut-tearing pain in my abdomen. My knees give out; my legs fold under me. I drop to the tiled floor, landing on my side.

I lie.

Motionless.

Somehow managing to keep the phone pressed to my ear. My field of vision: the living room, utterly consumed by flames.

"It's the same," I whisper. "The fire. It smells the same."

Arturo

I jump out of my SUV, my gaze flying to the house beyond the blocked gate and the remnants of a bullet-riddled vehicle. The flickering orange light dances inside, while thick smoke billows from the broken windows, turns the blood in my veins into ice.

No!

The thunder of my beating heart drowns out the sounds of the chaotic gunfight all around me as I race toward the raging inferno.

"Tara!" I yell into the phone. "You need to get out of the house. Right now."

Pain tears through my arm as a bullet grazes my shoulder. I block it out. Don't even stop to shoot back. There are almost a hundred and fifty yards between me and the burning house. And my wife is inside.

"Do you hear me, Tara? Can you get out?"

She takes a shallow breath. "I can't forget it." Her tone is strangely serene. Peaceful, even.

"Tara!" I roar, hoping it will jar her out of the obvious stupor she's in. She's probably in shock, panicking. The night Greta lit the fireplace in Tara's bedroom, my wife appeared to be rooted in place until I wrapped my arm around her.

"This smell. This… hellish heat. It was the same on the night we lost Dina. My parents. Twenty years. Twenty years and I can't forget."

A man with an automatic weapon is kneeling on the ground to my right, using Tara's helicopter as his cover. He's changing the magazine and getting ready to open fire. I shoot him in the head as I continue to run. "You have to get out of there, *gattina*! Please!"

"Drago should have taken Dina out first." Tara's voice remains calm, as if she doesn't even hear me. "I cried. She didn't. So he picked me. He chose the wrong sister. Dina would still be alive if I'd been braver, then Drago could have picked her instead of me."

"Tara!" I yell, desperate to get through to her. There are now fewer than twenty feet between me and the front door.

"I messed up." Her voice is so small, so mournful. "I always mess up."

At the far edge of the driveway, I notice Tony supporting a woman as they flee from the house. For a split moment, I think it's her. But no, it's Greta.

"Where is she?" I roar as I run to them.

My housekeeper looks up, her face ashen. "She's"—she coughs—"she's still inside."

Crushing fear squeezes my heart, spreads into every cell of my body faster than the flames destroying my home. I take off, closing the distance, and kick in the front door.

Thick, black smoke and unbelievable heat surge into my face. I toss the gun and lift the flap of my jacket over my nose, stepping inside.

Seems that most of the Molotov cocktails were thrown through the living room windows, because the whole area to the left of the front door is engulfed in flames. The blaze has spread along the entire span of the west wall, consuming drapes and furnishings, climbing to the ceiling.

Urgent calls replace the sounds of gunfire outside, and I recognize Nino's voice among many others, yelling my name. Screaming for me to get out.

I'm not going anywhere without my wife. Even if it means we both burn to ash inside the damn house.

"Tara! Answer me, baby. Where are you?" I shout into the phone, but no sound comes from her end of the line.

The flames have reached past the main stairs, eating their way across the other side of the ground floor. We're mere moments from the whole thing turning into a life-size furnace, and I can't see her! Can't find my wife! With all the smoke and blistering heat, I can't see shit.

The phone.

I still have the phone.

Half blinded, I barely manage to cut the call, then immediately hit redial. Smoke fills my lungs, and I stumble, praying I'll hear the ringing over the crackle of flames and the beating of my own heart. Access to the second floor is completely blocked by a floor-to-ceiling wall of fire. *Madonna Santa,* please, please don't let her be upstairs.

A faint melody, only just audible over the frantic noise. From somewhere in the kitchen. I turn around.

There. Just behind the breakfast bar, curled on her side, my wife lies on the tiled floor. Thank God the blaze hasn't yet reached her.

"Tara!" An animalistic roar leaves my chest as I run and scoop her into my arms. I can't even clearly see her face at this point, but I detect the rise of her chest under my palm.

She's alive.

"I've got you, baby," I murmur. "I've got you."

Cradling my precious cargo, I carry her through the fires of hell that are destroying our home. Thanking God and every saint above for letting me find my wife. For not being too late. For giving me a chance to save her. Without her, there is no me.

"Arturo!" Nino yells, running toward me once I step outside.

"I need to get her to a doctor," I cough out as my eyes scan her body, checking for injuries. "She must have inhaled a lot of—"

The words die on my lips. Panic. Overwhelming panic slams into me like a freight train. The sight before my eyes cannot be real. Blood. The entire front of Tara's dove-gray sweater is saturated in blood.

"TARA!" I roar.

CHAPTER
Twenty five

Tara

VOICES. SEVERAL. DISTINCT. EVERYONE IS SPEAKING AT the same time. It's hard to decipher what they are actually saying. Everything sounds muffled, as if veiled by a dense fog. Their energy, though, is unmistakable. Alarm. Haste.

Where am I? What's going on?

One voice in particular rises above the others. It's loud. Way too loud. Booming out commands. I know that voice. I've heard it angry. Soothing. Turned on. But now, there is a quality to it that's unfamiliar. It's shaky. Breaking on certain words. That's... odd. My husband's voice never shakes. Dear God, is he alright?

"Fucking floor it, Nino! Faster, or I swear I'm going to fucking kill you with my own hands!"

Oh. He's spitting out multiple curses in the same breath. Something bad did happen. There's no way he'd cuss this much otherwise. Not with other people around, at least. At me, because I'm awesome at driving him bonkers, that's normal. I guess I have a way of bringing out the devil in him. With others, he always refined.

"Shit. The bleeding won't stop. Fuck, baby, hang on." A hand strokes my cheek. "Don't you fucking dare leave me, *gattina*." A hard press of lips to mine. Quivering lips. Yet, still, so familiar. Except for the salty taste they leave behind. "Get us to that fucking hospital already!"

Images start flashing through my mind. Short clips, like brief scenes from a movie trailer. The sounds are so jumbled that I can't connect them to the plot. Gunfire. Running. A ringing phone. Glass, breaking over and over. The overwhelming smell of smoke. Flames. Flashing, twisting, climbing. Over drapes, the floor, up the walls. So mesmerizing, but frightening at the same time. Then, darkness. A man. A man with a gun in the window. Pain.

How strange. I don't feel it anymore.

Not the pain. Not the heat. Not the—Wait, was that real?

"How much longer, Nino?"

"Less than ten minutes. Keep pressure on the wound."

My husband. My husband in the midst of the flames. Like Satan himself, unfazed by the fire, he runs to me through the raging storm. Did he really barge into a burning house? To save me? Nah. Must be another dream.

"Ten minutes, baby." His lips are on mine again. "You need to hold on. Ten more minutes and we'll be there. Please, please hold on."

His voice sounds strange. The tone is… pleading. I've never heard Arturo plead for anything before. As I crack my lids open, my vision blurs, but I make out my husband as he leans over me. His hair is beyond disheveled, and there are black and red smears all over his frantic-looking face.

He looks like shit.

"*Gattina*?" he chokes out.

Mmm, I love it when he calls me that. It makes me want to curl up in a ball and purr. That would be nice because I'm so, so cold. And my eyelids feel so heavy. A little nap would be so good right now.

"No. No! NO!" Fingers spear through my hair at the back of my head. "Stay with me. Open your eyes, baby!"

I want to. I want to so much. But it's hard.

"Please, Tara. Look at me."

Damn, he's persistent.

"I'll kill Drago!"

What?

"I swear, if you don't open your eyes, I'll kill your brother." His voice shakes so much that it's definitely breaking. Kinda puts a damper on the threatening vibe.

"You're... full of shit, Arturo," I whisper, lifting my lids just a crack.

"I know." He nods.

His face is so close. Right in front of mine. Swaying a little. I must be imagining things because his eyes are red and puffy, and it looks like there's moisture on his cheeks.

My hand feels as if it weighs a ton, but with the last speck of my strength, I raise it. Trace my fingers across the whisker-roughened skin. It *is* wet.

"Why are you crying?"

He smiles. A sad smile. A smile that never reaches his dark, glossy eyes.

"I can't imagine my life without you, *gattina*. Please, don't leave me," he rasps.

My fingers feather over his lips, over that soft little smile. A smile that I wanted to be part of my very own happily ever after.

"Your shiny armor is showing," I whisper just as the lights go out.

Arturo

One minute and forty-seven seconds.

Eternity.

That's the span of time I burned in hell as my wife lay dead on the operating table after she flatlined. Until CPR and epinephrine restarted her heart. Until mine resumed its beating.

She died.

My wife died.

"I need a clamp. Now!" Ilaria's voice booms across the operating room. "Shit. She's bleeding too much. We'll need another bag of O neg."

"That's the last one we have, doctor."

My head snaps toward the nurse who uttered those words. "What?"

"We used up our supply on Riggo. He was crashing, so there was no time to get him tested before he was rushed into the OR."

"Then test Tara and give her the right blood!"

"We already did. She's O negative. She can't receive any other type."

O negative. Like me. "Get the blood extraction kit," I bark. "You're going to take my blood and give it to her."

"Direct blood transfusions are not done, Mr. DeVille. It's too risky. The donated blood needs to be tested and processed before it can be given to the patient."

"More risky than *my wife* dying of blood loss?" I roar. "Bring the kit!"

"Doc?" She throws a scared look at Ilaria.

"Do it," Ilaria says without taking attention off her work. "Just one unit. He's wounded too and can't give more than that."

I drop into the chair after dragging it to the observation window overlooking the OR so I can continue watching over Tara on the operating table and then start rolling up my sleeves. A technician rushes in, bringing the necessary supplies for blood collection. Once everything is set up and she has me prepped, she inserts the needle into a vein in my left arm. The blood starts flowing, and she's just about to take off when I extend my other arm.

"Now, the right one," I order.

"But, the doctor said—"

"Fucking do it!"

She swallows, nods, and rushes off for another extraction kit. I start pumping my fist to make the blood flow faster. Still, the process feels painstakingly slow.

Once the tech has the second needle in me, and another bag is slowly filling, I sit there—desperate—watching the don's mother as she tries to save my wife. Minutes feel like hours until the first bag is full and the tech rushes it over to the operating room. She returns to check my progress and eventually takes the second filled bag away.

"Let's get you finished here," she says when she pops back in.

"No. Take two more. And then another round. Whatever blood my wife needs, you take from me. Do it."

"Mr. DeVille. You've already donated twice as much as medically allowed. And that's ignoring the fact that you are wounded. I can't possibly—"

"I'm going to take that needle," I rasp, "and dig it into your fucking eye! Do as I tell you!" I kick the stool the tech sat on while she worked on me, and it flies across the observation room, hitting the nearby wall. "Draw my blood! Right now!"

"Get your shit together, Arturo!" Ilaria snaps from the operating room, her voice carried by the two-way intercom speaker. "I won't have both of you die on my watch."

"If my wife dies, Ilaria, I can assure you: no one present will leave that OR alive. You have my word on that." I give the tech a pointed look. "And that includes you."

"Hook the idiot up," Ilaria yells. "You can drain him dry for all I care. Damn lunatic."

By the time the second set of blood bags is full, the tech is semi-hysterical. She's frantic over the drop in my blood pressure, and my elevated heart rate. I do feel lightheaded, and my breathing is shallow, but I'll fight all the demons in hell not to pass out. The stupid woman doesn't understand that I'd give the very last drop of my blood for a chance that Tara might live.

My vision is getting blurry. Sweat soaks my skin. I hear Ilaria holler to get a Ringer's lactate solution IV in me. As more people buzz around me, more tubes get connected to my arms, my eyes lock on the OR monitors, and I listen for even the teeniest change in the beat of Tara's heart.

Each time a machine triggers an alarm, a cold shiver runs down my spine, and my lifespan gets shortened by another ten years. Still, I keep watching, trying to catch glimpses of my wife.

Tara, come back to me.

"Arturo." Ilaria's voice pulls me out of my daze.

It's a struggle to even move my head enough to meet her eyes through the glass. "Yes?"

"There was damage to major blood vessels, and she sustained a shattered rib. The bullet also nicked her right lung. In the end, she needed three and a half units of blood…"

I'm suddenly not able to take a full breath.

Swallow.

Wait for the prognosis.

"If her recovery progresses as planned, your wife will need to endure many decades of your annoying behavior. Unfortunately, I can't prescribe her anything for that."

CHAPTER

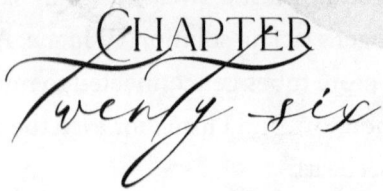

Tara

I TILT MY HEAD, TAKING A CLOSER LOOK AT THE MAN SLUMPED in the chair next to my hospital bed. His hand lies possessively over my sheet-covered thigh while his head, facing toward me, rests on the narrow space beside my hip. He's asleep, breathing evenly. But, something tells me this slumber is far from tranquil.

Dark under-eye circles mar his face, which looks gaunt and a bit yellowish under the layers of soot and smears of dried blood. His usually perfectly swept-back hair is a tangled mass of strands sticking out every which way, and some are caked together by what I suspect could also be dried blood. His clothes are in an even worse state. The once-pristine white shirt is now tattered and torn, covered in all kinds of stains (dirt, blood, sweat), and reeking of smoke. The only clean thing on him is the white bandages wrapped around his shoulder and elbows.

How long has he been here? How long have I? My last clear memory is tracing my fingers over his face. The rest is a bit of a shambles. The attack. The fire. The sound of his voice. Yes, in the car… He was yelling, urging someone to get us to the hospital. And then—

His voice echoes through my mind so clearly. First, his

commands, then his pleas for me not to leave him. I remember his words. Him telling me that he couldn't live without me. Something I've yearned to hear for a long, long time. But… But he didn't say the words I wanted to hear the most. He didn't say that he loves me.

Here's the thing about words. Saying them hardly ever requires a great deal of effort. People have been known to say whatever pops into their minds, whether it is the truth or not. A lot of times, words are used to manipulate a situation in someone's favor. In my life, a few men have told me that they loved me just to get me into their beds. They lied, and I knew it, but pretended they were being honest. I wanted that illusion. Living in a fantasy can be a beautiful thing sometimes.

Telling someone that you love them is so easy. Meaning it and showing it, that's the hard part.

This man risked his life for me.

Was that Arturo's way of showing that he has feelings for me? Dare I hope that maybe… just maybe, he loves me but can't voice it just yet? Or show me that he cares in a way that would be more obvious? I certainly haven't made it easy for him to go down that route. Can't blame him for keeping mum when I did everything in my power to convince him that I can't stand him. All because I am too scared to lower my defenses and admit that I'm in love with him.

Across from me, the door cracks open, making me glance up. A nurse steps into the room carrying a bag of saline solution. Her footfalls are nearly silent on the linoleum floor as she walks around Arturo to get to the IV stand by my bed.

"How are you feeling, Mrs. DeVille? Any pain or discomfort?" she whispers as she replaces the meds.

I manage a small smile and shake my head.

"The doctor will be by shortly to see you. I'll remind him to check up on your husband, too." She gestures to Arturo with her chin. "His vitals weren't too good after that stunt he pulled while you were in the OR. Passed out shortly after you were wheeled in here. Wouldn't leave your side. Not even to get cleaned up."

She must read the confusion on my face.

"Our supply of O negative blood was depleted," she elaborates. "That's your blood type, by the way, if you didn't know. It's special. O negative can be given to anyone, regardless of their blood type, but people like you, with O negative blood, can only receive that type. So while you were in surgery, your husband"—her gaze fixes on Arturo as she continues in a reverent tone—"made our technician draw the blood for the transfusion from him. He's your match, you see. And, it wasn't just a single donation. He made them take four units of his blood. That's extremely dangerous. I heard he actually had to be subdued before he went into hemorrhagic shock." A serene smile pulls at her lips. "He must love you very much."

Stunned speechless, I watch her retreating back as she departs, before my eyes dart to my sleeping husband. Arturo hasn't even stirred this entire time.

A stab of pain shoots up my arm from the IV site when I reach out to brush away a strand of hair that has fallen over his forehead. Instead of the usual softness, my fingers encounter brittle texture and soot. My throat feels raw, as if I haven't had water in days. Speaking seems like an impossible feat, but I manage to rasp, "Arturo."

His head snaps up so suddenly that I nearly jump out of my skin. His gaze immediately finds mine and locks in place. Not a single facial muscle of his moves. He doesn't even blink. Just… stares.

"Arturo?"

Nothing.

I'm not even sure if he's breathing. His tired-looking, bloodshot eyes pierce me with that silent, frantic look, scouring my face with disturbing intensity.

It's weird as fuck.

Slowly, I move my hand to lay it over his, where it still rests on my thigh. At the moment of contact, a violent shudder works its way through his body, but otherwise, he remains motionless. He just… keeps looking at me. What happened to him? Something had to. In these past few months, I've gotten to know Arturo enough to know that this isn't normal. I've never seen him behave like this. It makes me seriously question his present state of mind.

"Um… maybe we should call a doctor?"

That gets me a blink. Then, he practically springs off the chair as if he's been shocked and rushes out of the room. Within seconds, he's back and half dragging, half carrying a middle-aged guy in a white coat. Without a single word, he deposits the hyperventilating man next to my bed.

"I meant for you," I mutter. "I feel fine."

Another blink, and the poor doctor gets shoved out of the room. The door slams shut with a loud bang, and then Arturo is back at my side. Slowly and carefully, he picks up my hand, covers it with his other palm, and resumes his silent, bizarre vigil.

"You're freaking me out, Arturo."

The hold on my hand tightens. He leans forward, ever so slowly, until his face is mere inches from mine.

"You died." His voice is so quiet, it hardly qualifies as a whisper. "For a minute and forty-seven seconds, your heart stopped. And during each of those one hundred and seven seconds, I died a thousand deaths. It fucking broke me, *gattina*."

I suck in a breath.

I've never really thought about dying. Well, I never contemplated what happens to our bodies and souls after death. There were times, though, when I did wonder if my life would have any impact on this world. The answer was always: unlikely. I haven't done any great deeds. Nothing that would leave behind a legacy that could be carried on. No amazing feats to speak of.

Since I'm not what most would call a "likable person," my death would probably not affect many people at all. Drago and Keva, certainly. They'd take it hard. Perhaps also a handful of friends. Jelena. As of a few months ago, Sienna. And, maybe, my mechanic. He'd only miss me because he earned a small fortune over the years fixing my old car. That's what I figured, considering my role.

Never in a million years did I expect that my death would break the mighty Arturo DeVille.

"I can't live through that a second time," he continues in an unsteady voice. "I'd rather die than experience it again. Do you understand me?"

It's my turn to stare at him, stupefied. The only thing I can do is nod, too shaken by his tone and the tremble in his voice to manage anything else. He sounds devastated and absolutely serious.

"Good." He swallows the distance until our foreheads touch. Cupping my face with his hands, he closes his eyes and lets out a long exhale. "Jesus fuck, baby."

Tilting my face, I brush my mouth over his. When he pulls my lower lip between his lips, he does it with such tenderness that my heart swells in my chest. This must be the softest, most gentle kiss we've ever shared. It shakes me to the core.

"You need to rest," he whispers against my lips, still brushing them with his. "Ilaria will be back in a couple of hours to give you a checkup."

"Okay." I am tired, kind of groggy. A nap sounds heavenly right now. Whatever meds I'm on must be causing the drowsiness I'm feeling. "Where is Drago?" I ask before settling in.

"He's in the waiting room. Security had to restrain him, but I'll make sure he's here when you wake up."

"Mmm… thank you." My eyelids feel so heavy.

"And then, I have some paperwork you'll need to sign."

Of course, even in death, one can't escape bureaucracy. "Sure."

I nuzzle my face into his palm and let sleep take me.

"I'm going to fucking kill that son of a bitch."

I glare at my brother. "No, you won't."

"You almost died because of him!" he snarls.

The last thing I want to do is see Drago as distraught as he was when he barged into my hospital room ten minutes ago. *Scared shitless* would probably be a better way of describing the expression on his face. Still, I'd rather deal with that than his current murderous ire. I'm seriously worried that he might really kill Arturo. Reaching out, I take his hand in mine.

"No. I nearly died because I froze up. There was time for me to flee, and the path to the front door wasn't yet blocked. I could've run out of the house as soon as the fire started, then none of this would have happened." I squeeze his fingers. "I'm sorry I scared everyone."

He shakes his head and kisses the top of my head. "I'm still beating the shit of that asshole."

"You won't lay a finger on my husband. I love him, Drago."

"Don't you think it's about time to cut this crap?" he growls. "I know Ajello was behind this sham of a marriage. The bastard told me so himself. He came to see me a couple of weeks before your wedding, spitting out crazy ideas about setting up DeVille and you together so you'd fall in love. Christ! I'll never forgive myself for going along with his nonsense instead of—"

"Instead of fixing my problem for me?" I interrupt him. "By probably ripping the heads off both Ajello and Arturo, right?"

"Gutting them is what I had in mind, but cutting their fucking heads off would've worked, too."

A long and heavy sigh escapes me. I don't need to ask if he's being serious because I know he is.

"The reasons that brought Arturo and me together don't matter. None of them change things. I love him. And he loves me." A pang hits my chest as I say this. Arturo hasn't actually said that he loves me. And I know actions speak louder than words, but still… "So I'd appreciate it if you'd leave my husband's head where it is. Thanks."

"You deserve a man who would cherish and protect you, Tara. Who will love you so much that he'd—"

"He'd charge into a burning building and risk his own life by carrying me out through a wall of flames?" I ask. "Just as you had done for me? Is that what you were about to say?"

"Yes! That's exactly what—" He cuts off mid-sentence and looks away. "Fuck. I hate that motherfucker."

I can't help but laugh, even though it makes me ache from pulling on my stitches. "This isn't a competition, Drago."

"Right."

"And if you two would set aside this stupid pissing contest between you, maybe you'd both realize how much alike you are."

He gives me a look filled with incredulity and utter disgust. "God forbid. And for the record, I don't buy it one bit that you're truly in love with DeVille."

"Hmm… Well, maybe I should ask Mirko to set up a camera in my and Arturo's bedroom? One with a live feed to your laptop? You know, so you could see for yourself how much we love each other. Then maybe you'd be convinced?" I bite the inside of my cheek to keep the grin from breaking across my face. "Of course, one camera may not be enough. I'll have to have him add another in the bathroom. And the entry hall. The kitchen, definitely. Oh, the stairwell, too! We also quite often—"

"For fuck's sake, stop! Seeing that dickhead groping my sister in the middle of the driveway was enough. I really don't need to know every location where the two of you do the nasty. Jesus!"

"Sex, Drago. S. E. X. The same thing you can't get enough of with your wife. And if you don't want to know more about my sex life, I suggest you have Mirko kill the connection to our security systems. And for your record, that was a shitty move, big brother."

"I'll think about it," he grumbles.

"Alright. I'll just tell Arturo that from now on, all of our fun carnal times are happening on the front porch. He'll love it. All that fresh air will bring out the wild man in him."

"You wouldn't."

I raise an eyebrow.

"Fine." He grits his teeth. "Where is the pretty boy, anyway?"

"Ilaria dragged him away to give him a checkup and get some follow-up blood work done. She had to threaten to restrict all visitor access to me if he didn't obey her medical orders."

"What the hell does he need a checkup for? Making sure every strand of his hair is still in place?"

"Ha! Funny, but no. Considering he almost suffered a hypovolemic shock by donating all that blood for my transfusion, she needed to make sure he's alright, and that his pigheadedness didn't cause him complications."

Drago blinks at me as if my words left him mildly stunned, but that surprised expression on his face quickly morphs into irritation. "I'm your brother. They should have called me to do blood donation."

"Oh, for the love of God." I look toward the heavens and sigh. "Get lost, Drago. And send Keva in."

He kisses my cheek and rises to leave, just as a thought occurs to me. I bite my bottom lip.

"Hey." I grab his forearm. "Do you think Dina would have liked Arturo?"

A serene smile pulls at his lips. "Yeah. I think she would have. Unfortunately."

He crosses the room to the door, but before pulling it open, he turns abruptly. His eyes—worried yet resigned—sweep over me. What is he thinking? About Dina? Our past? Regretting the choices we both made?

"You really love that asshole?"

"I do. I really, really do."

The nightstand lamp beside my hospital bed casts soft light on the stack of papers in my hand, making the pristine white slightly yellowish. Sickly. Diseased. My mind can't quite comprehend the text before my eyes, so I stare at it a little harder. Trying to... understand.

How could I have been so wrong? Was I really that dopey from the meds that I completely misunderstood Arturo's words? My gaze slides to the bottom of the page. Below the bold section heading. The date. Our names. Focusing on the two lines. The upper one already holds my husband's neat signature.

I can't live through that a second time.

I thought that was him confessing that he loves me.

Obviously, I was mistaken.

That realization slams into my chest like a sledgehammer, and the pain is a thousand times greater than the actual physical discomfort after my surgery.

It's agony, but infinitely more.

Not wanting him to see the effect this is having on me, I sink my teeth into my lower lip to stop it from trembling. Then, I look up, meeting Arturo's piercing stare.

"You want a fucking divorce, DeVille?"

"Yes."

His instant response feels like a finishing blow, absolutely annihilating me. There's no hiding the shaking of my fingers as I slip free the pen clipped to the top edge of the file folder and set the ballpoint on the blank line. The ink flows blue across the page, but my vision blurs, distorts, and morphs what I'm seeing into red. In my mind, I'm signing another deal with the devil. This time, with my blood.

"There." I close the flap of the folder over the document and keep my attention fixed on the wretched thing. *I will not let him see me cry.* "What about my money? We agreed on a million for each month of our marriage."

"We did. And since I'm breaking the term, all twelve million was deposited into your account an hour ago."

I swallow. Barely. "Perfect. And Ajello?"

"I'll handle the don."

He'll handle the don. Great. "I'm keeping the rings."

"I wouldn't have it any other way. In fact, I insist that you do."

Bastard. I'm going to have them melted, just for that. "Well, I wish I could say it's been nice doing business with you, DeVille, but…"

"Likewise."

His voice rings with amusement. The jackass is having fun. Of course he is. First, he wrecked my life. Now, my heart. But sure, glad I've been able to entertain him. God, why can't he just get the hell out of here so I can break down in peace? Is that too much to ask? Is it?

My eyes stay glued to the folder, but I finally catch a slight movement in my peripheral vision. Except… He's not leaving. What… what is he—?

Snapping my head up, all I can do is gape at Arturo with stunned, wide-eyed amazement. He's down on one knee right beside my bed. He's wearing one of his fancy suits after, apparently, showering and changing while I slept, and he's kneeling on the hospital floor like he couldn't care less about that.

"What are you doing?"

"Patience, *gattina,*" he says, reaching into the pocket of his pants.

I'm just about ready to tell him to get lost when he clears his throat. His eyes capture mine, and there isn't a shred of mirth in them. He actually looks kind of—

"I fucked up," he blurts, running a hand through his hair like he's nervous. "Big time. Made a mess of everything because I was stupid. And stubborn. And because I was afraid." His voice cracks a little on the last word. "You told me once that you always screw things up, but that's not true. Drilling holes in the drywall or taking apart the coffee machine with a butter knife, that's not messing things up, baby. It's just you being you. You're independent and resourceful. Some things might not go your way, but you don't shy away from a challenge. You don't give up, and I love that about you. I love everything you do. Even when it involves bizarre hair antics. I get a kick out of seeing what insane idea you'll come up with next, and I want to keep experiencing that for the rest of my life."

He falls silent, but I have a feeling he's not done. His eyes keep bouncing between mine like he's soundlessly trying to tell me something. Imploring me to understand his every word. It's as if he's taking a deep breath before a plunge. Getting ready to light a match in a room filled with hydrogen instead of air. And I'm left gasping, struggling to breathe. Waiting for the spark that will blow my world apart with his next exhale. His next sentence.

"I love you, *gattina*."

B

O

O

M

"Tara, for over a decade, aside from my sisters, the Cosa Nostra Family was the most important thing in my life. But then you thundered into it like a beautiful storm. My precious hazard. And I realized that you eclipsed everything. The Family—if I had to make a choice, I would have betrayed them for you. My life—I would have given it to save yours in a nanosecond. I would give up everything for you, baby, everything. And that thought scared the living shit out of me. Having that kind of weakness, it was simply incomprehensible. But that's what you became. My Achilles' heel.

"And so, I lashed out. Tried to push you away when all I really wanted was to hold you in my arms, keep you safe, and never let you go. Because I love you. Desperately." He sucks in a sharp intake of air and pulls a ring from his pocket, lifting it in front of my face. "I'm so sorry, Tara darling. Will you marry me?"

I gasp. Astonishment, anger, and dizzying happiness surge inside me, battling for supremacy while I continue to gape at the beautiful gold ring with another dazzling emerald at the center, even more beautiful than the one in my current ring.

"Are you fucking kidding me?" I finally manage to spit out. "You just served me with divorce papers!"

"I want to make it right, *gattina*. Want every step of our life together to be real. One day, our kids should hear the story of how their daddy proposed to their mommy while kneeling before her.

Not that he was an asshole and blackmailed the love of his life into marrying him," he smirks. "But how can I ask you to marry me if we're already married? Please, Tara. Do me the honor of becoming my wife."

I grab the folder with our divorce papers, swinging and hitting him upside his head.

"Is that a *yes*?" He smiles sheepishly and squints his eyes.

"I've been going through hell, thinking I've fallen in love with a jerk who doesn't give the slightest fuck about me!" I bark. "No, Arturo. It's definitely *not* a yes."

That mischievous smirk morphs into a frown as confusion takes over his face. Springing to his feet, he leans in until he's eye level with me.

"What?"

It's my turn to smile. Fisting the lapel of his jacket, I pull him down for a breath-stealing kiss.

"If you thought I'd make this easy for you, you're oh *so* very wrong, darling." I smile against his mouth. "You'll have to earn that *yes,* this time." I graze his lower lip with my teeth. "The ring is pretty, though. I'll take it."

EPILOGUE

 Arturo

Several months later
Milene Ajello's birthday bash
New York

CAN'T FUCKING BELIEVE SHE SAID NO. AGAIN.
I don't break our kiss as I kick the bathroom door shut and then lock it.

"Something tells me the don won't be pleased with us ditching his wife's party," Tara says breathlessly while fumbling with my belt.

"I'll apologize for not giving a fuck." Wrapping my arms around her waist, I carry her toward the vanity counter.

"You might want to reconsider your attitude there, darling. After all, you have to stay on his good side so he won't be too pissed about you delegating the review of all the business docs to me."

"Ajello already knows. He even mentioned he'll be dumping his own shit on you, too." I crush my mouth to hers. "Now, no more work talk. All I want right now is to fuck my wife senseless."

"Ex-wife."

I growl. She just loves bringing this shit up. It annoys the crap out of me, and she knows it. She also knows that *technically* our divorce was never finalized because I refused to file the papers. None of that stopped me from trying to win over my wife. I've wooed her, dated her, made all her favorite meals, which she now has no problem indulging in night after night, and continually tried to convince her to accept my marriage proposal. No coercion this time. Just my love.

Including my initial attempt at the hospital, I've tried my luck exactly nineteen times. Regardless of the time, date, or place, the answer has been *no, no, no.*

I tried it during the *Preslava* celebration at her brother's place, figuring that asking her in front of her crazy family and friends would do the trick. *Preslava* is basically another version of the *Slava* but with fewer guests. Still included the pig roast, unfortunately. Nevertheless, I went down on one knee and asked Tara to marry me in front of fifty people. She declined. But she kept the ring. Frustrating woman. The day spiraled into a bit of a disaster after that. While trying to romance my wife, I sort of abandoned my duties as the pig roaster. The thing ended up burned to a crisp. Which led to Drago and me exchanging blows in the middle of the party tent, and we managed to knock over and roll around in the cake Keva made for the occasion. It didn't really matter who came out on top. I think everyone just enjoyed the entertainment, as if we were a couple of clowns there to amuse the crowd. Someone started a list of requests for the next family event.

That forced me to change tactics. The next time I gave proposing another shot was while we were having dinner at one of Tara's favorite restaurants in Manhattan. I was sure that a more upscale place would make her more receptive, especially if it reminded her of something out of those books she likes to read. I even hired a string quartet to play her favorite song in the background. People around us cheered and clapped as she beamed that maddeningly beautiful smile at me. But that noise quickly died down with her resounding *no*.

My follow-up crack at asking her to marry me was at the opera, during the intermission between the first two acts. Then, at the local bookstore as she browsed in the historical smut section. The movie theater. In front of the lingerie shop.

No, Arturo. No. No, and stop interrupting the movie. No. You're causing a scene.

Nineteen fucking times! I've poured my heart out while down on one knee. Every attempt was met with a negative answer. But each time, she made sure to accept the ring. At this point, I have a standing order with my jeweler in Rome. A new, custom-made emerald ring every couple of weeks.

All the engagement rings I've presented her with are lined up on top of our bedroom dresser, in our newly rebuilt home. They are a sad testament to all my failed attempts at convincing Tara to choose me. Each time I look at them, I can't decide if I want to laugh or kill someone. My only salvation? She's never taken off my original ring. Or the wedding band I gave her. Both are always present on her dainty finger.

"No hickeys," Tara mumbles into my neck. "And please, try not to ruin my outfit this time."

"I make no promises."

The pink dress she's wearing is close-fitting, but somehow, I manage to pull the hem up to her waist without tearing the fabric. No panties. Perfect. I deposit her naked ass on the marble and pull out my cock.

"Maybe I should just fuck you until you're mindless and

pliant." Her hair is a waterfall of gorgeous waves, reaching halfway down her back, all soft and silky. As I fist a handful at the back of her head, the strands slip through my fingers. "I should push you to the edge and simply keep you there until you say *yes* to my proposal, *yes* to marrying me all over again."

A wicked smile spreads across her lips, and I'm once more bewildered by how fucking breathtaking she is.

"Interesting strategy." Gripping the edge of the counter, she leans back and spreads her legs wide. "You should most certainly try it, darling."

"Maybe I will." I thrust inside her in one smooth motion. Home. Fucking bliss.

Her skin is so silky under my palm as I trail the delicate column of her throat. Perfect. Bloody perfect. Just like the whole of her. Angling my hips, I plunge deeper, then pull out, leaving only a fraction of an inch. She loves it when I pound into her mercilessly, retreating almost completely before driving back in.

Not tonight, though. Tonight, I'm going to get her to agree to marry me even if it makes my poor aching dick explode in the end. Her pulse picks up under my fingertips, and I sense the rapid rise and fall of her chest. *Yes, baby, yes.*

Gliding my other hand up her thigh, I slip it between our bodies, running my fingers over the folds of her pussy, up to her sweet swollen clit. Such a sensitive little spot, pulsing with each stroke of my thumb. Tara is so damn wet, the slapping of our flesh fills the room. Loud and lewd. I love it. The smell of her arousal is making me crazy. Hungry. Yearning for more. I pick up my pace, thrusting faster, but pulling back when I feel her getting too close to the precipice.

Sharp nails dig into my neck, for sure leaving red crescent moons that will mark my skin for hours. Branding me as hers.

That's not really necessary. I've been hers from the moment my eyes fell on my wildcat, and I'll be hers until my dying breath.

"Maybe you'd like to reconsider my offer?" I graze my teeth along the edge of her chin, then down her delicate throat, the swells of her breasts.

"No." Her response comes out as a drawn-out moan rather than a clearly spoken word.

Damn it.

I shift again, changing the angle once more. My hips ram harder, faster. I'm pressing as deep as I can while her inner walls clamp down on me, squeezing me like a vise. The overhead lights cast a bright glow over her beautiful tits. Tits that are right now nearly spilling out of the bodice of her dress. I curse inwardly for not having enough hands to do all the things I want to my woman. Touch her everywhere. All at once. I'm forced to abandon her throat so I can grab her right breast, kneading it lightly. Matching the squeeze of my fingers to the rhythm of my thrusts.

"I can keep this up for hours," I lie. That tingle at the base of my spine is already spreading, nudging me ever closer to the edge. I urge myself to hold on, drawing out her pleasure, all while the sweet, intoxicating smell of our lovemaking wraps around me, diminishing my resolve.

"Liar," she pants next to my ear. "We both know I can break you, and I only need to do this."

Her teeth sink into the soft tissue between my neck and shoulder, sending an electric jolt through every part of my body. I snap. Grabbing her knees, I push them open wider, and then I'm pounding into her like a man possessed.

Her back arches toward me as she moans. The most beautiful sounds leave her sinful lips as I claim her. With every thrust, I can feel her core spasming around my cock. She detonates. Shaking, shivering, riding the swells of ecstasy while calling out my name.

Mine. Only mine.

Gritting my teeth, I pull out, and the sudden loss of her heat almost sends me to my knees. I cradle her face with my palms, coaxing her slightly dazed eyes to meet mine. Every single muscle in my body is strained. The need to plunge back into her is overwhelming. A visceral urge that can't be denied. I want to fill her with my cum, brand her completely. But I also need her to understand.

"I love you more than anything else in this world, *gattina*," I rasp. "Anything. Can you comprehend that?"

That emerald gaze burns into me while her lips quiver. No matter how many times she's said it back before, the fear that this time she might remain silent nearly chokes me. Doubt creeps in that I somehow ruined everything for us after all. I need to hear her speak the words or I just might fucking die.

"I love you too, Arturo."

Relief pours into my system like a life-giving rain. Every time she says it, a shockwave goes through me. Letting out a groan, I plunge back inside her pussy, so deep and forcefully that I almost come right then.

Tara's passionate scream explodes into the room. It's loud, and I bet everyone in the banquet hall probably heard it. Above the music, chatter, and all. Tremors rack her body as she falls apart in my embrace. Again. I hold on to her tightly, just as I intend to hold on to her for all eternity. Keeping her safe and protected in my arms.

Only after she starts coming down from her high do I resume pounding into her, seeking my own release. Just two strokes get me there. My balls draw up, and I roar as my hot cum explodes into her, filling her with my seed.

My witch.

My precious little hazard.

 Tara

One month later
Piazza Navona, Rome

As I approach the center of the square, the magnificence of centuries-old buildings on all sides takes my breath away. The cobblestones under the soles of my heeled sandals are warm with the heat of the afternoon sun. Clusters of tourists are gathered everywhere, their voices blending into a harmonious hum of several different languages. The air smells faintly of roasted chestnuts, and the slight breeze carries the delicious aroma of fresh bread from nearby cafés.

I can't believe I'm in Rome!

"It's the most beautiful thing I've ever seen," I whisper, soaking up the view.

"Couldn't agree more," Arturo says behind me.

I turn around, finding him leaning his shoulder on the stone wall, watching me. Earlier, he ditched his suit jacket in our hotel suite, choosing to head out without it. The sleeves of his dress shirt are rolled up, the top two buttons are undone. The open collar shows off a touch of his bronzed chest, his sexy-as-fuck collarbones, and his scruff-covered neck with the golden cross around it.

As I look at my man, I'm reminded of that not-so-long-ago day at Naos. Back then, it was the glint of the lights instead of the sun's rays on his necklace that captured my attention as I walked up to him. All these months later, he still has the power to take my breath away.

"Are you going to finally explain why you insisted we come to Rome, of all places, this weekend?" I ask.

"Last week, after Drago mentioned the vacation he's taking Sienna on, you taunted him about never taking you anywhere fun." He pushes away from the wall and prowls toward me with slow, predatory steps. "And well, you know how much I love pissing him off. So I decided you deserve a getaway before them," he chuckles. "I left a postcard for him with the hotel reception, with orders for it to be sent as priority mail."

"You're still ticked at Drago for scheming with Ajello? Or do you still think he sold the Greeks' property to you on purpose, setting in motion everything we went through?"

"Both. But also, I just don't like him."

"We've been over this, Arturo."

"Mm-hmm. But the twisted dick still thinks he loves Sienna more than I love you."

"You two really need to stop this childish behavior. Who loves who more is a ridiculous competition to be in." I sigh. I guess it's better than the other shit they continue to argue about. Sienna and I have been trying to resolve the ongoing animosity between our brothers. So far, with little success. Drago holds Arturo responsible for my getting shot and nearly dying. And Arturo is dead set on the idea that the entire clusterfuck wouldn't have happened at all if Drago had better business sense. As far as exploiting the Greeks' collateral, that is. "Is there any news on Stavros's father?"

Arturo's face contorts into a mask of rage. "No. The motherfucker seems to have vanished and no one has been able to locate him. But he'll surface eventually. And when he does, I'm going to make sure his death is slow and extremely painful." He cups my cheek with his hand while his other palm settles over my heart. "I'm still plagued by nightmares about that night. I almost lost you."

"I'm fine. I'm here. With you." Lifting onto my toes, I press my mouth to his.

He briefly pulls my lower lip between his teeth, but then, with a rather amused look on his face, lowers himself to one knee.

"Another reason why I picked Rome is because my jeweler is here. That way, when you once more tell me 'no,' I can pick up the new ring right away and ask you again." He smirks, lifting an emerald ring in its velvet box before me. "Will you marry me, *gattina*?"

My heart flutters as it does every time he asks me. He's been trying to correct his wrongs, starting with a romantic proposal that I never received before we agreed to wed. Once I agree, he wants us to renew our vows. To say the words of love to each other, and this time, we'll both mean them. To date, he has proposed more than a dozen times, approaching twenty, maybe. I've honestly lost count. But it's time. He's redeemed himself enough.

I smile and reach for the ring. The long-awaited *yes* is ready to leave my lips when Arturo's gaze snaps to the side. The mirth in his eyes transforms into frustration as he stares at something behind me.

"You've got to be fucking kidding me."

"What?" I look around, not seeing anything amiss. "I don't… What's going on?" I gape at Arturo as he rises, throwing out a bunch of Italian curses under his breath, and stuffs my ring back into his pocket. "Hey! Give that back!"

"Nope. The little shit somehow followed me all the way here. I won't allow any bad luck to spoil this for us."

"What the hell are you talking about?"

"That." He juts his chin to the right.

My gaze shifts in the direction he indicated. Darting past the tourists huddled in groups. Searching, searching. Until it stops on the ornate trash can near a restaurant.

On top, hind leg straight up in the air, sits a scrawny black cat. One who's vigorously licking his ass.

I slam my palm over my mouth to stifle a laugh. Fail. Chuckling at the all-mighty Arturo DeVille. My man is superstitious?

"Why are you giggling? It's not funny," he grumbles.

Shaking my head, I grab the front of his shirt and pull him down for a kiss.

"Just give me the ring," I murmur into his lips.

"No," he rasps.

I rear back. "What do you mean 'no'?"

"I want to make it perfect. And this is definitely not."

"But, I was just going to—"

His mouth slams against mine, cutting off the rest of my words.

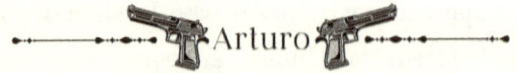

Arturo

Sometime later
New York

"Yes, I know it's urgent, boss." I shove the door shut with my foot and lug the bag of groceries to the kitchen. In my hurry to get home, I almost forgot to pick up the ingredients for the lasagna I'm teaching Tara how to make tomorrow. While Ajello yammers in my ear, I quickly put everything away and set off in search of my wife. "Tara has already gone over the contract and picked it apart. Those assholes tried to sneak in a higher rate than we originally agreed on and added a penalty to the delay clause. My guess is they figured we wouldn't notice. I'll see if—"

I jerk to a stop halfway to the stairs, not quite believing my eyes. Water is streaming down the steps from the upper level and cascading off the landing like a small waterfall.

"I'm going to have to call you back." I cut the line.

As I take the stairs two at a time, the soles of my shoes splash through the running water that quickly soaks through to my feet. Ridiculous squishing sounds beset me as I head down the hallway in search of the source of the leak.

"Tara!" I barge into our bedroom. "Baby, what's going on here?"

"Oh, hey, darling." My wife sticks her face through the doorway, grinning sheepishly. "You're home early. How about you go back to the office and try again in an hour? Or maybe three. Tomorrow would be better."

Her wet hair is gathered at the top of her head, several strands plastered to her rosy cheeks and forehead. The gray T-shirt she's wearing is soaked through, clinging to her breasts and stomach. No bra today. Lucky me.

"I think I'll stay."

"Absolutely not!" She slips out of the bathroom through the narrowest gap, shutting the door in her wake, then leans on it as if she's Cerberus guarding the gate. "The plumber is already on his way, and everything will be fixed in no time. I'll text you as soon as it's all done."

A smile threatens to break across my face, but I keep it in, biting the inside of my lip. Throwing my jacket on the back of the recliner that's started to absorb water at its base, I cross the flooded floor and lean down to kiss my wife.

"What did you do, Tara darling?" I whisper while nibbling her lower lip. "Leave the tub to fill up, but forgot about it?"

"Uh-uh. The pipe under the sink was dripping," she explains while she climbs up my body to wrap her legs around my waist. "I knew your day was full of meetings and things, and that you'd be dog-tired when you got home. So I tried to fix it myself because I didn't want you to have to deal with the issue. Um… It didn't go as planned, though."

"Can I have a look?"

Letting out a frustrated sigh, she buries her face in the crook of my neck. "Please, don't. It's a disaster."

"I'm sure it's not that bad." I adjust my hold, shifting Tara so I can support her ass with one hand while I reach for the bathroom doorknob with the other.

And open the portal to utter chaos.

Several jets are projecting from the cracked pipe under the sink like geysers, gushing in almost every direction. The largest is blasting the opposite wall, resulting in secondary sprays as the stream ricochets and drenches everything in sight, including my toolbox, which is half-submerged right next to the open vanity.

"I… I tried turning off the under-the-sink valve, but I must have done something, and the handle kinda broke off," she continues in a small voice, with her face still pressed into the hollow between my neck and shoulder. "I'm so sorry. I promise I'll fix this mess."

I kiss her forehead, then take her chin between my fingers and tilt her head so our gazes connect. "It's okay."

"It's not *okay*, Arturo. What about the new flooring? It's hardwood. And the entire house was just redone. What about the furniture? And…"

She continues spitting out concern after concern at a rapid pace as I wade across the water-sodden floor, carrying her to the towel cabinet while trying my best to avoid the worst of the spray. It appears like the safest spot, so I set my wife on the counter.

"…if it can even be fixed, that is. Shit. What if we need to replace all the pipes in the house?"

Water splashes my back as I reach into my pocket and pull

out a small velvet box. I've been carrying it around since we returned from Rome, waiting for the perfect time.

Perfect. The only perfect thing in my life is my wife. With her, everything else becomes perfect.

"And what if insurance won't cover it? And—Arturo? What the fuck? Get off your knee. You're getting completely wet!"

I smirk and lift the ring up to her. "Will you marry me, Tara darling?"

She gapes at me. "Really, Arturo? You're asking me now?"

"Really. The timing doesn't get more perfect than this." I shrug.

"We're in the middle of a major plumbing disaster, in case you haven't noticed."

"I did. So? Will you be my wife, my precious little hazard?"

Her lips press into a flat line as she stares at me for a long moment before a beaming smile breaks across her stunned face. Those beautiful green eyes of hers fill with tears as she starts nodding.

"Yeah," she sniffs, then lifts her hand. "I'll marry you."

Well, thank fuck!

I slide the ring on her finger until it rests butting up against the very first one I chose for her. The ring I gave her before my mind fully understood what this incredible woman meant to me, yet my heart already knew she was priceless.

As soon as the two center emeralds connect over the wedding band, sitting slightly askew to inadvertently form an infinity symbol, I spring up and scoop my wife into my arms, then scurry to our bedroom.

"Um… Can we skip mentioning the major leak and the flood when we tell our future kids about this moment? We can just say I agreed to marry you in Rome," she offers as I peel her wet T-shirt off her.

I smile and capture her mouth with mine.

"Absolutely not."

Meanwhile in Boston

Adriano

Ruffo Enterprises headquarters
Seaport District

The constant skull-pounding pain throbs in my temples, making my damn brain feel like it's turning into mush under the pressure. I squeeze the bridge of my nose and lean back in my office chair, hoping this latest migraine will pass quickly if I keep absolutely still. Just as I settle in for an agonizing hour, a sharp knock on my door sends my misery into overdrive.

"Great," I sigh.

Considering the late hour and the strange, muffled wails that can be heard even behind the closed door, this could only be one person. My courier.

With another squeeze to my nose and then my temples, which accomplishes fuck all as far as my migraine is concerned, I straighten in my chair.

"Enter."

The door opens to reveal a middle-aged man with greasy shoulder-length hair and a stringy gray beard. And a sniveling bastard curled up at his feet. Somehow, despite the dirty rag stuffed into his mouth, the roughed-up man's whining sounds like thunder in my head.

"I have your package," the bearded guy declares. His voice is tinged with a slight French accent; the articulation is crisp and utterly at odds with his unkempt looks. "Here you go."

As if to underline his point, he grabs the whining guy by the scruff of the neck and shoves him over the threshold. The poor bound and gagged schmuck rolls across the floor.

I cock my head, assessing the state of my newest acquisition. He seems to have passed out. My gaze shifts to the courier, scrutinizing him from head to toe. By the condition of his dirty, torn clothes, I'd guess he spent at least a week sleeping on the streets. I wonder if he actually did.

"That's new." I shift my gaze toward his hair, to the tresses that look as if they haven't seen soap and water in at least a month. "And I especially like the fake beard."

The man's eyes narrow into slits. They are the only flaw in his disguise. One can change many things about themselves, but the look in their eyes usually gives them away. The courier's eyes are clear. Young. Very young. Staring back at me with fire shining in their depths. Wild flame. He hasn't yet learned to control his emotions. Which only emphasizes his astonishing skills of deception. That includes the expertly applied makeup on his face. The crafty mask makes him appear more than twice his actual age.

"So? Are we even now?" he growls.

"Yes. We're even, Zacharie." I nod, immediately regretting it when a piercing pain shoots behind my eyes. "Did you have a chance to reconsider my offer to work for me full time?"

"No. I'm satisfied with my new employer."

I *tsk*. Bullheaded. Just like his father. And loyal. I should have tried harder and beaten that damn Sicilian to getting the boy out of the Chinese prison. "Alright, pass my congratulations to DeSanti. He gained himself quite an asset."

The kid's eyes flare in surprise. "That's not the kind of information that has been made widely known."

"As long as there are agents willing to sell intel and parties with means to pay for it, all information is obtainable. Remember that."

Once Zacharie Allard departs, I head over to the floor-to-ceiling windows, looking out at the Boston skyline lit up at night. My delivery is still curled up in the center of my office, stinking up the place with the stench of fear.

It took months and a small fortune, but my sources finally found Tobias Katrakis hiding in some dump in Athens. Another chunk of cash went to arrange a private flight to get him on this side of the Atlantic. It was worth it. The old loan shark has plenty of connections in New York that could prove useful, and the information I can get from him makes up for all the money I spent to hunt his ass down. And then there's the added bonus. The Cosa Nostra underboss wants the Greek's head for almost killing his wife. I'm still contemplating how to wield that leverage, but it's a good card to have up my sleeve.

I glance at my wristwatch. It's very tempting to stay and start on the first round of questioning right away. However, my priorities seem to have changed recently. Taking my phone out of my pants pocket, I send a text to the security guard downstairs. My staff knows that I expect prompt action, so he'll be here momentarily to collect Katrakis.

The Greek is starting to come around, something I cannot allow. Can't have him getting any crazy ideas at this time.

I approach the semi-conscious man and squat beside him. Young Zacharie Allard roughed him up quite a bit, but there's still a risk when it comes to Katrakis. And I understand all too well the value of mitigating residual risks.

Grabbing ahold of his foot with my right hand, I lay my left just above his ankle. Some pressure, and a loud snap resonates through the room. Immediately followed by the scream of a poor dumbass unlucky enough to suffer a broken bone.

That'll do.

Straightening up, I stride across the office, collecting my jacket on my way to the door.

I've always been pragmatic. Unhealthy fixations, desires, and petty delusional feelings have never existed in my life. Those are for the common man who cannot aim higher to reach his ambitions. Too easily swayed, distracted, and turned useless, incapable of separating fiction from reality.

Which makes it impossible for me to comprehend my new, inexplicable, and all-consuming obsession. This fascination I've developed and can't seem to shake off no matter how hard I try. Like a junkie, I keep thinking that one more fix will be enough to break me out of my addiction. Only to be proved wrong.

It all started with a single cellophane-wrapped confection. An Italian cookie. Half-squished when she offered it to me. Yet, the tri-colored layers of the filling were still distinct. Still tempting. Magical.

Rainbow.
The symbol of her name.
Iris.

The End

Bonus Scene 1
Kidnapped

This bonus scene is from Kurt's point of view.

For the story below to make sense, you need to have read Book 5 (Stolen Touches) and the previous bonus scene (Kurt), which can be accessed on my website.

Kurt

Clink...

I crack open one eye.

The sound is barely distinguishable, but I recognize the turning of a key in a lock. Are the love birds returning already? That'd be good because I've had enough of this uncomfortable recliner. The Mean One had shut every door to other parts of the penthouse before taking Milene on some fancy date and leaving me trapped in the living room. I'm certain he did it on purpose. He doesn't want me in any of the bedrooms. Too greedy to share the fluffy pillows that are piled on top of the soft beds. Rat-bastard.

The front door closes with a muted thud.

Yup, they're back.

Squeezing my eye shut again, I push the Mean One's phone charger under my belly so he won't notice it. The furless meatstick just loves taking away all my toys. But I really like this one. I've got it chewed up so nicely. The stringy thingy is now almost flat. Like bacon.

Ahhhh... I love bacon! Nearly as much as I love tuna. But cuddly Milene put me on a diet last month. *Hiss.* It's because of that vet bitch. She told my human that I was slightly overweight. Overweight! Me? How dare she insult me! I do not need any changes to my nutritional plan. Unless it means more tuna and bacon. I am the prime specimen of a male feline. Strong, and agile, and perfectly groomed! I lick my balls and asshole daily. Would an overweight cat have the flexibility for that?

Tap. Tap.

I crane my neck, glancing in the direction of the entry hall, listening to the sound of approaching footsteps. It's dark in the room, but that makes no difference to me. My vision is as sharp as my claws, and my hearing is better than that of the subway mouse. Just the slightest off-squeak is enough for me to determine the source. And those footfalls are too even. They don't belong to the Mean One's gait. And they are too heavy to be Milene's.

Intruder!

Hairballs! We have a problem!

Alert! Alert! Alert!

I leap onto the back of the recliner, then jump over to the top of the bookshelf. My movements are swift and graceful—definitely way beyond what a tubby cat could ever pull off. (You can't convince me otherwise. I've seen the video evidence. The record of fat cats trapped inside the screen of Milene's phone. Some of them were even called... Cheezburger. For shame, I say, for shame!)

But there's no time now to contemplate the poor choices made by the less-sensible felines in the world. I take up my observation post. Listening. Waiting.

Tap. Tap.

A man, dressed in a strange black outfit, looking like one of the lunatics the Mean One sometimes watches on TV, turns the corner, sneaking inside the room. He halts, looking around in the dark, then removes something from his belt.

A weapon!

Mayday! Mayday! Mayday!

He has a weapon!

By God's fleas! The stupid Mean One picked today of all days to whisk Milene on a date instead of protecting his lair! Useless! No instinct at all.

Click.

A beam of light extends from the intruder's hand, sweeping across the room from corner to corner.

Oh. It's a flashlight.

I flatten myself on top of the bookshelf, keeping utterly still. Not even a whisker twitches on me as I watch this strange interpoler snooping about my territory.

Is he a thief? He's not opening any drawers, not pulling out anything. An assassin? Sent by a Mean One's enemy to take out Milene's mate?

Darn it, I have such horrid luck!

You should have come over an hour ago, you idiot! Before the Mean One left!

I continue observing the intruder as he walks around, checking out every nook and cranny. Under the furniture, behind the curtains, even between the cushions of the couch. Is he searching for something?

Not an assassin, then.

When he's done with his weird-ass inspection, the snooper takes out his phone and heads to the kitchen.

"Fred," he says quietly into his device. "Are you sure it's supposed to be in the living room? Because it's not here. Should I check the rest of the place?"

The man is too far away for me to hear the answer, but that reply must have been some kind of instruction because the intruder moves toward the cupboard. My cupboard!

He is a thief!

"Alright. I'll try that." He nods as he reaches inside. Taking out a can I'm all too familiar with. He sets it on the counter. Opens it.

What the fuck? Did he feel like having a snack in the middle of his dumb robbery or something? Whatever. No one comes into my den uninvited. No one steals my food! I shall deal with him immediately and without mercy. I shall—Fuck! I'm starting to sound just like the Mean One. That's terrible. Back to the issue at hand.

I'm judging the distance between my hideout and the hungry burglar. Calculating how many leaps would be needed to land on his back. Plotting the force required to—Oh, what is that wonderful smell?

Yum, yum, yum! The divine scent of tuna fills the air.

Suffering nine lives! Drool spills out of my mouth. I've been getting nothing but tasteless kibble shit and zero treats for weeks, and a mere sniff of that mouthwatering aroma makes me want to rev up my purr engine.

"Here, kitty, kitty…"

The intruder lowers the can of tuna to the kitchen floor.

Nope. Ignore him. It's some kind of a trick.

Everyone knows not to take fish from strangers.

But dog's balls, it smells so good! Tempting me. Tempting me.

This dumb forced diet has turned my poor tummy into the size of a pea. How much can a starving cat be expected to handle? *Mmm…* Maybe just a sniff? A quick little bite—to recoup my power—before I turn my focus to disposing of this unwanted visitor.

Intoxicated by the heavenly smell, I dismiss the dude, no longer caring who he is or what he's after. Following my nose, I jump down off the bookshelf and rush toward the feast.

The initial bite of the perfectly flaked tuna is pure bliss. So good that in my hurry to gulp it down, I nearly choke on it.

Divine. So scrumptious that—

Thick, heavy fabric drops over my head.

MEOOOOW. HISS. GROWL.

"Got you!"

• • •

"Jesus fuck, Marv! Will you get that thing to calm down? I'm trying to drive here!"

"What the hell do you think I'm doing?" my catnapper shouts back while I thrash inside the trap, hissing and trying to scratch my way out. "This bag won't hold. We should have brought a fucking cage!"

A cage! How dare he! I let out another furious meow and dig my nails into what I hope is the mutt's crotch. This stupid canvas bag is no obstacle for my immaculately pointy claws. I didn't spend the last two days sharpening them on the Mean One's bedposts for nothing.

"Fuck! The little shit just dug his nails into my balls!"

Bingo!

Changing my position as much as the confined space inside the bag allows me, I puncture the fabric again.

A painful wail echoes through the interior of the vehicle.

"*Shiiiit!*" Marv the interloper groans.

Ha! There you go, you overgrown cockroach! Another exclusive ball-shredding, just for you.

My excitement is short-lived, though, because the asswipe pushes me off his lap and I tumble headfirst onto the floor. *Ouch!*

Rat tails, I can't believe I'm being catnapped! Are these scumbags going to ransom me to the Mean One? Is this a ploy to steal me from my humans?

I had a feeling that bozo was bad news soon as I saw and smelled him. He stinks like the sun-baked heap of horse shit I ran past one time at the city park.

"Screw the contract." Marv again. "Let's just kill it. I don't wanna drive out of state with this hellspawn on my lap just to dump it somewhere."

I freeze. My fur rises instantly.

Kill it?

Me?

"Good thinking, Marv. We'll just—"

The tires screech, and then the car jolts to a stop. That sends me tumbling inside the bag until I hit something. Never one to waste the opportunity, I toss from side to side, trying to find a way to escape. Nothing. The route to my freedom is rigidly tied.

"What the fuck is wrong with people? This asshole just cut me off! He almost ran us off the fucking road!" Fred yells.

"Shit, man. It's him." Marv's voice sounds slightly hysterical. That stench around him is morphing into something new. "What the fuck is he doing here? Oh, crap, he's coming this way. Did we fuck up?"

"Ah… Hi. Is there a prob—"

A piercing whoosh splits the air, followed by another right away. I keep very still, very quiet. Listening to hear what's going on.

The car door creaks as someone opens it, and then the bag I'm in is lifted off the ground. No! What is happening? Am I being catnapped from my catnappers?

Well, I am not going down without a fight!

HISS. GROWL. SNARL. HISS.

I trash around, scratching at the fabric of the bag.

"Stop that!" a low, commanding voice orders. "Damn defective cat."

The Mean One?

A long, delighted meow leaves me. I am being saved!

I patiently wait as he unties the bag, all while oscillating between relief and irritation. I'm thrilled that soon I'll be returned to Milene, but the fact that I'm being rescued by my nemesis feels somehow degrading.

Yeah, I know. There were two against one, but I should have been able to best them. My easy life with Milene has made me too soft. Shit, if the word spreads in the streets, about how a human had to save me, that would kill my reputation. I'd be tossed out of the Alley Cat Society.

The sides of the bag are finally loose. I shake, stretching my limbs and pushing my head through the folds. As soon as I pop out, I come face-to-face with the Mean One. The Usurper.

Took you long enough! I meow, swiping my paw at his chin. But the meatstick moves away just in time.

"I should have let them take you." He slips his hands around my belly, lifting and turning me side to side. "Did they hurt you?"

Yes! They smashed my self-esteem to smithereens, and then you arrived and buried it completely! How dare you help me, human? I would have managed to free myself! Eventually.

"You seem fine. Alright. Let's go home, little pest."

Pest? Me? Maybe I should stay with the catnappers. They obviously have a better sense of my worth.

As the Mean One carries me away, I crane my neck and turn my head to see the catnappers, wondering why they aren't making a fuss about losing me. Both mutts, though, are slumped in their seats, sporting identical red splotches at the center of their foreheads.

Dead?

The Mean One killed them!

For me?

I lift my chin a little higher, assuming a more dignified pose. Of course he killed them. No one fucks with the Ajello family, and I am a valued member of the clowder. Integral. Irreplaceable. Riggs doesn't count, of course.

That cat is a disgrace. And I'm glad that Milene realized that. She'll never make the same mistake again. There's only one top cat in our den, and it's me!

"You need to start behaving, pest," the Mean One prattles on as he sets me on the passenger seat after sliding behind the wheel. "No more swiping for shits and giggles. As of tomorrow morning, you're a big brother to a litter of baby kittens. Milene can hardly contain herself."

Noooo!

BONUS SCENE 2
THE LOVE GURU

Host: Good evening, everyone. I'm James Williams, and I want to welcome you to this week's episode of *Love is Just Around the Corner*. Tonight, we have a special guest with us in the studio. However, due to the sensitive nature of his business, we're not able to share his real name with you. Instead, we'll call him Don.

Nice to have you here, Don!

… [Nothing but silence greets the audience over the radio waves.]

Guest: Hi.

Radio Host: Ladies and gentlemen, please don't hold that against him. I believe Don might be just a little nervous. Prior to coming on air, he confided to me that he'd never done a radio show before.

Let's get started. Could you tell us why you chose to accept our invitation to appear on tonight's program? As I understand, you run a major conglomerate, so I do not doubt that your time must be very limited.

Guest: That's correct. I'm here because I have been blackmailed and coerced to come.

Radio Host: No way! Coerced? I had no idea. Could you elaborate on that?

Guest: One of my business associates thought that my appearance on your show would be helpful. Unfortunately, he shared this harebrained idea with my wife. She liked it. And then made me do it.

Radio Host: Oh, she's listening, then? Hi, Mrs. Don! Sending you much love and—

Bam!

Guest: That's just a little warning for you, James. No man other than me sends love to my wife. Got that? Next time, I won't stop at a mere black eye. Understand?

Radio Host: Absolutely. [*Groan.*] One hundred percent.

Guest: You may continue.

Radio Host: Um... yeah, sure. You seem to be very much in love with your wife, Don. Since this show is all about providing relationship advice, maybe you could share a few words of wisdom? Tell our audience how you met the love of your life, and your experiences courting her. Are there specific things that worked for you, or anything you wish you could have done differently?

Guest: Alright. We met in the parking lot of the hospital where she used to work. It was a brief encounter, lasting about ten minutes. But that was more than enough time for me to realize that I'd do whatever it took to make her mine.

Radio Host: That sounds so romantic. Tell me, what was your first move?

Guest: I did background research and then observed her.

Radio Host: Oh, you got to know the things she liked and places where she enjoyed spending time? That's sweet. I don't think enough people make the effort to get to know a person these days. We're very much living in a culture of instant gratification, don't you agree?

Guest: No. I meant I had my chief of security complete a thorough investigation of her and arrange video surveillance so I could watch her around the clock.

Radio Host: Uh… You mean… you… stalked her?

Guest: Yes.

… *[Ahem. Cough. Cough.]* … *[The host seems to be having a bit of an issue. Trained first aid personnel are on standby.]*

Guest: That was definitely one of the things that worked. In order to achieve the outcome you want, it's important to gather and analyze all pertinent info, James. Once you have a better understanding of your chosen person, it's that much easier to reach your goals. I fully recommend this approach.

Radio Host: Um… Right. I see. You're not a proponent of conventional means. Like giving flowers, for instance.

Guest: I tried that.

Radio Host: Oh, you did? How did that go? And, what did you get her? Roses?

Guest: Everything the florist had available. But my mistake was not writing the note. So she had no idea they were from me. That should be a lesson for your listeners. Always include a signed card with the flowers.

Radio Host: That's sound advice, right there. Well, since wooing your lady love with flowers seemed to fail, what was the next thing you tried?

Guest: I broke into her apartment and filled up her fridge.

Radio Host: Huh. Interesting. Not what I figured you might say. And why did you do that?

Guest: Her eating habits were extremely unhealthy. Each time I saw her on the cameras pulling out crap food from the fridge or eating fast food takeout, I cringed.

Radio Host: Cameras? At her place? Isn't that illegal, Don?

Guest: Is there a point to your question?

Radio Host: Oh, no. I was just, you know, wondering. Let's continue. Did your future wife know that you were… uh… interested… in her? Did the two of you happen to see each other, in person, during that time?

Guest: No. It was some time later that I decided the timing was right for us to finally meet face-to-face again. It happened to coincide with some creep stepping up his unwelcome pursuit of her and not taking "no" for an answer.

Radio Host: She had *another* stalker? Other than you, I mean.

Guest: Yes. But, luckily, that issue was swiftly resolved. Once I shot the guy, he quickly got the message that stalking another man's woman was wrong. My advice in that situation is to take care of all obnoxious creeps with the utmost expediency.

Radio Host: But… you stalked her yourself. You watched her without her knowledge.

Guest: I was making sure my future wife was alright. Totally different situations.

Radio Host: I see. And once you met again? Did she fall in love with you right away, or did you have to work to earn her affection? How long have the two of you dated before you proposed?

Guest: We had one date and got married the following day.

Radio Host: One day? She agreed to marry you after one date?

Guest: That's nothing remarkable. People tend to acquiesce promptly, and practically to anything, when their entire family is threatened with obliteration. Possessing excellent persuasion skills is essential for dating. This has been my greatest strength, I believe.

Radio Host: Right. Good to know. Um… I take it you've been married for quite some time now. So, I gather, she did develop feelings for you, in the end?

Guest: Of course.

Radio Host: Seriously? I mean… How can you be sure of her love? Did she express it in some grand manner or—

Guest: She took a bullet for me. Grand enough for you, James?

Radio Host: Whoa! That's… huge. Um… May ask what happened to the person who shot her?

Guest: A bit of filleting action.

Radio Host: I'm not sure I get what you mean.

Guest: Have you ever seen a fish gutted and then turned into fillets?

Radio Host: A couple of times, sure.

Guest: Then you get my meaning.

. . .

Producer: James, we're still *live.*

Radio Host: [*Ahem*] Right. Well, our time is almost up. I... ah... have one more question for you, Don. As a man who is very much in love with your wife—

Guest: Understatement.

Radio Host: Of course. I can see that. Could you tell me, is there anything about your wife that you might... not like? A pet peeve, perhaps?

Guest: My wife is the embodiment of perfection. I worship every single thing about her. Except Kurt.

Radio Host: Kurt?

Guest: Her defective cat. I am constantly tempted to strangle the little devil. Unfortunately, she loves the damned thing. And because she does, even though I hate him with a passion, I can't bring myself to harm him in any way. And, all my passive attempts to neutralize him failed. Leaving the doors open in hopes that he would flee. Windows, too. Nothing. Even the kidnapping and forced relocation scheme.

Radio Host: You tried to kidnap your wife's cat?

Guest: Don't be ridiculous. I just said I wouldn't lay a hand on him. Weren't you paying attention?

Radio Host: Um—

Guest: I hired a professional team. Top-notch mercenaries.

Everything was planned out to the minute detail. I had taken my wife out for a romantic dinner, gave the home security personnel a night off, and provided means of entry to the perpetrators. All they had to do was go in, collect the damn cat, and drive him out of state. Easy pickings.

They had the little pest safely in their grasp in under fifteen minutes. I received a confirmation call as they were heading out of the city on the interstate. My wife and I were still enjoying our main course—

Radio Host: Oh my God! You actually had your wife's cat kidnapped!

Guest: That's absurd. I got off the line and excused myself, letting my wife know that I needed to deal with an urgent matter. Then, I caught up with the kidnappers and disposed of them.

Radio Host: Hold on a minute. What do you mean by "dispose of them"? You didn't actually...?

Guest: Of course I did. And once that was done, I brought the pest home. Told my wife I simply needed to have Kurt checked out by the vet, but that I didn't want to needlessly worry her. [*Ahem.*]. If you are listening, *cara mia*, I'm deeply sorry.

Radio Host: Wait, wait. I'm not sure I'm following, Don. *You* hired the kidnappers in the first place! And then *you* chased them down and... offed... them? For taking the cat?

Guest: I'm not sure why you're confused, James. This is very simple. No one kidnaps my wife's cat. Or gets away with it.

WHAT'S NEXT?

Dear Reader,

The next book will feature Adriano and Iris. Both appeared first in *Sweet Prison*. You can expect tropes such as age gap, stalker hero, opposites attract, and an extremely OTT jealous and possessive hero. This is the story of a man who was raised to be ruthless, who didn't shy away from doing whatever was necessary to ensure the continuation of his family's legacy. His life's path led him to great wealth and tremendous respect, but in the process, he lost something very important. His heart. Or maybe… it wasn't lost. Maybe it was simply frozen.

The next book will be the last in the main series and it will release on April 30, 2026. And for those who might wonder why the wait is so long (since I've released books a lot faster in the past), the main reason is the book length. The first few books in the series were around 50,000 words each. However, as the series progressed, the books became longer, with the last few being over 120,000 words, which is more than double in length compared to the first books. With this in mind, it's not realistic for me to keep the same publishing pace as before. I'm sorry for the wait, but I would rather take more time to write the story and make the book as perfect as possible, than rushing it. Thank you for understanding.

The title for book 12 is ***Frozen Heart***, and you can read the blurb here:

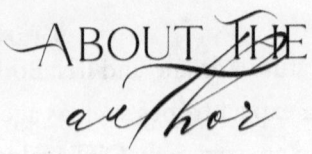

ABOUT THE author

Neva Altaj writes steamy contemporary mafia romance about damaged antiheroes and strong heroines who fall for them. She has a soft spot for crazy jealous, possessive alphas who are willing to burn the world to the ground for their woman. Her stories are full of heat and unexpected turns, and a happily ever after is guaranteed every time.

Neva loves to hear from her readers, so feel
free to reach out:

Website: www.neva-altaj.com
Facebook: www.facebook.com/neva.altaj
TikTok: www.tiktok.com/@author_neva_altaj
Instagram: www.instagram.com/neva_altaj
Amazon Author Page: www.amazon.com/Neva-Altaj
Goodreads: www.goodreads.com/Neva_Altaj

www.ingramcontent.com/pod-product-compliance
Lightning Source LLC
Chambersburg PA
CBHW030239030726
47493CB00023B/170